Praise for *The Fourth Horseman*

"David Hagberg consistently delivers thrillers that truly thrill, with an uncanny ability to anticipate future headlines. Skill, experience, knowledge, and a dedication to quality long have been hallmarks of Hagberg's novels, and *The Fourth Horseman* exceeds all expectations."   —Ralph Peters,
Fox News strategic analyst and
New York Times bestselling author of
Valley of the Shadow

"David Hagberg is the pros' pro, the plot master we all wish we were."   —Stephen Coonts,
New York Times bestselling author of
The Art of War

"Hagberg knows how to get the reader to turn the page, and those who enjoy action-oriented spy thrillers involving government insiders will find much to enjoy here."   —*Booklist*

Praise for David Hagberg

"Bleeds action on every page . . . Outstanding in every respect."   —*The Providence Journal* on *Retribution*

"Exciting . . . Hagberg's extensive research and background [in the military] heightens the realism."
                —*Publishers Weekly* on *Retribution*

"The action is nonstop, and McGarvey is always a compelling protagonist."
                —*Booklist* on *Retribution*

BOOKS BY DAVID HAGBERG

Twister
The Capsule
Last Come the Children
Heartland
Heroes
Without Honor*
Countdown*
Crossfire*
Critical Mass*
Desert Fire
High Flight*
Assassin*
White House*
Joshua's Hammer*
Eden's Gate
The Kill Zone*

By Dawn's Early Light
Soldier of God*
Allah's Scorpion*
Dance with the Dragon*
The Expediter*
The Cabal*
Abyss*
Castro's Daughter*
Burned
Blood Pact*
Retribution*
End Game*
The Fourth Horseman*
The Shadowmen†
24 Hours†
Tower Down* (forthcoming)

• • •

FICTION BY BYRON DORGAN
AND DAVID HAGBERG

Blowout
Gridlock

NONFICTION BY DAVID HAGBERG
AND BORIS GINDIN

Mutiny!

* Kirk McGarvey adventures
† Kirk McGarvey novellas

THE FOURTH HORSEMAN

DAVID HAGBERG

A TOM DOHERTY ASSOCIATES BOOK
NEW YORK

This is a work of fiction. All of the characters, organizations, and events portrayed in this novel are either products of the author's imagination or are used fictitiously.

THE FOURTH HORSEMAN

Copyright © 2016 by David Hagberg

All rights reserved.

A Forge Book
Published by Tom Doherty Associates
175 Fifth Avenue
New York, NY 10010

www.tor-forge.com

Forge® is a registered trademark of Macmillan Publishing Group, LLC.

ISBN 978-0-7653-7000-6

Our books may be purchased in bulk for promotional, educational, or business use. Please contact your local bookseller or the Macmillan Corporate and Premium Sales Department at 1-800-221-7945, extension 5442, or by e-mail at MacmillanSpecialMarkets@macmillan.com.

First Edition: February 2016
First Mass Market Edition: January 2017

Printed in the United States of America

0 9 8 7 6 5 4 3 2 1

FOR LORREL, AS ALWAYS

AUTHOR'S NOTE

The facts are that Pakistan does have an arsenal of more than one hundred nuclear weapons and the means to deliver them throughout the Indian subcontinent.

Pakistan is an unstable government. For years its secret military intelligence service, the ISI, has been funding Islamic fundamentalist terrorists, including the Taliban, to harass Indian military forces on its border with Kashmir. But now those terrorist organizations have turned on their former master.

The United States has the means to swoop into Pakistan, find the nuclear weapons and disable them if the government were to fall into rebel control. The operation wouldn't play out so neatly as the raid to eliminate Osama bin Laden did—almost certainly, American lives would be lost.

The problem is, according to U.S. military sources, we could guarantee finding only around ninety of the weapons, which would leave at least ten, and possibly more, nukes. A formidable arsenal.

I have not divulged the locations of our strike forces nor the exact methods they would use to neutralize the weapons. Suffice it to say, for the sake of the story, the scenario is current and real. All it would take is one spark. One man.

And when he had opened the fourth seal . . . I looked, and behold a pale horse; and his name that sat on him was death, and Hell followed with him.

—REVELATION 6:7–8

PART
ONE

The Messiah

ONE

At midnight a private Gulfstream biz jet that had just arrived from Paris touched down at the newly opened Gandhara International Airport near Pakistan's capital city, Islamabad. David Haaris, the only passenger, made a telephone call.

He was a slightly built thirty-eight-year-old man wearing khaki trousers, an open-necked white shirt and a dark blue blazer. He had the long, delicate fingers of a concert pianist and a round, pleasant face, slightly dark, as if he'd been spending his weekends in the sun. His eyes were wide and jet black, and held intelligence and power that were immediately obvious to anyone meeting him for the first time. His voice was soft, cultured, with a hint of an upper-class British accent, and his vocabulary and grammar were almost always perfect. At the Pakistan Desk in the CIA his was the last word on proper usage.

His call was answered on the first ring by a man speaking Punjabi, Haaris's first language. "Yes."

"I've arrived."

"I'll expect you in my office the moment you're clear. Good luck."

"Are you looking for trouble?"

"These are difficult times, my friend, as you well know. The Aiwan-e-Sadr came under attack just three hours ago. There is no telling what will happen next. So it is good that you are here, but take care." The

Aiwan was the residence and office of Pakistan's president. It served the same purpose as the White House in Washington.

"Have you sent a car?"

"Yes. But keep a very low profile. Short of sending a military escort—which would just make matters worse—you will be on your own until you reach me."

"Perhaps I could order a screen of drones."

"Anything but."

"As you wish," Haaris said, and he broke the connection, a slight smile playing at the corners of his mouth. His cell phone conversation with Lieutenant General Hasan Rajput, who was the director of the Covert Action Division for Pakistan's intelligence agency, was primarily for the benefit of the U.S. National Security Agency and the Technical Services Section in the CIA directorate where he worked. They were listening in.

The pretty flight attendant, who'd been aboard since Andrews, came aft as he took the SIM card out of his phone and put it in his pocket. Her name was Gwen, and like Haaris she worked for the CIA.

"The captain would like to know how long you expect to be on the ground, sir," she said.

"Probably no more than a few hours, luv. You might have him refuel in case we have to make a hasty retreat."

The young woman didn't smile. "Should we be expecting trouble?"

"Not out here at the airport. At least not for the short term."

Haaris glanced out the window as they taxied to a hangar used by the government for unofficial flights. The night was quiet, and he could almost smell the place even over the faint stink of jet fuel. A host of memories passed behind his eyes at the speed of light. Good times, some of them when he was a child in Lahore, but then horrible times after his parents died and his uncle brought him first to London to study in public school, then on to Eton and finally Sandhurst. He was a "rag head," an "Islamic whore," and in prep school the older boys used him in just that way.

And so his hate had begun to build, centimeter by centimeter, like a slowly developing volcano rising out of the sea.

He unbuckled and got up as the aircraft came to a complete halt, and he gave the attendant a smile. "I'm here to do a little back-burner diplomacy, see if I can't point the right way for them to extract themselves from the mess they're in."

Gwen nodded. She was a field officer and had been under fire in the hills of Afghanistan. "Good luck, then, sir."

Pakistan was a powder keg ready to explode at any moment. Nearly every embassy in Islamabad had been stripped to skeleton staffs, the ambassadors recalled. Attacks by the insurgents had been happening throughout the country for the past week. Haaris's recommendation to the president's security council three days earlier was to have its nuclear readiness teams put on high alert. It had been accomplished within twenty-four hours.

Gwen went forward, opened the door and lowered the stairs as a black Mercedes S500 pulled up and parked ten meters away, just forward of the port wingtip. She said something to Ed Lamont, the pilot, then stepped aside as Haaris came up the aisle.

"I thought they'd send an armed escort," Lamont said. He was a craggy ex–air force fighter pilot who'd flown missions in Iraq and Afghanistan. A steady man.

"We didn't want to attract any attention," Haaris said. "But I want you to refuel and stand by in case we have to get out in a hurry."

"What if the Pakis deny our flight plan?"

"They won't," Haaris said, careful not to bridle at the derogatory term for a Pakistani.

He stepped down onto the apron, the summer evening warm, the sky overcast, the air close. This far out from Islamabad the country could have been at peace, but the KH-14 satellite real-time images he'd seen yesterday at Langley showed a starkly different picture. Pakistan was on the verge of an all-out war, and the conflict promised to be much worse than any that had ever happened here. It's why he'd been sent: to try to make the ISI, Pakistan's Inter-Service Intelligence agency, come to its senses and to work with the fundamentalists so that civil war could be avoided.

But it was not the real reason he'd come.

An old man wearing the traditional Pakistani long loose shirt over baggy trousers held open the Mercedes' rear door.

"Allah's blessing be upon you, sir," he said in Punjabi.

Haaris answered in kind, and as soon he got in the car, the driver closed the door and went around to the front.

They headed past several large maintenance hangars, the service doors closed. This side of the airport seemed to be deserted.

"What's the situation?" Haaris asked.

"The highway has been closed, no one is allowed to pass."

"Does the government hold it?"

"No, sir. It's the Lashkar-e-Taiba, and they are murdering people trying to get out."

The group, once funded by the ISI, was allied with the Taliban. Their main purpose was to get their hands on at least one working nuke. The CIA considered them the main threat to Pakistan's arsenal, which was for the most part spread around the country at air force and navy bases. So far security at the nuclear sites was holding. But it had long been rumored that some of the weapons had been moved to other locations, most often in unmarked vans or panel trucks, without armed escorts. And it was these weapons that had the Pentagon most worried.

At this hour the KH-14 was twenty degrees below overhead to the east and so could not pick up images, even in the infrared from straight down. As well, no surveillance drones were scheduled for flybys out here until later the next morning, and then only if the trouble from inside the city spread to the airport.

The driver made a leisurely turn to the right, along the west side of one of the hangars, and pulled up next to a battered old Fiat, its blue paint mostly faded or rusted away. Two men stood beside it, one of them about the same general build as Haaris and similarly dressed in khakis, a white open-necked shirt and a dark blue blazer. The other man was dressed much like the Mercedes' driver. He held a pistol.

Haaris got out, and the man with the pistol prodded the other man to get in the front seat next to the driver.

"With God's blessing," Haaris said.

"Fuck you," the man in the blazer said. His voice was slurred.

As soon as the door was closed the Mercedes took off toward the main highway into the city.

"I'm Lieutenant Jura," the man said, putting away the gun. "Welcome to the Taliban. Your clothes and beard are in the backseat."

TWO

ISI Lieutenant Usman Hafiz Khel presented his credentials to the senior enlisted man at Quetta Air Force Base Post One—the main gate—shortly after midnight. The base was midway between Islamabad to the northeast and Karachi to the southwest. At twenty-three he was young, but he knew how to follow orders. The directorate had been his home since he'd been recruited at the age of fourteen to attend a special technical school in Islamabad, followed by university and finally his commission.

"May I ask the lieutenant the purpose of his visit at this hour?" the acne-scarred corporal technician demanded. It was the same rank as a master sergeant in the West. He'd joined the air force when Usman was nine.

"I have orders to meet with Group Captain Paracha." The GP was the commander of the top-secret nuclear storage depot here on base.

"Not at this hour."

Usman was driving a Toyota SUV with civilian plates and no markings that had been waiting for him at the international airport. The windows were so darkly tinted that the interior of the car was all but invisible to anyone looking in. He'd been stopped at the barrier, and the sergeant along with an armed guard who stood to one side had come out to see who'd shown up. Security across the country was tight because of the troubles.

"Call him."

"Impossible."

"He needs to know that I am here."

Another of the guards came to the door of the gatehouse. "A call for you, CT," he said.

"In a minute."

"Sir, it's Paracha."

"Shoot the lieutenant if he moves," the CT told the armed guard, and he turned on his heel and went into the guardhouse.

Usman understood the physical facts of his orders, if not the reason for them, though if he had to guess he figured this move tonight was only one of many similar operations across the country in response to the terrorist attacks. But this was desperate. Like leaping off a tall cliff into the raging ocean because a tiger was at your back. And he felt naked because he wasn't wearing a uniform—only big-city blue jeans and a T-shirt.

The CT returned almost immediately. "You're late. The group captain is at headquarters waiting for you. Do you know the way, or will you require an escort, sir?"

"I can find it," Usman said.

The CT stepped back and motioned for the barrier to be raised. He looked green in the harsh lights.

Group Captain Kabir Paracha, at forty-seven, was an unlikely military officer. His desert camos were a mess, he'd forgotten his hat, and his sleeves were rolled up to just below the elbows, the straps that were meant to hold them higher poking out. But he was the correct man for the job because his primary training had been as a nuclear engineer at the Dr. A. Q. Khan Research Laboratory. He understood the nature of the devices he was meant to guard. Especially the consequences if they ever had to be used.

He was waiting next to his Hummer, a driver behind the wheel.

"You're late," he said as Usman got out of his SUV. "And in civilian clothes."

"Pardon me, sir, but there were only three lightly armed men at Post One. This place should be crawling with patrols."

"We are told that the problems are confined to the north. I was ordered to maintain a low profile. And your trip makes no sense. It's insanity."

"Do you mean to disobey orders?" Usman demanded.

The GC's face fell and he looked away for just a moment. "No. But I will send two of my people with you. For the weapons—the *mated* weapons. Do you completely understand the sheer folly?"

Usman could guess. Almost all of Pakistan's nuclear weapons were stored in the unmated configuration: the trigger circuitry was stored in one spot, while the Pit—the physics packages that contained either highly enriched uranium or plutonium fissile cores plus the tritium accelerators that greatly increased a nuclear weapon's explosive power—were stored elsewhere. The procedure was for safety's sake, and it was something that the leadership assured the Americans was standard.

"I agree with you, sir. But I too must follow orders. These are difficult times."

"Indeed," Paracha said. "Follow me."

Usman followed the group captain across the base to a series of low concrete bunkers inside a triple barrier of tall, razor-wire-topped electric fences. Guard towers were located at fifty-meter intervals, and from the moment they approached the main gate, they were illuminated by several strong searchlights.

All of it was wrong. Anyone watching the bunkers and the high-security perimeter had to know what was here. And now the lights and the two vehicles were nothing short of an invitation. Insanity. Paracha was right: what was happening here and across the country was sheer folly.

Once they were passed through the triple fences, a thick steel door leading inside one of the bunkers rumbled open with a loud screech of metal on metal that had to be audible for miles.

Four heavily armed soldiers, one of them a flight lieutenant, motioned for Usman to drive inside what appeared to be a loading area about thirty or forty meters on a side. At the rear was a large freight elevator, its steel mesh gates open.

A small tug towing a cart on which were strapped four small nuclear weapons shaped like missile nose cones emerged from the elevator and the driver came around to the rear of Usman's SUV.

Paracha spoke to the four armed guards, then came over to where Usman had gotten out of his vehicle and opened the tailgate with shaking hands.

"Do you recognize what these are?" he asked.

"Nuclear weapons meant to be carried by rockets."

"Plutonium bombs for the Haft IX missiles. And do you know the significance of that fact? The exact meaning of the thing?"

Usman only had his orders to pick up four weapons, drive them to the airport at Delbandin, a small town three hundred kilometers to the south, and deliver them to a Flight Lieutenant Gopang, who would load them aboard a small transport aircraft and fly away. Once the delivery was made he was to return to Islamabad.

"No, sir," Usman said, his voice quiet. He was in the presence of something so overwhelmingly powerful that all of his certainty had evaporated.

"These missiles have a range of less than one hundred kilometers. Does this mean something to you?"

Usman shook his head.

"These weapons were not meant to be launched against India or against anywhere else *outside* of Pakistan. They have been designed to kill any force threatening us from *inside*. They are meant to be used against our own people."

"The Taliban. Enemies of the state."

"Save me the propaganda, Lieutenant. These people were once our allies."

"And now they are our enemies," Usman said. And the fault rested entirely with the ISI. Just as the CIA was at least partly to blame for bin Laden. The Americans had funded the fundamentalists in Afghanistan, who drove the Russians away, and when the war was over the same Stinger missiles had been turned against Americans, which in turn had finally led to the attacks on New York and Washington. The events of the last two weeks were Pakistan's 9/11, and nothing short of a miracle would stop Islamabad from falling.

"I won't push the button, I only helped design the things and now I'm in charge of guarding them," Paracha said. "You won't push the button either, you'll merely deliver them somewhere."

Usman had nothing to say.

Paracha stepped closer. "Are our hands clean, Lieutenant?" he asked. He shook his head. "We'll never be clean."

THREE

The fires in the city became visible about ten miles from the airport, the night sky glowing unevenly beneath a low cloud deck. The situation was just as bad as the CIA thought it would be, and just as good as Haaris had hoped. Revolutions were not born on sunny days.

He was dressed now in long loose trousers, over which he wore a filthy long shirt and a kaffiyeh wrapped around his head, concealing his false beard and showing only the bridge of his nose and a hint of his eyes.

Virtually no traffic moved on the broad highway that had been built to service the new airport. But there had been intense fighting this evening: the shot-up, burned-out remains of several cars and pickup trucks littered the ditches in a quarter-mile stretch, and several bodies lay where they had fallen along the side of the road.

Haaris sat in the front seat next to Lieutenant Jura, a Beretta pistol holstered on his chest and a Kalashnikov propped up between his knees.

They came around a long sweeping bend to a half-dozen pickup trucks blocking both sides of the highway; at least twenty armed men dressed much the same as Haaris stood either in front of the trucks or in defensive positions behind the vehicles or in the ditches. Several of them were armed with American-made LAWs rockets, meant to take out tanks.

Although he had remained silent since leaving the airport, Jura now said, "I'll do the talking," and he slowed, coming to a stop a couple of meters from two men who stood ahead of the others.

One of them came forward, a Kalashnikov assault

rifle hanging casually from his right shoulder. He was tall and muscular, his face mostly hidden behind his scarf, his eyes behind aviator sunglasses.

"What are you doing here?" he demanded.

"There is to be another demonstration in front of army headquarters. We have been ordered to attend."

"Ordered by whom?"

"That is none of your business, brother. Your job is to attend to those fools who are trying to leave the city. Not freedom fighters ready for holy work this night."

The man shifted his weapon to a firing position, though he did not exactly point it at Jura. He leaned down and looked in at Haaris. "And who the hell are you?"

Haaris pulled out his Beretta pistol. "I have been in Paris, and I'm bringing good news to the revolution. We have our funding. Stand aside and let us pass."

"If you shoot me, you won't get five meters," the second man, with an AK47, said, but he didn't seem so certain.

"But then you would be dead, so whatever happened to us would be of no concern. Call your unit commander."

"I am in charge here."

Haaris pulled the hammer back, and with his left hand moved the end of the kaffiyeh from his face. "If you should make it to Paradise, remember me." He started to pull the trigger.

The man suddenly stepped back and waved them through. "Go with God," he said.

"And you, my brother," Haaris said.

They had to maneuver their way slowly past several pickup trucks, the armed warriors watching, until on the other side, the road clear, Jura sped up.

"Anyone aiming anything at us?" Haaris asked, decocking his pistol and holstering it.

Jura checked the rearview mirror. "Not yet." He glanced at Haaris. "The general said that you had balls. But you could have gotten us shot back there. Most of those guys were stoned. Opium. They chew balls of that shit all the time."

Haaris shrugged. "It doesn't matter." Since his parents had been killed in a rock slide—he'd been there when their mangled bodies had been dug out—and since his abuse at public school, he had been mostly indifferent to his personal comfort or well-being. He didn't know if he actually cared whether or not he survived to live another day, and he wasn't sure if this was a gift or a curse. But like a man who could feel no pain because of a medical condition, Haaris couldn't feel fear.

Just as well, he thought. But this night was important, and no matter what happened he had to present himself as invincible. Which made him smile.

The entrance to the sprawling Inter-Service Intelligence compound in Islamabad was next to a hospital, the gate guarded only by a plainclothes officer armed with a pistol. No sign identified the place, which looked more like the campus of a university—a number of mostly low slung modern buildings separated by well-tended lawns and fountains were grouped around the eight-story main headquarters building, on the top floor of which was the director general's office.

This area of the city was all but deserted now, most of the trouble centered around the Army Headquarters Building ten kilometers away in Rawalpindi.

The guard recognized Lieutenant Jura and waved

him through. On the other side of the gate completely out of sight from the main road, they were stopped by a half-dozen heavily armed soldiers and four bomb-sniffing dogs. They were made to get out of the car so that they could be searched with security wands of the same type that at one time had been used at airports and then thoroughly patted down.

Haaris's and Jura's pistols were taken, as was the Kalashnikov from inside the car, before they were allowed to proceed.

"They knew we were coming but they're jumpy because this place will probably get hit sometime tonight," Jura said.

"Maybe not," Haaris said, and the lieutenant gave him a sharp look.

"Pardon me, sir, your bravado got us past the roadblock, but the Taliban setting fire to the city might not be so easily convinced."

They were admitted to the parking ramp beneath the headquarters building after submitting to another, even more thorough search.

"Remember what happens tonight, Lieutenant," Haaris said, getting out of the car in front of the elevator. "Pakistan's future is at stake."

"Yes, sir. I know. We all know it."

"Stay here, I'll be back."

The ISI's Covert Action Division covered the entire third floor of the building. A hundred or more cubicles took up the center of the room. Offices, conference rooms and two data centers faced outward around the perimeter on three sides, and the fourth—the side facing toward the presidential palace—was taken up by General Hasan Rajput's large suite of offices, along with the offices of his deputy director and staff.

Anyone who had gotten past security inside the main gate and again either in the parking garage or through the ground-floor entrance was considered safe. No one bothered to look up as Haaris got off the elevator and made his way to the general's office. The secretary was gone and the door to the inner office was open. Rajput, the collar of his white shirt unbuttoned, was seated at his desk listening to reports from three of his staff. When Haaris walked in he looked up. He could have been a kindly grandfather, with gray hair and soft eyes.

"At last," he said. "Gentlemen, please leave us."

The staffers glanced at Haaris as they walked out but said nothing. The last one closed the door.

Rajput motioned for Haaris to take a seat. "Did you run into any trouble on the way in?"

"Not much. What's the current situation at the Aiwan? Is Barazani there?" Farid Barazani was the openly pro-Western new president of Pakistan. His election four months earlier was one of the reasons the Taliban had staged their attacks. Almost everyone in the West believed this was the signal for the dissolution of the government, which was why American nuclear strike force teams had been moved into place.

"Yes, I spoke to him less than ten minutes ago. The fool still thinks that he can talk his way out of this."

"Did you tell him about me?"

"He thinks that you're here from the CIA to offer him backing. He's waiting for you."

"Will he try to call Washington?"

"He might, but we've seen to it that the Taliban have cut all the landlines to the Aiwan, and we control the cell phone towers within range."

"How about satellite communications?"

"We have a good man in their computer section. Nothing will be leaving the Aiwan tonight."

"Except me," Haaris said. "Has it been reported to the CIA's chief of station here that I'm missing?"

"The metro police reported an incident on their wire, one of dozens this morning."

"No word from Langley?"

"No." Rajput picked up his phone and said, "Now, if you please."

A minute later a young man in army uniform without insignia of rank came in.

Haaris got to his feet and unwrapped the kaffiyeh. He stood still as the young technician secured what looked like a dog collar with a device about the size of a book of matches just below his Adam's apple.

"Say, 'My name is Legion.'"

Haaris spoke the words, but the voice coming from his mouth was nothing like his own. It was deeper, more resonant, the British accent almost completely absent.

FOUR

The four nuclear weapons, covered in wool blankets, were strapped to wooden cradles in the back of the Toyota SUV, the two uniformed guards sitting on top of them. They were south of Quetta, on the narrow highway to Delbandin, and Usman kept nervously looking in his rearview mirror. He could see the empty highway behind them, but he could also see the blank expressions on the faces of the two men, and he thought it was just like watching the zombie movies that were so popular.

"Aren't you afraid of getting radiation sickness, sitting so close?" he asked.

Neither one of them wore name tags, and they could have been brothers, with slight builds, narrow faces, dark complexions, wide, dark eyes.

"They don't leak," the one on the right said. "And if they did you'd be in the same trouble as us."

"You're not nervous?"

"Just drive, Lieutenant. I'm not nervous, as you say, just damned uncomfortable."

"And I have to take a piss," the other guard said.

"I'm not stopping out here," Usman said.

Ten minutes earlier they had passed through the town of Nushki, where nothing moved and very few lights shone. At this point they were fewer than thirty kilometers from the Afghan border, and Usman could feel the brooding hulk of the wild west country, once filled with friends of Pakistan who had now turned enemies. The mix of the nearness of the border and the weapons he was transporting had caused him to have waking nightmares: all he could see were hulking monsters, wave after wave of zombies, mushroom clouds, burning flesh, women and children screaming in agony. His armpits were soaked, his forehead was dripping, even his crotch was so wet it almost felt as if he had pissed himself.

He reached over and took from the glove box the SIG-Sauer P226 German pistol his father had given him as a graduation present from the military academy and laid it on the center console.

"There's no one out here," the one soldier said. "So you might as well let Saad take his piss, otherwise we'll have to listen to him forever."

"Thirty seconds," Usman said. "Any longer than that and I'll drive away without you."

He slowed down, pulled off the side of the road

and stopped. Immediately both soldiers got out and walked a few meters away.

Usman had asked for a radio in case he ran into trouble, but his request had been denied by his unit commander, Captain Siyal. He'd also been made to give up his cell phone.

"They have the capability of intercepting our radio transmissions and even our cell phone calls."

"What if I break down in the middle of nowhere?"

"See that you don't."

"That makes no sense, Captain," Usman had argued.

They were in Siyal's office, and the captain spread his pudgy hands. "Personally I agree with you, but I too have my orders. Balochistan has been fairly quiet. Pick up your cargo, drive three hundred kilometers, hand it over and you're done."

The captain's use of the word *cargo* bore no relationship in Usman's mind to the things in the back of the SUV. The fact that Pakistan had more than one hundred of the weapons had given him a certain pride, a nationalistic fervor—until now. These things right here were not an abstraction. They were real. They were meant for only one purpose—to kill a lot of people.

He looked over his shoulder in time to see both soldiers lighting cigarettes. He couldn't believe it. His nerves were jumping all over the place now, and the nearly absolute darkness of the night was pressing in.

Grabbing his pistol, he started to get out of the SUV, but for whatever reason he took the key from the ignition and put it in his pocket.

"What the hell are you men doing?" he shouted, walking around to the rear of the Toyota.

"A change of plans, Lieutenant," one of them said, and he turned around, a pistol in his hand.

Usman reared back, and at the same time the soldier to his left fired one shot that went wide.

Someone else from the darkness off the side of the road opened fire with a Kalashnikov, the rattle distinctive. The rounds slammed into the side of the SUV.

Usman ducked low as he raced across the road in the opposite direction and into the desert, the soft footing making it almost impossible for him to move fast.

Another burst of fire came from the highway, but then someone shouted something, and Usman continued running, as one of the soldiers answered.

"It doesn't matter, let the bastard go. We don't need him now."

Only then did Usman remember the pistol in his belt. He stopped and turned around as he drew it and fired four shots in rapid succession at the side of the SUV, about twenty meters away.

Someone cried out, and Usman took several steps back toward the highway, when another burst of Kalashnikov fire bracketed him, one round slamming into his left side, knocking him backward but not off his feet.

"Let him go!" an unfamiliar voice commanded.

"He's got the fucking key," one of the soldiers shouted.

"What?"

"The key to the ignition!"

Usman staggered to the left as the shooters opened fire, this time off to the right. He hunched over again, and holding the wound to his side with his left hand ran as fast as he could into the desert, the soft sand catching his feet, wanting to trip him up, make him fall. His only consolation was that the sons of bitches coming after him would have the same problem. And one of them had cried out. With any luck he had hit the bastard hard.

The sand suddenly dropped away and he pitched forward onto his face and tumbled five meters into a depression. When he ended up on his stomach he rolled over onto his back and looked up to the crest of the sand dune. He was at the bottom of a bowl, with no easy way out.

He had managed to hold on to his pistol so when they came for him he would take them out. Maybe all of them.

Someone shouted something to the left, over the top of the dune, and immediately someone else to the right shouted back, and then others picked up the cry. Maybe a half dozen or more men, some of them speaking with a variation of the Gilgit tribal accent, one Baloch, another Brahui and two Pashtuns—the soldiers from Quetta—without a doubt all of them Taliban.

This had been a trap from the beginning. Which meant that Captain Siyal or whoever had given the original orders was a traitor, as were the two guards from the air base, and possibly even the group captain.

But why put things like these into the hands of terrorists? All of a sudden he had at least one part of it: if the government fell American SEALS accompanying Nuclear Energy Support Teams would swoop down and disable as many of the weapons as they could. The highly trained NEST people, most of them nuclear scientists and engineers, were ready to mobilize at a moment's notice to anywhere in the world. So it came down to losing the weapons either to the Americans or to the Taliban

It would be a perfect opportunity for India to launch a preemptive strike, which would very possibly embroil the entire region in an unwinnable war.

Usman laid his head back for just a moment.

The weapons were too heavy simply to pick up and carry away. They would need the SUV.

He sat up, took the car key from his pocket and making sure that no one had crested the dune and was watching him, tossed it as far as he could.

They might eventually find it, though maybe not until dawn, but by then when he hadn't shown up at Delbandin the alarm might already have been sounded. Unless, of course, he'd never been expected to get that far in the first place. It never occurred to him that they might hot-wire the ignition.

He got to his feet, just a little dizzy now but not in any serious pain, and started for the wall on the opposite side of the depression down which he had fallen.

"I've got the bastard," one of the soldiers cried from the crest.

Usman turned and fired in that direction, and kept firing until his pistol went dry, the slide locked in the open position.

He felt the Kalashnikov rounds striking his body before he heard the noise of the shots, and he fell back, dead as he hit the sand.

FIVE

The attacks across the city and down in Rawalpindi, where the Army General Headquarters was located, had increased just during the time Haaris had been inside with General Rajput. Small-arms fire and the occasional explosion rattled in almost every direction around Diplomatic Row in the Green Section. But there were no sirens.

Haaris had changed back into his blazer, white

shirt and khakis, and he got off the elevator in the parking garage carrying a bright blue nylon shoulder bag, sealed with a U.S. State Department diplomatic tag. Word had finally come that the CIA knew that a man matching Haaris's description had been kidnapped by the Taliban on the way from the airport. Traffic between Langley and the ISI had suddenly become heavy.

He tossed the bag in the backseat of the Fiat and got in with it.

Lieutenant Jura turned around. "It might not be such a good idea for you to be seen dressed like that tonight."

"I'm back to being an American CIA officer."

"If the Taliban spot you they won't hesitate to kill you."

"We'll just have to take the chance. But this is the only way I'm going to get into the Aiwan to see Barazani."

"There's no way that the guards will let us through the gate, even if we could get to it. Right now there's a crowd on Constitution Avenue and it's growing."

It was just what Haaris was counting on. "We're going in from the Colony." The Aiwan-e-Sadr, located between the parliament building and cabinet block, was actually a compound of several buildings in addition to the president's main residence and workplace that were used as the residences of his staff and families, and was called the President's Colony, just off Fourth Street.

"The guards there are just as likely to shoot first and ask for credentials later."

"They've been told that I'm coming."

"Yes, sir," Jura said. "But if you're carrying a weapon, I suggest that you keep it out of sight. It wouldn't do you any good."

They headed out of the garage and around to the main gate, where the barrier was immediately raised and they were waved through. The streets were all but deserted; it was something else Haaris had been counting on. The growing crowd at the Aiwan was draining Taliban and ordinary citizens alike from across the city. The same thing had happened during the trouble in Beijing some years earlier, and during the problems in Cairo and a dozen other capital cities just lately. The world was starting to light up, and how big and terrible the fires would become before they died down was anyone's guess.

Haaris sat back in the seat. By now Charlene Miller, the president of the United States, would be assembling her security team in the Situation Room, if she hadn't already done so, trying to figure out if the situation here had gotten critical yet.

He expected that at the very least she would have ordered that the NEST teams be alerted for possible deployment. She was an intellectual who preferred the calm approach; she leaned toward thinking things out, getting the opinions of her staff, working out all of the options, before coming to a decision. But when she made one it was firm and final.

Her favorite line to her directors of National Intelligence and the CIA was that blowback, the unintended consequences that often came because an operation had gone in some direction no one had anticipated, "will never be an option on my watch."

The blowback this time was going to be more than any of them had ever imagined. Much more. And for a purpose.

Jura had to make a long detour around Constitution Avenue because of the crowd, which already stretched at least a kilometer from the Aiwan, to get to the rear of the compound and the heavily guarded gate into the Colony. Four soldiers from the president's Special Security Unit, armed with Heckler & Koch MP5s, surrounded the Fiat.

Haaris lowered the window and handed out his diplomatic passport. "I'm expected," he said in English.

Jura rolled down his window and he translated into Punjabi, but the senior guard handed back Haaris's passport. "Do you know the way?" he asked in good English.

"Yes, I've been here before."

"Don't leave the main driveway. And only you may go inside, your driver must stay with the car."

They eased through the gate and Jura followed the broad driveway around the side of the Presidential Palace past several of the residences. BMWs, Mercedes and Jaguars were parked in carports, but none of the buildings other than the palace showed any lights. The president's staff and their families were keeping a very low profile this evening.

With the windows of the Fiat down they could hear the low rumble of the crowd around front. So far the demonstration was peaceful, though no one thought that would last. The Taliban were attacking in a dozen or more spots around Islamabad and Rawalpindi, and possibly in other key cities, though information broadcast over television and radio was spotty at best. But the people were demanding that the government do something about it. The police and especially the army were nowhere to be seen. So far as the ordinary citizen knew the cowards had barricaded themselves inside their bases. Even the air force, which should have sent jets aloft to fire on the enemy, were absent from the skies.

They had gathered on Constitution Avenue and were marching on the Aiwan to demand President Barazani take control. Or at least give them reassurances that the government was doing something.

The people wanted someone to tell them that they were in charge. That Pakistan would survive. That their day-to-day lives would return to normal.

"Excuse me, sir," Lieutenant Jura said. "I know that you work for the CIA and are here at the orders of your president, but what is the U.S. going to do for us this time?"

"Show you the way out of this situation," Haaris said. He didn't mind the question, not this late in the game.

"Are you bringing the military?"

"Pakistan's answers are here, right in front of your nose, Lieutenant. And tonight you'll understand."

"Even the mob out front?"

"Especially them."

Lieutenant Jura pulled up in front of a gatehouse at one of the rear entrances. Two armed soldiers in the uniforms of the president's security service came out as Haaris stepped out of the Fiat, his nylon bag in hand.

"Good evening, sir," the taller of the two guards greeted him respectfully. "Your driver will have to remain here, but one of the president's aides will escort you upstairs."

"Thank you."

"Will you be requiring assistance with your bag?"

"I can manage," Haaris said.

At that moment a man in a British-cut business suit appeared at the door. "The president is waiting for you."

SIX

President of the United States Charlene Miller entered the White House Situation Room late in the afternoon, local, after getting off the phone with Walter Page, the director of the CIA. She was not in a good frame of mind, and combined with the fact she hadn't taken the time to freshen her makeup made her look like the Wicked Witch of the North. But she didn't give a shit. This was the first major crisis in her first year of office, and it was a whopper.

Everyone bunched around the long table were glued to the large flat-screen monitors on the wall, showing images of the mob in front of the Presidential Palace in Islamabad. Another monitor showed fires and explosions around the city, and in Rawalpindi about ten miles away the Army General Headquarters was under attack.

Miller took her place at the head of the table.

Her chief of staff, Thomas Broderick, nodded. "Madam President," he said.

"What about David? Any word yet?" she asked.

"No demands have been made. But we've confirmed that he was taken on the way in from the airport."

"I just got that from Walt Page."

The others around the table—Secretary of Defense William Spencer, a retired three-star army general who'd been commandant of West Point until he'd been tapped by the president; Secretary of State John Fay, a tall, lean, almost ascetic man with a thick shock of white hair, who'd been Harvard's dean and was undoubtedly the smartest and most liberal person in the room; the chairman of the Joint Chiefs, Admiral Harry S. Altman, a short man whom everyone thought looked and sounded like Harry Truman, and whose stewardship of the military was unparalleled in fifty years; and the president's adviser on national security affairs, Susan Kalley, a former professor of geopolitical affairs from UCLA who was the first "out" lesbian (although her significant other remained closeted) ever to serve at such a high level of government, who looked like a movie star and was beloved of the media—all looked up.

Notably missing was Saul Santarelli, the director of National Intelligence, who was on his way back from Paris.

"The situation in Islamabad is becoming critical," Kalley said.

"Is it possible that Barazani will fall?" Miller asked.

"It's likely."

"We may have another problem developing as well, Madam President," Sec Def Spencer said. "Units of the army and the ISI have been moving nuclear warheads out of their secure storage depots."

"As we expected they might. They've done it before."

"A risky business. But we got a series of satellite shots of a civilian vehicle showing up at Quetta Air Force Base and leaving twenty minutes later. We managed to track it south on the highway through the town of Nushki—which is practically on top of the border with Afghanistan—until it parked alongside the road. NRO analysts think they may have detected flashes from gunfire, and then nothing. The car—actually a SUV—is still at the side of the highway."

"Do you think it was carrying a nuclear warhead?" the president asked.

"We got lucky with a decent angle shot of the SUV before it reached Quetta and then afterwards. In the second series of images it was low on its springs, as if it were carrying something heavy."

"And?"

"There's been traffic leaving several other suspected nuclear weapons depots—at Chagai Hills, Issa Khel, Kahuta and Karachi. But we haven't picked up any signs of trouble, and we can't be certain that nuclear weapons were taken off those bases."

"I saw part of that report," the president said. "But have we followed any of those suspected vehicles—other than the one from Quetta—to their destinations?"

"We don't have the resources," Kalley said. "Neither does the CIA or NRO. Congress has cut their budgets the last three years in a row." The National Reconnaissance Office was responsible for putting spy satellites in orbit and maintaining them.

Miller had been warned by her top advisers, including Spencer and Kalley, that one day the reduced funding of such a vital component of the intelligence apparatus would rise up and bite the U.S. in the ass. Which it had now. But after the Snowden debacle, which had resulted in the sharp curtailment of the National Security Agency's ability to monitor telephone and computer traffic, Congress had been adamant that budget cuts across the board be made to the entire U.S. intel community. And it had been an issue that Miller, whose programs on poverty were most dear to her heart, and most expensive, wasn't willing to go to the mat with Congress on.

"What do we actually have over Islamabad and Rawalpindi?" she asked.

"An enhanced KH-14," Sec Def Spencer said. "It's one of our best assets."

"But not all-seeing," Miller said.

She picked up the phone and called Walt Page at Langley. She got him in the Watch, which was the section just down the hall from his office where a half-dozen analysts working twelve hours on and twelve off were tied into every available intelligence resource. They were the only people who knew practically everything that was going on in the world in real time.

His image came up on one of the flat-screen monitors, the connection completely secure from any outside eavesdropping. Or it was at least as secure as intel technology, and the extremely complicated quantum effects algorithms of the CIA's computer genius, Otto Rencke, could make it.

"Good afternoon, again, Madam President," Walt Page said.

"We're not getting as much help from our satellite resources as I'd hoped we would. We think that the Pakistanis are moving some of their nuclear weapons around the country."

"We're sure of it."

"I want to know where they're being taken and why," Miller said. "Especially the possibility that one of them may have been snatched from Quetta. Because if the Taliban gets their hands on even one of the things, everything changes out there."

"Ross has someone in the area and he's sent them to take a look at the SUV," Page said. Ross Austin, a former SEAL, was the CIA's chief of station in Islamabad. "We know that it was a rental from the Quetta airport. Possibly by the ISI."

Miller sat forward. "Son of a bitch," she said softly, but Page and everyone in the Situation Room with her caught it. "Is someone over there working with the Taliban again? Could this be a double-cross?"

"At this point I'd believe anything. Ross is running

a full-court press on the issue. Every asset he has in Islamabad and Rawalpindi are working the streets. Not only that but they're looking for Dave Haaris."

"Are we sure that the Taliban have him?" Kalley asked.

"Yes, nothing's changed to this point," Page said. "But no demands have been made."

"Thank you, Walter," Miller said. "Keep me posted."

"Madam President, perhaps it's time to alert our nuclear response teams."

"That's the issue we're working now."

"Yes, Madam President," Page said.

Miller cut the image. "Get me a Punjabi translator on the line, and telephone President Barazani."

Chief of Staff Broderick got on it and within a few seconds a young woman who'd been born, raised and educated in Pakistan before immigrating to the U.S. to get her master's in Middle Eastern languages from Columbia came on a split screen. She had been put on standby for just this occasion.

Moments later a man's image appeared on the other half of the screen. "Madam President," he said in English. "President Barazani has been expecting your call, but he begs your indulgence. He is meeting with his advisers on how best to handle the issue at hand. But he is most keen to talk to you."

"I'll wait for his call," Miller said. The connection was broken, and she thanked her translator. "Don't go far, we may still need you."

"Yes, Madam President," the young woman said.

Miller turned to her advisers. "Alert our nuclear response teams. I want them to be ready to go airborne the instant I give the word."

SEVEN

President Barazani's private secretary brought Haaris to the top floor and down the broad marble-tiled corridor to the anteroom. The palace felt almost deserted and was quiet except for the noise of the mob outside. Despite the warm early morning, fifty-five-gallon oil drums had been filled with trash and were burning down on the street. The flames sent odd flickers through the windows that played on the walls and ceilings.

"I'll just leave you here, sir. The president waits inside for you."

"Thank you," Haaris said.

President Barazani stood at the bullet-proof French doors looking directly out across Constitution Avenue. His hands were clasped behind his back, his shoulders hunched, his head bowed. His jacket was draped over the back of his desk chair, and the armpits of his white shirt were stained with sweat, though his office was air-conditioned.

He was a different man from the student Haaris remembered at Eton. Then Farid to his friends, F to Haaris's D, he was a hell-raiser. They both had been heavy drinkers and gamblers. Haaris had little money in those days, so F had bankrolled him. Of course it never mattered, because they always lost and yet they always had fun, usually ending up with a couple of whores just before dawn.

When Barazani's parents—his father was a major general in the army and his mother traced her lineage back to royalty—had enough of their son's antics and sharply reduced his allowance, Haaris had taken up the slack. He convinced his uncle that Barazani would one day be an important man in Pakistan—and therefore a good friend to cultivate. Anyway, his uncle had no children, and had heart problems; his money would probably go to his nephew. So why not spend a little of it now?

The logic was good enough for his uncle, who opened the financial spigot; not full flow, but enough so that Haaris could bankroll Barazani. And they had become fast friends who'd never completely lost touch with each other.

The president turned and nodded, a sad smile on his lips. He had already lost his country and he knew it. His entire range of emotions was written in deep lines on his brows, in the way he stood favoring his left knee, which he'd hurt in a rugby match, and in his general physical condition. Haaris estimated that Barazani had lost at least twenty kilos since the last time they'd met, the year before, in Washington. He looked ill.

"So here you are at last, an American spy come to offer his advice," Barazani said in English.

"An old friend come to help where he can," Haaris replied. He dropped his bag on the floor and crossed the room and they embraced.

"Maybe too late. But I understand the necessity of the ruse of your kidnapping. Was it your idea?"

"The ISI helped, of course."

"No doubt you and Rajput have become close over the past couple of years, but take some advice. Hasan Rajput is no friend of ours."

"Especially not you," Haaris replied, and Barazani smiled and nodded.

"But then he's still a valuable asset. Let's sit down so you can tell me exactly why you have gone to such lengths to get to me."

They sat in a pair of easy chairs at a low table with

a brandy service between them. Barazani poured them drinks. The room was large, the high ceilings hand-painted with a sunrise and clouds to the east, and a sunset and a few faint stars and a crescent moon to the west. The odor of incense hung softly on the air, none of the smoke from down on the street reaching this far yet. The large desk was littered with papers and file folders, most of them stamped with "Most Secret," orange diagonal stripes on the covers. Barazani was a busy man. Unlike Nero when Rome burned he had not been fiddling, he was trying to save his country.

The noise of the crowd had grown since Haaris had arrived, as he'd hoped it would. He needed as large an audience as possible.

"We're worried about your nuclear weapons. There's a fear—justified, I think—that one or more of them might fall into the hands of the Taliban. So my first job here is to get your assurances that your security systems are firmly in place."

"Your president telephoned me a few minutes ago, probably to ask me that very question. I didn't take her call, I wanted to talk to you first. We may have a problem. At this point I'm told that four of them have gone missing."

Haaris suppressed a smile. "My God," he said. "Rajput said nothing about it. Who has them, hopefully not the Taliban?"

"As I said, General Rajput is no friend. At this point all I know is that they may be missing, who has them is still in question. But if it is Taliban it's not likely they have the technical knowledge to explode the things. There is that."

"The North Koreans would be willing to help."

"We're watching for just that. Currently there are

seventeen North Koreans in Islamabad, Rawalpindi and Karachi. They are here as businessmen, but we're keeping a very close eye on their movements."

"Exactly who is doing this?"

"People in the SS Directorate personally loyal to me."

The ISI's SS Directorate's prime function was to monitor terrorist activities throughout Pakistan. It was one of the divisions inside the spy agency that Haaris had not been able to penetrate, and one that General Rajput had assured him was of little or no interest to the Americans. Of course, the general was playing both ends against the middle.

"You'll need to talk to President Miller and reassure her that you are in control of the nuclear arsenal."

"It would be a lie."

"Of course, but without that assurance she'll almost certainly send in our Nuclear Energy Support Team to disable as many of your weapons as our people can get to."

"That would not be so easy as the bin Laden raid."

"No one thinks it would be. Certain of our people on her staff and in the Pentagon believe that the losses we would suffer are worth reducing the risk of your weapons falling into the wrong hands."

"Which may already have occurred," Barazani said. "But why are you here? What you are telling me makes you a traitor. And just what is it that you are telling me? What's the U.S. strategy?"

"You need to look at the bigger picture, Farid. If the Taliban has gotten its hands on some nuclear weapons, Pakistan is finished. If President Miller does order our Nuclear Energy Support Team to neutralize what weapons they can reach, Pakistan will be doubly vulnerable—from the Taliban and also from India, which could very well mount a preemptive nuclear strike knowing that you could not retaliate." Haaris waved his hand toward the French doors. "Then there are the people who demand that something be done."

"A camera has been set up outside, and my image will be shown on the Jumbotron screen at the head of the front stairs. But what do I tell them? I was waiting for something substantive from you."

"What they want to hear."

"What are you telling me, David?" Barazani asked. "That I should step down? Who would take my place? Who would want to, except for the military, or maybe Rajput himself? What are you saying?"

"More to the point, what is the mob on Constitution Avenue demanding?"

"They're a mob."

"Pakistanis."

"Directed by the Taliban."

Haaris nodded.

Barazani looked like a trapped man. His eyes were wide and he breathed through his mouth. His face was wet. "Is this the message you have brought me from Washington?"

"Not exactly," Haaris said. "I have something more specific."

"What?"

Haaris got up and went to his bag. His back to Barazani he broke the diplomatic seal and took out a Glock 29 subcompact pistol, a suppressor attached to the muzzle. He turned around, walked directly back to Barazani, who reared back, and shot the president of Pakistan in the middle of the forehead.

EIGHT

President Barazani lay slumped to the left in his chair. Only a small amount of blood had leaked out of the wound in his forehead and dribbled into his left eye. Haaris felt the carotid artery, but there was no pulse.

The anteroom was empty, the door to the corridor closed. Getting a one-kilogram brick of Semtex and a contact exploder from his bag, he molded the plastic explosive to the outer door and set the fuse. When someone opened the door the Semtex would explode, killing anyone in the corridor within a few meters of the door.

He closed the inner door and molded a second brick of Semtex and an exploder to it.

From his bag he took the trousers, long shirt and kaffiyeh he'd worn in from the airport and put them on over his khaki slacks and white shirt.

Stuffing the pistol in his belt, he inserted the SIM card into his cell phone and called Rajput, getting him on the first ring.

"This is Haaris. I managed to get away from the bastards."

"My God, David, are you hurt?"

"No, but I'm on foot about five miles from the airport. I need to get to my airplane."

"The city is a mess. A big crowd has gathered in front of the Aiwan. They're calling for Barazani to come out and speak to them. But the coward is hiding in his office."

"He has to do it, General. There's no other way out for Pakistan." Haaris let some desperation into his tone. "Can't he see that?"

"It's our problem now, David. You've done all that

you could. We'll send someone to take you to your airplane and out of the country. Just hold tight."

Haaris shut off his phone and removed the SIM card.

He took the voice-altering device out of his bag and strapped it around his neck, centering the electronic package just beneath his Adam's apple, and readjusted the kaffiyeh to cover it and all but his eyes.

The remote control for the outside camera was lying on the small table next to Barazani's body. Haaris pocketed it, and finally he pulled a razor-sharp machete from his bag and went back to the president of Pakistan.

"Now it is time, my old friend, for you to actually do something worthwhile for your country," he said.

He swung the blade with all of his might, easily severing the flesh of Barazani's neck and cutting through the top of the spinal column. The president's head fell backward, thumping onto the floor behind the chair and rolling a meter or so before coming to rest on its right side.

Haaris wiped the machete on Barazani's shirt and laid it aside before he switched on the outside camera, picked up the severed head by its hair and walked to the door.

The radio in Lieutenant Jura's car came to life. "Special unit one."

He answered it. "Unit one."

"Get out of there right now. The situation is about to go explosive."

The only one who could use this channel was the directorate's dispatcher, under the personal control of General Rajput.

"What about my passenger? He's still inside."

"He's no longer your concern. Leave now, Lieutenant. That is an order."

"Roger," Jura said. He started the car and headed back past the residences to the rear gate. He had no idea what was going on, but he was relieved to be out of it. All hell was about to break loose; it was thick in the air and at this moment, he could think only of himself, and the hell with the bloody Americans.

As he approached the gate, he could hear a helicopter coming in from the south, but then three armed guards came out of the darkness and blocked the driveway.

"Halt," one of them shouted.

For some inexplicable reason the iron gate stood open just beyond the guards.

"Stop now!" the guard shouted.

Jura slammed the gas pedal to the floor and the Fiat surged forward, striking one of the guards before the others opened fire.

Haaris switched on the voice-altering device, opened the French doors and walked out onto the balcony. At the balustrade he raised Barazani's head to show the crowd.

For a seeming eternity the mob fell almost silent. In the distance to the south the ISI helicopter was arriving. The time for long speeches was past.

"This man was an instrument of our enemies in the West," Haaris shouted in Punjabi, the language that nearly 50 percent of the people spoke.

"But we have friends with us now. The Students." He used the Pashto word for "students" which was *taliban*. "Our only way to liberation is with them. They will help guide us when the Americans attack, which they will very soon, possibly even before dawn. But we will not allow another Abbottabad. The shame will not be ours to bear."

The crowd reacted with a low, ugly roar that slowly rose to cheers.

"I have come here to guide you. I am not a Student, but follow me, I will show you the way."

His image was on the huge Jumbotron, the head in grisly color, his altered voice amplified so that it rolled over the mob, seeming to fill every molecule of air on Constitution Avenue.

"Pakistan's leaders have been nothing more than puppets of the American regime. They in Washington are friends of New Delhi. It must not continue this way. Pakistan needs at long last to declare its independence. We are a sovereign nation, we are a sovereign people."

The mob roared but without anger. They were hearing something they needed to hear, something they had yearned to hear for years, but especially since the SEAL team raid on bin Laden's compound in Abbottabad.

The unmarked helicopter, showing no lights, passed to the west of the Presidential Palace, but few people in the crowd seemed to notice.

"I have come with a message for you. A message that I was given by Allah in a waking dream."

The mob released a collective sigh.

"We do not have to wait for Paradise because it is here now, within all of us. We need only strength: strong arms to do what is needed, strong resolve to stay the course, strong hearts and strong love to know for certain that what we do is right and just."

Someone close to the front of the crowd shouted, "Messiah!"

At first it seemed like no one had heard, but then

someone farther back in the mob repeated it: "Messiah!"

Then a woman screamed, her voice shrill, "My Messiah!"

"Look to each other for strength."

The chant, *Messiah!* grew.

"Look to your families, your friends, your neighbors for strength."

"Messiah!"

"Look to strangers for strength."

"Messiah!"

"Look to me, for I will be your right arm of justice," Haaris told them.

The helicopter came from the north, very low, flared suddenly just high enough to set down on the roof behind and eight meters above the balcony.

"I will leave you now in person but not in spirit," Haaris shouted. "Love Pakistan, love your neighbors, have strength. There will be more messages from me."

The mob was momentarily subdued.

"Allah be with you. Allah be with us. Allah be with Pakistan!"

He threw the head over the edge of the balcony at the same moment the Semtex charge on the corridor door exploded with a sharp bang.

NINE

President Miller watched in stunned disbelief as the man the mob on Constitution Avenue was calling "Messiah" tossed the severed head off the balcony. Moments later the image they were intercepting from the Jumbotron broadcast went blank.

"My God, who was that?" she asked.

"If you mean the head, I'm pretty sure it was Barazani's," Secretary of State Fay said. "I met him twice last year. But if you mean the one who tossed it, I haven't the faintest."

Miller called Page, who was still at the Watch. His image came up on one of the big monitors. "Do we have a positive ID on whose head that was?" she demanded.

"Photo interp gives it a ninety-eight-percent match, plus or minus nothing, Madam President. It's Barazani."

"What about the man who tossed it?"

"Taliban, probably. We're getting a lot of signals out of ISI and they're just as surprised as we were. But I do have a bit of good news. We think that Dave Haaris may have escaped. The ISI is trying to reach him so they can get him out to the airport."

"As soon as he's airborne I want to talk to him. He was right in the middle of it, he should have picked up something. But what about the man the crowd called 'Messiah'?"

"We don't have an ID, but one of our technical people is sure the voice was artificial."

"What do you mean?"

"He thinks the man's voice was computer enhanced. He's trying to re-create the real voice."

"We can do that?" Kalley asked.

"Otto Rencke's on it."

It was the second piece of good news, and the president said so. "We'll soon have an answer if he's as good as everyone says he is."

"He is," Page said. "But the bigger issue is why would he go through the trouble of disguising his voice in the first place? I'm told that his Punjabi was perfect."

"Excuse me, Madam President, but Mr. Page is correct," the White House translator, still on the Situation Room screen, interjected. "The Punjabi the man was speaking was educated. He's someone from an urban population center. I'd guess Lahore."

"That jibes with what my people are telling me," Page said.

"Have there been any hints about someone like that on the way up?" Miller asked. "He doesn't sound like run-of-the-mill Taliban."

"There are always rumors, but nothing that we've been able to substantiate. I spoke with Ross a few minutes ago and he's just as mystified as the rest of us. But we are working on it."

Kalley sat forward. "Was that an explosion we heard just before the signal was cut off?"

"We think so. Our best guess is that the president's personal security people blew the office door to get in."

"What about the Messiah?" Miller asked. "Do they have him?"

"Our spy bird picked up the image of an Mi-24 Hind attack helicopter landing on the roof of the Presidential Palace. It's just twenty-five feet above the balcony."

"Jesus, are the Russians somehow involved in this?"

"It's not likely. The angle was for the Jumbotron. We did some enhanced imagery and couldn't come up with any markings. But we think the speaker may have made his way to the roof and boarded the helicopter, which took off toward the south, where we lost it."

"Goddamnit, don't tell me what we can't do, tell me how," the president said in frustration.

"I'm sorry, Madam President, but current economic policy has tied our hands in some critical areas. Like the launching of new reconnaissance satellites."

"What did we do before the age of satellites?" Miller shot back.

"We had more personnel on the ground," Page said, not backing down. His message was clear: You get what you pay for.

"What resources do we have to send to help Ross?"

"Rencke suggests that we ask McGarvey for a hand."

Miller personally had never liked or trusted maverick operators such as McGarvey. But when she'd gone to the White House just before Christmas, a couple of weeks before she was inaugurated, the outgoing president had briefed her on highly classified assets she could count on if nothing else was working. Kirk McGarvey, the legendary operator who for a brief period had actually been director of the CIA, was one of them.

"He won't want to work for you, but if he does, never ask him a question for which you think you already know the answer," the president had told her. "The man has the bad habit of telling you the truth, no matter how much you don't want to hear it."

She'd started to object, but the president held her off.

"He's likely to do things his own way, not yours, and he's just as likely to ignore the law. Hell, I even had him arrested and put in jail. Lasted less than twenty-four hours before the shit hit the fan and I had to let him get back to work. And through all of it, I had the impression he let himself be arrested just to make his point."

"Isn't he getting too old to be running around shooting people?"

"No," the president said flatly. "And don't ever

question his loyalty or his motivation. He's been severely wounded several times in the line of duty. And he lost his wife, his daughter and his son-in-law to the cause."

"What cause is that?" Miller had asked. It was the last time she tried to be sarcastic when it came to discussing McGarvey. She had gotten over it that afternoon.

"His country and for what it stands. Jingoistic, even schmaltzy, but true nevertheless. Don't forget it, Charlene."

Miller focused on Page's image. "We're not quite there yet, Walter. First I'll decide if we'll send our nuclear response teams before the situation gets totally out of hand. Keep in contact. And let me know as soon as Haaris shows up."

"Will do," Page said, and the president shut down the connection.

For the longest moment, no one said anything.

"Discussion," the president said.

"I don't think that there's any question that we send in our nuclear response teams," Admiral Altman said. "But we will suffer casualties."

"We didn't when we took out bin Laden."

"They didn't know we were coming. This time they'll be expecting us."

"I don't know if I can completely agree. They've got their hands full trying to defend their military bases against attacks by the Taliban."

"People listening to what the Messiah told them might have bought into it," Kalley suggested.

"That the Taliban is suddenly the friend of Pakistan?" Miller asked sharply. The use of the word *Messiah* was bothersome to her.

"Yes."

"And we can only guarantee to neutralize ninety of their nuclear weapons," the admiral said. "And that's the best-case scenario. It would leave them with thirty workable weapons—including the ones that went missing in the last twenty-four hours. Could turn into an all-out war."

"Our response teams would create enough of a cause célèbre for them to declare war," Secretary of State Fay said.

"Not against us," Miller said.

"Against Afghanistan. Hamid Karzai is no friend of Pakistan."

"We still have people on the ground over there," Kalley said. "It could turn into an unholy mess. But I agree with Admiral Altman. We don't have any choice but to send in the teams. We just have to be prepared for the blowback."

Blowback was a term that President Miller hated more than any other, and she let her displeasure be known by the look on her face and the tone in her voice. "I want to talk to Haaris first."

TEN

The ISI's Russian Hind attack helicopter carrying Haaris touched down in Jinnah Park two miles southeast of Rawalpindi and trundled beneath a canopy of trees before its engines shut down.

The ephemeris data of the American KH-14 spy satellite that showed the exact position of the spy bird for any given latitude and longitude twenty-four/ seven had been programmed into the chopper's navigation systems. Two years ago, within ten days after the bird had been launched and went operational, the data set had been stolen by an ISI-paid computer hacker working out of a commune in Amsterdam. The pilot merely linked the data to his GPS receiver and he was showed the route that would avoid detection.

The gunfire and explosions around the Army General Headquarters had subsided a few minutes after Haaris's speech, and here in this isolated spot Pakistan seemed to be holding its breath.

Haaris pulled off his kaffiyeh, shirt and trousers and stuffed them in the nylon bag, from which he pulled out his blazer and put it on. He took the computer collar off, detached the microchip processor, which he pocketed, and then put the collar in the bag. The clothes and other things would be destroyed.

The only other person in the chopper besides the pilot and copilot was ISI captain Qadir Aheer, a totally disagreeable little rat-faced man whose complexion was pocked from teenaged acne. He was constantly chuckling as if he were in on a very big joke.

A yellow Toyota pickup truck was parked about ten meters away in a copse of willows.

"It has a half tank of gas," Qadir said. "But you will be on your own and you will have no weapon. You've been a Taliban prisoner tonight."

"Of course," Haaris said indifferently. The most difficult work had already begun. The next would be convincing the U.S.—but slowly, gently, with finesse—to take military action against Pakistan beyond the nuclear response raid that should happen sometime before dawn.

"But you will have to present the illusion."

"I need your help."

Qadir grinned. "Yes, you do. That part is unavoidable. You will simply be an American spy who got in the way and who luckily escaped with his life."

Haaris felt no malice for the man, who was simply doing a job he was ordered to do, except that the little bastard would enjoy inflicting the pain on someone he knew was his better.

Qadir yanked on the breast pocket of Haaris's blazer, tearing the material. He ripped Haaris's white shirt down the front, the buttons popping off, and he slapped Haaris in the face as hard as he could.

The pilot and copilot did not turn around.

Qadir picked up a Kalashnikov and slammed the butt of the assault rifle into the side of Haaris's face, nearly dislocating his jaw and breaking a couple of teeth. He then slammed the rifle butt into Haaris's chest, cracking a couple of ribs, and then raised it like a club.

Haaris grabbed the captain's hand and stayed the blow. "That will be enough." It hurt to talk.

"The Taliban wouldn't have been so easy on you," Qadir said, grinning ear to ear. "I think we need to complete the illusion."

"As you wish, Captain," Haaris said. He pulled out his pistol and shot the man in the face, just above the bridge of his nose.

Qadir fell back against the rear of the copilot's seat.

The pilot turned around. "What do you want us to do with the captain's body?"

"On the way back dump it out the door."

"How shall we report it?"

"He was a captain who exceeded his orders," Haaris said.

"Yes, sir," the pilot said.

Haaris shoved the pistol in his belt but left his bag

behind. He climbed down from the helicopter and went directly to the pickup, not bothering to look over his shoulder as the helicopter lifted off and swung back to the north toward ISI headquarters.

Gunfire to the north toward Islamabad had all but died down, but smoke from the fires that had been set earlier still flickered in the overcast sky, and the smell was everywhere, as Haaris drove east along a narrow dirt track through Koral and then Shaheen Town.

His face was on fire, and his ribs hurt so badly that it was difficult to take even shallow breaths.

He came over a low rise and stopped. In the distance, maybe five or six kilometers, Gandhara International Airport was still lit up. Closer to his position, where the dirt track met with the main highway from the city, he could make out several cars and pickup trucks.

He put the SIM card back in his phone and called General Rajput. "I need some help."

"Where are you, David?"

"A few klicks from the airport, but the highway is blocked. I think the Taliban still hold it."

"My hands are tied, you must understand this. I'm told that Captain Qadir, who got you out of there, was himself shot to death less than fifteen minutes ago. I've sent two gunships to retrieve his body."

"I'm more important than a dead man, god-damnit!"

"You're an American."

"An embarrassment to your government if I'm re-captured. Give me air cover, General, and clearance for my aircraft to take off and I'll be out of your hair."

Rajput was silent for several beats. When he came

back he sounded resigned. "Keep your head down and get word to your crew to start the engines. We'll clear the highway. Your window of opportunity will not last long. I suggest you take advantage of my friendship as quickly as possible."

"Go with Allah."

"And you too."

Haaris shut down his phone, but this time he did not remove the SIM card. There was no need for it now.

Within three minutes a pair of Bell gunships materialized from the northwest, and swooping fast and low, opened fire with their GAU-17/A 7.62-millimeter machine guns. In a single pass the vehicles parked on and off the road had been reduced to little more than burning sheet metal, and the Taliban fighters little more than blood mist and scattered body parts.

The choppers made tight arcs and came back, the gunners looking for targets, but there were none and the pilots peeled off and headed back the way they had come.

At the bottom of the hill, Haaris had to take care to avoid the carnage until he could get up on the highway and race to the airport. Passing the signs to the arrivals and departures terminals, he drove around to the military aviation side, no one coming out to challenge him.

The Gulfstream was on the tarmac in front of one of the closed hangars, its engines running, the hatch open and stairs lowered.

Gwen stood at the open hatch and when Haaris pulled up and got out of the pickup, she came down with the copilot, Dan Francis, and together they propped him up and helped him aboard.

"Get us the hell out of here," he croaked. The pain in his mouth was bad, but he made it sound worse.

"Get him strapped down," Ed Lamont said.

Francis helped with that, and then he raised the stairs and closed the hatch as they started to roll.

"We thought for sure that they had killed you," Gwen said.

"They wanted to," Haaris said.

"I'll get the trauma kit."

"First I need a large brandy, and as soon as we're out of Pakistan's airspace get me Mr. Page on the secure phone."

ELEVEN

Walter Page's call came into the White House Situation Room, his image up on the flat-panel monitor. It appeared as if he was still in the Watch at CIA headquarters.

"Madam President, Dave Haaris is in the air and on the way out of Pakistan. I just talked to him on an encrypted phone. They've been given permission to fly over Saudi Arabia and Egypt to our air force base at Incirlik, Turkey."

"Why there, why not Ramstein and then home?" Miller demanded, her impatience rising. There was always a certain rhythm and meter to crisis situations, a metronome that could not be altered without bad effects.

"They weren't allowed to refuel at Gandhara, so they'll have to make the stop. And Haaris was banged up."

"How badly?"

"His says that his injuries are uncomfortable but not life-threatening."

"I want to talk to him."

"As soon as they're safely on the ground in Incirlik a secure circuit can be arranged," Page said.

"Now," the president said.

"They haven't cleared Pakistan's airspace yet."

"That doesn't matter."

"He needs medical attention."

"And I need to talk to him," Miller insisted. "I know Haaris. He's a good man who's been in the middle of a situation for which I need more information. Doing nothing at this moment is not an option, but neither is doing the wrong thing."

"As you wish," Page said. "May I listen in?"

"Of course," Miller said. Several moments later Haaris's image came up on the split screen, Page to the left.

"Madam President," he said, his voice distorted. His face was red and swollen.

"Where are you at this moment?"

"We haven't been in the air very long. I suspect we're about one hundred miles south of Islamabad en route to Karachi, where we'll fly up the Gulf of Oman to Saudi Arabia."

"How are you?"

"I've been better, but I'll live. The bastards aren't terribly civilized, you know."

"You can save your full report until you get home, but I need to know what the situation on the ground is. Do you know about this Messiah who showed up out of nowhere?"

"Only what General Rajput told me. Is it true that he murdered President Barazani?"

"Unfortunately, yes."

"Incredible," Haaris said. "And let me guess, he admitted openly that he killed the president and probably that the Taliban are in reality Pakistan's friends."

"Yes, did you see the broadcast?"

"No, but the group that captured me suddenly got up and left. Five minutes later a squad of ISI security showed up and got me out of there."

"What else can you tell me?"

"There were many explosions and a great deal of gunfire, but from where they took me I couldn't say if it was more concentrated in Islamabad or Rawalpindi. But it stopped just before my captors took off. I can tell you that they were happy. One of them wanted to shoot me, but another one—I think he was probably the leader—said something to the effect: 'Why bother?'"

"You had no trouble taking off from the airport? No one challenged you?"

"No. I think it must have been the ISI's doing, but frankly I don't see how they'll be able to hang on. They used to be friends of the Taliban, but that relationship hasn't existed for several years."

The president looked around the table at the others. They were grim-faced. "I'm in the Situation Room."

"Yes, I can see that, Madam President."

"I'm considering launching our NEST people. They're standing by now."

Haaris sat forward. "Have there been any reports yet of missing weapons?"

"Unfortunately, yes."

"There'll be more. Launch the teams immediately."

"More? How can you be sure?"

"If this Messiah claims that the Taliban are friends of Pakistan, his first move will be to get as many WMDs into their hands as quickly as possible. It's no secret that our intention is to neutralize as many as we can."

"Yes," Miller said. "My concern is an Indian preemptive strike. The entire region could go up in flames. The loss of life would be nothing short of catastrophic."

"Telephone Mr. Singh," Haaris said. Manmohan Singh was India's prime minister, who held the actual executive power. "He'll listen to reason. And have you spoken with Sabir?" Nasir Sabir was Pakistan's PM.

"Not yet."

"Then, Madam President, I strongly suggest that you send the teams in immediately. And once they have accomplished their mission, contact both PMs to let them know what you have done and that the U.S. will continue to stand by as an ally to both nations."

"It's possible that India will strike as soon as they find out I've launched the teams."

"Not while our personnel are on the ground there. But every minute that you delay could mean the loss of more weapons to the Taliban."

"They wouldn't have the means to launch them."

"If they have the cooperation of the air force they will," Haaris said.

"Thank you, David. Have a safe trip home."

Page remained on screen after Haaris was off.

"Let me know as soon as he clears Pakistan's airspace," Miller said.

"Okay."

Miller cut the connection.

Everyone around the table stared at her, their expressions even darker than before, their mood easy to read.

"Discussion," she said.

"There's no question but we launch now," Kalley said. "Haaris was right, we mustn't delay."

"He's a CIA analyst."

"Whom everyone trusts," Secretary of State Fay said. "Haaris is the last word on the Pakistan question. The agency has built an entire desk around him."

"No one at the Pentagon doubts his expertise,"

Secretary of Defense Spencer said, and Admiral Altman agreed.

"The man has never been wrong."

And that was one of the main sticking points for Miller. The man was never wrong. It was a condition in people—especially in her advisers—that she'd always found disturbing.

Before her election, she'd been only a one-term junior senator from Minnesota, but before that she had been the dean of the University of Minnesota. It had been an important job, heading one of the leading universities in the U.S., the job made more interesting because of the geniuses who answered to her administration.

But she had, for the most part, let them do their own thing. Before she had taken the job, a friend of hers who was the dean of a small but prestigious Northeastern college had given her a piece of advice that she'd always thought was sound.

"Venerate your geniuses—the straight-A students who will go on to do major things, win prizes, bring honor to your school. But take special care of your C and even your D students because they are the ones who will go out into the world and make millions with which they'll endow your new library or science wing."

It was the same for her in the White House. She was bombarded by geniuses—eggheads—but it was the workers in the trenches, the ones with real-world experiences, that she most admired. The problem was that Haaris was both an egghead and a man of the world.

"If the Taliban are truly in charge—or at least are partners—they will retaliate," she said.

"We don't have a choice," Secretary of Defense Spencer replied. "We have to strike now."

"We won't get them all."

"No," Spencer said. "But we'll get most of them."

Politics, Miller had decided early in her campaign for president, was like chess. The opening moves for control of the center board were decisive. A master against a mere journeyman could force a checkmate in the first four or five moves. But against an out-of-control wild man who was likely to do the totally unexpected, even the superior player sometimes had serious trouble.

Like now.

The screens lit up in red, and a moment later Page was back on. "Madam President, we've had a nuclear incident in Pakistan on the border with Afghanistan. It may be a detonation of the weapon taken from Quetta Air Force Base. We have a WC-135 Constant Phoenix aircraft operating out of Kandahar that is measuring particulates in the atmosphere, and we've a seismic confirmation of a ten-kiloton-plus event."

Haaris came on. "We can see it off to the north," he said. "Definitely a nuclear explosion."

"Have you been affected?" Miller asked. She felt numb.

"Physically we're okay. Have you sent the teams?"

She looked at the others, and nodded. "They're on their way."

PART
TWO

The Mission

TWELVE

The Gulf water one hundred yards off Florida's west coast was in the mid-eighties, and Kirk McGarvey, just finishing his five-mile swim for the day, was warmed up—his body heat keeping just ahead of the drag from cooler water. Sometimes like this in the mornings just after dawn, he felt that he could swim day and night forever. Across the Gulf to the Bay of Campeche if he wanted to.

He was fifty with the solid build of an athlete, the stamina of a man much younger and the grace of a world-class fencer, which in fact he had once been. He was not an overly handsome man, but a certain type of woman found him very good looking because of his almost always calm demeanor even under the most trying of circumstances. When McGarvey—Mac to his friends—showed up you just knew that everything would turn out fine. It was an aura that he radiated.

After his air force days with the Office of Special Investigations, he'd been snapped up by the CIA, where at the agency's training facility outside Williamsburg, Virginia, he had gone through the field operator's course with the highest marks ever recorded. He'd been a natural for special operations from the beginning. And he'd been groomed to think on his feet, which came naturally to him, and to kill with a variety of weapons, including sniper rifles, pistols, knives, garrotes, and if the need arose, with his hands.

A sailboat heading south toward the Keys was low on the horizon, just a couple of miles out, and McGarvey considered taking out his own forty-two-foot Island Packet ketch, docked behind his house on Casey Key, about seventy miles south of Tampa. Maybe down to the Dry Tortugas, then ride the Gulf Stream up to the Bahamas, maybe spend a month or so before the hurricane season started in earnest.

It was a trip that he and his wife, Katy, had taken several times since moving down here from the Washington, DC, area. But she was gone now, assassinated with an IED meant for him. They'd been attending the funeral at Arlington for their son-in-law, Todd, a CIA officer killed in the line of duty. Mac was riding in a separate limousine from Katy and their daughter, Elizabeth, when theirs in front ran over the powerful explosive before his eyes. There'd been little or nothing left of the car, and almost nothing of Katy, Liz and their driver.

Since then he'd taken a few freelance assignments for the Company, but his heart had never really been in them, let alone the day-to-day business of enjoying life as he had before their deaths.

Nor did he think now that he was ready to solo his boat to places where people—couples—would be enjoying themselves. Laughing, playing, making love.

He would head back to his house just across the road from the beach, take a shower, have a little breakfast and then head up to his office in the philosophy department at the University of South Florida's New College campus in Sarasota. He taught Voltaire during the fall and spring semesters to a bunch of gifted kids, who were so liberal in their views that sometimes it was all he could do to stop himself from smiling indulgently at them. But most of them were seriously bright, and they had the habit of asking some seriously difficult questions. He loved the challenge.

But before September rolled around he needed to put some work into the book he was in the middle of writing, about Voltaire's influence not only on Western thought since the eighteenth century, but especially on the United States' fledgling democracy. It would be a hard sell to the kids, but he'd had a personal connection with the Frenchman's philosophy and its direct effect on the U.S., starting with the Civil War.

He was about to start back toward the beach when he glanced again at the southbound sailboat in time to spot a speedboat heading from the north almost directly toward him. It wasn't uncommon to see boats like that coming so close to shore, especially along Casey Key, where a lot of millionaires maintained seasonal homes. Tourists who wanted to get a glimpse of someone famous sometimes came up on the beach and walked around.

McGarvey angled back toward the shore and put real effort into his swimming, his progress aided by an incoming tide and a light westerly breeze. A woman standing on the beach began waving at him. She looked vaguely familiar, but the distance was too great for him to make out more than the fact that she was a woman and that she was gesturing.

Two minutes later he could feel the buzz of the outboard motors as well as hear their high-pitched drone—two of them, he thought, maybe two-fifty or three-hundred horsepower each—capable of pushing a boat with the right hull shape to speeds in excess of fifty miles per hour.

He glanced over his shoulder in time to see the

center-console boat just a dozen yards away and heading directly for him.

The water here was less than ten feet deep, and he immediately dove for the bottom, jackknifing with a powerful kick.

A couple of seconds later the boat passed over him, its propellers roiling the water and setting up a double-helix current that sent him tumbling up and then downward again, totally out of control, his shoulder slamming into the soft sand of the bottom.

Kicking off he reached the surface in time to see the speedboat making a tight turn back toward him, one man at the helm, another hanging on to a side rail on the console. But making such a tight turn was a mistake. It had cost them a lot of speed for the sake of the distance the wide turn had taken.

He maintained his position low in the water, bobbing up and down with the residual wake.

The second man aboard pointed toward him, and the guy at the wheel gunned the engines. But they were too close for the boat to come back up on plane and gain any real speed.

As the boat reached McGarvey, its bow was high, impairing the helmsman's sight line straight ahead.

At the last possible moment, McGarvey kicked to the right like a matador stepping aside to let the charging bull pass, allowing the bow of the boat to just brush his shoulder.

He hooked his left arm over the gunwale of the boat, just ahead of its stern, and allowed the building momentum to yank him out of the water and deposit him just aft of the transom.

Both men were dark-skinned, and Mac got the immediate impression that they were Middle Easterners—

Afghanis, Iranians, Iraqis, Pakistanis—before the lookout twisted around, a big Glock 17 in his hand.

McGarvey lurched forward and to the left, slamming his bulk into the back of the helmsman just as the lookout fired a shot that went wild.

The helmsman, shoved off balance, held on to the wheel so he wouldn't fall. The boat turned sharply to the left and headed back toward the shore.

It was what McGarvey had expected would happen and he'd braced himself against the rail.

The lookout fired again, the second shot going wide, and in an instant McGarvey was on him, snatching the pistol out of his hand and tossing it overboard. He butted the man in the face with his forehead, then pulled him forward and down, smashing a knee in the guy's jaw.

Shoving the man aside, Mac turned to the helmsman, who was trying to turn the boat away from the beach, which was getting alarmingly close.

With one hand on the wheel the man looked back, a Glock 17 in his left. Just before Mac could reach him he jogged the wheel sharply to the left and then to the right.

Mac was thrown off balance back against the rail.

The boat steadied, and the helmsman aimed at McGarvey's chest, center mass.

At that moment a bright red spot materialized just above the bridge of the man's nose and he fell backward against the console, blood spurting out of the bullet wound in his forehead.

Mac regained his balance at the same moment the boat's keel lurched against the bottom, less than ten feet from the beach, the engines wide open.

He managed to leap off the boat and stay clear of the props as it reached the beach, hurtled up over the first dunes and smashed into a large palm tree, the force of the impact ripping both engines free of the transom, the dual fuel tanks going up with a bright flash and an impressive boom that echoed off the fronts of the houses just across the beach highway.

THIRTEEN

McGarvey picked himself up from the surf as the woman who had been gesturing came toward him at a run. He was a little dazed from the second impact against the ocean floor, and it took him just a moment to realize that the woman was Pete Boylan. She was dressed in jeans and a white polo shirt.

"Jesus, Mac, are you okay?" she demanded breathlessly. She was an attractive woman in her late thirties, with dark red hair, blue eyes and movie-star looks. She had started her career in the CIA as an interrogator, but by happenstance over the past couple of years she had worked on a number of assignments with McGarvey. She was holding a Wilson nine-millimeter compact tactical pistol in her left hand.

"I'll live," he told her, brushing the sand off his chest and shoulders. "That was a hell of a shot at a moving target at that distance. I don't think more than a handful of people in the Company could have pulled it off. Thanks."

She laughed more in relief than in humor. She was in love with McGarvey and she made no bones about showing it. "It was my fifth try, and I thought there was just as good a chance that I'd hit you instead. But the advantage was his. I had to try." She looked critically at him. "Are you sure you're okay?"

"Yeah," he said. He gave her a smile. "The right time at the right place, but what are you doing here?"

"Walt Page sent me down to talk to you. But who were those guys?"

McGarvey always expected that someone out of his past—someone who'd either been partners with or the control officer of one of the people he'd taken down—would come looking for him to settle the score. It had happened a couple of times, but this one was about the closest he'd come to being taken out.

"I don't know. Might have been Middle Easterners."

"Pakistanis?"

McGarvey shrugged. "It's a possibility. But with the trouble going on over there I think I'd be low on their list." But then he had another thought and he glanced at the furiously burning wreckage of the boat. In the distance they could hear sirens.

"You wouldn't know more unless you'd talked to Otto overnight," Pete said. "Miller sent in our NEST people, and it was a disaster. We managed to shut down less than ninety of their nukes before all hell broke loose."

"Casualties?"

"Out of ninety-four operators, thirteen are either KIA or wounded, but our SEALS got everybody out. The Pakis knew we were coming."

"Miller waited too long," McGarvey said. The woman had been a competent president to this point, dealing decisively, for the most part, with immigration, health care and employment issues. But ordering the U.S. military into harm's way was completely different.

Pete nodded. "She did." The look on her oval face was a combination of resignation, that what was done was done; of shame, that perhaps the CIA could have provided better, even more timely intelligence; and of something else, maybe fear.

McGarvey had learned to read her emotions, which were almost always clear in her eyes and in her body language—unless she was conducting a debriefing or an interrogation, during which times she was nothing short of efficient and even ruthless. He knew that she was in love with him, and had been for at least a year, probably longer, and he had held her off as best he could.

He'd never had any luck with the women in his life. In the beginning of his CIA career, after he had returned from an assignment in Chile, where he'd assassinated a powerful general and the man's wife, Katy had given him an ultimatum: it was either her or the CIA.

She was sick to death of his frequent absences, not knowing where he'd gotten himself to or if he'd ever come back. She knew about the stars on the granite wall in the lobby of the Original Headquarters Building at Langley. They represented fallen field officers whose names and assignments could never be made public. They'd died in the line of duty; it was the only thing that their wives or husbands and families could ever be told. Katy didn't want to end up as one of those widows.

That day, confused, angry and hurt, McGarvey had run away to Switzerland, where he'd hid himself in plain sight for a few years until the FBI came calling for his particular talents.

In the meantime the Swiss Federal Police had sent a woman to get close to McGarvey, which she did. But she'd also fallen in love with him.

He'd walked away from her too, but she'd followed him to Paris, where she'd been killed.

Something similar had happened not long after

that, when another woman had fallen in love with him and she had been killed in a bomb blast that destroyed a restaurant in Georgetown.

Then Katy and their daughter and son-in-law had lost their lives because of him.

He couldn't allow something like that to happen again—which in his heart of hearts he knew would. So he kept his distance. It hurt Pete, because she could sense that he had feelings for her. But it was better than identifying her body on a slab in a morgue somewhere.

"I haven't turned on my computer, or watched much television in the past ten days."

"And you've shut off your landline and cell phone. It's why I'm here. We need your help."

The sirens were closer now. McGarvey led Pete across the road to his house. Here the island was less than a hundred yards wide, and they were inside by the time the fire trucks and rescue squad had arrived.

They sat at a table on the lanai overlooking the pool, beyond which was the gazebo where Katy had loved to sit at dawn with her first cup of tea to watch the birds. The Island Packet was tied to the dock, behind which a small runabout sat out of the water on its lift.

"It's pretty," Pete said.

McGarvey felt a little odd having her here but not terribly guilty. He brought them Coronas with pieces of lime. She'd once told him that she wasn't always a lady; sometimes she liked to drink a cold beer straight out of the bottle.

"Yes, it is," McGarvey said. "Help with what?"

"It's complicated," Pete said. She quickly sketched everything that had gone on over the past twenty-four hours, including Haaris's trip to Islamabad, his kidnapping and his escape a few hours later. "Barazani is dead—beheaded by this guy who the crowd in front of the presidential palace called 'Messiah.' He told them that the Taliban were no longer the enemy. That they needed to work together for a new Pakistan."

"How about Sharif?"

"No one can reach him, and the ISI is keeping off of the radar for now. Their headquarters along with the Army's General Headquarters have been surrounded, as have most of the government buildings in Islamabad and Rawalpindi."

"What about the air force and navy bases?"

"No troop or ship movements," Pete said. "For all practical purposes Pakistan's government, military and intel services have been shut down. And for now India is biding its time. But if Pakistan so much as twitches, they promise to protect the sanctity of their borders using any and all means at their disposal."

"That sounds like a quote."

"A spokesman for India's prime minister," Pete said. "But there's more. We're pretty sure that at least one nuclear weapon was stolen from the air force base at Quetta last night. It was detonated about fifty miles south in an unpopulated area close to the Afghani border. Page thinks it was a demonstration by the Taliban that they not only have nukes, but that they know how to use them."

"What else?" McGarvey asked, though he had a good idea where this was leading and why she had been sent to ask for his help.

"The hell of it is that life is going on as usual. Kids are in school, the shops are open and, from Ross's accounts, doing a brisk business. There've been no further incidents of rioting or explosions or gunfire."

"What about the Messiah?"

"The television stations keep rebroadcasting his

speech and promising that he will be talking to the people again very soon, and that he has the reins of government firmly in control."

"It was a coup, and less than twenty-four hours later the country has calmed down," McGarvey said. "So other than the nuclear demonstration the only real problem is the Taliban and what they'll do next."

"Directed by the Messiah, and no one thinks it'll develop into a 'let's all lie down with the lambs.' At least not for long."

"What about our embassy?"

"Ready for business, soon as the ambassador and his staff return."

"Ross and his shop?"

"Hunkered down in place. He sent a field officer to Quetta to confirm the bomb, but he hasn't been heard from so far. Other than him and Dave Haaris's kidnapping there've been no aggressive acts toward Americans other than the NEST casualties."

"So what does Page want from me this time?"

"It's the White House. The president wants to see you right now. None of us know for sure what she's going to ask you to do, but we think it's a safe bet she's going to ask you to assassinate this Messiah."

"Otto thinks that too?"

Pete nodded. "He's already working on something. The voice the Messiah used to speak to the people was artificial. Altered electronically. Otto's trying to clean it up. But the question up in the air is, why would he need to change his voice? To fool whom?"

"Us," McGarvey said. "Because we know who he is. And the guys in the boat were no coincidence."

FOURTEEN

Haaris sat reclined in a dentist's chair at All Saints in Georgetown. The hospital was the place where wounded intelligence agents were brought when their identities needed to remain secret. The facility, discreetly located in a three-story brownstone, was equipped with the latest medical technology and the best doctors, surgeons, dentists and nurses in the business.

Dr. Rupert Marks straightened up and lifted his clear goggles to his forehead. "Nothing terrible in there," he said, patting Haaris on the shoulder. "Two teeth damaged, which I've temporarily capped for you, but that's the worst of it, except for the bruising. You're not going to be so terribly handsome for the next few weeks, but as soon as the procaine wears off your speech will get back to more or less normal."

"Nothing permanent?" Haaris asked. He'd come back to DC, his CIA mission definitely not accomplished; but he had come back, nevertheless, and as a wounded hero—even better.

"No. We'll have the permanent caps back from the lab tomorrow. Any time after that stop by and we'll finish up. Won't take more than twenty minutes."

"Thank you, appreciate your expertise."

Rupert smiled. "I'll send you my bill in the morning."

Rupert's assistant took off Haaris's bib and raised the chair. "You'll sound a little lispy for a half hour or so."

Haaris grinned. "That a real word, luv?"

"It's my word," she said. "Before you go, Dr. Franklin would like to see you, he's just around the corner in his office. It's next to the lab."

"I'll find my way, thanks."

Dr. Allan Franklin, the chief surgeon and administrator of All Saints, was seated behind his desk in his tiny, book-lined office on the ground floor, just across from the security station in the lobby. The door was open.

Haaris knocked on the door frame. "You wanted to see me?" he asked.

"Come in and have a seat," Franklin said. "And close the door." He was a slender man, his hairline receding, his fingers long and delicate.

"Bad news about my ribs?" Haaris asked, sitting down.

"How are you feeling?"

Haaris started to shrug, but then thought better of it. "What is it?"

"We took some pictures, routine for chest injuries. We found something else. A tumor on your pericardial sac that has probably been there for some time—maybe a year or longer. Operable in itself, but the cancer appears to have spread to your spine and three of your ribs. One of the reasons they didn't fracture. They're too soft."

Haaris crossed his legs and shrugged. "Prognosis?"

"We can remove the tumor, but as for the bone cancer you'll need chemotherapy, and it won't be pleasant."

"I meant the overall prognosis, Doctor. Am I going to beat this and live a long-enough life to have a dozen grandchildren?"

Franklin was used to dealing with intelligence officers, most of whom were tough-minded, pragmatic people; nevertheless, his simple and direct reply gave even Haaris pause.

"No."

"I see. Assuming I choose not to go the route of chemotherapy, how long do I have to live?"

"There's no way to say with any degree of certainty. A year, maybe longer, maybe less."

"Let me put it another way. I'm in the middle of something quite important. It has to do with the situation in Pakistan. And I can't walk away from it. How much viable time do I have? Mental acuity as well as physical? I must be able to think straight."

"Frankly, that'll depend on your tolerance for pain."

"I've been there before."

"Six months tops, I'm afraid."

"I see." Haaris paused. "Thank you for telling me straight out," he said. "Now, I don't suppose I could convince you to withhold your diagnosis from my employer?"

"I can't do that."

"Maybe a delay for a week or so?"

"Marty Bambridge is here with your wife," Franklin said. "I phoned him to come over." Bambridge was the deputy director of the Clandestine Service, also known as the Directorate of Operations.

A moment of intense rage threatened Haaris's sanity. For just that moment he was on the verge of coming around the desk and killing Franklin. But it vanished as quickly as it arose. "I will take care of letting my wife know. Are we perfectly clear on this, Doctor?"

"Your call, Mr. Haaris."

"Yes, my call, as you say."

Haaris stopped for a second just before the frosted glass door to the visitors' lounge to gather his wits. The deputy director was a complete idiot, who'd had the solid reputation of caring more for the mission than the man, so getting past him would present no obstacle. He would be perfectly willing to keep the news to himself, so long as the job was being handled. He'd make some noise, of course, and possibly bounce it up to the seventh floor. But six months was more than enough time for Messiah to set things in motion. Payback.

The biggest problem would be Deborah. She and Haaris had been married five years, after a whirlwind romance. She'd been a student at the Farm, where he'd given a brief series of lectures on developing and using psychological profiles of the opposition's field agents. That included the Chinese, who thought differently than Westerners, and spies sent by America's "friends" in Canada, England, France and Germany.

She'd been an indifferent student at best, completely in awe of the CIA in general and Haaris specifically, whom she thought was the most sophisticated, kind and gentle man she'd ever met since she'd graduated from Stetson University law school in Florida.

And for his part, he was in need of a bullet-proof cover if he was ever going to be promoted to a high enough level within the Company where his opinions mattered. Single men might make for good field officers, but working at headquarters, they made a lot of people nervous. Where did their loyalties lie and all that?

The woman had been incredibly boring to him from the start. Their sex unimaginative and mechanical. Her cooking, Midwestern meat and potatoes— she was from some small town in Iowa. She lacked any practical education vis-à-vis intelligence work. And most of all, her professed unconditional love and absolute devotion and loyalty were nothing short of stifling. But anyone from the Company who'd ever met her fell totally in love at first sight. She was the quintessential American wife. From the beginning he'd thought of her as a lap dog. The CIA needed people like her for background noise.

He opened the door and went in.

"There he is at last, in one piece," Bambridge said, getting up. The deputy director was short and slender with dark eyes that were usually angry. He always moved as if his feet were hurting him, and his expression suggested that just about everything he heard or encountered came as a surprise. "Clean bill of health and all that?"

"The doctor says I'll live at least until the end of the year," Haaris said. "He'd like to have a word with you."

Bambridge gave him a searching look, but then nodded. "Are you up for your debriefing this afternoon? Say, four?"

"I'll be there.

"Lots to tell?"

"Indeed."

Bambridge left, and Deb, who was five-three, blond and a little on the *zaftig* side, jumped up. She was shivering, her face a study of emotions from happiness to fear. She was dressed in a short skirt, with a frilly white blouse and flats, because she'd never learned how to walk in heels.

Haaris opened his arms to her and she came to him. He winced in more pain then he actually felt when she put her arms around him, and she cried out.

"Oh, God, David, I've hurt you!"

"It's all right, sweetheart. I'm just glad to be home in one piece with you."

FIFTEEN

A car and driver were waiting for McGarvey and Pete at Joint Base Andrews when their CIA Gulfstream landed and taxied to a navy hangar. They thanked the crew and walked over to the Cadillac Escalade, where a very large man in a plain blue jacket opened the back door.

"Welcome back, Mr. Director," he said. "Don't know if you remember, but I used to drive you places."

"Tony," McGarvey said.

"Yes, sir, good to see you again."

On the drive out to Langley, McGarvey came to the realization that he would not have answered the summons from the president if he hadn't been attacked that morning. "How many people knew that you were coming to talk to me?" he asked Pete as they got off the Beltway and took the George Washington Parkway toward the CIA's main entrance road.

"The president and at least some of her staff. Me, Marty, Walt Page, and Otto, of course."

"Whose call was it?"

"I guess the president asked Walt to contact you."

"Last night?"

"I imagine so. Marty called me about three in the morning, said you weren't answering your phone, so he wanted me to go to Florida and talk to you. Thought you might need some convincing. "

"The guys who tried to run me over did that. Apparently someone doesn't want me meddling in this business. Someone who has a contact either at the White House or in our shop."

Pete nodded. "I was thinking the same thing, but it could also be someone who suspected that you might be called in and wanted to stop your involvement even before you got started."

"That too," McGarvey said. "But it still points to an insider."

Haaris and his wife had a nice two-story Colonial just west of Massachusetts Avenue and within a few blocks of the Finnish and Dominican Republic embassies. She drove him home from the hospital, chatting all the way about how she hoped that he would feel better real soon. She was hoping they could fly out to see her parents in Des Moines and maybe even take them for a surprise vacation to Hawaii.

At home he took a quick shower and changed into a suit and tie, Deb dogging his every step, even sitting on the toilet seat while he dried off.

"My God, they beat you terrible," she said. His chest was black and blue and his face was still puffed up. "We help them and how do they repay us?"

"It's okay," Haaris told her, and he had a little twinge of sorrow for her. She would be lost when he was dead, and he felt as if he almost cared.

"No, it's not. And now you're going back to work."

"I was sent over to try to make a difference."

"Did you?" she asked, her voice sharp, only because she was hurting for him.

"I hope so," he said.

He kissed her on the cheek and took his Mercedes CLS500 down to West Potomac Park, where he walked over to the Vietnam Memorial wall with its fifty-thousand-plus names. It was three on a weekday afternoon, but the weather was good and a lot of people were in the park, many of them seated on the steps of the Lincoln Memorial.

A man something over six feet tall, with the frame of a footballer, wearing jeans, a polo shirt and a Yankees baseball cap, stood at a point at the wall where several KIAs named Johnson were engraved. He was Colonel Hasan Kayani, who controlled all ISI activities in the U.S. from his offices at the UN in New York. The FBI knew him as a low-level diplomat with the Saudi delegation, but when he left the city he traveled with a British passport under the name Wasif Jones. His English was spot-on, in part because he'd always been a quick study, but in a larger measure because he, like Haaris, had been educated in the UK. And also like Haaris, had been bright enough to hide his radicalism when he had been recruited by the Pakistani intel service nine years earlier.

Haaris had been a walk-in recruit up in New York and had been feeding Kayani information about the CIA's activities in Pakistan for the past three years. The colonel knew that Haaris had been sent to work with the ISI in Islamabad, but he did not know that Haaris was the Messiah. Only General Rajput knew that secret.

"The general said that you had received some rough treatment," Kayani said, glancing over.

"I'll live," Haaris said, that old phrase of his sounding odd in his ears now.

"My God, Page will be beside himself. Your trip to Islamabad completely backfired. Have you been debriefed yet?"

"I'm on my way over."

"What do you think of this Messiah business? Crazy, if you ask me."

"The people in the street are behind it. And we're finally going to have peace with the Taliban. So who knows where it'll lead?"

"Not me. But no one else knows what to make of it either."

"Thanks for taking care of the McGarvey business. That bastard could have created some trouble. He usually does wherever he goes."

"The mission failed," Kayani said. "I thought that you would have heard by now."

Haaris forced himself to remain calm. He needed only one thing from this buffoon, and the man had screwed it up. "What happened?"

"I don't have all of the details at this point, except that the powerboat my two people rented in Sarasota crashed on the beach and exploded. I've not heard from them since, so I assume they died in the crash."

"What beach?" Haaris asked, his voice even.

"Apparently directly across the street from Mr. McGarvey's house."

"Send someone else to do the job."

"Don't you think that he will be alerted to the fact that someone is trying to kill him? The CIA will certainly take notice."

"I want the bastard dead within the next twelve hours—twenty-four at most. And I don't give a damn how many assets you have to burn." Haaris turned to the man. "Have I made myself clear, Colonel? Do you understand what's at stake?"

At stake was Haaris continuing to feed solid-gold intel to the ISI in the person of Colonel Kayani. The pipeline from the CIA had made the man's career.

"Consider it done."

The Cadillac SUV was passed directly through the main gate, and driving up the road through the woods to the Original Headquarters Building—the one always shown in TV and in the movies—McGarvey had the same sensation he always had coming back like this. It was part excitement to be back in the hunt, part nostalgia for days past and sometimes just, at some point way in the back of his head, the tiniest bit of fear, or more accurately, concern, that sooner or later he was going to screw up. Sooner or later he would go up against someone, or someones, better than he was.

They parked in the underground VIP garage, and Pete went up to the seventh floor with him. She left him at Page's office. "They're expecting you."

"What about you?"

"They want me to sit in on Dave Haaris's debriefing."

McGarvey's ears perked up, though he didn't let it show. "They suspect him of something?"

"Good heavens, no," Pete said. "I've known about the guy for a few years now, and without him we wouldn't have a Pakistan Desk. But he was over there in the middle of it; the Taliban picked him up on the airport road, and the ISI managed to get him released. We just need the details. Might be something that could help. He'll point the way."

SIXTEEN

McGarvey was shown straight through by the DCI's personal secretary. Page was sitting on one of the couches in the middle of the large office, facing Marty Bambridge and the CIA's general counsel, Carlton Patterson, who were seated on the other. Otto was perched on the edge of Page's desk.

"Oh, wow, Jim Forest is looking for you," Otto said. He was a barrel-chested odd duck of a computer genius, with long red hair tied in a ponytail. He wore jeans and a KGB sweatshirt. He was McGarvey's best friend, and they had a long history together.

"I expect he is," McGarvey said. Forest was the chief of detectives for the Sarasota County Sheriff's Office, and he and McGarvey also had a history together. He would be taking the boat accident as no coincidence.

"Good afternoon," Page said, gesturing McGarvey to an empty chair. "You weren't injured?" he asked. He'd run IBM until the president before Miller had tapped him to take over the CIA, and the new administration saw no need to replace him.

"It was close, but Miss Boylan was waiting for me on the beach, and she helped out."

"She told me," Bambridge said. "A pretty big chance for her to take, wouldn't you say?"

"Don't start, Marty, I didn't come up here to play your games," McGarvey said. He too had a history with the deputy director of the Clandestine Service, not much of it any good. In his estimation Bambridge was a damned good desk jockey but not much of a field officer, though he fancied he was.

"My dear boy, have you been brought up to date on the situation in Pakistan?" Patterson asked. He was a tall slender man, with thinning white hair and the patrician manners of an old-school gentleman. He'd been the Agency's general counsel for what seemed like forever. In his early eighties, everyone in the business was much younger than he; his "dear boys" and "dear girls."

"Miss Boylan briefed me on the flight up, and Otto sent me some material while we were still in the air. But I don't know what the president thinks I can do about it."

"You're not an analyst, Mac," Otto said. "But I

think the woman is off her rocker if she's going to send you out to do what I think she will."

Page's jaw tightened. Like just about everyone else on the campus he tolerated Rencke mostly because he had a great deal of respect and even awe for the computer guru. And it was once suggested to him that since it was Otto who had designed the advanced computer systems for the entire U.S. intelligence community—including the National Security Agency's telephone and Internet monitoring capabilities—he could also destroy them.

McGarvey let Otto's comment slide for the moment. "What's Dave Haaris recommending?"

"Nothing yet," Bambridge said. "He's being debriefed at the moment. Soon as he's done he wants to get back with his people and come up with a plan. He said we're going to need one to get ourselves out of this mess." He hesitated.

"But?" McGarvey prompted. It wasn't like the deputy director to hold back.

Bambridge glanced at Page, who nodded.

"The Taliban beat him up. Dislocated his jaw, broke a couple of teeth with a rifle butt. Cracked a couple of ribs. We took him to All Saints, where they fixed his teeth and took some X-rays of his chest to see how bad the damage was." Bambridge looked away for a beat, the gesture also uncharacteristic for him. "The thing is, Franklin says Haaris has cancer, and it's spreading. Chemo and radiation therapy would prolong his life but not by much. Anyway, Dave declined."

"How long does he have?"

"Less than a year, six months of which he'll be on his feet. But after that he'll probably go downhill pretty fast."

"It's why he wants to get back with his people to help figure out what our response should be," Page said. He shook his head. "It's a damned shame, when we need him the most."

"You gave him the option to quit?" McGarvey asked. He knew almost nothing about Haaris except for his reputation, which was as sterling as his impeccable manners.

"Of course," Page said. "I spoke to him a half hour ago. Told me he was a little rushed for time, so he excused himself and left."

"Extraordinary man, by all accounts," Patterson interjected. Yet there was something in his tone of voice and the look in his eyes that didn't sit quite right. But McGarvey let that slide as well.

"Here's the situation as I see it. The president wants to see me. Since I shut down my phone and computer—I wanted to be left alone—Miss Boylan was sent to talk me into coming up here."

Bambridge started to say something, but McGarvey held him off.

"Did anyone at the White House know I wasn't taking calls?"

"Her chief of staff, Tom Broderick, I would imagine," Page said. "It was he who phoned to ask if you were in town."

"Who else here on campus?"

"All of us in this room—except for Carlton," Page said.

"A couple of people on my staff, including the housekeepers who arranged the aircraft," Bambridge said.

"Me and Louise," Otto said. Louise was Otto's wife, who sometimes did contract work for the Agency.

"Someone knew Miss Boylan was coming to see me, and they didn't want that to happen," McGarvey said. "Means two things: there's a leak here or at the White House, and whatever the president's going to ask me to do involves the situation in Pakistan."

"We don't know that for sure," Bambridge said.

"There were two guys in the boat. Small, dark. Almost certainly Middle Eastern."

"Inconclusive," Patterson said, but without much conviction.

"Enough for me," McGarvey said.

"That being the case, what do you propose?" Patterson asked.

"Well, we're not going to invade Pakistan. From what Otto gave me they still have thirty nuclear weapons and the means to launch them on rockets, from aircraft, from surface ships and possibly even from their Hamza submarines. The Indians know this also so it's not likely they'll launch a preemptive strike. And from what this Messiah character told the mob in front of the Presidential Palace, the Taliban are once again friends of Pakistan. Trained well enough, or helped by someone in Pakistan's military—probably someone from Quetta Air Force Base—to set off one of the weapons as a demonstration."

"So what's left?" Page asked, but it was a rhetorical question and everyone knew it.

"That's up to the president."

"We'll provide any sort of backup you need. And our COS Ross Austin in Islamabad should be able to fill you in on what's going on."

"I'd like to talk to Haaris before I head over to the White House, maybe get together with his team."

"And I might have something more for you," Otto said.

"I have a foolish question, my dear boy," Patterson said. "Since you believe the attack upon your person has something to do with the Pakistan issue, would you like some help, maybe a couple of bodyguards?"

McGarvey had to smile. "As you said, a foolish question."

"They could try again."

"I hope they do. It'd mean that I was irritating someone."

Bambridge couldn't hide a slight smile. "Are you armed?"

"I will be when I leave the building."

"Let us know what the president wants of you, if you would," Page said. "If it involves what we all believe it will, we'll need to adjust our thinking, and Ross will have to be given the heads-up."

"The president is going to ask me to assassinate the Messiah," McGarvey said.

"Indeed," Page said.

"I don't know if I'll do it."

SEVENTEEN

Pete walked across the connecting walkway from the Original Headquarters Building into the new building, past the cafeteria that faced the inner courtyard with its copper statue "Kryptos," which had recently been totally decrypted. The debriefing room was on the second floor, its windows also facing inward to the pretty courtyard with its walkways, statues and landscaping.

Haaris was seated at the end of a small conference table for six when Pete walked in. He was faced by Don Wicklund and Darrel Richards from the Directorate of Intelligence. His product and in general his conclusions on the Pakistan issue over the past several years had been so stellar that whenever he came back in from the field he was treated with kid gloves.

Both Wicklund and Richards were well-seasoned officers in their mid-forties who had done their stints in the field and had come in from the cold to take important administrative positions. They were respectful and pleasant. Just three friends having a little discussion. Could have been about the weather.

They all looked up. Wicklund and Richards had expected her, but Haaris hadn't, though he didn't show much surprise.

"Welcome back, Dave," she said. "Looks like a rifle butt to your chin. Must have hurt like hell."

"It stung a bit."

Pete sat at the opposite end of the table. "I'm Pete Boylan. Mr. Page asked me to sit in on your debriefing. Just a little bird in the corner. He's concerned not only about your well-being but about what the hell just happened over there."

"Miss Boylan, your reputation precedes you," Haaris said.

"Good, I hope."

"Nothing but."

The man was in pain, she could see that, but something else was bothering him, something deep at the back of his eyes, in the set of his mouth, in his mannerisms, which were nothing less than pleasant. No artifice that she could detect, just something bothering him.

She had read his jacket on the way up from Florida, and the only real anomaly, the only fact that didn't seem to fit, was his wife, Deborah nee Johnson. The woman had dropped out of recruit training at the Farm before she was flunked out. And a few months later she and Haaris were married. Haaris, the smooth, urbane, educated and worldly man. And

Deb the farm girl from Iowa with a law degree, just barely, though she'd never taken or passed any bar examination in any state. The two as a couple didn't gel in Pete's head.

His latest psych eval was mostly good, as were all the previous ones, and there didn't seem to be any hint of marital troubles. He and his wife didn't entertain much, nor did they accept many invitations, but they came across as a happily married couple.

It just didn't fit in Pete's mind.

"We have your written report that you sketched out on the flight back from Incirlik that says you weren't aware of this Messiah nor did you see the dramatic speech he made at the Presidential Palace," Wicklund said. He looked and acted like a professor of history.

"Not at the time. But I did watch the recording later. The man is a maniac, assuming he killed Barazani."

"He tossed the president's head over the rail."

"Might have been an accomplice who did the actual murder," Haaris said. "We can't discount any avenue of investigation."

"Is that the recommendation you're going to give to your desk?"

"I'll give them the same recommendation that I always give: Keep an open mind. Do not jump to conclusions. Spend a little time with your thinking."

"They still have thirty-plus nuclear weapons at their disposal, plus the means to deliver them," Pete said. "Do you think that time might not be on our side?"

"Pakistan is not preparing to attack India or any other country in the near future," Haaris said to her. "What we have witnessed is a coup d'état. A long time coming, in my estimation. And, Miss Boylan, I have given that much thought over the past several years—ever since the departure of Pervez Mush-arraf."

"So where is Pakistan going?"

"I'm not sure, but it is something very high on my list of priorities."

"Should we go to war with them?" Pete asked.

"Good heaven, no," Haaris said, genuinely surprised. "No nuclear power goes to war with another nuclear power in this day and age. In this case it's likely that India would become involved after all, and possibly even China might climb aboard ostensibly as our allies. It would give them a foothold into the region." He looked at Wicklund and Richards. "In that direction lies only madness."

"So your recommendation to the president would be wait and see," Wicklund said. "Not very insightful from where I sit. But believe me, Mr. Haaris, I don't want to come across as confrontational. We're all just trying to come to some conclusions about the situation, and you not only had your boots on the ground there, you are the go-to person on Pakistan."

"I understand," Haaris said. "I'll prepare a few notes by this evening and email them to you as soon as I have time. But for now my people are waiting to get started."

"We may have a few further questions."

"I think we all will," Haaris said. "Are we finished here?"

"Of course," Wicklund said.

Haaris got up and walked out of the conference room, and Pete caught up with him before he reached the elevators.

"Do you want to buy a girl a coffee?" she asked.

Haaris smiled. "Miss Boylan, are you coming on to me?"

Pete laughed. "Your accent drives women nuts, I

hope you know that. I'd like to ask you something personal, away from the recording equipment back there."

"I am rather busy."

"Only take a minute, promise. We can go back to the cafeteria, and I'll buy."

Haaris smiled again. "I suppose that it's an offer I can't refuse. And tit for tat. A good-looking woman drives me nuts."

Pete suppressed a smile.

They walked back down the corridor to the cafeteria, where she got them coffee and they sat at a table by the windows. Only a few other people were there at this hour of the afternoon.

Every window in every building on campus, even the cafeteria, was double-paned, with white noise piped in between the panes to cancel out any surveillance attempts.

"Who do you think this so-called Messiah is?" she asked. It was only an opening ploy to get him talking comfortably about a difficult subject.

"Hard to say this early."

"Your gut feeling, if you were to be pressed."

"Not Taliban, I think. He's likely using them only as a tool."

"For what?"

"It's a coup d'état, Miss Boylan, as I've already stated. The Taliban hates the U.S., and hate can act as a very powerful adhesive to hold a mob together. He or someone like him was probably inevitable."

"And an aphrodisiac," Pete suggested. He hadn't said that the Taliban hated "us," but that they hated the U.S. The U.S. as a third party distinct from himself as well as the Taliban.

"That too, but I wouldn't suspect that the average Pakistani would think of it that way."

Pete gazed out the window, sipping her coffee, letting the silence between them grow. It was an old interrogation technique. Subjects almost always wanted to fill the void by saying something.

"So, it's been interesting meeting you," Haaris said, rising. "Now if you'll excuse me."

"Something's bothering you," Pete said, looking up at him. "Call it woman's intuition or whatever."

"That's a personal statement."

Pete smiled. "It's the business. Goes with the territory. And trust me, none of what's been said here will be written down. You have my word."

Haaris hesitated for just a second then shrugged. "Doesn't matter, I suppose, for someone else to be in on my little secret. It's already arrived at the seventh floor."

Pete waited.

"Fact is, I'm dying. Cancer, I'm told. And I probably have around six viable months left to me."

Pete was taken aback. It was nothing close to what she had expected.

"Now, I must get back to my people. Time waits for no man, Miss Boylan, not even for me."

EIGHTEEN

McGarvey went down to Otto's third-floor suite of offices, where no one ever worked except for the special projects director. The three rooms were filled with sophisticated computer equipment: two-hundred-inch ultra-high-def flat-screen monitors on the walls, one horizontal flat-panel about the size of a pool table in the middle of the inner room and smaller screens, keyboards, printers and several laptops and tablets scattered on various desks and worktables. In addition, several large tables were filled to overflowing with printed maps, files, books, newspapers and magazines. Most of the chairs were stacked with folders. Other books were piled just about everywhere.

"Not everything is digitized." Otto had been saying this for years. "And probably won't ever be, provided there's a need for secrecy. A computer can be hacked from ten thousand miles away, but a piece of paper in some obscure file somewhere ain't so easy to access."

Several of the monitors showed various colors as backgrounds, ranging from light yellows and reds to deep violets, which lately meant his search programs—his little darlings, he called them—were running into something that could potentially be dangerous to the U.S.

One of the programs was working on the Messiah's brief speech; the image was on a screen, the voice low in the background.

"Pink picked up the fact that the voice was artificially enhanced," Otto said. "I didn't hear it myself. But I set her to filter out the enhancement, leaving only the original. Not so easy even for her since we have no idea, not even a clue, what the original sounds like, except its Punjabi seemed to be clipped, odd vowels here and there. Maybe someone who'd learned British English."

"About half the educated males in Pakistan," McGarvey said.

"Eighty percent," Otto said. He entered several commands from a keyboard. "I'm trying to translate what the guy was saying into English—the way his voice might sound if he were speaking in English."

"Are you making any progress?"

"It's coming, but slowly. And even if Pink does

come up with a credible voice, whose will it be? Any one of millions."

"There's only one reason he went to the trouble to disguise his voice, and it's because we'd recognize it. But if we could find out whether his English was Punjabi accented or not, it would give us a direction of sorts."

"My program has a seventy-eight-percent confidence that Punjabi is his native language."

"What about the voice-enhanced technology he used? Was it anything that you're familiar with?"

"Nothing that stood out. You can buy the basic chips and other circuit elements at your local Radio Shack."

McGarvey stepped right up to the monitor showing the Messiah. Nothing was visible of the man's face—if in fact it was a man—and even the eyes were in deep shadows under his kaffiyeh; nor were his hands clearly visible, except for a brief shot of him holding Barazani's severed head.

"His hand," McGarvey said.

"I tried enhancing it for at least a partial print on one of the fingers, but no go. It was his left hand but I couldn't find a wedding ring. Though I got the impression of a light band around his wrist."

"He wore a watch or bracelet?"

"Probably. But the mark isn't deep, so it could mean he doesn't spend a lot of time outdoors with his sleeves rolled up."

McGarvey stared at the image. "What's your snap judgment?"

Otto perched on the edge of one of the desks. He liked to think on his feet, he'd said, but he also liked to relax. "It was a brilliant move on his part bringing in the Taliban, or at least offering them a place in the

new government. The attacks on the army's headquarters in Rawalpindi stopped almost immediately
after his speech. And commercially Pakistan went
back to normal. But if you're asking what his agenda
is, I don't have a clue. Maybe Miller knows something I don't know."

"We're the ones who brief her, so if you don't
know—if the CIA doesn't know—then she doesn't
either."

"That's a scary thought," Otto said, "considering
what she'll ask you to do."

McGarvey looked away from the screen. "Is anyone saying Pakistan has become a credible threat
against us?"

"No. And from what I understand our CIA guys
have shed their tails. I talked to Ross just before you
came in, and he says it's gotten spooky over there.
The only trouble he's run into is the disappearance of
the guy he sent to check things out in Quetta."

"Could be he was too close when the bomb went
off."

"That's what Ross is worried about," Otto said.

Someone was at the door. Otto glanced at a monitor. "It's Pete," he said and buzzed her in.

"Thought I'd find you here," she said to McGarvey.
"Haaris just finished with his debriefing—and it was
brief—and afterwards we had a little one-on-one in
the cafeteria. Franklin says he has cancer, gives him
only six months on his feet."

"Marty told us that much," McGarvey said. "How
was he handling it?"

"He's dedicated. Said that time waited for no man,
not even him. So he scurried back to his people."

"Too dedicated?" McGarvey asked. He'd never
liked things that didn't add up.

"I guess if I were in his place I'd want to spend my

last months with someone I loved, maybe lying on a beach somewhere, drinking piña coladas. Listening to some good reggae. Or maybe eating and drinking my way through Paris."

"Unless he has an agenda."

"Love or hate, your choice, Mac," she said. "I'll give you a lift over to the White House."

"I want to have a word with Haaris first. I'll meet you in your office."

"I don't have an office here."

"Where do you work?"

"I have a place in Georgetown. Not too far from your apartment. I'll wait for you in the cafeteria."

The Pakistan Desk consisted mostly of a dozen cubicles, each with a specialist, surrounding a central meeting space that doubled as a library and tripled as a computer work center. Haaris's office was behind a glass wall on the side of the room opposite the door.

McGarvey had been given a blue badge, which gave him access to every office on the entire campus. When he walked in, Haaris was seated in the middle of the meeting space with his staff—most of them young men, along with an older woman, her gray hair up in a bun.

Haaris looked up with a scowl. "We're in the middle of something," he said.

"Sorry to barge in," McGarvey apologized. "But I'd like to have a word with you."

"Well?"

"What's your thinking on the situation?"

"We're discussing it, as you may well expect."

"I've been called to the White House. They want my opinion. I want yours. What's going to happen in the next twenty-four hours? Forty-eight? Seventy-two? One week? One month?"

"The million-dollar question, Mr. McGarvey. What do you think will happen?"

"Depends on whether something were to happen to the Messiah, and if it were to be blamed on us."

Haaris laughed, though it was obvious his mouth hurt. "We were crude in Vietnam, were crude in Afghanistan and Iraq, so it wouldn't surprise me if we botched this as well. We'll have a position paper for the president first thing in the morning. In the meantime you may tell her, if you wish, that you are exactly the wrong sort to get involved."

"I'll do that," McGarvey said. "Because I happen to agree with you."

NINETEEN

"The man's peckish," McGarvey said on the way over to the White House. Pete was driving her BMW three hundred series convertible. She'd flown to Munich and bought the made-for-Europe model, and drove it for a month so that when she had it shipped back to the States it came in as a used car. She'd left to try to get over McGarvey, and she had come back with a car.

"Wouldn't you be?" she asked.

They were on the parkway across the river, and McGarvey was in what almost amounted to a funk. He knew damn well what the president was going to ask him to do, and even some of the why of it, and he was almost 100 percent certain that getting close enough to the Messiah to put a bullet in his brain, and then getting the hell clear, was the wrong thing to do.

Except that the president would consider him expendable. If he killed the Messiah and then was caught, she could deny any knowledge. McGarvey was a rogue agent. There'd be no compunction in the White House about tossing him to the wolves. And if it came to pass that he was arrested and placed on trial, someone would show up to silence him.

It put him in a "damned if he did, damned if he didn't" position. Which, he thought, he ought to be accustomed to by now. He'd been in similar situations just about all his professional career. Starting with taking out the general and his wife in Chile, what seemed like a couple of centuries ago.

"A penny," Pete prompted.

"The president is going to make some wrong decisions over this thing because of the missing nuclear weapons. And I don't know if she'll be willing to listen to me."

"Like you said, you can just walk away if it doesn't feel right. But she does have a point: at least thirty nukes are unaccounted for, and we're in no position to demand to be told who's holding the triggers."

"That's one of the parts that bothers me the most. Our people went in and neutralized a lot of them, and yet other than the firefights on the ground, the government hasn't said a word. It's business as usual over there, according to just about everyone. For all intents and purposes Pakistan is at peace."

"The calm before the storm?" Pete asked.

"Maybe," McGarvey said. "But whatever happens, could be it won't turn out so well for us as we want it to."

They were expected at the East Gate and were allowed through. Pete parked at the foot of the stairs at the east portico and went up with McGarvey; one of the president's staffers, who did not identify himself, escorted them to the West Wing.

"Just you, Mr. McGarvey," the staffer said.

"I'll wait out here," Pete said.

President Miller was seated behind her desk, and when McGarvey walked in she picked up her phone and told her secretary that she was not to be disturbed. They were alone in the Oval Office.

"Thank you for coming so soon," Miller said. She motioned for McGarvey to have a seat across from her.

"A call from the president is something difficult to ignore."

Miller smiled faintly. "For you, not so difficult sometimes."

McGarvey shrugged. There was no answer. "Madam President, will someone be joining us?"

"No. This meeting is just between you and me."

"Considering what I expect you'll ask me to do, I think a witness might be wise."

"For exactly that reason there will be no witness," the president said. "I want you to find and assassinate the man the Pakistanis are calling the Messiah. The one who beheaded President Barazani. I assume that you've seen the tape."

"Before I agree to take on the job, I think that you have to consider what might come of it, whether I succeed or not."

"I have," the president said coolly.

"Such an act, even if it could be done, could spark a regional war. India might not sit on its hands if Pakistan's government fell apart. So far as I've been briefed, this Messiah has not threatened to retaliate for the attacks by our nuclear response teams. Send

Don Powers back to talk with him." Donald Suthland Powers, Jr. was the U.S. ambassador to Pakistan, and his father had been a legendary director of the CIA a number of years earlier. He and most of his staff had left the embassy shortly after the attacks by the Taliban had begun.

"This Messiah murdered the legitimate president in cold blood with his own hands. Nasir was murdered as well. And two hours ago I got word that the supreme court has granted the man executive and legislative authority for the next four years. He's become a dictator."

"The same thing happened with Musharraf in two thousand, and the country settled down. They avoided a war."

The president was sharply angry. "Don't try to teach me history or politics, Mr. McGarvey."

"I'm sorry, Madam President," McGarvey said. "But don't try to teach me my business."

The president started to say something, but McGarvey held her off.

"Someone on your staff, or possibly at the CIA, knowing that you had asked for me, tried to have me killed."

"I'm told that many people and even a few governments would like to see you neutralized."

"Two most likely Middle Eastern men, both of them dead. Maybe the autopsies will give us a clue where they were from. For now I'm betting Pakistan."

"I told no one at the CIA why I wanted to talk to you."

"That's right."

The president got it, and she flared again. "No one on my staff has any knowledge of who hired someone to kill you."

"Before I agree to do this thing, I'll first do as you suggested and eliminate the other possibilities. If someone else is gunning for me, I'll find out who it is."

"We don't have time. The situation is too unstable. It won't last. And at this moment I have to consider the primary threat that Pakistan poses—that of her thirty or more remaining nuclear weapons, and her ability to deliver them. And you must know that a good number of those weapons are tactical only—with ranges under one hundred miles. They're meant for only one thing, and that's to kill their own people."

"Is that what your advisers are telling you?"

"No one expects India to send ground troops across the border."

"Do you actually expect me to take on an entire country?"

"No, Mr. McGarvey, just the man; the country will follow."

McGarvey got up.

"I'm not finished with you, mister," the president practically shouted. "If need be you'll sit this one out in jail."

"That would be much easier for me."

Miller sat back and ran her fingers through her short dark hair, a calculating look in her eyes as she considered her viable options.

At that moment McGarvey almost felt sorry for her. Just about everyone who wanted the presidency was shocked and disappointed at exactly how little actual power they had. They were mostly administrators, who hopefully would, from time to time, come up with some idea that actually worked. Truman had been right: the buck did stop in this office, though a lot of presidents after him had tried to sidestep the responsibility.

"Tell your staff what you've asked me to do."

Miller started to object, but he held her off again.

"Tell them, and say that I'm thinking about it. In the meantime get Powers in motion to head back to Islamabad with most of his staff—just the volunteers—plus one."

"You."

"Yes. But I'll need a day or two to see who might come out of the woodwork after me. And this time I'll try to keep them alive long enough to ask some questions."

"Let the CIA know," the president said.

McGarvey shook his head. "Just the opposite. I'm going to tell them that I'm not taking the job."

"I see," the president said. "Isolating my staff from the CIA's."

TWENTY

Haaris stopped at a 7-Eleven just off Massachusetts Avenue and bought the early edition of *The Washington Post* before he drove the rest of the way home. It was coming up on three in the morning and not a lot of traffic had been moving on the parkway down from the CIA or anywhere in the city.

Steering his team into coming up with the recommendation that the U.S. should take a wait-and-see attitude on the Pakistan issue for at least the next forty-eight hours had been relatively easy, considering their respect for him, and considering he had hand-picked each of them, not for their intelligence and certainly not for their ability to think outside of the box. They'd also agreed to recommend that the entire U.S. embassy staff be sent back to Islamabad, and that an attempt at a dialogue with the Messiah be initiated.

Deb had heard the garage door open, and wearing only one of his old T-shirts as a nightgown, was waiting for him in the kitchen. Her blond hair was tousled and she was half asleep but she was smiling.

"I was getting worried about you," she said, coming into his arms.

She was warm and soft and for just a moment he responded. She was a dolt, but she was sometimes comforting, and her love for him was unconditional. He knew what he was doing and why he was doing it—that hate burned deeply—but every now and then, like right now, he wavered.

He kissed her deeply, and when he withdrew she didn't want to pull away.

"Come to bed, darling," she said, her voice husky.

"Fifteen minutes. First I have to do something at my desk, and then I'll take a shower."

"Haven't you done enough work for one day?"

"Fifteen minutes."

She smiled again. "Maybe I'll go back to sleep."

He pecked her on the cheek. "I'll figure out some way of waking you."

She laughed and went back to their bedroom.

Haaris poured a glass of wine and went into his office, which overlooked the large backyard and flower garden that was Deborah's second leading passion. It was pleasant here in the summer, when on rare occasions they sat outside listening to the night sounds, the traffic and the troubles they represented seemingly in another universe.

He turned on his computer, and once he was on-line entered a forty-seven-character alpha-numeric-case-sensitive totally random password that he changed on a regular basis. Almost at once a Pakistani ISI Web site came up through remailers in Sri Lanka, India and the Czech Republic.

He turned on the computer's camera and held up the morning's *Washington Post*. The lead stories were about the confusing issues unfolding in Pakistan. The main headline read: PAKISTAN'S BARAZANI CONFIRMED DEAD NEW MESSIAH TAKES OVER. Only the center of the front page itself, not the borders and not his hands, was visible in the image.

Entering another long password, he brought up a sub-program that contained four speeches that he had prepared five months earlier.

He clicked on one and opened it. The room was dark, the background anonymous except for a computer-generated image of Pakistan's green and white flag with the crescent moon and a single star. He was seated on an easy chair, only his head and shoulders visible. His face was almost completely covered by a kaffiyeh, his eyes in deep shadows. The image he presented was meant to be ominous, and it was.

"My friends, we have reached the first of many way points in our blessed journey together," he said in English.

He picked up a *Washington Post* from off camera and held it up. It was dated five months earlier. Haaris clicked on the newspaper and moved it off screen, replacing it with the morning's front page.

"We are at peace. Across our great nation the guns and bombs have stopped. We are no longer at war with each other or with our neighbors. And yet America still sees us not as equals but merely as a client state."

His image on the screen let the newspaper fall away.

"Our commerce is back to normal. We have asked the other nations to return their ambassadors and staffs so that we may all continue our peaceful coexistence.

"My dreams for Paradise here in Pakistan continue. Allah has spoken to me with his message of strength.

"Be strong of heart, for the way ahead may be difficult.

"Be strong of mind, for we will face many problems.

"Be strong of arm, for the tasks that we are faced with will seemingly be without end."

Purely bullshit, Haaris thought. Karl Marx had written that religion was the opiate of the masses. Well, this is exactly what he was giving them.

His speech went on in the same vein for a few more minutes, until in the end he promised that he would be among them. He would be a man on the street, a simple wayfarer on the highways, in the hills, on the deserts, by the sea.

He used a translation program to render his words into Punjabi before taking the speech processor out of his sealed attaché case and downloading it to the program that changed his voice to the same one he'd used on the balcony of the Aiwan.

Ten minutes after sitting down at his desk, he attached the speech to an e-mail—also sent through the remailers to the PTV, Pakistan Television Corporation, the main government-controlled network of stations throughout the country. Within minutes it would be broadcast as a flash bulletin and be rebroadcast dozens of times over the coming days.

Haaris sat back. "The Messiah has spoken again."

"I don't understand," Deb said at the door.

Haaris controlled himself not to overreact. He turned to her and smiled. "I thought you had gone to bed."

"What was that all about?" she asked.

He couldn't see any anger, just confusion. He got up and went to her. "I wish I could tell you, but it's stuff for work. We're doing a disinformation operation, trying to sow a few seeds of doubt about this guy calling himself the Messiah."

"That was you on the computer."

"Yes, it was. My idea."

She looked up at him, searching his eyes for the truth of what he was telling her. "What about the shower you mentioned?" she asked.

To the outside world looking in at them, their marriage must have seemed odd. They were mismatched. And yet it had to be obvious that they were very much in love. Deb believed it. And now it was coming to an end as all things must.

He slipped off his shoes and led her back to their bedroom suite, where in the bathroom he took off her T-shirt and kissed the nipples of her breasts.

"I'd like the water hot," he said.

"I love you."

"And I love you too."

She stepped into the shower and started the water.

He waited for just a second or two then got in with her. She started to laugh because he had not undressed. He kicked her feet out from under her, grabbed her shoulders and slammed her face down onto the raised lip of the shower stall with every ounce of his strength. The side of her head cracked like an eggshell, blood poured out of the wound and her legs jerked several times before they were still.

When he was certain that she was dead, he went into the bedroom and phoned 911.

"My God, my wife fell in the shower and hit her head," he cried. "She's not breathing! I don't know what to do!"

"Who is calling?"

"Please hurry," Haaris sobbed. He gave the address then left the phone off the hook, turned on the front porch light and unlocked the door, then went back to his wife.

TWENTY-ONE

It was late when McGarvey heard a soft sound on the stairs outside his Georgetown apartment. He unlocked the door then sat down in the dark in his living room, a cognac at hand, his Walther PPK in the nine-millimeter version on the small table beside him.

After he'd left the White House, he phoned Walt Page's office and left a message for the director as well as for Bambridge that he'd turned down the president. He told them that he would stick around Washington for the next day or two and then head back to Florida.

He'd not answered Pete's calls and had dinner alone at a small place a few blocks away down on M Street. Afterward he made a show of drinking too much at the bar before he staggered back home to his third-floor apartment in a brownstone across from Rock Creek Park.

But he hadn't been drunk then, nor was he drunk now.

He'd phoned Jim Forest at the detective's home. "How are things going?"

"I was wondering when you were going to call," Forest said.

He and McGarvey weren't exactly friends, but they did have a mutual respect. Mac thought the kid was a good cop, though sometimes a little too earnest.

"I wanted to give you time to get the autopsy results."

"You got out of Dodge before I could get to you. A Gulfstream left SRQ for Andrews. I assumed that you were aboard and that you were definitely involved. But the one guy had a forty-five-caliber slug in his head, and you carry a Walther. Mind telling me what the hell you're involved with this time and who was helping you?"

"I can't tell you a lot, except those two guys came to kill me, and I think they may be Pakistanis."

"Holy shit," Forest said softly. "They rented the boat at Marina Jack up in Sarasota under the name Walter Smith. One of them showed a New York driver's license and left a deposit with an American Express gold card in the same name. But the rental agent said neither guy's English was very good."

"Anything show up in their dental work?"

"Nothing yet. But a coroner's jury wants to talk to you."

"Later, once I get something settled."

Forest was silent for a beat. "Is this about what's going on right now in Pakistan?"

"You don't want to know."

"Just tell me that you're not bringing any more shit down here. I have my hands full as it is. The chief knows that I know you, and he's asking some very pointed questions. You come back to Sarasota and bring another shooting war with you, we'll probably both end up in jail."

"I don't know what to tell you. A lot depends upon

what happens here in DC over the next twenty-four hours or so. Could be it'll all blow away."

"But you don't think so."

"No."

"Shit," Forest said. "Anyway, for what it's worth, take care of yourself, Mac."

"I'll try."

Someone knocked.

"It's open," McGarvey said, hanging up. He snatched his pistol, got up and moved quickly across the room so that when the door opened he would be behind it.

"It's me, so don't shoot," Pete said softly. She opened the door and stepped in.

"Are you alone?" McGarvey asked. He could see the hallway through the crack at the edge. It was empty.

"Yes," she said and came the rest of the way in.

Pointing his pistol down and away, McGarvey reached around her and locked the door.

"How about some light?" she said.

"Were you followed?"

"I don't think so."

At the window McGarvey carefully parted the curtains and looked out. Nothing moved on the street below; the same cars that were parked there earlier were still there. "Where's your car?"

"I left it down on Dumbarton a couple of blocks away," she said. "I knew that you were lying the minute you came out of the White House. Why didn't you at least tell me or Otto?"

McGarvey laid his pistol on the table and switched on the small reading lamp. "I didn't want to get either of you involved. Especially not Otto, he's a terrible liar. And I needed the illusion to hold for at least until tomorrow."

Pete stood flatfooted, her blue eyes wide. "I'm a pretty good liar. And not so bad at covering your ass. I have a vested interest that I want to protect, you know."

A number of years ago McGarvey had been shot up pretty badly and had lost one of his kidneys. Then during an incident that had gone bad a few months earlier, McGarvey had lost his remaining kidney, and Pete, who by happenstance was a close enough match, donated hers without hesitation.

"They won't take the bait now."

"Would have been stupid if they had, anyway," she said. "Otto wants to talk to you, but your phone is off and he didn't want to turn it on in case you were in the middle of something. But he knew that you were here or at least that your phone was here."

"So he sent you?"

"I volunteered," Pete said. "The Messiah came on PTV in Islamabad. When Otto couldn't reach you he sent the recording to me. But he said he thinks something was wrong with it."

"What, exactly?"

"Something about the newspaper. He was holding up this morning's *Washington Post,* but Otto says it was dubbed."

McGarvey turned on his encrypted cell phone and called Otto, who answered on the first ring. McGarvey put the call on speaker.

"Pete's okay?"

"She's here. What have you come up with? She says something about the *Post* was wrong?"

"It was this morning's early edition, but the bottom right edge didn't line up. You won't be able to see it on a small phone screen, but one of my programs picked up on it, and when I put it up on the table it was there. The message was recorded sometime in the past. How long ago I don't know."

"Did he have anything significant to say?"

"Just that he wanted peace, and he invited everyone to send their embassy staffs back. Business as normal."

"With thirty-plus nuclear weapons still on the loose," McGarvey said, piecing it together. "He probably said something like he'll be around, but he wouldn't be making any public appearances."

"He said that he's going to be the invisible man on the street, in the hills, out in the desert. Anonymous."

"How about the voice?"

"We're working that," Otto said. "The spectrum analyzer I'm using says it's a match with the speech he made at the Aiwan. But it's too perfect a match."

"Do you have a confidence level? Eighty or ninety percent would be good enough."

"Just gut instinct, but something else came up in the past few minutes that I just don't know what to make of. The timing is all wrong, unless the same people who want to shut you up want to get to Haaris."

"What else?" Pete asked.

"Haaris's wife slipped and fell in their shower. Hit her head, and by the time a paramedic crew got there she was dead."

"Was he there when it happened?" McGarvey asked.

"Apparently he'd just gotten home and found her," Otto said, then hesitated.

McGarvey picked up on it. "And?"

"Maybe I'm getting to be an old lady hearing rats in the attic, but I got the real funny feeling that Dave Haaris might just be the Messiah."

Two minutes later, McGarvey's phone rang. It was Otto again. "Dr. Franklin just called. Haaris had his wife's body brought to All Saints. You might want to go over there."

TWENTY—TWO

A distraught, angry Haaris charged out of the waiting room when they came in. "The sons of bitches murdered her just to get at me," he said. "I want both of you in on this, because no matter what I said before, my advice to the president is different now." His clothes were still wet.

"How do you know someone killed her?" McGarvey asked.

"Dr. Franklin figured it out. And if it really is Messiah's people who did it to keep me off balance there's no possible way the political situation will ever get back to normal in Islamabad. That's clear to me. The bastards. The dirty bastards. She never hurt a soul in her life. She was incapable of doing anything mean. To anyone."

Dr. Franklin, his jacket off, his shirt collar open, got off the elevator from the second-floor operating theater, a long look on his face. "Good morning, Mac, Miss Boylan. I assume that David has filled you in."

"Did you find what I asked you to look for?" Haaris said, a little more in control of his emotions.

"I'm sorry I missed it earlier. She could have fallen with enough force to cause the damage to her skull. But you were correct in assuming that someone was in the shower with her. I found a displacement of her left ankle. Whoever the killer was probably grabbed her by the shoulder with one hand and the back of her head with the other, and kicked her legs out from under her, forcing her down."

"My God," Pete said. "Could it have been someone she knew?"

Haaris's face colored. "She wasn't having an affair, if that's what you meant to imply."

"I'm sorry, I was just looking for options. It would have been a very big deal for someone to send killers after your wife, unless they were specifically looking for you, and she got in the way."

"There's no accounting for stupidity."

"You and your think tank are our reigning experts," McGarvey said. He'd been watching for any signs that Haaris was faking his emotions, but he couldn't see it.

"We can see trends, possibilities, likelihoods. But for whole systems. One rogue operator changes everything. People are unpredictable, nations usually aren't. They're too ponderous, too slow to react or change in any fundamental way."

"The Messiah is fundamental."

Haaris stopped for a beat.

"If you'll excuse me," Dr. Franklin said. "It's been a very long day and I'm going home to bed now."

Haaris shook the doctor's hand. "Thank you for confirming something I'd already suspected."

"I'm terribly sorry, David. For everything."

"I appreciate it."

Franklin left down the hallway to the rear parking area.

Pete touched Haaris's wrist. "I'm truly sorry too," she said. "We all are. As hard as an accident is to accept, something like this is a million times worse."

Haaris nodded.

"What's next?"

Haaris gave her a look. "If you mean what's next vis-à-vis Pakistan, I don't know for sure, but I have some ideas."

"Anything that you'd care to share?" McGarvey asked.

"The president asked you to assassinate the Messiah, and the word is you turned her down."

"I may rethink it."

"Because of my wife?"

Again McGarvey tried to read the man, but he came up blank. Haaris was either a consummate liar. Or he was filled with genuine hate. "In part."

"And the rest?"

McGarvey shrugged. "From all accounts your wife was a gentle soul. Whoever killed her was a bully. And I don't like bullies."

"The world is full of them, didn't you know? Or are you a Don Quixote, tilting at windmills?"

"Something like that," McGarvey said, letting it hang there.

"I'm going now," Haaris said.

"Home?" Pete asked.

"No, the office, I recalled my team," Haaris said. "We need to revise our position for the president this morning." He started down the hall the same way Dr. Franklin had left.

"What's next?" Pete called after him.

"A reception for diplomats at the Pakistani embassy this evening," Haaris responded without looking back. "I'm going to stick it to them, see who reacts."

It was coming up on six, and McGarvey was tired.

"How about some breakfast?" Pete asked.

"Sure."

They walked outside from the rear exit, where

Pete's car was parked. "This isn't the end of it," she said.

"It's just started," McGarvey said, mulling over the entire situation. The ISI killing Haaris's wife made no sense, unless they had stumbled on her while waiting for Haaris to show up. But if that had been the case the operation had been incredibly sloppy, unlike the one off Casey Key. It was an anomaly, something he neither trusted nor liked, except that anomalies usually pointed to something, some direction no one expected.

They drove over to a Panera Bread restaurant.

"He wasn't distraught," Pete said before they got out of the car.

"They wanted him, but they took out his wife instead."

On the surface it made no sense. The situation was almost the same as one he'd encountered on his first wet assignment for the CIA at the beginning of his career. He'd been sent to Chile to kill a general who'd ordered the murders of thousands of innocent civilians. But when he got to the general's compound in the middle of the night, the general was making love to his wife. The alarm had been sounded and McGarvey had only seconds to react. Out of necessity he had assassinated both of them.

Later he had beaten himself up thinking about the woman, until he'd learned that she'd fancied herself a devotee of Joseph Mengele's wife—the Nazi who'd personally butchered thousands of Jews. Mengele's wife had many of the victims' skin removed, had tanned the pieces—most often taken from their backs—and had painted pictures on some of them and made lampshades from others. She was as monstrous as her husband. As was the wife of the Chilean general, and she'd deserved to die. But McGarvey had never gotten over it.

"I held his hand for a few seconds," Pete said. "I could feel his pulse. It should have been fast, but it wasn't. His heart rate was that of a man at peace with himself. What do you make of that?"

McGarvey went back to Pete's apartment with her, where he sacked out on the couch for a few hours. It was against his better wishes to get her involved, but she'd at least had a half night's sleep and she kept watch.

Otto called at a little after eleven as Pete was fixing them an early light lunch. He took the call at a window of her second-floor apartment from which he could look down at the street. But the traffic seemed normal. No one lurking in a doorway or on a rooftop with the glint of sunlight off the lens of a scope.

"Page has been trying to get in touch with you all morning and so has Marty. Broderick has been putting a lot of pressure on us. They want you to act right now. The situation in Islamabad is starting to spin out of control. None of the EU countries are in any hurry to return their embassy staffs, and from what Austin is sending us, it looks as if Taliban committees are being set up at all the key governmental offices, and more importantly, at all the major air force and navy bases. The bases where nuclear weapons are being mated for deployment."

"Has Haaris briefed the president yet?"

"He went over there around ten, And so far as I know he hasn't returned," Otto said. "The metro cops were all over his wife's murder, but he knows someone at the Bureau who took over the case. And he's agreed to be interviewed, but only briefly, so that he can get on with his work."

"Anything new from your analysis of the Messiah's voice?"

"It was the same guy who spoke at the Presidential Palace. But my darlings are having a tough time re-creating the original voice. Whatever equipment he used was well above the over-the-counter Radio Shack lash-up. Professional-grade stuff. Shit that only a government is likely to come up with."

"The Pakistani embassy is hosting a cocktail party for diplomats tonight. Get me a pass for it."

Pete had come to the kitchen door in time to hear McGarvey's request. "Me too," she said.

McGarvey started to object, but Otto overheard her.

"She'll be good cover," he said. "Anyway, two sets of eyes and ears are better than one. And they've promised to have the new prime minister there. He's flying in this afternoon."

"Who is it?"

"I don't know yet, but I'm working on it."

"Will Page be there?"

"No, but Fay and his wife will be."

"Black tie, I assume," Pete said after McGarvey hung up.

"Of course."

"I can hardly wait."

TWENTY-THREE

The main reception hall of the Pakistani embassy was packed with more than 250 people, a significant portion of the top diplomats in the city, almost all from nations that did regular business with Islamabad. A long buffet table was spread out along one side of the large circular room. White-coated waiters moved through the crowd with trays of hors d'oeuvres, sweet mint tea in small cups and glasses of Dom Pérignon.

McGarvey in a tux and Pete in a simple black over-one-shoulder cocktail dress and a tasteful diamond necklace stood to one side of the entry, sipping champagne. Neither of them was armed.

"I haven't spotted Haaris yet," Pete said.

"It's going to be interesting to see Haaris's demeanor if and when he does show up," McGarvey said. "Especially if he publicly pins the blame for his wife's murder on the ISI."

"It still doesn't make sense to me that he could think the ISI was behind it. Otto has the recordings of him talking with General Rajput, and they seemed like old friends, or at least allies. And it was the ISI who supposedly rescued him from his Taliban captors."

"He changed his tune this morning."

"A strange man," Pete said. "Did you know that he was born in Pakistan?"

"Otto said something about it. His parents were killed when he was very young, and a rug-merchant uncle brought him to London and put him in the best schools, including Eton."

"When he came to us he was a British citizen. But what's most curious to me is that he was willing to share what he learned with the British Secret Intelligence Service. Technically made him a traitor."

"I've not seen his entire jacket yet."

"I have and you need to look at it soon," Pete said. "Read between the lines. The guy is filled with hate for what they did to him as a kid in school."

"British public schools are notorious, but they've graduated some pretty substantial people."

Pete looked up at him. "You're playing devil's advocate again."

"I guess I am. I don't trust him either, but just because he was used hard as a kid in school, and he's filled with hate, as you say, doesn't make him bad. Nor does the fact that he was born in Pakistan, and raised by an uncle, make him suspect."

"But?"

"I don't know," McGarvey said. And he really didn't. "But before I pack my bags I'm going to press him. Maybe Otto's right."

"My God, you're not seriously thinking about going over there to take out the Messiah?"

"I don't think that even a SEAL Team Six unit with all the right intel and a lot of luck could do it. And get back out."

"That's not what I asked, Mac," Pete pressed. She took his arm. "No screwing around now. What the president wants you to do is crazy."

"Less crazy than sending troops over there."

John Fay and his wife came over. "Mr. McGarvey, your name came up again in a strategy session this afternoon," the secretary of state said. He was of the old school of diplomats, among the last of a certain class defined by breeding, refinement and intelligence.

"I imagine it did," McGarvey said, and he introduced Pete as a CIA special projects officer.

"A serious title," Jeanne Fay said. "If it implies what I expect it must."

"There've been interesting moments," Pete said, smiling pleasantly.

"Excuse us, ladies, but I'd like to take Mr. McGarvey aside for just a minute or two," Fay said.

"Miss Boylan is privy to everything that I've done or have been asked to do over the past couple of years," McGarvey said.

Fay was just a little vexed, but he didn't press. "Have you come to a decision? The president is running out of viable options."

"Like the situation when Russia invaded the Ukraine?" Pete asked.

"Worse. Kiev had no nuclear weapons and not much of a military."

"They're not going to start a nuclear war," McGarvey said.

"Did you see the Messiah's latest broadcast?"

"Yes."

"What did you think?"

"I was surprised that he was inviting everyone back—especially us," McGarvey said. "Our taking out a significant portion of their weapons had to be viewed as an act of war."

"Yet there has been no mention of it, officially or unofficially," Fay said. "What do you make of that?"

"I'm not a political analyst, Mr. Secretary. Just a tool."

"At this point a very important tool. The question is, will you do it?"

It dawned on McGarvey that Fay was frightened, but it was impossible to tell if the secretary of state was more frightened of the situation in Pakistan or of the president's decision to have an assassin kill the Messiah. "Do what?"

"Don't be crude, Mr. McGarvey. The order was put on the table, and you are a volunteer. You can either carry it out or simply turn your back and walk away. Though from what I understand happened in Florida, the latter might not be an option for you."

"Do you think something like that will happen again if Mr. McGarvey turns down the assignment?" Pete asked.

"You don't think that it's a good idea?"

"I think it's stupid."

Fay smiled faintly. "As a matter of fact, so do I. To this point Pakistan has shown no aggression towards us."

"They want our financial support," McGarvey said. He was fascinated with the secretary's verbal maneuvering.

"Shahid has called for a continued cease-fire, in this instance with no time limits." Shahidullah Shahid was the primary spokesman for the Tehreek-e-Taliban Pakistan, the organization of militants in the country.

"I would think that's good news. Are we sending Powers back to Islamabad?"

"He leaves in the next day or two."

"What's his brief?"

"To open a dialogue with the new prime minister, whoever he turns out to be," Fay said.

"Will Powers be here tonight?" Pete asked.

"No, Miss Boylan, for reasons that should be obvious to you and Mr. McGarvey."

Pete started to say something, but McGarvey held her off. "Has he been told what the president suggested?"

Fay hesitated. "No."

McGarvey had never considered himself a political animal, but he'd seen equal amounts of what he took to be brilliance and sheer idiocy coming from just about every office in Washington and the Beltway, including the National Security Agency, the CIA, the Pentagon and the White House.

"Every time we've had one agenda for an ambassador and another either for our military or intelligence services, it's almost always turned out for the worse. I would have thought that you guys understood that by now. Especially after Benghazi and the aftermath."

"One mistake."

"Supplying bin Laden and his fighters with Stinger missiles to use against the Taliban—after which they were and still are used against us. Going into Iraq with no intention of rebuilding their infrastructure. Getting bogged down in an unwinnable war in Afghanistan. The list isn't endless, Mr. Secretary, but it's long."

Fay took a moment to answer. "Mistakes have been made, but we do what we can do. Have you never made an error?"

"Plenty," McGarvey said.

There was a flurry across the room. The Pakistani ambassador to the U.S., Idrees Burki, came to the middle of the room and held up a hand. The guests fell silent. "Ladies and gentlemen, it is my pleasure to present to you the new prime minister of Pakistan, General Hasan Rajput."

TWENTY-FOUR

Rajput, dressed in a British-cut dove-gray suit, with a blue dress shirt of horizontal white stripes and a plain gray tie, shook hands with Ambassador Burki and then turned to face the crowd, his eyes lingering one by one on the guests.

McGarvey stepped to one side so that Fay wasn't blocking his line of sight to Rajput, and the new PM spotted him, with no hint of recognition.

"Who is he?" Fay asked.

"Until two days ago he was the general in charge of the ISI's Covert Operations Division," McGarvey said.

"I'll be damned," Fay replied, and he started forward, but McGarvey laid a hand on his arm.

"Just a minute, Mr. Secretary. What are you going to say to him?"

"I'll merely introduce myself. It's customary in these circumstances."

Other diplomats approached Rajput and the Pakistani ambassador, forming what amounted to a receiving line.

"You have a little time yet. And considering what our SEAL teams did to their weapons, and the loss of lives on both sides—none of which has been made public—it might be better if you didn't get to him first."

"I thought that you weren't a political animal."

"I'm not, but first I want to see if Dave Haaris shows up."

Fay gave him a sharp look. "He blames the ISI for murdering his wife. He wouldn't dare show his face here."

"Well, he just walked in the door," Pete said.

Haaris, perfectly dressed in what was obviously an expensive tuxedo, an unreadable expression on his face though his lips were set in a tight smile, stopped to get a glass of champagne from a waiter then headed across the room to where the receiving line was forming.

He passed McGarvey and Pete without acknowledging them but nodded to the secretary of state and his wife. "Mr. Secretary, good to see you here this evening," he said without pausing.

"Stay here, Mr. Secretary," McGarvey said, and he headed after Haaris, Pete at his side.

"What are you going to say to him?" she asked.

"Depends on what he says to Rajput. But no matter what, I want the new PM to get a good look at my face."

"He's probably read your file."

"Yeah, but I want him to see me in person," McGarvey said.

Pete stopped him. "You're going through with it."

"I don't know yet," McGarvey said, though that wasn't exactly the truth.

He hurried to catch up as Haaris walked straight to Rajput and the ambassador, bypassing the line. Both men looked up with interest.

"David, I didn't expect to see you here this evening," Rajput said. He introduced Haaris to the ambassador, who offered his hand, but Haaris ignored it.

"I thought not, considering that your people tried to have me killed last night."

A hush spread across the big room. McGarvey and Pete stood only a couple of feet behind Haaris.

"I have no idea what you're talking about," Rajput said.

The ambassador said something to the new PM that McGarvey didn't quite catch. The look of puzzlement on Rajput's face turned to sadness.

"But that's terrible news about your wife. You've often spoken to me about her. But I can give you my word of honor that I knew nothing about such an attack. And I'm in a position to know about such things."

"He's telling the truth," Pete whispered in McGarvey's ear.

"So far as he knows it."

"You're a liar," Haaris said at the top of his voice. Shock rippled across the room.

The look on Rajput's face didn't change. "You're distraught, David. You don't know what you're saying." He reached out a hand but Haaris batted it aside.

"But you've made a terrible mistake, General. I have the president's ear, and she agrees with me that the Messiah is an ISI creation, and that Pakistan is surely sliding toward nuclear war."

"Insanity."

"Yes, it is, only this time Pakistan has miscalculated my country's intentions."

Fay struggled through the crowd, elbowing past McGarvey and Pete. "Pardon me, Mr. Prime Minister, Mr. Ambassador, but Mr. Haaris does not speak for the president."

Haaris turned on him. "Pakistan is no friend of the United States. And it's time that the president understands it."

"If you rightly remember it was under my direction that you were rescued from the Taliban," Rajput said.

"More of your intrigue, General."

"Why in Allah's name would I want to cause your death? You're making no sense."

Haaris stepped closer. "I can guarantee you, General, that the United States will do more to your regime under this dictator you call the Messiah than simply neutralize most of your nuclear weapons. Perhaps I'll be flying to New Delhi in the very near future."

The ambassador motioned to someone and almost instantly two large men in plain Western business suits arrived.

"Mr. Haaris was just leaving," the ambassador said. "Please show him out."

"He was just leaving with us," McGarvey said.

The entire room was silent.

"I will of course lodge a formal protest," the ambassador told Fay.

"I understand," Fay said.

"Time to go," McGarvey prompted.

Haaris glared at Rajput, but then turned and stalked across the room, the crowd parting for him.

"Someone tried to kill me too, Mr. Prime Minister," McGarvey said. "Quite a coincidence, wouldn't you say?"

"We all have enemies."

"Yes, and you should keep it in mind."

Fay started to say something, but McGarvey nodded pleasantly. "Mr. Secretary. Gentlemen."

Haaris was waiting for the valet parker to bring his car when McGarvey and Pete came out.

"I didn't expect to see you two here," he said. He had a grim set to his features.

"We were waiting for you to show up," McGarvey said.

"I don't think I made Fay happy. I'll be surprised if I keep my job."

"Walt Page will probably want to have a word with you first thing in the morning. He'll need an explanation."

"I thought that would be obvious. I was provoking the bastard."

"He was your friend," Pete said.

"No, I was mining him."

"A two-way street," McGarvey said.

"You know how the game is played. I've fed him some hand-crafted disinformation and he's done the same for me."

"A zero-sum game," Pete said. "No one wins."

A faint smile played at the corners of Haaris's mouth. "Ah, but I'm smarter than he is. That's how the game is played in the majors."

His S-class Mercedes arrived, and he tipped the valet and drove off.

"The entire thing was staged," McGarvey said.

"How do you mean?"

"The PM and ambassador spoke English to each other the entire time for our benefit."

TWENTY-FIVE

Pete had parked her car around the corner from McGarvey's brownstone, and when they reached it she hesitated. The night was early and there was a fair amount of traffic, but nothing suspicious, just the usual weekday flow.

"I don't want to be alone tonight," she said.

She'd been quiet ever since they'd left the Pakistani embassy. "What's the matter?" Mac asked.

"The willies, I guess," she said. "I keep looking over my shoulder expecting to see someone gaining on me."

"No one on our tail tonight."

She smiled. "I meant it metaphorically."

They were double-parked, and a cabby passing them honked his horn.

"Do you want me to follow you home?"

"Only if you'll come up with me and spend the night," she said. "But I have to warn you that my fridge is mostly empty, so we'd have to eat out."

"You can stay with me. I'll take the couch and you can have the bed."

"Switch the sleeping arrangements and it's a deal."

McGarvey drove around the block and found a spot two doors down from his apartment. Something of Pete's willies had transferred to him, and he was especially careful with his tradecraft. His apartment was swept every week, but after the incident at the embassy he figured that both he and Haaris were fair game. It was exactly what he wanted. This time when someone came calling he would do everything in his power to take him alive.

Upstairs Pete took off her cocktail dress and put on one of McGarvey's long-sleeved shirts. While he was changing out of his tuxedo she made them bacon and eggs and toast, and opened a bottle of Pinot Grigio from the fridge. They sat at the small table in the kitchen.

"I've haven't cooked for a man in a long time," Pete said.

"You were married, weren't you?"

She smiled a little. "It didn't work out the way I thought it would. Probably because I was too much of a romantic. Still am, I suppose." She sipped her wine. "Fairy tales. Ride off into the sunset, all of that. Just like the end of *An Officer and Gentleman*."

"Katy loved the movie too," McGarvey said. She'd made him watch it one Sunday afternoon at their place on Casey Key. Afterward they made love, a sea breeze coming in from the Gulf. Happy times.

"From what I know of her, I expect she did."

McGarvey looked away.

Pete reached across the table and laid a hand on his. "It wasn't your fault, Kirk. I read the file. They wanted to stop you and they were willing to do whatever it took."

"I understood Todd's death. He got involved with something and they killed him for it. In the line of duty. He understood it when he held up his hand and took the oath. But Katy and our daughter were senseless. The only reason they died was because of me. Not because of something they were involved with, just me."

"So you're still beating yourself up?"

"No. I evened the score for them, but it's happened before. Too often."

"And you're afraid that I'm next?"

"I know you are," McGarvey said.

"My tradecraft is pretty fair. And I'm a good shot."

"I know that too."

"You let me tag along to the embassy tonight. So what's your point? Do you want me involved, or do you want to keep me locked up somewhere until this business is finished? I'm a field officer. If you don't want me in this thing that's your prerogative. But if you don't want me to be involved with you, you're out of luck. Fact of the matter is, I love you, and I have a feeling that if you would admit it for just a New York minute you'd realize that you were in love with me."

But he didn't have a New York minute. He wouldn't allow himself the introspection, even though he had to admit that he would have been in big trouble off Casey Key if she hadn't taken the shot. "Not yet."

"You mean not this time. But you're going to Pakistan, and if you survive there'll be another time. And another. It's what you do, who you are. One of the reasons I fell in love with you in the first place."

"Leave it be, Pete."

"I can't. So now it comes down to, am I going to Pakistan with you, or am I staying here in Washington?"

McGarvey had given that question a lot of thought over the past day or so, in part because he hadn't entirely made up his mind to take what would be the most impossible assignment of his life, but also because he knew that he would have to give Pete an answer that made sense to her.

"If I go, Otto will have to backstop me, and the ISI will know it. To stop me they'll go after Louise, and Otto will have to jump in and they'll get him too. I'll need you here to ride shotgun for both of them."

Pete wanted to object, but she couldn't and it was obvious from her expression. She nodded.

McGarvey telephoned Otto and brought him up to date.

"Interesting choice for PM."

"Dave Haaris showed up."

"I expected he would," Otto said. "Was he surprised by Rajput? They worked together for the past couple of years."

"He didn't seem to be; in fact he publicly accused the ISI of murdering his wife."

"Let me guess, he even told them that he was going to change his policy advice on Pakistan."

"Something like that. Anyway, the ambassador tossed him out, and John Fay made his apologies."

"What about you?" Otto asked.

"I don't know."

"That's not like you, Mac."

"I'm still figuring out how to find this Messiah, whoever the hell he is, and then get the hell out with my hide intact."

"Are you coming over in the morning?"

"I'm going to stick it out here, take a run in the park, and pack a few things for Casey Key."

"With a big target painted on your back."

. . .

Pete took a shower first and over McGarvey's objections made up the couch. "I'll get out of here first thing in the morning," she said. "I want to have a little talk with Haaris."

"Do you want me to drive over with you?"

"I'm a big girl, but thanks for putting me up for the night."

After his shower he took a turn at the front window for a few minutes to make sure no one was out there. Pete was apparently already sleeping, because she didn't look up. And ten minutes later he was just drifting off, when she came to the bedroom door.

"It's me," she said softly, as he automatically reached for the pistol on the nightstand.

"Is something wrong?"

"I'm not sleeping alone tonight," she said. She took off the shirt and slipped into bed with him. "Don't send me away."

She came into his arms, and her softness, her breasts, the feel of her legs against his, her breath on his face as she kissed him, were as good as he'd imagined they would be. And they made love, slowly, elegantly, even though he could feel the same urgency in her as he felt in himself. And in the end he almost lost his fear for her life.

TWENTY-SIX

Pete got up shortly before dawn and after she got dressed she went back into the bedroom, where McGarvey was lying awake. "I'm sorry I woke you," she said. She'd not slept well the entire night, worrying about him going into badland.

"I'm usually up by now."

"Not at five in the morning, liar."

"Do you want me to follow you back to your place?"

"No, but I'm going to borrow one of your guns, just in case. I want to get to the Campus before Dave Haaris does."

McGarvey sat up and handed her the Walther he usually kept by his bedside. "Watch the corners."

"Yeah," she said, stuffing the small pistol into her purse. She bent down and kissed him on the cheek. "Thanks for last night, Kirk."

"It was a two-way street," he said. "Why the hurry to talk to Haaris this morning?"

"I want to know why a man like him is so eager to get back to work even before his wife is in the ground." The instant the words left her lips she realized what she had just said and to whom she had said them. "Oh, Christ, I'm sorry."

"Don't ever be sorry for asking a legitimate question. I've asked myself the same thing for a long time now, and the best I could come up with is revenge. Plain and simple. Get the bastards who did it."

Pete sat on the edge of the bed. She could feel heat coming off his body, and the sight of him so close, his chest bare, started to arouse her. Sometimes field officers who were in love backed each other up when all hell was raining down on their heads, but too often their feelings put them in danger. They dove in to save someone who could not be saved and lost their lives or their freedom.

"Something's not right with him. Working with Rajput and then suddenly accusing him of ordering the killing? Especially like that in public. What was he trying to accomplish?"

"He was pushing the general to see what kind of a reaction he'd get."

"He got nothing, at least nothing as far as I could tell."

"Haaris is a professional."

"So am I," Pete said. "Everything I've seen in his jacket gives him high marks. Page says the guy's sophisticated. Old-world educated. Last night's display was anything but. I want to know why."

"Maybe I should go in with you."

Pete shook her head. "Let's keep up normal routines. It's my job for the Company to find out what's eating people. Your job is to sleep in, have breakfast and take your morning run. Everything as usual."

"I'll come out later this morning, I need to work out a few things with Otto, and talk to Walt and probably Marty."

Pete looked at him in the dim illumination from the night-light in the bathroom. He seemed calm, at ease with himself, despite what he was facing. This time she didn't think it would be quite so simple for him as going up against an assassin somewhere, or even an organization, like the group who'd tried to kill all the SEAL Team Six guys who'd taken bin Laden down. That had been a German terrorist group, all ex-military special operators who'd been hired by the ISI. This time, he would be taking on an entire nation, with just about every other person over there wanting to kill him.

"I might have something to add," she said.

"Watch your back," McGarvey said.

"You too," Pete told him, and she almost said "darling."

A few doors down Pete looked over her shoulder. McGarvey was in the window watching her. She smiled and waved, then hurried around the corner to her car.

She lived close and it took less than an hour to take a quick shower and change into a pair of khaki slacks, a white blouse and light jacket, before she was back to where she'd parked her car.

It was still dark, but the morning was coming alive with traffic, mostly garbage trucks, a street-sweeper machine and delivery vans for the bars and restaurants down on M Street. Nothing or no one threatening that she could detect.

She kept Mac's pistol in her shoulder bag but laid her Glock 27 on the passenger seat as she took the Key Bridge across the river and started up the parkway to CIA headquarters.

In the east the sky was beginning to lighten, no clouds, and the trees and other vegetation along the side of the highway were lush. She'd read somewhere that because of various government projects in the past two hundred years there were more species of North American native trees here than anywhere else in the country. In the fall with the colors it was fabulous, but she preferred the full bloom of summer.

She glanced in her rearview mirror as an eighteen-wheeler, black smoke belching from its twin exhaust pipes, came up and pulled left to pass her. She got the vague impression of a figure behind the wheel and perhaps another riding shotgun. They were trying to make time, and she didn't bother to keep up or get ahead of them even though the truck would slow down for the hill coming up less than a half mile away. Haaris probably wouldn't be on Campus this early anyway.

The cab came even with her and she looked up into the face of a dark-skinned man with a narrow face and black hair as the truck swerved directly across the center line toward her.

On instinct she reached for her pistol, but she was forced off the side of the pavement and onto the apron before she could reach it. In the next instant her right-side wheels dropped down onto the grass strip and suddenly she was fighting to control the car.

The truck slammed into the side of her car again, sending her down a steep hill and across the drainage ditch ten feet lower. Before she could straighten out the wheels, the car tipped over on its side and continued rolling for forty yards until it broke through a swatch of bushes, finally smashing roof-first into the bole of a large tree.

For a seeming eternity she could only wonder that she was still alive—or at least she thought she was, nothing seemed to hurt but there seemed to be an awful lot of blood rolling down her face and neck.

"The fucking ISI," she mumbled and dropped down into a dream-like state in which she was vaguely aware that she was still awake, but she couldn't move. If the bastards who had done this wanted to come down and finish the job, she couldn't do a thing about it.

Too bad, Kirk.

TWENTY-SEVEN

Pete's cell phone rang once before the message came up that the call had been forwarded to an automatic message system. "It's me, give me a call," McGarvey said and hung up, an odd feeling between his shoulder blades that someone was taking a bead on him.

He'd phoned her apartment with no success and had left a message at her office. The automatic bar code scanner on the main gate of the Campus had not shown her arriving.

He called Otto. "Pete left here about an hour ago, and now I can't reach her on her cell phone. The main gate says she hasn't scanned in yet."

"You try the back gate?"

"No reason for her to go that way."

"Hang on."

McGarvey went to the window and looked out toward the Rock Creek Park across Twenty-sixth Street. It was just dawn and already the morning joggers and bicyclers were out in full force.

Otto was back. "She didn't come in that way. What are you thinking?"

"How about accidents between here and the Campus?"

"Is she still driving the three-hundred Beemer?"

"Dark green, convertible. DC plates: P-two-thirty-eight-five-seven."

"I'm checking," Otto said. "Was she armed?"

"I gave her one of my pistols before she left here. Presumably she still has it, and possibly the Glock from her apartment."

"A half-dozen fender benders in the city and one accident with injuries on the Beltway down by Alexandria, but nothing on the parkway heading up here. Could be she just stopped somewhere for breakfast."

"She wouldn't have shut off her phone. It's not like her."

"Maybe she has something on her mind. Wants a little room to think it out."

"Maybe," McGarvey said. But that wasn't like Pete either. If she had something to say, she wouldn't be shy about it. Just like last night and this morning.

"Do you want me to give it to Security?"

"Just keep checking. I'm going for my run, and I'll come out around ten. I want to talk to Walt."

"You're going to do it?"

"I don't know how many other choices we have, after the obvious stage play last night," McGarvey said. "How about Haaris?"

"He's been with his gang all night."

"If there was any doubt in Islamabad what our position is, he gave it away."

"I'll keep trying to find Pete, but watch yourself, I shit you not. Your being at the embassy last night makes you even more of a target than you were in Casey Key. Somebody figured that you might get involved so they thought they'd take you out, just in case. But now that they know you've jumped in, it's not likely they'll give it up. They'll keep sending people until they get lucky."

"I'm counting on it. But she was with me, so she's a target too."

McGarvey put on a Kevlar vest under his sleeveless sweatshirt, stuffed his Walther in his belt at the small of his back and his cell phone in his pocket, and left his apartment. He waited for a break in traffic then jogged across Twenty-sixth Street and into Rock Creek Park, which ran from the Potomac up to Oak

Hill Cemetery, where it blended with Montrose Park and finally the National Zoological Park.

This was a favorite place for him. In Florida he swam in the Gulf and ran on the beach. Here he jogged every morning he possibly could in the park. It was his habit, his routine. Anyone who had him under surveillance for even a short length of time knew it.

More than once in the past few years he'd been attacked while he ran along the river. It was like going fishing. He tossed in the bait and waited for the strike. And just like real fish, the guys wanting to take him out never seemed to learn from each other's mistakes.

But Otto was right: Sooner or later they'd either send enough people to make the odds overwhelming. Or a decent sniper hiding somewhere across the creek would get lucky with a head shot.

Once he was on the path he took a fighter's stance, bobbing and weaving as he ran, air boxing, ducking left and right, slipping punches. This too was sometimes part of his routine. It kept him loose. Other joggers had their own styles, and no one thought anyone else was odd. They were all out here for the same thing, to stay healthy. Though he figured that this morning no one else but him would be a target for some hitman.

He crossed under the Rock Creek Parkway so that he could take the path along the creek. A few hundred yards north he came to the P Street Bridge, where he pulled up and shadowboxed in place.

For a moment he stopped moving. Cocking his head he listened to the sounds of the building traffic, under which was the soft gurgle of water over rocks, and somewhere a dog barking, a horn tapping twice.

No one had followed him nor had there been anyone obviously ahead. Nor had he spotted anyone seated at one of the picnic benches or lurking in the trees.

A shot from a rooftop to the west in Georgetown was certainly possible. But if a sniper had been set up there waiting for him to come out of his apartment, he could have taken the shot almost immediately. To the east toward Dupont Circle most of the sight lines to his position were partially blocked by trees.

If he was going to do it, he would be somewhere in the park, or in a car or van driving along the parkway. But traffic was still not heavy, and McGarvey had not spotted anyone suspicious passing by.

He turned and started back. It was possible that a sharp ISI analyst had worked out the likelihood that he would actually come to Islamabad. He'd been there before. They knew him, they knew what he looked like, how he moved.

Taking him out here would be chancy. Florida was easier. Running him over in the water could be defended as an accident. Inexperienced boaters not spotting a head in the waves; accidents like that had happened before.

And that same analyst could also have come to the conclusion that if McGarvey was running in the park, after the incident in Florida, he would be offering himself as a target in order to catch the gunman. A possibly no-win outcome if the shooter missed, because despite opposition to what the Company called enhanced methods of interrogation, such methods were still used when necessary. If McGarvey captured an ISI contractor, the truth would come out.

Still weaving and bobbing as he ran, McGarvey reached the parkway when his cell phone rang. It was Otto.

"I found her. She's banged up but not seriously. They're taking her to All Saints right now."

A cool, dispassionate anger came over him. "What happened?"

"I sent a chopper up to find her. Looks like she was forced off the road a few miles south of our front gate. She rolled down the hill and up against a tree. No one could see her from the parkway because of the heavy brush."

McGarvey jogged across the road. "Is she conscious?"

"Our guys who got to her first said she was in and out. Lots of blood but it looked like superficial scalp wounds. Could be a concussion but we won't know until Franklin takes a look at her."

"I'm going to change clothes and get over there. Tell Page I'm taking the president's assignment."

"The ISI will spot you the minute you get off the plane."

"No. they won't," McGarvey said. "I'll see you as soon as I can."

It was after ten by the time Franklin came out of the operating theater on the second floor and walked down to talk to McGarvey in the waiting room at the end of the hall.

"She'll have a couple of black eyes and a lot of bruising on her legs and thighs, but there were no broken bones nor any brain trauma."

"She's hardheaded."

Franklin shook his head. "You all are," he said. "How's Dave Haaris doing?"

"He's back at work."

"Too bad about his wife on top of his own problem." Franklin shook his head again. "I don't see how you guys do it. Patching you up is a hell of a lot easier job."

"When can I see her?"

"They're cleaning her up now. She wants to go home, but I'm keeping her overnight just to be on the safe side. You can try to talk some sense into her as soon as they get her up to her room. I don't want her getting dressed and walking out of here."

McGarvey went up to Pete's room on the third floor as soon as she was wheeled up from the operating theater. Her smile was lopsided but she was as glad to see him as he was to see her. He kissed her lightly on her cheek.

"Franklin says you'll be okay, but he's keeping you overnight."

"Not a chance in hell," Pete said, her voice a little slurred.

"I'm taking your old clothes, they're a mess, and bringing you some clean clothes and some other stuff in the morning. You'll be staying on Campus for the time being. They tried to take you out to make me think twice."

"You've decided?"

"No other choice," McGarvey said, and an expression he couldn't read came over Pete's face.

TWENTY-EIGHT

McGarvey passed the spot where Pete's car was forced off the road, broad furrows cut in the grassy slope all the way down into the bush and trees that no passing motorist had spotted. The ISI—and now he was almost 100 percent certain it was they—had tried to kill her to get to him. And from their point of view it had been the right thing to do, given his history. But if they had meant to distract him by a repeat performance of something that had happened to him three times before—killing someone very close to him—they were dead wrong.

Vengeance hadn't worked for them when they'd sent a German assassination squad to the U.S. to kill all the SEAL Team Six operators who had taken out bin Laden. But here and now for McGarvey, vengeance was a powerful motivator.

He was given a VIP pass at the main gate and he drove up to the Old Headquarters Building and parked in the basement garage. The elevator stopped at the security station on the first floor, where he had to surrender his weapon before he was issued a pass that allowed him access to just about every office on the entire campus. Many former DCI's retained that badging privilege because they often worked in unpublicized advisory capacities. And every time McGarvey walked through the door, the security people welcomed him back.

He'd phoned ahead and Walt Page was waiting for him upstairs on the seventh floor. The DCI's secretary passed him straight through. No one else was present. It was just the two of them, as McGarvey had insisted be the case.

"How's Miss Boylan?" Page asked.

"Banged up but not serious. Franklin's keeping her overnight to make sure. I'm going to bring her out here soon as she's released, have Security keep an eye on her."

"Good idea."

"Were you told what happened at the Pakistani embassy last night?"

"John Fay filled me in. Said that you and Miss Boylan were there too. Are you going to tell me that the attack on her this morning had something to do with what went on there?"

"I think that the ISI wants to keep me out of the mix. It's why they tried to kill me in Florida, and it's why they went after Pete—to distract me. Have you seen Dave this morning?"

"I wanted to talk to you first. Susan Kalley called from the White House, wanting to know what the hell happened. The president is ready to discount just about everything Dave's told her. And she's pulling the records of every meeting he had with her, even during her campaign."

"What'll she find?"

"Nothing but solid advice, so far as I know. But his wife's murder has hit him very hard. I'm thinking about putting him on administrative leave."

"Might not be a bad idea, but give it a day or so. I'm going to talk to him this morning."

"You don't trust him."

"No," McGarvey said. Both he and Pete had got the strong impression that Haaris's performance last night had been staged, and he said as much to Page.

"You and Otto think that he might be the Messiah," the director said. "But it could be that you're cherry-picking him. Focusing on every little bit that supports your notion while discounting everything else. Suppose it was an intruder, a burglar, who his wife surprised, and not a hitman sent by the ISI?"

"The ISI didn't kill her, nor did a burglar."

"Who then?"

"He did it."

Page sat back. "Good Lord almighty. Do you have proof?"

"No, but their marriage could have been a front all along. Could be she walked in on something he was doing or saying that she wasn't suppose to know about. He wouldn't have had much of a choice."

Page's secretary buzzed him. He picked up the phone. "Not now." But then he looked at McGarvey. "Dave Haaris would like to have a word with you as soon as possible."

"Five minutes," McGarvey said.

Page gave his secretary the message and hung up.

"As soon as Dave Haaris disappears I think the Messiah will show up. But it won't happen until the staff at the Presidential Palace has been purged of everyone who supported Barazani, including just about everyone in the compound."

"It's not been in the news yet, but the purge has already started. Quietly, but it won't be long before word of it gets out."

"I'm going down to talk to him now." McGarvey got up and went to the door. "When does our ambassador and his staff leave for Islamabad?"

"Two days."

"You're a friend of Fay's. Have him include me in the delegation."

"Not a chance they'd take you. And even if they did you'd be recognized the moment you got off the plane."

"I'll be an assistant to the military attaché. Different name, different appearance. No one will recognize me."

"Once you're there, then what?"

"I'm going to kill the Messiah."

A haggard-looking Dave Haaris was alone in his office reading a summary report on the developing situation in Islamabad that had been sent down to him from the Watch, when McGarvey was buzzed through.

"Thanks for coming to see me," Haaris said. "I want to apologize to you personally for my behavior last night. I wasn't myself."

"No need to apologize to me, but you might want to have a word with the Pakistani ambassador and with your old friend Rajput, who's filed a formal complaint with the White House."

"I'm rather afraid that I've lost the ear of the president."

"What was the point of confronting Rajput so publicly?" McGarvey asked. "What sort of a reaction were you looking for?"

Haaris took a moment to answer. "The general has never been a friend of mine, old or new, but I have met with him a sufficient number of times to have made a measure of the man. And there've been the odd psych reports, which contained some nuggets. But I didn't get what I was looking for. Either he's a better liar than I thought he was or he truly knows nothing about my wife's assassination."

"So now what?"

"Deborah is being cremated this afternoon, and I'm taking her ashes to London. She thought it would be elegant if her remains were to be spread on the Thames. Actually, she'd always thought it would be both of us. Mine because she thought I wanted to go home, and hers because she wanted to be with me."

"When are you leaving?"

"Tonight. Since I'm no longer required to be at the White House, I thought I'd see some old friends at the SIS and get their take on the situation. Pass it along to my people here."

"What about the Messiah?"

"What about him?" Haaris asked.

"The president has asked me to assassinate him."

Haaris was taken aback. "How extraordinary."

"The same order was given for bin Laden."

"I meant how extraordinary that you would tell me such a thing, unless you firmly believe that I'm the Messiah."

"Where did you hear that?"

Haaris smiled. "Good heavens, you were the director of Central Intelligence once upon a time. Didn't you learn as DCI that there are more leaks here on Campus than there are in a peasant's roof?"

"I could ask you who you heard it from."

"I don't recall, but perhaps it was from Miss Boylan. We had a chat a couple of days ago, she might have mentioned it. I understand that she was involved in an automobile accident this morning. How is she?"

"Dead," McGarvey said.

TWENTY-NINE

McGarvey went back up to Page's office, where he briefed the director on his conversation with Haaris.

"I'll have Tommy Boyle put a tail on him," Page said. Boyle was the CIA's London chief of station and a friend of Haaris's. "But I don't understand the part about Miss Boylan."

"As long as most everyone thinks she's dead, she'll stop being a target," McGarvey said.

"If Marty's in on it he'll want to use her as an asset."

"I don't want to worry about her, so keep Marty out of it."

"I understand how you feel," Page said. "But she's a capable field officer who's proved her worth on more than one occasion. From what I understand she was of some assistance to you in Florida a few days ago."

"Have our media people pass it along to the Virginia Highway Patrol. They can make the announcement that one of our officers was killed in a car crash on the parkway. It was an unfortunate accident."

"I'll do it, but you're the only one who'll be able to convince her to lie low."

"Have you talked to Fay yet?"

"I was waiting until you spoke with Haaris. You still mean to go through with the president's request?"

"Like I said, Walt, I don't think we have much of a choice."

"You understand that this won't be like the bin Laden op. You'll be totally on your own. If you're captured or taken out, we'll deny your orders. And I got that directly from Kalley. Not in so many words, of course, but her meaning was clear."

"I'll have Otto send up a passport name, photo and number later today or first thing in the morning. You can tell Fay to tell the ambassador that I'm a CIA officer, but I'll be tagging along purely as an observer."

"What about our station staff at the embassy?"

"I don't want to interact with them unless it becomes necessary. If this thing goes south I want Austin to stay in the clear."

"I suppose if I briefed Carlton he would say that you had finally gone completely out of your mind," Page said. "And I'd have to agree with him." Carlton Patterson was a longtime admirer of McGarvey's.

"You're right, so don't bother him," McGarvey said.

"One of these days when you walk out of this office you won't come back."

"You're almost certainly right about that too. But it's what I signed up for at the beginning."

"Take care of yourself, Mac."

Otto was in his office monitoring the same feeds from Pakistan that the Watch was receiving when McGarvey showed up.

"Louise has been bugging me about Pete. How's she doing?" Louise and Pete had become fast friends over the past couple of years.

"She'll be okay. I'm bringing her out here first thing in the morning as soon as Franklin releases her."

Otto had to laugh. "Do you think she's going to stand for it—putting her on ice so you don't have to worry about the pretty little woman? I can just hear what she'll say about that move. Even Louise will think you're nuts."

On the feed was the image of a stern-looking man in traditional Punjabi dress, seated behind a desk, the national flag behind him, the translation of what he was saying in a crawl across the bottom of the monitor.

"Shahidullah Shahid," Otto said, "official spokesman for the Tehreek-e-Taliban Pakistan. He's been speaking for the past hour and a half about unity. But it's not so important who he is but *where* he is."

"Could be anywhere."

"The Aiwan," Otto said. "In fact he's seated at the president's desk."

"The ISI has finished its purge."

"Mostly a bloodless coup so far, except for Barazani."

"Any sign of the Messiah?"

"Not yet, and Shahid hasn't even mentioned him,

at least not by name. But he admits that he's not the only man in charge of the government. And if Haaris is the Messiah, all we have to do is keep a tight rein on him, which shouldn't be so tough so long as he stays in Washington."

"He's taking his wife's ashes to London tonight. Says that she wanted them to be spread on the Thames. Page will have Tommy Boyle put someone on him."

"Okay, same difference. As long as we can see him anywhere but Islamabad he won't be able to get into much mischief."

"I need a new ID set—driver's license, credit cards, passport, family photos, medical insurance card. I don't want to use ones I've already fielded."

"By when?"

"In the morning at the latest. Page is going to get me a slot on Power's team when they return to Islamabad. Should be tomorrow or the day after."

"Everybody knows your face, so we'll need to change it. Saul Landesberg over in Technical Services is about the best around. I'll give him the heads-up. When do you want to do it?"

"Now. I want to see how it plays here first, because if it doesn't I'll have to find another way."

Otto gave him a long, odd look but picked up the phone and called Technical Services. "Saul, Otto. I have a job for an old friend. But this would have to be totally off the grid. And quick. Like right now."

Landesberg was a short, slightly built man with thinning fair hair and wide, serious eyes, who seemed to have a perpetual broad smile plastered on his wide face. He'd cleared the two technicians from his small studio before McGarvey and Otto showed up.

"Judging from Otto's call, I thought it might be you, Mr. Director, but I didn't breathe a word to anyone. Where are we off to?"

McGarvey had never actually met the man, but he'd heard of him. He'd been named by a number of NOCs as the "Artist."

"Pakistan, in a couple of days," McGarvey said.

"Good Lord, not as a Paki? You're too damned big."

"No, I'm going in with our embassy staff as an observer."

"So everyone will know that you work for the CIA but as a wonk, not a spook. An intellectual. An academic. Maybe Harvard or some such on contract to the Intelligence Directorate."

He had McGarvey take off his jacket and shirt, and sat him down in a swiveling salon chair in front of a bank of mirrors, some of them reflecting close-up views of McGarvey's face, neck and upper torso.

"Do we have a name?" he said, brushing his fingers through McGarvey's hair. Feeling the structure of his forehead, cheeks, nose, chin. Peering into his eyes.

"Travis Parks."

"Dr. Parks. Cultural anthropology, but only as the first layer of your cover. It's a subject almost nobody knows anything about. Your real specialty, of course, is government studies. You're on board to take a close look at what's really happening in Islamabad. Friend or foe."

Landesberg shut off the lights in the mirrors so that they went blank. "We'll make you a little older, gray at the sides, shorter hair. Do you tolerate contacts?"

"I don't want to fuzz out if I'm in the middle of a shooting situation," McGarvey said.

"No contacts. Gray green it is. A little broader

nose, thicker eyebrows, heavier cheeks, maybe a jutting chin. Sallow complexion. A little sagging of your jowls, a few wrinkles on your neck, same complexion on your chest and back, gray hair. Nothing over the top, but cumulatively the effect should be enough that your own mother wouldn't recognize you, and yet you'll have complete mobility." Landesberg laughed. "Won't run or fall off. You'll even be able to take a cozy shower for two."

THIRTY

Haaris never had trouble adjusting to time zone changes. His body clock was on U.S. eastern, where it was one in the morning, while it was six in the morning when he arrived at London's Heathrow Airport. He'd only napped for an hour or so, but walking through the concourse to Immigration Control he was alert.

Several international flights had arrived at about the same time and the terminal was very busy; even so he spotted his tail within twenty-five feet of his gate.

He presented his U.S. passport to the agent at one of the windows.

"Good morning, Mr. Haaris. What is the purpose of your visit to Great Britain?"

"I've brought my wife's ashes over, she wanted to be buried here."

The uniformed agent looked up, startled. It was an answer she'd not often heard. "I'm terribly sorry, sir. Was she a British citizen?"

"No. But she loved everything here, especially the countryside in spring and summer."

"You might need a permit, sir."

"Actually, no, unless you want to scatter them on private property or in a public park."

The woman stamped the passport and handed it over. "Do you have friends here?"

"Yes," Haaris said, and he pocketed his passport as he moved down the hall to Baggage Claim and Customs.

Deborah's ashes were in a small cardboard carton that he had packed into a zippered nylon bag. The only other luggage he'd brought over was a wheeled bag. When it was his turn at one of the counters, he handed over his passport and customs declaration.

"Anything to claim, sir?" the agent asked. "Tobacco, spirits, plant matter?

"Only my personal belongings plus my wife's cremated remains."

"May I see?"

Haaris opened the nylon bag. The box had been sealed in Washington with tape from the funeral parlor. He handed the agent the death certificate.

"Sorry to do this, sir, hope you understand," the agent said. He handed the box to another agent, who stepped across to a baggage scanner and ran it through. A few moments later he brought it back.

The customs agent cleared both bags. Haaris walked out into the main terminal and headed toward the ground transportation exit, where the man in the dark blue blazer and open-collared white shirt who'd tailed him from the gate unobtrusively fell in behind him.

Just at the doors to the cab queue, Harris suddenly turned and walked up to the agent. "I assume that Tommy Boyle has sent you to watch over me."

The CIA officer, caught out, smiled and shrugged. "Mr. Boyle thought you might spot me, sir. But considering what happened to Mrs. Haaris, he thought it might be wise to watch your back."

"Good enough. I assume you have a car?"

"Yes, sir."

"Then you can save me the cab fare and drive me into town. I'm staying at the Connaught, actually, just around the corner from our embassy."

"Yes, sir, I know it."

Haaris arched an eyebrow. "You do?"

Caught out again the young officer could only smile. "I meant to say I know where it is."

The officer's car was a white Ultima, and he was a good driver. The traffic was heavy on the M4 into the city center, and they didn't speak much except about the weather in London versus Washington.

At the hotel a uniformed bellman opened the door for Haaris while another opened the boot and took out the two pieces of luggage.

Haaris looked back through the open door. "Tell Tommy that I'm sorry but I don't want any company this time around. But if he wants to keep a tail on me, stay out of sight. He'll understand."

The young officer didn't know what to say.

Haaris had made reservations for five days in a corner suite, and after check-in he ordered a bottle of Dom Pérignon. He took off his jacket and tie and laid them on the bed. When the wine came he sat by the window looking out of one eye down on Mayfair toward Buckingham Palace and out of the other toward the nylon bag with his wife's remains.

He'd felt no remorse, killing her. It had been a necessity. Nor had he ever felt any love for her. She had been another necessity for his cover. The union had been perceived as odd by others, which was exactly the sentiment he'd wanted to promote. Looking too closely at something unusual diverted attention from reality.

Things like that, people's perceptions of him, were another thing he'd hated about the West—especially Great Britain and even more so the U.S. Narrow-minded, provincial bastards, all of them, who couldn't see past their own self-perceived superiority. The white man was the world's salvation. Always had been.

Of course life wasn't any better in Pakistan, or India, or China or even the new Russia with its oligarchs. But he'd worked all of his adult life to pit the East against the West. Pakistan against the U.S., who was the real enemy, not India. The ISI against the CIA. The man on the street in Rawalpindi or Lahore against the man from West Point or Des Moines.

It had always been a grand game for him. Revenge. Making England and the ISI the sparring partners for his game was far too tame. But antagonizing the U.S., which still held out hopes that by sending massive amounts of military aid to Islamabad that Pakistan would actually be a moderating influence on the Taliban and the dozens of other terrorist societies in country, was actually sweet.

Washington had never learned the folly of its ways. The Pentagon supplied bin Laden and al Qaeda with Stinger missiles and other weapons to kick the Russians out of Afghanistan, apparently never really understanding the first principle of blowback. The generals never dreamed, or never wanted to admit, that someday those same Stinger missiles would be used against its own forces.

Just as they could not see that all the military aid to Pakistan would one day come back and bite them in the arse.

Payback time was coming, and Haaris had a

front-row seat for the most over-the-top game on earth: revenge for all the shit he had taken since his uncle had brought him to England.

Sitting now drinking his wine he understood that he'd never really considered the possibility that he was insane. Stark raving mad, as one of his teachers at Eton had railed. "All wogs are barking mad. Happens at birth."

It was the same when he was eight and nine, and being raped by the older boys. No matter that his grades were in the top 5 percentile, he was a wog. A thing. An object to be used.

And he'd bided his time.

He took a shower and changed into a pair of khaki slacks, a light yellow V-neck sweater and a comfortable pair of walking shoes. He arranged for a rental Mini to be brought to the hotel and took the nylon bag with Deb's ashes downstairs.

Ten minutes later he drove off, all the way down to Pulham, where he parked in the lee of the Putney railroad bridge and dumped Deborah's ashes in the river. They floated on the surface and spread out as scum, along with the oil slicks and other industrial flotsam. It was several minutes before the broad patch disappeared downstream.

One of Boyle's minders, driving a shiny gray Vauxhall had pulled over fifty yards away, and when Haaris got back in his Mini and drove off the CIA officer pulled in behind him, staying three or four cars behind.

For a time Haaris drove around south London as if he were merely trying to escape the memory of tossing his wife's ashes in the Thames, but then he drove back to the Connaught, where he turned in the car and went up to his suite.

A man who could have been his twin, dressed in

khakis and a yellow V-neck sweater, was sitting on the bed, and when Haaris walked in he got up without a word and walked to the window, where he sat down and poured a glass of champagne.

Haaris changed into a pair of jeans and a blue shirt with rolled-up sleeves that buttoned into place. He left his passport, other IDs and money on the dresser, and without a word left the suite. Taking the service elevator down to the basement level he left the hotel via the loading dock. A dark blue Mercedes S500 with deeply tinted windows was waiting for him, the rear door open.

He got in, closed the door and the driver headed away.

THIRTY-ONE

McGarvey rode with Otto out the back Campus gate at three in the morning, and they drove directly over to Haaris's house in Embassy Row just off Massachusetts Avenue, in light traffic. They'd managed to get out of the OHB without being spotted by anyone who knew Mac, and the gate guards hadn't paid much attention to who was driving. Their main brief was to vet everyone coming onto the Campus.

After Landesberg had finished, around one-thirty, he'd turned on the lights in the big mirrors and swiveled McGarvey's chair around. The effect was nothing less than stunning, and even for someone who'd used disguises before, a little disorienting.

"Tamp down your west Kansas drawl, Mr. Director, and your own mother wouldn't recognize you."

Otto had gone over to the cafeteria for some coffee and doughnuts, and when he'd come back he'd almost dropped the lot, a large grin animating his face. "You're a genius, my man," he'd said to Landesberg.

"What do you think, Mr. Director?"

"I have to agree with Otto," McGarvey said. "It's me, but it isn't."

"That's the point."

Otto had phoned Louise to meet them at All Saints at seven sharp, and when she'd pressed he told her that he was with Mac on the Pakistani thing.

Crime scene tape still blocked the front door of Haaris's place, but not the driveway, when they pulled up. The houses in the neighborhood were all dark, except for the carriage lights out front. And before they'd come around the corner Otto had pulled over and brought up the security systems, including cameras and motion detectors, in every house, shutting them down with a universal password of his own design. The security services would show that the systems were operating as normal, but the view from the eaves-mounted cameras would show only a street with no traffic.

Otto followed McGarvey around to the rear of the house, where Mac picked the lock to the kitchen hall in under twenty seconds, and they were in. They'd checked with London Station earlier and were assured that Haaris had arrived in the morning, had spread his wife's ashes in an industrial section of the Thames and had returned to the Connaught, where he remained.

"Find his computer. I'll take the master bedroom," McGarvey said.

Otto went to the study, while McGarvey found his way to the master suite. The curtains were tightly drawn so he switched on a light in one of the bathrooms.

The bed had been made up, and Deb Haaris's

walk-in closet, crammed with clothing and maybe two hundred or more pairs of shoes and boots, was a total mess. Clothes were piled on an upholstered chair, lying in heaps on the floor and stuffed in jumbled, sloppily folded piles on the shelves.

Haaris's closet, on the other hand, was precisely organized. Slacks were hung in order of color right to left, shirts the same, the fronts all facing left, as were the sport coats and blazers, first, a dozen suits and two tuxedos next. Shoes were on low shelves. Racks held belts and ties; drawers, socks, or underwear. Nothing seemed to be missing.

McGarvey was not able to find a wall safe or floor safe or any other place to hide something in either closet, in the separate bathrooms or the bedroom itself.

Otto was just coming out of the study when McGarvey passed through the living room.

"Anything?"

"Nada," Otto said. "He's a careful man."

"What about his computer?"

"Empty."

"Even if he erased the hard drive, you can retrieve some of it, can't you?"

"You don't understand, Mac. His computer is empty. The hard drive is missing as are the RAM chips. Nothing left but a keyboard, screen and hard-frame wiring."

McGarvey looked toward the front windows at the neighborhood, still asleep. "He did tell us one thing at least."

"What's that?"

"He's not coming home. At least not soon."

They stopped at an all-night McDonald's not too far from the old Columbia Hospital for Women just off

Pennsylvania Avenue. A few people were having early morning breakfast and coffee. Several of them were outside smoking at the picnic tables.

"We've come a long ways together, you and I," Otto said.

"Yes, we have," McGarvey said, not really hearing yet what his friend was trying to say.

"There was a time in France when I didn't think I was going to make it. No one knew what hacking was all about then, but I was really on the verge of being one of the true assholes. Doing that kind of shit out of pure spite. Boredom, maybe. I was pissed off at the world and really didn't know why. Then you showed up on my doorstep one day and gave me my purpose."

"It was a two-way street. I was having my own troubles then, before Katy and I got back together."

"But then the two of you did."

"Not for long enough."

"But you had each other," Otto said, looking away momentarily. "I was really jealous of you, until Louise. Mostly because I didn't understand what it was like to . . ."

"To be in love?"

"Yeah. And here we are again, on the actual brink, you and I. We can't do it alone, Mac. Never could. Of all people I thought that you would understand most."

Suddenly McGarvey understood what his old friend was getting at. "Two things," he said, maybe a little too sharply. "Don't write me off just yet, and second of all, leave Pete out of it."

Otto managed a smile. "I haven't on the first, and I won't on the second."

Louise was already at All Saints when they arrived. Breakfast was being served to the half-dozen patients on the third and fourth floors, but Franklin hadn't arrived yet. It was he who signed all release orders. Pete wasn't going anywhere, no matter how much she protested, until the doctor said so.

Last night Louise had stopped by Pete's apartment to pack a couple of bags for at least a few days, maybe as long as a week, on Campus. "If she needs anything else in the interim, I'll get them," she told McGarvey.

She was waiting upstairs in the second-floor visitors' lounge, watching *Good Morning America,* when McGarvey and Otto got off the elevator and came down the corridor.

"Is Pete awake yet?" Otto asked.

"Awake, dressed and pissed off," Louise said. "She wants out now." She turned to McGarvey. "And who are you?"

McGarvey and Otto exchanged a glance.

"Travis Parks," Otto told his wife. "He's been assigned to act as Pete's minder."

Louise guffawed. "Lots of luck, Parks."

McGarvey smiled. "Maybe I can take her by surprise for a change," he said, reverting to his Kansas drawl.

Louise's expression changed by degrees. "My God, it's you," she said. "I can see it in your eyes, but I didn't notice at first."

"That's a good thing," McGarvey said.

He went down the hall to Pete's room. The door was open and he knocked on the frame before he walked in.

Pete was fully dressed, sitting on the edge of her bed, her breakfast tray untouched. She looked up. And for just a moment her mouth pursed in irritation, but suddenly she brightened.

"Kirk, you look worse than I feel."

THIRTY-TWO

McGarvey showed up at Joint Base Andrews in a CIA Cadillac Escalade with civilian plates and was dropped off on the tarmac where a C-32A military VIP transport aircraft was boarding the Islamabad embassy staff for the overnight flight. The twin-engine jet was the military version of the Boeing 757, which the vice president and sometimes even the president used. In this case it was meant as a show of the U.S. commitment to diplomacy with Pakistan.

A pair of embassy security officers in civilian clothes were checking the passengers according to a boarding list.

"Travis Parks," McGarvey told the men. He handed one of them his passport.

"We understand your mission, Mr. Parks, but Ambassador Powers isn't particularly pleased that you're along for the ride," the officer said. He checked McGarvey's well-traveled passport closely before handing it back. "Will you be a part of our detail?"

"I'm just going over as an observer. I'll try to stay out of everyone's hair."

"Do that," the officer said.

Hefting his single bag McGarvey went up the stairs and inside the plane a steward directed him to a rear section of the cabin that contained general business-class seating for thirty-two staffers. Most of the seats were taken and the staffers looked up with curiosity, some with a little animosity as he stowed his bag in an overhead bin and took a seat in the last row across from the galley.

No one said anything to him, and once he was seated the other passengers went back to their conversations or to their laptops or telephones.

He phoned Otto. "I'm aboard, but it's a little frosty."

"Powers talked to you yet?"

"Probably not till we're airborne."

"I suppose it would be stupid of me to tell you not to annoy the man. He could send you back, no matter what Fay has to say about it. When he gets to his embassy he's the boss."

"I'll go in the front door and right out the back soon as we get there."

"To the Presidential Palace?"

McGarvey had thought quite a bit about what his first moves would be once he got in country. His target was the Messiah, but first getting to General Rajput and the Shahid of the TTP who'd taken up residence in the palace would probably be necessary.

"What's the latest on Haaris?"

"As of an hour ago he was still in London."

"In the hotel?"

"He had lunch at a pub in Notting Hill and then drove down to Charing Cross, where he parked in the station lot, and from what I was just told he's taking a leisurely stroll along the river. But he's being very careful with his tradecraft, almost as if he were trying to hide in plain sight even though he's already been made."

"Whatever moves he makes, tell Boyle to stay out of his way."

"He already burned one of Boyle's people at the airport, and in fact had the agent drive him to his hotel."

"Whatever happens I want Tommy himself to stay away from Haaris. They're old friends and I don't want anything to interfere with Dave's plans. And tell Boyle that if Haaris makes contact and wants to get together to beg off. I want to give him all the room in the world."

"Sixty-four-thousand-dollar question, *kemo sabe*: what if we're wrong, and Dave Haaris is not the Messiah?"

"Then we're wrong. Still leaves the Messiah, whoever the hell he is," McGarvey said. "Are your programs making any progress identifying the voice?"

"Sometimes they're going around in circles. It's almost as if the speaker disguised his voice that was inputted to the device. Maybe like adding a Southern accent, or an Indian accent, that was then altered. We may get to the false accent he used, but it might not tell us anything we can use. Could be he's smarter than us."

"Or thinks he is."

They departed around four in the afternoon. The flight plan would take them to Ramstein Air Force Base in Germany for refueling, and a layover, before they started their second leg to Islamabad. Touchdown was scheduled for eight in the morning.

A half hour later a steward came back with the drink cart, and McGarvey was told that there would be no alcohol service on the flight in respect for the Muslim tradition. He had a coffee instead. Still no one else bothered to speak to him or even look his way.

At six when they were well out over the Atlantic the same steward came back. "Ambassador Powers would like to see you in conference section," he said.

McGarvey went forward to where Powers was seated at a small table. No one else was with him, and when the steward withdrew he pulled the curtain.

The ambassador, unlike his namesake father, was a short, stoop-shouldered man, slight of build. His face was square, his eyes deep-set, and he looked like a scholar, like a professor of history in some Northeastern school. He motioned for McGarvey to sit down.

"I argued against taking you along. The CIA chief of station is a capable man and runs a very tight operation. We don't need a rogue operation out of the embassy. Not now, not under the present circumstances."

"You mean of course the beheading of Pakistan's president, the detonation of a nuclear device and the top Taliban terrorist in the Aiwan."

Powers was vexed. "Don't presume to tell me my job, Mr. Parks."

"Nor should you try to tell me mine, Mr. Ambassador. We both have difficult assignments."

"What exactly is yours?"

"To observe."

"You work for the CIA, therefore in Pakistan you work for Mr. Austin. I want no mistake about that."

McGarvey took out his sat phone and called Walt Page's private number.

"You can't use a telephone while we're in the air," Powers said.

McGarvey put it on speakerphone when Page answered.

"You must be in the air now, and I assume that you're sitting across from Ambassador Powers, who has read you the riot act."

"Something like that. He wants to put me under Austin's umbrella."

"Actually I want your Dr. Parks to leave my delegation as soon as we touch down at Ramstein," Powers said. "We don't need another spy just now. Diplomacy is the best defense for a situation that has spun nearly out of control."

"I can call John Fay."

"Secretary Fay is not in charge on the ground, I am."

"You're absolutely right, Mr. Ambassador," Page said. "I'll telephone the White House. Dr. Parks is working on a presidential mandate. I'll call back."

Powers sat forward. "For goodness' sake, wait just a minute now," he said. "There's absolutely no reason to take this any further."

"I'll stay out of your way, Mr. Ambassador. You have my word on it," McGarvey said. "In fact I won't even be staying at the embassy."

"In heaven's name, where do you expect to go? I need to know what my staff is up to."

"I'm not on your staff."

Powers blustered for a moment or two.

"What's your pleasure, Travis?" Page asked.

"I think that Ambassador Powers and I will come to an understanding, Mr. Director," McGarvey said. He ended the call and got up. "I'm just hitching a ride to Islamabad. Once we're there I'll disappear. It will give you plausible deniability. You never knew who I was or even why I was on your flight."

Before Powers could reply, McGarvey went back to the aft section, where he stopped at the galley to talk to the stewards. He did not raise his voice nor did he whisper.

"I'll have a cognac. I think a nice Rémy will do. And with whatever you're serving I'll take a split of Dom if you have it, Veuve Clicquot if need be. But it damned well better be cold."

McGarvey turned to go.

"Sir, we have our orders," one of the stewards said.

"Am I going to have to shoot you?" He smiled.

PART
THREE

The Operation

The flight to Pakistan went without incident. They were directed to the military side of the airport, where they were met by an honor guard of Pakistani army, air force and navy at strict attention as Ambassador Powers came down the stairs.

A black Mercedes limo and five white vans were parked at the end of a long red carpet, the drivers also waiting at attention.

Powers and several of his top aides were met by Prime Minister Rajput, who was dressed in his army uniform.

No civilians had gathered for the arrival, but the fact that Rajput was in uniform was not lost on one of the men who had been seated just in front of McGarvey. "The general is making his point," the man said to his seatmate. "Whatever else is going on here between the Messiah and Taliban, the army is still in charge."

"They're the ones with their fingers on the nukes," McGarvey said, getting up and taking his bag from the overhead bin.

The two field service officers glared at him as he made his way to the front of the aircraft. Two men whom he'd not noticed earlier were waiting at the main door as others on Powers's team left the plane.

The taller of them stepped forward to block

McGarvey from leaving. "A word if you please. Dr. Parks. I'm Bob Thomas."

"We don't want any trouble," the other man said. They were both young and well built, with the no-nonsense attitude of ex–Special Forces.

"Sounds good to me."

"Mr. Austin asked us to escort you to the embassy, where he'd like to have a word before you leave Pakistan," Thomas said.

"I'm surprised he didn't come out here himself to meet the ambassador. But I suppose he's a bit busy trying to figure out what the hell is going on."

"Are you armed?" the second officer said.

"I don't think it'd be very smart for an American to be running around Pakistan without some protection. Unless you guys were sent out to act as my bodyguards."

"We'll have your weapon," Thomas said.

"No," McGarvey said.

The man stepped forward. "We were instructed to take it, sir."

"I don't think you guys really want to have an incident here and now. Lots of people out there would take notice."

A dozen foreign service officers were backed up in the aisle waiting to get off, but none of them said a word, waiting for the little drama to play out.

The limo carrying Powers and two of his top aides pulled away, escorted by two Hummers in the lead and two in the rear filled with armed Pakistani Special Forces troops.

"What say we just hitch a ride to the embassy," McGarvey said. "I'm carrying a personal message for Ross from the director. And once he has it I'll be out of your hair. No trouble. Promise."

"Yes, sir," the taller of the two said. "We'll hold you to your word."

The run into the diplomatic section of Islamabad went without incident. Life in the city had gone back to normal. No evidence of the disturbances over the past week were visible, nor were angry crowds lining the highway with protest signs. Traffic was heavy, but no one seemed to be in a hurry, no one seemed to be angry. No one honked their horn.

"It's almost spooky," one of the FSOs commented.

"Like the city is holding its breath waiting for the shoe to drop," another one said.

"How long has it been like this?" McGarvey asked his minders.

"Ever since the Messiah took over," Thomas said. "The place was under martial law until the parliament named General Rajput as acting PM and he lifted it." He glanced at McGarvey. "It looks peaceful, but no one thinks it's going to last. It's why Mr. Austin didn't want someone from Langley coming over here with an attitude, and carrying."

"They invited us back."

"The diplomats. Not us. Ever since Lundgren went missing we've been keeping a low profile."

"Was he the one caught in the nuclear incident?"

"He was out there, and we haven't heard from him since."

"What about you guys? Is the ISI dogging you? Or are you being left alone?"

Thomas hesitated for just a moment. "If they were on us, I'd understand it; we've always had our rat packs. Twenty-four/seven, usually four teams rotating. In and out of the embassy, to and from our quarters, restaurants. Christ, even if we had to take a dump someone was always watching. But not in the past couple of days. Same with the British embassy staff, the French, Germans, Italians, everyone."

"Unless they got better and no one has made them," McGarvey suggested.

"I wish it was that simple," Thomas said. "At least we'd know what to expect. But trust me, Parks, no one is following us. It's one of the reasons Mr. Austin wants you to go back home. If you create an incident there's no telling what the ISI will do. It's like walking across a field of broken glass with bare feet: the wrong move and it'll be a bloody mess."

Powers was already inside the embassy, his limo and the four military escort vehicles gone when the five vans pulled up and their escorts left. Two marine guards at the main entrance stayed out of sight as much as possible, only opening the gate electrically when the drivers radioed ahead.

Thomas and the other escort brought McGarvey into the embassy past the security desk and up to the third-floor rear, where the CIA maintained a suite of offices under the guise of the American Information and Cultural Exchange Section.

Chief of Station, Pakistan, Ross Austin, alerted that they were on the way up, was waiting at the open door to his office, his jacket off, his collar open, his tie loose, sleeves rolled up: the pose of a man, who looked like a Packers' linebacker, obviously deeply at work. He was a career intelligence officer who hoped one day to raise to at least a deputy director slot. His mentor was Marty Bambridge and at forty Austin fashioned himself after the DDO—pinch-nosed, disapproving, feigning surprise whenever something was set before him. But despite all of that the scuttle-butt was that he was a damned fine COS.

But, and it was a very large *but,* in McGarvey's thinking, Ross Austin, like many chiefs of station, *was* the CIA in Pakistan. He was not only bright, he knew Pakistan and its government and especially its secret intelligence services better than just about anyone—other than Dave Haaris. At the very least he deserved the truth.

"Thank you, gentlemen," he told Thomas and the other officer, and motioned for McGarvey to join him.

Austin's office was a mess of files, maps, newspapers and the translations of dozens of Pakistani magazines and television and radio broadcasts. He went behind his desk and McGarvey sat across from him.

"I talked to Walt Page last night, and he asked me to at least hear you out before I sent you away. I have an aircraft standing by to take you to Turkey—Incirlik—right now. Talk to me, Parks."

McGarvey had met Austin twice before, once at the Farm and once at Langley. The first time McGarvey had been deputy director of operations, and the second time he'd been the DCI. In each instance the meeting had not been one-on-one.

"I'm leaving the embassy within the hour, but I am not leaving Pakistan. I have a job to do here."

"No."

"There's not much you can say about it, Ross."

"Where the hell do you get off addressing me by my first name? Who the hell do you think you are?"

"My name is Kirk McGarvey. I'm here to assassinate the Messiah and I've just put my life in your hands." He took out his pistol and laid it on the desk.

THIRTY-FOUR

McGarvey left the embassy on foot shortly before noon and walked down the driveway and out the gate past the two marine guards, who watched but said nothing. The streets here in what was known as the diplomatic enclave of the city were as safe as any streets could be right now in Pakistan, but McGarvey still felt naked without his pistol, though he understood the theater of leaving it with Austin. An unarmed McGarvey was no immediate threat. It was what he wanted the COS to believe.

Two blocks away, he got a cab in front of the Canadian embassy and directed the driver to take him to the Marriott Hotel near the Aiwan and the prime minister's residence. A lot of foreign businessmen and journalists stayed there, and with its double walls and bomb-proof entrance gate, it was among the most secure spots in the city.

Otto had made the reservations for five nights. "It'll be a reasonable jumping-off place for you, but you might run into a problem right from the start. They scan people's luggage at the gate. If they find your gun, they'll hold you until the cops get there. But the good news is they profile. And you don't fit the image of a suicide bomber."

"I'll leave it at the embassy until I need it," McGarvey had said.

"You'll have to let Austin in on your plans."

"He's a good man. He won't want me there, but if Page tells him that I'm staying, he'll wash his hands of the op but he won't do anything stupid to put me in harm's way."

"Just being in Pakistan puts you in harm's way."

"Keep an eye on Pete for me."

"Louise wants her to stay with us."

It went against McGarvey's better judgment, but he'd agreed. "Make sure that she stays out of sight, she's supposed to be dead."

Passing the Aiwan on Constitution Avenue he saw no signs of the mass demonstration that had taken place only a few days before. Traffic was normal. Like the FSO in the van had said: it was spooky.

The nation was waiting for the Messiah to show up, to tell the people what to do next. Haaris had said that he was betting that the man was going to push Pakistan into war with India, which was in itself a bizarre position for him to announce so openly if he was in fact the Messiah. Something was missing. But Haaris was probably insane because his advice to the president was to make preemptive strikes on Islamabad and Rawalpindi.

"Cut the head off and the monster will die," he'd said.

The president was certain that Pakistan wouldn't dare start anything. With their reduced nuclear arsenal, they'd lose.

Neither Rajput nor anyone else in the government had made any mention of the U.S. strikes against their weapons. Not even the international press corps had broken the story, though there were plenty of witnesses on the ground. Nearly everyone's attention was still focused on the nuclear incident near Quetta, for which no one in the government had offered an explanation.

Security at the Marriott's front gate was tight. One of the uniformed security officers led a bomb-sniffing dog around the cab, while another checked McGarvey's diplomatic passport and a third looked inside the trunk.

"If you want to check my luggage I have no objection," McGarvey told the officer.

"It is not necessary, Dr. Parks," the officer said.

The busy lobby was sleek and new, and the check-in went smoothly. He was given a suite on the fourth floor that looked out toward the Margalla Hills. which at night would be alive with the lights of homes.

As soon as the bellman left, McGarvey used his encrypted phone to call Otto. "I'm in. Has Powers scheduled a news conference yet?"

"One-thirty local, you'll have just enough time to get over there. How'd it go with Austin?"

"He didn't like it, but he wasn't about to go head to head with me. Did he call Page?"

"No. But what'd you tell him?"

"Everything."

"Jesus," Otto said softly. "You just unzipped your fly. Care to tell me why?"

"Haaris has been Austin's chief adviser."

"I'll check the embassy's phone records, see if he's called the Connaught in London. But it might not prove anything."

"It'd prove that Haaris is still there," McGarvey said. "But I have a hunch that whoever Doyle's people are watching is a double, and that Haaris is already here or will be soon. Everyone is waiting for the Messiah to show up."

"Including you."

"Including me," McGarvey said. "Where's the news conference being held?"

"At the Aiwan with Rajput. And I've worked out your secondary cover, including a seven-month back story. You're a geopolitical blogger on a site called PIP—'Parks's International Perspective.' Right-wing, hawkish. Your basic tenet is that since the Second World War the U.S. has stepped into the role of the world's benevolent police force. It's something you believe anyway. I've posted almost one hundred articles."

"No one at the news conference will have heard of the site."

"They do now. Last night when I finished setting it up, I inserted nearly one million hits. An hour ago the number had gone up by two hundred thousand, and it's still climbing because of your most recent posts on the Messiah wanting to go to war with India. The journalists in the room might never have heard of you until now, but none of them will admit it. Especially not to each other. Not for a while, anyway."

"Anybody making any significant comments?"

"If you mean Dave Haaris, no. But I'm pretty sure that our people here on Campus are aware of the site. I have a filter on it to screen for anyone interesting. But the only posts against you are coming from unknowns or people who didn't care to identify themselves. I'm working on tracing some of them back to their sources, but nothing much is coming up."

"How do I get to it?"

"Google 'PIP.' You'd better read the last half dozen or so posts to get yourself up to speed. But like I said, I didn't put any words in your mouth that you haven't already spoken at one time or the other."

McGarvey had to smile. "Have I always been that obvious?"

"Yes."

"Keep an eye on Pete. I don't trust her."

Otto evaded the comment. "I can have a pistol sent in a diplomatic pouch from Jalalabad. Be there by dinnertime."

"Don't do it. I'd have to ditch it every time I came back to the hotel," McGarvey said. "And if I get into a situation where I'd need a weapon, it'd probably be worthless to me."

On the short drive over to the Presidential Palace McGarvey brought the PIP site up on his phone and scrolled backward through several days of articles before the Messiah had made his first appearance. Pakistan, according to what Otto had written, had never been a U.S. friend. Nor had the U.S. been theirs.

The United States had provided their military with billions in aid so that the U.S. would be allowed to make air strikes on al-Qaeda positions in the rugged mountains on the border with Afghanistan. All the while the ISI gave rock-solid assurances that Pakistan's nuclear weapons were perfectly safe under the protection of the Strategic Plans Division—a separate security service whose sole purpose was guarding the nation's nuclear arsenal.

But he argued that the same high-ranking officers in the ISI who had promised nuclear security had also promised that they had no idea of Osama bin Laden's whereabouts, even though the man's compound was less than one mile from Pakistan's main military academy.

The military had not officially reacted to the raid on bin Laden's compound, prompting a lot of text messages to the effect that: if you honk your horn, do so lightly, because the Pakistani army is asleep. The ISI, however—even though it was military intelligence— had worked an under-the-table agreement with a German assassins-for-hire group to kill all the SEAL Team Six operators who'd participated in the raid. And it had very nearly succeeded.

Into this mix had come the Messiah.

THIRTY-FIVE

Pete took care to make as little noise as possible as she got dressed in a pair of jeans, loose untucked blue button-up shirt and boat shoes. She went to the window and looked down at the backyard that bordered on some woods.

The night sky was clear, the moon full, and so far as she could tell nothing moved below. She'd half expected Marty to send some minders from the Campus to watch over her, but last night Otto had assured her that no one had put her on any sort of a leash. He had promised Marty that she wouldn't do anything dumb.

"Define 'dumb,'" she'd asked, but Otto had just laughed.

The last word she'd been given was that Haaris was holed up at the Connaught in London and Mac had arrived in Pakistan and had checked in at the Marriott. Which put Haaris—if he was the Messiah—at Mac's six o'clock. And that was totally unacceptable.

Walking was difficult for her. Her thighs were deeply bruised and just pulling on her jeans had been painful. In addition she had headaches that came and went; sometimes they were so intense that she had to close her eyes and sit down, lest she fall.

At the moment her head was clear, Mac's image bright in her mind. Even with his disguise she'd recognized him immediately at the hospital. It was his eyes; everything that was inside him was there to read like an open book. A window into his soul, some poet had written. Her soul.

She turned to get her overnight bag and purse.

Louise, in one of Otto's floppy KGB T-shirts, her legs bare, one of her quirky smiles on her long, narrow face, stood at the open door.

"I didn't mean to wake you."

"I've been reading," Louise said.

"Otto asked you to keep an eye on me?"

"He talked to Mac and so far everything is going okay, and last we've heard Haaris is still in London, but you know that."

"So I'm busted, now what?" Pete asked. "You know I can't just sit on my hands here."

"Otto figured you'd want to go to London first, to make sure it's really Haaris and not some imposter. Boyle has been ordered to personally stay out of it. If it is Haaris, Tommy might get himself killed. Or at the very least he would change the dynamic and force Haaris to do something unexpected."

"What's expected?"

"We think Haaris is either already in Pakistan or on his way. It's something Mac needs to know."

"I think so too," Pete said.

Louise smiled again. "He's really going to be pissed off when you show up in Islamabad."

"He'll get over it."

"Driven men are not easy to love. I could write a book on the subject. But they're worth every pound of trouble. In Mac's case it has to be doubly hard because of what he's already lost. And now he's frightened out of his head about losing you."

Pete was at a loss for words.

"He's in love with you, that's obvious to the most casual observer, so he wants to keep you in a cotton-batten lined box, tucked out of harm's way."

"He's wrong about keeping me locked up."

"Of course he is," Louise said. "But good luck trying to argue with him. Just keep your ass down and your eyes peeled. Come downstairs, Otto sent something over for you and I'll put on the coffee."

It was three in the morning. "I want to get to Dulles as early as possible."

"No rush, your flight doesn't leave till nine-thirty. Otto's booked you a business-class seat on Lufthansa. You'll get to Heathrow around eleven this evening."

Pete wasn't really surprised, but something must have shown on her face, because Louise laughed.

"You think being in love with a field operator is tough, you oughta try being in love with a genius. Sometimes it's downright scary."

Pete brought her overnight bag and purse down to the front hall. Louise handed her a small leather bag with a diplomatic seal.

"Your Glock, a couple of magazines of ammunition and a silencer. The seal will get you through Customs in London." She handed Pete a manila envelope. "Your tickets, confirmation number at the Connaught for three days, a new passport and other papers, plus air marshal creds, which you'll need to carry your weapon aboard for the flight to Islamabad. What happens once you get there could be another story, but you'll just have to take it a step at a time. In the meantime I suggest you take a look at everything—your work name will be Doris Day, and your home address, Hollywood."

Pete had to laugh. It was an old tradecraft trick; give them something so glaring that it would direct their attention elsewhere. A NOC, non-official cover agent, would never travel into badland with such an outrageous ID—therefore the ID had to be legitimate.

In the kitchen, Louise put on the coffee, and Pete sat at the counter.

"You haven't asked what I'll do if the guy is an imposter," Pete said.

"It'd mean that Dave is almost certainly the Messiah. You'd have to prevent the stand-in from warning him." Louise turned around. "You were an interrogator before you were a field officer. Do you think that you can do whatever is needed if the situation arises?"

Pete had thought about just that possibility. Mac had once explained to her that the thought of killing someone, anyone, was opposite of everything he was and everything he stood for. But the people he had eliminated were bad, many of them beyond any sort of redemption or even incarceration. If he hadn't pulled the trigger, other very bad things would surely have happened.

"I have to look at it like a soldier on the battlefield," he'd said. "For every life I take I have to figure that I've saved ten, maybe fifty, maybe even one hundred or more innocent lives."

"Haven't you been afraid of making a mistake?" Pete asked. At that time she'd been in the process of falling in love with him, and she wanted to know everything. Some of her questions had been reckless. But he'd taken them in his stride.

"All the time," he'd answered.

Admitting something like that had to have been hard for him, but he'd explained another time that in the business, partners had to be completely honest with each other. No secrets whatsoever. By then she had been head-over-heels and the only word of his that had really registered was *partners*.

"I'll see when the time comes," she answered Louise. "But first I'll have a couple of questions for him."

"Like I said, keep your ass down."

At first light Louise drove Pete out to Dulles, weekday traffic already building on the Beltway. On the way she phoned Otto, who had spent the night in his office.

"We're on the way to the airport. Have you had any word from Mac?"

"He's at a news conference with Powers and Rajput," Otto said. "Are you on speakerphone?"

"I can hear you," Pete said. "How did he sound?"

"Fine, but he doesn't know that you're on your way to London."

"Anything new from Boyle's people?"

"They're wary of the guy, so they haven't been crowding him."

"Someone should have gotten close enough for a positive ID. Maybe a telephoto lens?"

"Boyle says Haaris's tradecraft is too good for something like that. And anyway, they're one hundred percent sure that it's him."

"Christ," Pete said.

"It's the reason for you going to have a look for yourself. Mac needs to know what's coming his way—what might already be gaining on him. But watch yourself, Pete. The ISI is playing for very big chips."

THIRTY-SIX

McGarvey had to show his passport before he was given his press credentials for the news conference. When he got to the main briefing room an aide to President Rajput had just come to the podium. The hall was filled to capacity with more than one hundred journalists seated and perhaps a dozen or more standing at the back.

"Good afternoon, ladies and gentlemen," the aide said. His English was as crisp as his Western-cut suit.

An attractive woman with short, unkempt blond hair standing next to McGarvey wore an ABC pass on a lanyard around her neck. She glanced at Mac's pass, and her eyes narrowed. "Dr. Parks," she said in a low voice. "I'm a bit surprised to see you here. I would have thought they'd turn you away at the door."

"Freedom of the press."

The woman chuckled. "I read a few of your overnight blog posts about the situation here. Pakistan's new prime minister is no friend of the U.S. and neither is the Messiah—who probably is nothing more than a stooge of the ISI."

"Well?"

"All I can say is you've got balls showing up in Pakistan, let alone here." She looked at the PM's aide. "If they spot you this'll be interesting."

"Ladies and gentlemen, Prime Minister Hasan Rajput and the Honorable Donald Suthland Powers, ambassador from the United States."

The journalists applauded briefly as Rajput and Powers strode into the room and took their places at podiums placed only a few feet apart. Rajput spoke first.

"I'll make just a brief statement, after which Mr. Powers will have a few comments, at which time we'll open the floor for questions."

Like Powers, Rajput's smile and easy manner were obviously forced. The political situation in Pakistan had radically changed, but the relationship between the two countries had deteriorated. The U.S. still needed Pakistan's cooperation in going after the terrorists along the border with Afghanistan. And Pakistan needed the billions in economic aid from Washington to prop up its military.

"Extraordinary events in recent days have propelled Pakistan into a new era—one, we hope, of peace and prosperity. My deepest wish is for the guns to go silent. All of the guns and bombs which will make drone strikes a choice of the past." Rajput turned to Powers. "Which is why we invited you and your staff to return to your embassies—along with the ambassadors of all the other nations—so that we can get back to work. Welcome, Mr. Powers."

"It's good to be back, Mr. Prime Minister, and I wholeheartedly share your desire for peace—but not peace at all costs." Powers turned to the audience. "It's also my hope that the violence which has swept across Pakistan for the past several years may have finally come to an end. The events of the past few days, as Prime Minister Rajput said, have been nothing short of extraordinary. In Washington we looked with some alarm on the happenings, wondering if Pakistan would dissolve into chaos—into the same sort of civil war that has gripped so many other countries recently. But it has not happened. Though the circumstances were nothing short of extraordinary, the results are even more stunning." Powers turned again to Rajput. "President Miller sends her warmest regards, and her commitment to aid Pakistan on its road back to a lasting peace."

Rajput and Powers shook hands and held the pose for photographers to catch the shot.

"And now we will take a few questions," Rajput said. He pointed to a journalist in the front row, but McGarvey raised his hand.

"Mr. Prime Minister, can you tell us the whereabouts of the Messiah? I would have thought that he'd be here today."

"I'm sorry, sir. You are?"

"Dr. Travis Parks, PIP. I'd like to ask him a few questions. Perhaps even a one-on-one interview."

"I'm sorry, Dr. Parks, but the Messiah's exact

whereabouts are unknown to me, except that he is somewhere in Pakistan walking amongst his people, as he said he would do."

"With no security?" McGarvey pressed. "Aren't you afraid that someone might assassinate him?"

"No. It was the people who named him, and it is the people who will protect him from interlopers who wish to harm us, as has happened so many times in the past."

"Is it your government's intention to follow the Messiah's call for an alliance with the Taliban?"

"Perhaps you would allow someone else to ask a question," Rajput said. He pointed again at someone seated in the front row.

"Thomas Allen, Reuters," the journalist said. "But I would like to hear your answer to Dr. Parks's question."

If Rajput was flustered, he didn't show it, but Powers was fuming.

"Yes, we are exploring commonalities that we might be able to exploit to prevent any future violence," Rajput said. "I hope that answers your question."

"Why aren't representatives from the Tehreek-e Taliban Pakistan here today?" McGarvey pressed. "Or from the Lashkar-e-Taiba or the Harkat-ul-Mujahideen? All of them terrorists organizations whose stated purpose was to bring down the government."

"That will be all the questions for today," Rajput said.

"The U.S. has helped Pakistan hunt these people down, will that now change, Mr. Powers?" McGarvey asked. "Has the White House issued a new policy that you have come here to present to the prime minister, and perhaps at some point the Messiah? Are you willing to sit down with the Taliban leaders and open a dialogue?"

For a moment Powers was at a loss for words, handicapped because he had been led to believe that McGarvey—as Travis Parks—was a CIA analyst who'd tagged along only to observe.

"My readers would like to know, because it would be a tidal wave change that could have a serious impact on our relationship with India."

"I'm the ambassador to Pakistan, Dr. Parks, not India."

"I understand, sir, I'm merely asking if that consideration was in your brief before you left Washington?"

"We have much work to do now, as you must suspect, but another news conference will be scheduled within the next twenty-four to forty-eight hours," Rajput said. "You will be notified."

He and Powers walked out, and the aide, clearly distressed, announced that briefing packages were available in the press room, along with secure Wi-Fi connections for those wishing to file their stories from the Aiwan.

"Jesus, you hit them pretty hard," the woman next to McGarvey said. She stuck out her hand. "Judith Anderson, ABC."

"Evidently not hard enough," McGarvey said, shaking her hand.

A mob of other journalists clamoring for attention surrounded them.

"I'm sorry, people, but I don't give interviews. You can read about it on my blog."

"Did you actually think that someone from the Taliban would be here today?" one of them asked.

"Why not? This Messiah said they were partners, and except for the nuclear explosion outside of Quetta,

Pakistan appears to have gone back to business as usual."

"I'd say that what's happening on the ground, at least here in Islamabad and Rawalpindi, is anything but business as usual," someone else said.

"What do you know about the explosion?" another journalist asked.

"What, you want me to share sources?" McGarvey said, laughing. He turned away and walked out of the room. Before he reached the broad marble stairs, Judith Anderson caught up with him.

"Care to share a late lunch?" she asked.

"I don't think that it would be such a hot idea to stick close to me. At least not right now."

Her eyes widened a little. "You think the ISI might send someone to whack you?"

"It's happened out here before."

She thought about it for a moment. "I'll take my chances," she said.

THIRTY-SEVEN

Judith Anderson followed McGarvey outside, where she hailed a cab. "I'm bunking at the Serena, and lunch and drinks are on me," she said.

Most of the other journalists had stayed behind to pick up their briefing packages and some of them to file their stories. It didn't matter much that the ISI was monitoring the Wi-Fi connections in the Aiwan. They did it all over the country. No place was secure.

"What do you want with me, Miss Anderson?" McGarvey asked her.

"My friends call me Judy. But you've become the story now, because you challenged the ambassador."

"He'll get over it."

"But you came down even harder on Rajput and he won't get over it. Aren't you afraid that he'll send someone after you? Or at the very least order you out of the country?"

"If that happens it means I wasn't very far off the mark."

"No one thought that you were, but everyone else had the good sense not to push it. More than one journalist has been killed in Pakistan."

A taxi pulled up and Judy opened the door. "Just lunch and a beer, and I promise all I want is a back-grounder. Besides, you'll stick out if you don't mingle."

Otto had warned that journalists, unlike CIA operatives, ran in packs. "I'll hold you to it," McGarvey told the ABC correspondent and got into the cab with her.

"Good," she said.

The Serena, only one of three hotels in Islamabad that served alcohol, was just off Constitution Avenue, and the ride was short. The bar was furnished with low cocktail tables and large easy chairs. A handful of other Westerners were finishing their late lunches and cocktails.

"A civilized oasis in the middle of insanity," Judith said.

A waiter came with menus and McGarvey ordered a Heineken. She ordered a Pinot Grigio.

"This isn't your first time in Pakistan, is it," the woman said as a statement of fact, not a question.

"I've been here before."

"Funny, we haven't run into each other. You're provocative, and I tend to gravitate toward the type."

"It's a big place."

"Journalists usually stick together. Same news conferences, same stories, same hotels, especially the same watering holes. I just got back from Quetta, which was a wasted trip, but I didn't see you there."

"They had a nuclear event, and they sure as hell weren't going to share it with a bunch of Western news people. The real story is here."

"The Messiah tops a nuclear explosion?"

"In my world, yes," McGarvey said. He'd come with her in part because of Otto's advice, but also in a large measure to find out what she knew. Whatever it was would be something everyone else in the media knew or suspected. But she hadn't brought up the attacks on Pakistan's nuclear arsenal. Incredible as it seemed to him, the raids were still a secret known presumably only by the government and the ISI in Islamabad, the White House and the CIA in Washington, plus the Seal Team Six operators and NEST team.

"Do you know what I think, Travis?"

"No, but you're going to tell me."

"Until yesterday I never heard of you. But I should have. Your blog posts are nothing short of brilliant. Right on the mark. And history says that you've been around for a couple of years now. Which either means you've created something out of whole cloth or I'm a lousy journalist. But I'm damned good. So what gives, Parks, if that's your real name?"

"Why are you here?"

"You mean here in this restaurant with you or here in Pakistan? Because the answers to both questions is you. You're not a journalist, your blog is good but it's a scam, so who are you? My guess would be CIA."

"How many others at the news conference do you suppose share your suspicions?"

"Just about all of them," she said. "If we're right you're a marked man. Why else do you think they didn't follow you outside?"

"But you did," McGarvey said. "And I came with

you to find out what you thought you knew. Trust me on this one, Miss Anderson, stay as far away from me as you possibly can. I'm going to lean on some important people who aren't going to like it very much. They'll push back."

"You're here to find the Messiah."

"Yes."

"But there's more. You want to find out who he is, because it's a safe bet that he didn't show up as some sort of an Islamic savior. He's not here to save Pakistan. He has another agenda, and you want to know what it is."

"Something like that."

"Fine, it's the same thing I want. Same as just about every reporter over here wants to know."

The waiter came with their drinks.

"We'll order later," Judith told him, her eyes never leaving McGarvey's. She sat forward. "My people in New York tell me that this guy's voice was probably altered by some electronic device. They're trying to decrypt it now. But you already know this."

"Stay away from me," McGarvey said, getting to his feet. He'd learned what he needed to know, and it wasn't going to make his job any easier. Once the Messiah came out into the open, if he ever did, he would be surrounded not only by palace guards but by the same horde of news people as were at the Aiwan.

"Look, we can collaborate. In fact I'd rather share my sources with someone from the CIA than I would with another reporter."

"Someone will either try to kill me or have me arrested."

"And it's the first option that you want. I can help."

"No," McGarvey said. "And if you try to follow me, I'll have you deported."

"It's not so easy to push around a reporter."

McGarvey walked out of the hotel and headed down one of the side streets that eventually wound up back on Constitution Avenue in the direction of the Aiwan. The moment he had emerged, he knew that he'd picked up a tail. Two men in a yellow Fiat 500, not making much effort to hide the fact that they were following him.

Two blocks away, through heavy traffic, he sprinted across the street and entered a narrow alley, the second stories hanging over the pavement, the shops here mostly silversmiths and rug merchants, plus a CVS pharmacy, and next door an outdoor barbershop.

He waited until the Fiat turned the corner before he entered a tobacco shop so narrow that if he stretched out his arms he'd touch both walls, and walked straight back and out the rear door, which opened onto an interior courtyard filthy with garbage and the carcass of a dog that had been dead for at least a month.

The only way in or out was through the tobacconist's shop or above through the second-story windows of what were apparently apartments. Laundry hung drying from lines that stretched from building to building. No one was in sight.

McGarvey stepped to the side as two men, both of them wearing jeans and khaki shirts, came out of the tobacco shop.

They stopped short, McGarvey leaning against the wall behind them.

"Looking for me, gentlemen?" he asked.

Both of them turned at the same time, and the taller of the two pulled a pistol from a belt holster under his shirt.

McGarvey was on him in an instant, grabbing the big Sig-Sauer, a long suppressor tube on the barrel, out of his hand, and smashing the butt of the gun into the bridge of his nose, knocking him backward.

The second man was just reaching for his pistol when McGarvey jammed the muzzle of the silencer into his forehead.

"Who sent you?"

The man had his pistol out and he was raising it, when McGarvey fired one shot. Before the man crumpled to the dirt, the first officer had recovered enough to press his attack, a crazy, failure-is-not-an-option look in his eyes.

"Who are you?" McGarvey demanded, but the guy kept coming, and McGarvey fired another shot, catching him in the bridge of his bloody nose, and he went down hard.

"Shit," a woman said from just inside the tobacco shop.

McGarvey spun around, bringing the pistol to bear.

Judith Anderson stepped back half a pace, her empty right hand coming up.

THIRTY-EIGHT

McGarvey lowered the pistol. "I told you to stay away from me."

"Saying something like that to a journalist hot on a story is like throwing petrol on an open fire," Judith said. She stood flatfooted, her eyes wide, her mouth half open. She looked vulnerable.

In the not-too-far distance they heard sirens. She looked over her shoulder. "Someone must have reported this. We have to get out of here."

McGarvey stuck the pistol in his belt under his

jacket. He turned one of the bodies over and came up with a wallet in the man's back pocket. The ISI card, with its wreath and crescent moon emblem, and the service's motto, "Faith, Unity Discipline," identified the officer as Kaleem Babar. The other ISI officer was Raza Davi.

"ISI?" Judith asked.

"Yes," McGarvey said.

The sirens were a lot closer. "The stupid bastards left their keys in the Fiat. And unless you know the city better than I do, I'll drive. But right now, the last place you want to be is in an interrogation cell in Rawalpindi."

McGarvey followed her through the tobacconist's shop to the narrow street where the yellow Fiat was parked, its engine idling. No one was in the immediate vicinity, though traffic one block away seemed to be flowing normally.

Within a minute Judith had driven to the corner and tucked behind a three-wheeled truck and other traffic heading in the opposite direction of the Aiwan. The day was bright and hot, the air polluted with a combination of dust, charcoal smoke and something else with a pungent smell.

The ISI had always been in firm control of the government here, and if something, anything happened that displeased the military intelligence service it reacted. In McGarvey's estimation a few pointed remarks from an American journalist rated an expulsion order. But the two ISI officers who had followed him into the dead-end corridor had been ordered to kill him, not arrest him. And the main problem at the moment was staying alive until the Messiah showed up and then somehow getting close enough to put a bullet in his brain.

Ambassador Powers was at the U.S. embassy, and

Prime Minister Rajput was at his post. Both of them primary movers and shakers. If anyone knew when the Messiah would show, and where, they would.

"You're not just another blogger," Judith said. She was driving them out of the diplomatic sector, the traffic even heavier here. Mopeds competed with cars and with trucks and buses of all sizes, no one obeying traffic laws or the white-gloved cops standing at busier intersections.

Again McGarvey got the strong impression that the country—or at least the capital—was at peace with itself. The riots of just a few days ago were completely forgotten, and if anyone was making any noise about the nuclear event in the northwest, it was below the background level of business as usual.

"Those guys were trained intelligence officers. Taking you out should have been easy as pie. But you disarmed one of them and killed them both without a moment's hesitation. Says to me my first impression was right."

"Where are you taking me?" McGarvey finally asked.

"A reporter friend of mine has an apartment here in the city. The AP's bureau chief. He's still up in Quetta trying to interview someone at the military base where we think the nuke must have come from. There've been no reports of any recent Taliban activity up there, so it could mean the government moved one of the weapons for some reason. It's Randy's theory that the nuclear depot has been infiltrated, but by whom is anyone's guess."

A police car, its lights flashing, its siren blaring, came up behind them and bulled its way through traffic, then disappeared through a red light around the corner onto the Avenue G8.

"It'd be a good idea to ditch this car as soon as possible," McGarvey said.

"I think you're right," Judith agreed. "Randy's apartment is just a few blocks from here."

She turned down another avenue in what was known as the G7-3 section of the city, and a few blocks later came to the Al Habib Market, mostly empty of shoppers at this hour, the morning and noon crowds gone, and the afternoon trade not yet picking up.

Finally stopping at the rear of the market, Judith took a long scarf out of her purse and covered her hair, wrapping the extra length once around her neck and over her left shoulder.

"You might want to wipe the gun down and leave it behind. If you're caught with it you'll definitely be tied to the killings."

"They were sent to take me out, so that's not an issue," McGarvey said.

The street back here was quiet, and at the moment no one seemed to have noticed them. McGarvey walked with Judith in the opposite direction of the market, turning back toward the broad Luqman Hakeem Road two blocks to an eight-story apartment building.

"No doorman here, which is one of the reasons Randy picked the place."

The building was modern and seemed well maintained. The AP bureau chief's small, well-furnished apartment was on the fifth floor facing a long strip of businesses: a pizza place, a FedEx office, banks and offices for several airlines, including United of Holland and Saudi Air. Beyond that was a large green space in the middle of which was a building in the general shape of an X that housed offices of the United Nations.

Judith tossed her scarf aside and laid her purse on the table near the windows. "Randy always keeps his fridge well stocked. How about another beer?"

"Sounds good."

She went in the kitchen and McGarvey went through the woman's purse, coming up with an old Russian-made 5.45-millimeter PSM pistol. He removed the eight-round magazine, unloaded it into the bottom of her purse and ejected the round out of the firing chamber.

He'd just closed the purse and stepped away from it as she came out of the kitchenette with the beers.

"Do you need a glass?" she asked.

"No, and I don't need this now," McGarvey said, taking the ISI officer's pistol out of his belt and placing it on a shelf of one of the bookcases flanking a small flat-screen television.

She handed him a beer and perched on the end of the couch. "CIA?" she asked.

"You thought so at the news conference. What gave it away?"

"Your blog, partially. Some of the others claimed they'd been reading you from the beginning, but that's a line of bullshit. I should know about you but I don't. And unless I miss my guess you're here to assassinate the Messiah."

McGarvey just shrugged, sure now who she was and where she was going.

"That's a pretty tall order, but beyond that I want to know why," Judith said.

"You want to know or your viewers want to know?"

"Two speeches and he's brought calm to this place. Something neither the government nor the ISI has been able to do. So what's Washington worried about, the alliance with the Taliban? Because if that's what's put the bug up Miller's ass then she and her advisers ought to rethink the thing. If the Taliban is willing to lay down their arms and work in a real partnership with General Rajput to bring a lasting peace, isn't that exactly what Washington wants?"

"If that's what this Messiah wants we have no objections."

Judith smiled in triumph. "I knew you were CIA. But you don't think that's what he and the new PM want."

"I'd like a chance to ask him."

"Before you assassinate him."

McGarvey took out his encrypted sat phone and called Otto, who answered immediately. "Judith Anderson. ABC correspondent."

"Are you in a safe place?"

"For the moment."

Judith put her beer down and went over to her purse. She pulled out the pistol and pointed it at McGarvey. "You're under arrest, Dr. Parks, or whoever you really are."

"Never mind," McGarvey told Otto. "She's holding a gun on me, she's almost certainly ISI and I'm under arrest. But if she was sharp enough she'd have realized by now that the gun is too light. No bullets."

Judith racked the slide back.

"What do you want to do?" Otto asked.

Judith went for the gun on the bookcase, but McGarvey grabbed her arm, pulled her away and got the pistol himself. "Sit down, please, Miss Anderson, or whoever you really are."

She did as she was told, but she only sat on the arm of the couch as before.

McGarvey gave Otto the address. "Get someone down here to pick her up and take her across the border to Jalalabad. I want her to disappear for the time being, but I don't want to shoot her if possible."

"That'll take a few hours, *kemo sabe.*"

"Fine. In the meantime she and I are going to get better acquainted. I'm sure she has lots of stuff she's willing to share. After all, we're allies."

"I'm on it."

THIRTY-NINE

Pete's flight landed a half hour early at Heathrow and it was only a few minutes before eleven at night when the cabby dropped her off in front of the elegant Connaught hotel in Mayfair. She hadn't been able to get much sleep, worrying about Kirk in Islamabad, even though Otto had assured her two hours earlier that he was still in one piece.

"Where is he right now?" she'd asked.

"In an apartment with a beautiful woman the ISI sent to find out who he is and arrest him. But it's okay, she'll be on her way to Jalalabad within the next hour or so."

Pete almost laughed, except for the fact that the ISI was already on to him. "He must have made some waves."

"The understatement of the year. He showed up at a news conference for Rajput and Powers at the Aiwan and asked some pretty pointed questions about the Messiah and the Taliban. He made international headlines."

"Jesus."

"It's exactly what he wanted to do, call attention to himself right off the bat. He thinks it'll draw the Messiah out in the open."

"So how did he end up in some apartment with the woman?" Pete asked, her voice a little bit edgier than she wanted it to be.

"That's the tough part," Otto said, and he told her what McGarvey had told him.

"Two dead agents and one who'll turn out missing, all in his first afternoon there. The ISI is going to shoot him on sight."

"Which means you're going to have to press on to see if the guy at the Connaught is actually Haaris."

"Is he in the hotel for the night?"

"Last I heard he came back a half hour ago, had a late dinner and went up to his suite. You'll have to somehow dig him out of there tonight."

"I'll let you know as soon as I'm checked in, and then I want you to let Tommy Boyle in on what we're doing. If the guy turns out not to be Dave, which I'm betting will be the case, I'll need some muscle to put him on ice somewhere without making a fuss."

"If it is Haaris, Mac might want Tommy to ask him for help."

"You don't think it's him."

"No. And when you find out, Boyle's not going to like it very much."

"I'll tell him what's going on, but Marty will have to back me up."

"Page will handle it personally."

"One more thing, Otto: has anyone on Campus figured out that Mac is in Pakistan in disguise? You said he made the news; will anyone in our shop recognize him?"

"I don't think so."

"I did," Pete said.

"But you're special," Otto said. "Watch yourself with this guy."

"Will do."

Pete secured her reservations for three nights with a platinum AMEX that Otto had got for her under the name Doris Day, to match her passport. She only had the one bag but a bellman in a black apron carried it up to her elegantly furnished third-floor room that looked out toward Hyde Park, just a few blocks away. She tipped him, and when he was gone she called Otto again.

"I'm in," she told him.

"Haaris's minders think that he might be in the bar."

"Are they here in the hotel?"

"No, across the street in a van, but they have a clear view of the lobby."

"I'm on my way down."

"What have you got in mind?"

"If it's Haaris he knows who I am and we'll have our little chat. If not, I'll strike up a conversation and seduce the bastard. Let's just hope he isn't gay."

"I'll call Tommy now and give Page the heads-up."

Pete had brought along a revealing scoop-neck, thigh-high black Spandex dress, silver hoop earrings and four-inch spikes, for just this sort of an encounter. It gave her no place to hide her pistol, even though it was a subcompact conceal-and-carry Glock 24, but if she got into a shooting situation her part in Mac's op would be over before it began.

She touched up her makeup, fluffed up her short hair and took the elevator downstairs. crossing the lobby to the corridor to the Coburg bar. At this late hour the room was mostly empty, a few of the low tables filled with well-dressed men and women. When she came in, a number of the patrons looked up. She'd gotten their attention.

A man with light hair and small shoulders sat alone at one of the tables, his back to her. He did not turn around to look as she crossed the room to him, but if he wasn't Dave Haaris he was a hell of a good stand-in.

"David?" she asked.

He looked up. "Do I know you?"

It wasn't Dave, but his facial features and voice were nearly perfect matches. Pete sat down across from him. "No, but David does. The question is, what the hell are you doing impersonating him, and when did he leave for Pakistan?"

"I don't know what you're talking about, Miss—"

"I think you do," Pete said. A waiter came over and she ordered a Pinot Grigio.

The man laid a fifty-pound note on the table and got up.

"The problem for you is that you're in a room that Dave paid for, and so far as the hotel staff is concerned, you are him. Makes you guilty of fraud at the very least. And at the most it puts your life in jeopardy. Please sit down."

"Bugger off," the imposter said.

Pete's phone went off and she took it from her purse. It was Tommy Boyle.

"Are you with him?"

"Yes, and he's not Dave. You might want to have the two gentlemen from the van parked outside come in."

"Ten seconds."

"Sit down," Pete said.

The imposter deflated all at once. "It was a simple job of work. Nothing more."

"Who hired you?"

"Mr. Haaris. A gentleman."

"To do what and for how long?"

"Act as if I were him. Move around, see the sights. For two more days and then I was to leave."

"Did he warn you that someone like me might show up?"

"No."

Two men in dark blue blazers walked in and came over. "Miss Day?" the larger of the two asked. "Mr. Boyle sent us. Is there a problem?"

"No, except that this guy isn't Dave Haaris."

"My name is Ronald Pembroke, I'm a stage actor," the imposter said. "So far as I know I've broken no British laws."

"Yes, sir," the one CIA agent said. "We'd like to have a little chat with you."

"You have no authority here, you're Americans."

"If you'd like I can have someone from New Scotland Yard handle it," Pete said. "I'm sure that they'll figure out something to charge you with."

"We just want to ask you a few questions, sir, and then you'll be free to go," the CIA officer interjected.

The other officer smiled. "Of course, if you've actually threatened this lady, who is a close personal friend of mine, I'll be forced to break one of your bones. Won't be pleasant."

"Shit."

"Yes, sir."

The imposter gave Pete a bleak look but then got up. "You're CIA, right?" he asked.

The shorter of the two officers took his elbow. "Just outside, sir. It'll only take a few minutes and then you can get your things and check out. We'll even drive you home, if you'd like."

They left as the waiter brought Pete her drink.

Boyle was still on the line.

"They're off," Pete told him.

"I'll meet you at the embassy and you can tell me what the hell is going on."

"Sorry, Mr. Boyle, I'm still in the middle of something, but I'm sure that Mr. Page will fill you in when he feels that the time is right. In the meantime, whatever you do, don't let this guy near a phone or a computer."

FORTY

The private jet that had been arranged for Haaris touched down at the old airport outside Rawalpindi around two in the morning. The French crew had been solicitous, but after they had taxied to an empty hangar across from what had been the main terminal, and the engines spooled down, he dismissed them for the rest of the day.

"I may have need of you late this evening or first thing in the morning," he told the pilot, who was an older man with gray hair and a large mustache.

"We'll need to find accommodations," the pilot said.

Haaris smiled at him and the copilot, and the pretty flight attendant who stood just behind him in the tiny galley. "Actually, a car is waiting to take you to the Serena. A pair of suites has been booked for you. When I have need of the aircraft I'll leave word."

"Yes, sir," the pilot said.

In ten minutes they secured the aircraft for the night, got their bags and left. A pair of Toyota SUVs with deeply tinted windows waited just inside the hangar. They got into one of them and left.

Two men in dark blue blazers got out of the second SUV and stood at attention near the open rear door on the passenger side. One of them held an H & K submachine gun.

Haaris had worn his American civilian clothes over on the flight. He changed into the long loose shirt, baggy pantaloons and headgear he'd worn at his first appearance on the balcony of the Aiwan. He strapped the voice apparatus onto his neck, adjusted his scarf to conceal it and retrieved his bag containing some personal items and a change of clothes, plus a nine-millimeter Steyr GB Austrian-made pistol with a pair of eighteen-round box magazines. The reliable semiauto had always been a favorite of his, in large measure because it was accurate and could be disassembled for cleaning in under six seconds.

He checked the weapon's load then stuffed it in his belt beneath his shirt and went to the open door of the plane.

If the two men by the black Toyota had suspected who their passenger was to be they didn't make a big deal of it. The man with the weapon involuntarily stepped back half a pace, while the driver's mouth dropped open, but only for a moment.

Haaris went down the boarding stairs, and he held up a hand. "There will be no conversations," he told them in Pashtun. "You will not address me by name or title, nor will you speak of my presence with anyone. You are simply to take me to the Aiwan, stopping for no one, for no reason."

The driver nodded and stepped away from the open rear door.

"I'm sorry, sir, but I must ask if you expect trouble this morning?" the man with the H & K asked. He was young, possibly in his early twenties, but he had the thousand-yard stare of someone who'd taken incoming fire somewhere.

"No," Haaris said.

"There have been people on Constitution Avenue

off and on ever since you . . ." He hesitated. "For the past several days."

"Avoid them," Haaris said, and he got into the car.

Within minutes they drove away from the airport and took the old main highway up to Islamabad. The morning was cool, as were many mornings in this part of the country. It was a contrast to muggy Washington. Haaris neither liked nor disliked Pakistan and its people, nor had he ever thought that he would be returning until eight years earlier when he first began to conceive a plan not only for revenge against too many people for him to count—except that he knew all of their names and positions—but for his immortality.

He did not believe in Paradise with its willing virgins and endless milk and honey, but as a boy in school in England he had developed the notion of an existence after life. The history professors taught him that. Almost no one remembered most of the players in the Trojan War, but everyone knew the name Achilles. Everyone knew the names Caesar and Marc Antony, but especially that of Caesar. German generals were famous, but Hitler's name rose to the top of every schoolboy's list of the most recognizable. George W. Bush was known, but not as well as Osama bin Laden. And in the end no one would ever forget the name Messiah.

The Presidential Palace was in the Red Section of the city, the area where most of the government buildings and foreign embassies were located. A small crowd of several hundred people were gathered in front of the imposing building, and as before they burned trash in barrels. Armed guards on the street just outside the fence looked out at the people but did nothing to send them away. The foreign press had dubbed them "the Messiah's people." It was they who had named him and it was they who continued to keep watch for his return.

They drove around to the rear entrance that led into the president's colony, where his staff and families were housed. Though the gate was guarded by two armed soldiers—who admitted them without question—the colony itself seemed to be deserted. After President Barazani's assassination his staff had fled for their lives.

According to Rajput the Aiwan itself had been deserted as well. Not even a maintenance staff had remained. It was as if the seat of power had been deserted so that the prime minister could govern Pakistan without interference.

Ghulam Kahn was the first president to live there, in 1988, and Barazani was the last. But Pervez Musharraf had lived elsewhere during his presidency. The real seat of Pakistan's power was gone from this place. The PM was the chief administrator of the country, but the president had been the leader.

Until now.

They pulled up at one of the service entrances. The armed guard riding shotgun jumped out and opened the rear door.

As Haaris got out the guard saluted. "Do you wish us to stay here, sir?"

"No, you are finished for the morning. Thank you. And remember, do not discuss this with anyone. My reasons will become evident soon enough."

Haaris waited just inside what had been a security vestibule, with a heavy steel door leading into the main floor of the building. Under normal circumstances the door would be opened electronically from the inside, but only after the visitor was positively identified and searched for weapons or explosives. This morning it stood wide open to a marble-floored corridor that led straight to the ornate entry hall where visiting heads of state or other VIPs arrived.

He could see the SUV through one of the small bullet-proof windows but could not see the driver or the armed guard because of the deep tinting of the car's windows. After a moment or two, however, the Toyota moved off and disappeared around the corner.

Haaris remained for a full three minutes longer to make sure that guards did not return.

He walked down the long corridor to the ceremonial staircase and went up to the president's residence on the third floor.

The building was totally deserted, but the electricity hadn't been shut off, the security cameras were still operating and the battery-powered emergency lighting had not activated.

Enough light came from outside that he could make his way to a window that looked down on the street to the people gathered there. They were actually very stupid. He had held Barazani's severed head for everyone to see—the severed head of the properly elected president—and one of Rajput's shills had shouted "Messiah" a couple of times and the sheep had taken up the chant.

He'd made a brief speech that was broadcast over television, and here they were camping out on Constitution Avenue. Waiting for him to show up, to give them meaning in their meaningless lives.

That fact of the matter was, none of them realized that all life was pretty much without purpose unless you were willing to make it so for yourself.

He didn't bother with lights as he got undressed, took a shower and went to bed. In a few hours the situation would change, because he would make it so. In a few hours he would lead the country in exactly the direction he'd planned for it to go.

When he slept it was without dreams. The sleep, he told himself when he awoke briefly just before dawn, of a man with a clear conscience and an even clearer purpose.

FORTY-ONE

Upstairs it took Pete less than ten minutes to change into jeans, a white blouse and dark blazer. When she was done she phoned Otto, who answered on the first ring as he usually did.

"Oh, wow, that went fast."

"The guy's a stage actor. He admitted that Haaris hired him to hang out. But the point is he told me that his contract would be up in two days. So whatever Haaris is trying to pull off, having an imposter here won't matter because it'll be too late for us to change anything."

"Did he give you any hint what that might be?"

"None, but Haaris wouldn't have told him something like that in any event," Pete said. She went to the window. Nothing looked out of place on the street. "Get word to Mac, he'll want the timetable. In the meantime I need to go to Islamabad as fast as possible and I don't think a commercial flight will get me there in time."

"You don't want to go there." Louise had come on the line. "Mac already has his hands full, he won't be happy to have you jump into the mix."

Pete wasn't surprised that Louise had joined in. "Otto's already filled me in, and it's exactly what I need to do. The ISI won't know about me, so I'll be the loose cannon watching his back."

"Ross Austin knows about Mac's situation. You're not going to be of any use out there."

"I'm going with or without your help," Pete said, the strident note again in her voice. She felt as if she were standing on the edge of a cliff overlooking the sea, huge waves crashing into the rocks below. If she fell she knew that she would be dashed to pieces, and yet Kirk was there. She could see his head in the crest of a wave. He was motioning for her to stay away from the edge, but at the same time she knew that she would have to try for him. Because of her love.

"I'll arrange something," Otto said. "But first you'll have to get past Boyle; he's already on his way to your hotel."

"I thought Walt talked to him."

"He did, but Boyle insisted that he needed the chance to meet with you. Haaris is a good friend of his, and he's not convinced that Dave could be the Messiah."

"I'm not going to try to convince him of anything."

"He knows that too; I spoke to him just two minutes ago. He knows that you want to get to Islamabad as quickly as possible, and he's willing to help. He has a Gulfstream at his disposal, and he's already given the order for the plane to be prepped and a crew to get out to Heathrow. The RAF at Northolt is arranging it. He wants you to try to convince Mac to back off before it's too late."

Too late for what? she wanted to ask, but didn't. "Does he know Mac's cover ID?"

"I'm sure that he's talked with Austin in Islamabad, and I can't see any reason why the COS would hold anything back."

"Damn," Pete said softly. "Mac shouldn't have told him."

"He had to do it," Otto said. "If everything goes south, and Mac is outed as CIA, Austin will need to cover his ass."

"That's why you shouldn't go over there," Louise said. "You'll just complicate things."

"Will Boyle try to contact Haaris, to warn him?"

"Page specifically ordered him not to," Otto said.

"Not much comfort," Pete replied. "I'll call when I get there, and you have to let me know where Mac is."

"I know why you're doing this thing," Louise said after a beat. "Can't say I object on those grounds, except that you'll be putting yourself in serious harm's way, and we all know exactly how Mac will react. But good luck."

"Thanks."

Tommy Boyle strode into the lobby just as Pete was finishing checking out. He was tall and very slender, his face all sharp angles, his hair thinning on top. He was dressed in a tweed sporting coat, iron-gray slacks and highly shined half boots of the sort that were popular in the sixties. He looked every bit the English gentleman.

He kissed her on the cheek as if they were old friends. "I have a car just outside."

"I talked to Otto."

"Your aircraft crew will be aboard by the time we get out to Heathrow. I thought I'd ride along so that we could have a little chat."

"About Dave Haaris?"

"More specifically about this fellow they're calling the Messiah."

"Not the Messiah of the Second Coming, but the 'just for the moment' Messiah," Pete said. "A very big difference."

The car was a light blue Jaguar XK sedan. Doormen were holding the rear doors open for Pete and Boyle to get in. Pete hung on to her overnight bag. Their driver headed away immediately, traffic still fairly heavy even at this hour.

"I'll need to call in your passport number," Boyle said. She took it out of her shoulder bag and gave it to him. He phoned someone and recited the name and number, and the fact that it was diplomatic.

When he was finished he handed it back without comment.

"Other than the fact that Dave is a friend of yours, what makes you so certain he couldn't be the Messiah?"

"What makes you so certain he is?"

Pete didn't answer.

"And what do you hope to accomplish by going out there? Whoever this guy is, you'd never get close to him."

"I'll work something out."

"My God, you're going to try to assassinate him," Boyle said. "Of all the goddamn harebrained ideas . . . Let me guess, it's McGarvey. And he's already there or on his way. You're just going over to confirm that the guy we picked up wasn't Dave."

"Why do you suppose that Dave Haaris hired someone to impersonate him?"

Boyle was troubled. "I don't know, but I'm going to ask him just that."

"Have you tried to contact him?"

"I left a message at his desk the moment I learned that the man we were ordered to watch wasn't him. All of this is bad business. The director is holding something back, I'm sure of it."

"What about Ross Austin, have you spoken with him?"

Boyle gave her an oddly pensive look. "No reason for me to have, is there?"

"I meant about you having arranged transportation for me."

"I was going to give him a call once you were off, in case I couldn't talk you out of whatever nonsense you were up to."

"Don't call him," Pete said. "Especially if he's another one of your friends."

"We've bumped into each other, but he and Haaris are fairly close," Boyle said. "Ross will have to be told about the incoming flight."

"Have Marty do it," Pete said. "I'm asking you for my safety's sake, and for Mac's, just stay out of it. In the meantime lean on Pembroke to see if he knows anything else—though I doubt he does."

"Whatever Dave was up to he would not have divulged anything."

"No, but the transition went smoothly enough so that your people didn't catch it. Maybe Pembroke heard or saw something."

"Like what?"

"A phone call. Perhaps Dave met someone in the lobby. Maybe a car came for him, maybe he took a cab and Pembroke remembered the time. Anything we could use."

"You were a good interrogator, from what I've been told. How about staying behind and questioning him yourself?"

"Don't try to look down my trail."

"Other than the flight, I'm washing my hands of the entire business."

Pete wished that she could believe him.

FORTY-TWO

McGarvey sat at the window watching for someone from Jalalabad to show up and take the woman off his hands. The sky to the east was beginning to lighten, and he was anxious to get on with it. Every hour that went by was to the ISI's advantage. They'd tried to kill him once—because of his questions at the reception, not because they suspected who he really was—and he was certain they would try again.

If the woman didn't report soon to her superiors, someone would come here looking for her.

He glanced at her. She was asleep on the narrow couch, but when his sat phone chirped she stiffened slightly. She was awake.

It was Otto. "The guy was an imposter."

"It means that Haaris is almost certainly here. He'll probably show himself sometime today."

"He'll have to, because according to the guy he hired as his stand-in, the job was going to last only two more days."

"What about the people who were supposed to pick up the woman? I can't sit around here much longer, especially not now, knowing Haaris has a timetable."

"They must have run into trouble; I'll check on it. But the air force is paying a lot better attention than they did before the bin Laden raid, and even more since the ISI's botched attack on the SEAL Team Six operators."

Judith opened her eyes and sat up, obviously measuring the distance to McGarvey.

"But you have another problem," Otto said. "Pete is heading your way, and there was nothing that anybody could say to talk her out of it."

"Is she already en route?"

"In the air. Boyle arranged an RAF Gulfstream for her."

"He knows that the guy they've been watching is an imposter?"

"Yes, and he was willing to help Pete because he wants the issue with Dave to be settled one way or the other. He's betting that Haaris is working on something but not as the Messiah."

"I'm going to ask him. In the meantime have Page call someone at the State Department to meet the plane and take her to the embassy. Put her in handcuffs, if it's the only way."

"Won't be easy. And Austin knows who you are. He's bound to come to the conclusion who she actually is and why she showed up in Islamabad."

McGarvey was afraid of something like this happening. Every woman he'd ever been involved with had been strong-willed, and sooner or later had lost her life because of it.

"Have Walt call one of his friends in London; maybe they can get their Home Office to convince someone from their embassy here to meet the plane and pick her up. It'd be more convincing that way since it's a RAF flight."

"She's carrying a U.S diplomatic passport."

"They'll have to work around it," McGarvey said. "Make Walt understand how important this is to me."

"I'll see what I can do," Otto promised. "But getting

around Pakistan's passport control will be a lot easier than getting around Pete."

"Tell them they can do anything they want, short of shooting her."

"Okay. In the meantime I'll see what's holding up our people from fetching your prisoner."

"I need her gone as soon as possible," McGarvey said and hung up.

"Who is Haaris?" Judith asked.

"You don't want to know."

"CIA like you and whoever the woman is who's coming apparently to help you? Maybe Haaris is a rogue CIA agent. Out of control. Someone you need to stop, for whatever dark reason."

In the early morning light her complexion and features were fair, her blond hair tousled from sleep she looked anything but Middle Eastern. "You don't look like an ISI operator."

She smiled. "What's a nice girl like me doing in a place like this?"

"You don't look Pakistani. More like someone from Ohio."

"Close, actually. Indiana. Michigan City. My dad, brothers and uncles worked in the steel mills and were union all the way. And Catholics. The workers and the priests versus the bosses. Made for interesting dinner table discussions."

"But not your cup of tea."

"No. The men were getting screwed in the mills, and their sons were getting raped by the priests."

"There were other places you could have gone to. Other churches," McGarvey said. "Why here where a girl who marries the wrong man can be stoned to death by her own father? Almost every day some sort of violence. Bombings, assassinations, coups—your own president had his head cut off."

"It's a long story, which I promise to tell you if you'll hand over your pistol."

"Then what?"

"You'll be debriefed and probably be declared persona non grata," Judith said. "We are allies, after all." She smiled faintly. "So, I'll take my chances. Who is Haaris and what is he doing in Pakistan?"

"The ISI tried to kill me."

"Because they thought that you were a troublemaker."

"Is that how your father and his friends treated troublemaking journalists in Michigan City?"

"We have a great deal of respect for the CIA."

Someone was on the stairs below. McGarvey glanced out the window. A newer red Mercedes E350 was parked in front.

At that moment Judith leaped up and was on him in two strides, shoving him aside and grabbing the pistol on the window ledge beside him, then stepping back out of the way.

She nodded toward the door. "If you warn them, I'll kill you."

McGarvey got up and took a bullet from his pocket. "You might need a few of these," he said.

She racked the slide, but the gun was empty.

"That's the second time you didn't notice the weight; makes me wonder what kind of training they gave you."

"You bastard," she screamed and she charged, swinging the butt of the pistol toward his face.

He easily grabbed the gun, twisted it out of her grip and shoved her away. "You'll be okay. We don't kill prisoners."

"The fuck you don't. How about renditions? How about Guantanamo? Waterboarding? Secret firing squads?"

McGarvey opened the door for two clean-shaven men in Western suits and ties. They could have been American businessmen.

"Who are you guys?" Mac asked.

"SEAL Team Six; we were told you needed an extraction," the shorter of the two said. His hair was above his ears and neatly combed, as was the other's.

"Good disguise."

"Makes us conspicuous, for all the wrong reasons," the operator said. "Where's the woman?"

McGarvey turned as Judith came full speed out of the kitchen, a butcher knife raised.

One of the operators pulled out a silenced Beretta nine-millimeter and fired one shot, catching her in the middle of the forehead. She fell back, dead.

"Gnarly," he said.

McGarvey truly hadn't wanted it to end this way. Katy had told him more than once that he had more respect for women then a lot of them deserved. But she loved him all the more for it.

"Take the body with you," he said.

"Will she be missed?"

"She was ISI."

Both SEALS fired several more shots into the woman's body.

FORTY-THREE

With the dawn Haaris got out of bed, dressed in his Messiah costume and donned the voice-altering device before he crossed the hall and went into the president's office. He wasn't hungry, which surprised him a little, because he hadn't eaten anything substantial since London, only a light snack on the flight over. But he was thirsty.

He found the small pantry hidden behind the rear wall. It was equipped with a wet bar and several top-shelf whiskeys, cognacs, gins and vodkas. A rack beneath the sink held a dozen or more red wines, and the cooler beside it was filled with whites.

A small fridge contained fruit juices, bottled tea and bottled water. He got a water and crossed to the windows. He stood to one side so it would be difficult for anyone to spot him but he'd have a decent sight line down Constitution Avenue. The crowd of a few hundred when he'd arrived had grown to a thousand or more people, many of them children. He had to wonder why, unless word had gotten out that the Messiah had possibly returned. With the rising sun some of them were eating flatbread for breakfast, while men sat smoking in the beds of pickup trucks. It did not seem like an angry mob to Haaris, rather a gathering of people patiently waiting for something to happen—or for someone to show up.

As a young student he'd learned from his teachers that the people of any nation deserved the government they had. If they were dissatisfied a revolution would occur. Sometimes the uprising took years, like in the case of the aftermath of Stalin and others in Russia, but unless it happened the people would be stuck with the likes of a Hitler, who had been replaced only by all-out war.

Haaris turned around as he raised the bottle of water to his lips but stopped short, not immediately recognizing the bearded man in white robes standing in the doorway. But then it came to him, and he smiled.

"The Tehreek-e-Taliban has sent you."

"Yes. I am Mufti Fahad. We were told that you returned to the Aiwan."

"Where is Shahidullah Shahid?"

"I am his representative."

"Are you a scholar?" It was what the title *mufti* translated to.

"Yes."

"Then am I to govern as a triumvirate with a prime minister and a man of learning?"

"And us with a man of mystery the people call Messiah? But your face is clean-shaven; you do well to cover it in public, lest a false impression be made."

The mufti was dark-skinned with deep-set eyes under thick eyebrows. He stood with a bamboo cane in his left hand, favoring that leg as he took a step closer. He had a white lace cloth covering the top of his head.

"We will rule in peace," Haaris said, the words sounding pompous to him.

"The jihad against the West will not be abandoned until sharia law is universal."

"Peace within our borders."

"The war here against our brothers is at an end for now," the mufti said. "But we will send our *fidayees* back to New York and Washington to continue their work."

"And to London."

The mufti raised an eyebrow.

"Great Britain is infidel America's staunchest ally," Haaris said. "When we strike it will be swift as lightning and just."

The mufti took a step closer. "Urge the people to join the jihad, but first study Islam, quote the Quran and then come to us; whatever your skills we shall put them to use against the infidels."

It was the same diatribe the Taliban had repeated over and over again, of which only since 9/11 did people in the West take notice.

"We will train you to stand with us."

Haaris turned again to look out the windows. People from the side streets were joining the increasing crowd, and it seemed almost as if they were in a celebratory mood. Some of the men were dancing in the streets. And unlike previous demonstrations no one was shooting Kalashnikovs into the air.

In came to him that the situation was unfolding just as he had planned for it to do. Despite all the variables, for which he had to deal with by hiring an imposter in London, this was working. Two days.

He turned back. "We will go to the prime minister now to complete our government and plan for jihad against the West."

"The whore will not give up military aid from the U.S. It is too precious."

"Money that was used to equip the war against you," Haaris said. "It ends now."

"You understand."

"I've always understood my people."

"Our people," the mufti said.

Downstairs in the main reception hall, where flowers wilted in vases around the central statue of Islamic figures, and a huge chandelier hung from the high ceiling in front of massive double doors of polished oak, Haaris stopped.

He'd been here before. A pair of ornate sofas in a corner, so large that the room did nothing to dwarf them, was where he'd sat sipping sweet tea talking with General Rajput for the first time shortly after he had conceived his plan for revenge. He remembered his first impression: the man was not particularly bright, but he was a good administrator, a decent leader, he had connections throughout the government and especially the military, but above all he was devious.

Haaris had decided on the spot that he would make good use of the man and had begun sharing intelligence that had allowed the government to anticipate every objection the U.S. raised to its policies, especially concerning Pakistan's movement of nuclear weapons around the country, and developing responses that if not believed were at least placating.

Pakistan was helping the U.S. continue the war against the terrorist groups within its borders, and with staging rights for the war in Afghanistan.

No one in Langley or especially in Washington liked the alliance, but no one was bright enough to see the liars for what they were and do something about it.

"Thou dost not trust General Rajput," Haaris said. The Punjabi words and grammar that had always seemed so formal, even ancient, to him had begun to sound normal. Even right.

"We have been enemies too long for that," the mufti replied.

"But you must trust me."

"Why?"

"Give me two days, and you will see."

The mufti laughed.

"I am the Messiah," Haaris said dramatically. "Pakistan's savior."

He adjusted the scarf over his features then threw open the doors and strode outside, down the broad stairs and across the complicated green spaces, past outer buildings, prayer halls and across the circular driveway up which VIP guests of state would be driven, and past the long, narrow reflecting pool.

The two soldiers manning the ceremonial iron

gates that opened to the sidewalk and broad Constitution Avenue turned around in surprise as the first shouts of "Messiah!" came from the crowds.

"Be careful what you aspire to," the mufti said to his left.

Haaris looked at him.

"Consequences that are unintended often arise."

Haaris almost laughed out loud. *Unintended consequences* indeed. It was a CIA term, which meant, in essence, be careful what you plan for because you just might get something else—something that could jump up and bite you in the ass. And it was especially funny to him at this moment, because the comment had come from a hated enemy of the CIA to a CIA operative.

The soldiers opened the gates and stood back to let Haaris and the mufti walk out onto the broad avenue. The crowd immediately surged forward, men touching Haaris's shoulders, women holding their babies for him to bless with a fingertip to their foreheads.

"Allah's blessing be upon you, my children," he said.

The mob went wild, chanting, "Messiah," over and over again, the volume rising.

"A lasting justice is at hand for all of us."

FORTY-FOUR

McGarvey wiped down the pistol he'd taken from one of the ISI officers who'd tried to kill him and put it in the woman's hand in such a way that at least a couple of partial prints could be lifted.

He laid it on the floor next to her blood, and as soon as the SEALs left with her body, he walked the couple of blocks up to Luqman Hakeem Road, where he got a table at a small café and ordered a coffee with milk.

The waiter was distant, but he came back immediately with the coffee.

It should have been the start of the morning rush hour, but the street was all but deserted of traffic, and he was the only customer.

"Where is everybody?"

The waiter shook his head and started to leave.

"Do you speak English?" McGarvey asked.

"Yes, sir," the waiter said.

"Where is everybody?"

"I do not know," the waiter said and again walked away.

McGarvey phoned Otto. "Something is going on, the streets where I am are all but empty."

"Oh, wow, Mac, the shit has started big-time now. Louise is with me. She's brought up real-time satellite images of the Red Section, right in front of the Presidential Palace. There's another mob there, and two figures are right in the middle of it."

"Haaris?"

"We can't tell. Austin is sending someone over to find out what's going on, but I think that it's a safe bet that it is Haaris as the Messsiah and he and whoever is with him are on the move."

"To where?"

"Straight up Constitution Avenue toward the Secretariat."

"Rajput's office," McGarvey said. "How long will it take them to get there?"

"It's not far. A hundred meters or so, but the crowd is slow, they're barely crawling. I'd say an hour, maybe longer."

An army jeep, a green flag on its radio antenna, its

blue lights flashing, turned the corner and headed at a high rate of speed toward the apartment building where McGarvey had been staying. Two men in civilian clothes, one of them talking on a radio, who could have been the twins of the two ISI officers McGarvey had taken out.

"A couple of ISI officers just went past me, and in a few minutes they're going to find Judith Anderson's blood all over the apartment, and the gun I took from one of the ISI officers I killed. Her fingerprints are on it."

"The SEAL operators finally showed up?"

"Yes," McGarvey said, and he explained everything that had happened, including her death. "They probably know that she was with me."

"You have to get out of there right now, Mac. I'll arrange a military flight out for you as soon as you can get out to the airport."

"I want you to get me an interview with Rajput in his office."

"Are you nuts?"

"I don't care how you do it, but I want to see him before Haaris and whoever's with him—and I'm betting that it's someone from the Taliban—get there."

"They'll shoot you on sight."

"I don't think so. Tell him that I know about the missing nuclear weapons at Quetta and the explosion, plus the disabling of most of their arsenal by our people. I'll make a deal with him for an exclusive interview with the Messiah and his Taliban friend. I think that Rajput will want to know what Travis Parks knows and how he came by his information."

"I can't go through the normal media channels; you're the competition, they wouldn't agree to help even if you offered to become a pool reporter. In that case you'd have to take along one of their cameramen. It wouldn't work."

"Goddamnit, Otto, I need this. Haaris is here and on the move; this is my chance, maybe my only chance."

"To do what, *kemo sabe*, kill him with your bare hands in the prime minister of Pakistan's office?"

"The bastard has a plan, and if I can push him hard enough maybe he'll give me a clue."

"He's smarter than that."

"He's vain. Whatever he came to do will be big, and he needs an audience."

Otto was silent for several beats.

"We're running out of time," McGarvey said. He could feel Otto's anguish and fear, almost like the roar of a distant waterfall. "This isn't a suicide mission, there'll be too many witnesses."

"Even if you get inside and interview them, once you leave you'd be a walking dead man."

"They'd want me to file my story first. Haaris would. And then they'd have to find me."

Again Otto was silent for a moment or two, but when he came back he sounded resigned. "Getting the media involved would open a can of worms nobody wants opened, especially not Page or Bill Myers." Air Force General C. William Myers was director of the National Security Agency. "Not to mention the White House. The blowback would be immense. We need to find another way."

McGarvey had considered another possibility, if the situation were to come to this point. It was the main reason he'd confided his real identity to Ross Austin. But it was last-ditch. "Austin knows who I am."

"He's pressed Walt to pull you out immediately."

"Have Page call Ross, right now, and tell him that I may have gone rogue. Have Austin convince Powers to tell Rajput that I could be another Snowden with information potentially damaging not only to the U.S. but to Pakistan's security."

"Rajput will have you arrested."

"He'll want to find out what I know. Putin gave Snowden asylum, maybe Rajput'll do the same for me."

"That's crazy, Mac."

"You're right. But just now crazy is my only option."

"It was your only option from the get-go."

"You have about twenty minutes to make it happen," McGarvey said, and he ended the call.

He sat nursing his coffee for a while, before he laid down a few coins and walked down the block until a taxi came and pulled over for him. The driver, an old man, seemed excited.

"I do not think I can take you to Constitution Avenue, sir," the driver said. "There are too many people. The Messiah has finally come to us, praise Allah."

"The Secretariat."

The driver stopped and looked in the rearview mirror. "You're American. I knew it. But you must know that this is a wondrous time for all of Pakistan."

"The Secretariat," McGarvey said. "They are expecting me."

The Secretariat was housed in a large stuccoed white five-story building just off Constitution Avenue near the northwest end of the Red Section. The foothills of the Himalayas rose to the east, and clouds were beginning to roll in, like an ominous gray blanket. A storm was on its way, and Mac could feel it coming in more ways than one.

He counted more than a dozen white domes at various corners of the L-shaped building as they approached, and they reminded him of the domes and spires atop minarets across the Muslim world.

He got the distinct feeling that peace would never come to Pakistan or places like this. He was not anti-Islam; in fact, he didn't care one way or another for any organized religion. But the extremists in any system were always the exception to the norm—Islam, Judaism or Christianity—yet they always accounted for the highest body counts. The primary purpose of terrorism was to terrorize.

The driver pulled up at the main gate. McGarvey rolled down his window and presented his passport to a guard, who checked the photo against his face.

"Yes, Dr. Parks, you are expected."

FORTY-FIVE

A pair of motorcycle cops escorted McGarvey's taxi up the long driveway to a side entrance of the Secretariat. Close up the massive pile looked more like a fortress or a prison than a governmental office. It felt ancient—and menacing: *Abandon hope all ye who enter these gates.*

He paid off the cabby, who was escorted back to the main gate. As he stood waiting next to an armed guard who was to take him inside, he could hear the chanting of a large crowd. He was around the side of the building, so he had no sight line down the broad avenue, but notably absent were the sounds of gunfire, which seemed always to be present at times like these.

"Dr. Parks," his guard prompted.

"It sounds peaceful."

The guard smiled faintly. "It is the Messiah, his message is one of peace."

"Someone is with him."

"The people."

"I meant that someone from the Aiwan is walking with him. Someone from the Taliban."

"I wouldn't know," the guard said.

"Sure, you do," McGarvey told him, but he followed the man inside, where he was searched with an electronic security wand before they went down a long, marble hall and took an elevator to the top floor.

The place was bustling with clerks and other governmental employees scurrying from office to office as if they were on missions of urgent importance, which considering who was heading this way, they were.

The anteroom to the prime minister's office was nearly half the size of a decent ballroom, with very high ceilings from which hung ornate chandeliers, gilded mirrors on the walls and vast Persian carpets on the wood parquet floor. An older man dressed in the morning clothes of a state functionary was seated behind the desk in the middle of the room.

He looked up, a pleasant expression on his round face. "Good morning, Dr. Parks," he said. "The prime minister will see you momentarily." He motioned for the guard to leave them.

"I imagine that he's very busy this morning."

"Indeed."

A pair of couches flanked by large tables topped with vases of flowers were set along one wall, but there was no place else to sit other than behind the secretary's desk. The length of time that someone wishing to see the prime minister was required to stand was related to his importance.

The secretary picked up his buzzing telephone. "Yes, sir," he said. "You may go in now, Dr. Parks."

A pair of massive ornately carved oak doors at least sixteen feet tall opened into the PM's office, which was nothing like what McGarvey had expected; very little of anything was ornate or pretentious about it. As he walked in, a service door to the left was just closing. Rajput was standing behind his desk strewn with papers, files, a telephone console and two computer monitors. Large windows faced toward Constitution Avenue, and on the wall between them was a wide flat-screen television that showed a view down the avenue from a camera mounted on the roof. Two library tables were piled with file folders and other documents. No paintings adorned the walls and the only real concession to decoration other than the ornately carved desk was a massive Persian carpet, the twin, or at least the cousin, of the one in the anteroom. This was a place of work, not ceremony.

Rajput motioned for McGarvey to have a seat in front of the desk. "Coming here just now, what struck you most about the demonstration out there?"

"So far as I know, this time your Messiah hasn't cut off anyone's head yet."

"It was a brutal act, but one that may have been necessary. Pakistan was going nowhere under its former leadership. And I believe you call such actions a 'clean sweep.'"

"Some would call it a purge."

"The guns have been silent. The suicide bombers have taken off their vests. Business goes on in peace. The ambassadors are returning to their embassies—

most notably your Mr. Powers—and next month we will be receiving a delegation from the Pentagon to open a new era of cooperation between us and your military."

Rajput wasn't rising to the bait—yet.

"What went wrong in Quetta?"

"A nuclear accident, regrettable, but the location was isolated enough, there were only a very few casualties."

"The driver and escort were moving the weapons somewhere. But it was my understanding that in cases such as that one the weapons would have been unmated—their nuclear cores and trigger mechanisms separated."

"In this instance that was not in fact the case. An investigation is in progress, the results of which will be classified."

"But there has been very little about it in your press or on television."

"We do not restrict our citizens from access to foreign newspapers, television or the Internet. If truth be told, the unescorted shipment was probably attacked by a Taliban group that got more than it bargained for. Because of the Messiah we have begun steps for rapprochement with them."

"Instead of supplying them with weapons."

Rajput sat back. "What are you doing here, Dr. Parks? What do you want from Pakistan?"

"Extraordinary things have been happening over the past days; I just want clarity for my readers on a number of issues that seem to have eluded the foreign press to this point."

"The nuclear incident in Quetta has been discussed with your government."

"It's my understanding that you stonewalled President Miller, which was why she ordered teams to disable as many weapons in your nuclear arsenal as they could reach. There've been no reports that I've seen on the effectiveness of those raids or of the casualties on both sides."

Rajput said nothing.

"How has that affected Pakistan's relationship with the U.S?"

"There has been no effect."

"How many weapons remain in your arsenal?"

Rajput smiled.

"What I meant to ask, does your military still present a credible enough threat to India that it will not make a preemptive strike?"

"It would be a mistake on their part."

McGarvey made a point to look up at the big monitor on the wall between the windows. The crowds had grown. Haaris and the Taliban representative were not visible, but there was a center to the mass that moved steadily up the broad avenue.

"What do you want here, Dr. Parks? I'm still not clear."

"An in-depth one-on-one interview with the Messiah. My readers want to know who he is and what his agenda might be."

"Even I do not know that yet."

"Then we'll ask him together when he gets here."

"But what is your agenda?"

McGarvey suppressed a grin. It was like fishing: hook, line and sinker. "To get a story."

"Do you know Ross Austin?" Rajput asked out of the blue.

"No."

"You're lying. He knows you and he knows why you're here."

McGarvey maintained his composure.

"Mr. Austin is in fact the chief of station for the

CIA's activities here in Pakistan. And he is concerned about you. In fact he wants me to have you arrested and turned over to Ambassador Powers immediately."

"We have a little thing called the First Amendment."

"He says that until recently you were an analyst with the CIA. He says that you fancy yourself as the next Edward Snowden, and that you have come to Pakistan seeking asylum in exchange for information."

FORTY-SIX

It was well after eleven in the evening when Otto Rencke left his office and took the elevator up to the seventh floor. The DCI had called fifteen minutes earlier to say that he was coming to Campus and wanted a meeting, not at all surprised to find Otto still at work.

Louise had gone home a couple of hours before, totally wasted after working nearly nonstop for the past thirty-six hours. She was just as worried as her husband was over the chances of Mac getting out of Pakistan alive, let alone finishing what he'd gone there to do, yet Otto expected the situation was harder on her in part because she didn't have the same history with Mac's abilities, and she wasn't at the center of CIA activities.

Page had just arrived by helicopter when Otto reached his office. Already there were Marty Bambridge and Carlton Patterson, whom Otto had come to think of as the DCI's unlikely war council.

"Don't you ever get tired, dear boy?" Patterson

asked, though he looked just as beat as everyone else. He was an old man, in his late seventies, and yet he had energy because, he'd once explained, his job was at least interesting if not exciting.

"No time for it," Otto said, taking a seat next to him on one of the couches in the middle of the room.

The DCI's office was laid out much like the Oval Office because Page often found it more comfortable to have discussions with his people not across his desk, and not around a long table in a conference room, but up close and personal.

Bambridge, who'd been down the hall in the Watch since late afternoon, looked sullen as usual, but Otto detected a hint of fear in his eyes. It was unusual even for the DDO.

"There've been some developments in the past hour or so that all of you might not be aware of," Page told them. "First off, the TTP's representative Shahidullah Shahid has disappeared."

"The Messiah and a Taliban mouthpiece, apparently the mufti Fahad, had a brief meeting this morning at the Presidential Palace before they set out on foot toward the Secretariat, presumably to meet with Prime Minister Rajput," Bambridge added.

"Yes, we know that much," Otto said.

"Then you also know that the blogger who identifies himself as Travis Parks is none other than Kirk McGarvey."

Otto looked to Page. "That was supposed to be kept secret, for his own safety."

Bambridge was puffed up. "Be that as it may, for whatever reason he revealed himself to my chief of station out there, who, duty-bound, reported it to me."

"And what did you do about it?" Otto asked.

"I told Ross not to get himself or his station personnel involved except to monitor the situation as closely as practicable and report anything of interest directly to me."

"Has he?"

"McGarvey's apparently already gotten into trouble. Ross thinks that he killed two ISI officers and was responsible for the death of a third—a woman—whose body is being transported from Pakistan by a team of SEAL Team Six operators out of Jalalabad."

"Did you know about this?" Page asked Otto.

"I arranged it."

"The White House didn't know and the president's national security adviser wants the mission scrubbed. She wants McGarvey recalled."

"I tried to make him get out," Otto said. "But he's not going to back off. We have confirmation that the man who we thought was Dave Haaris in London was in fact an imposter, which makes it even more likely that the Messiah is Dave."

"Not likely at all," Patterson said, surprising them all. "Before he took his wife's ashes to London he confided in me that he was tired, that he needed a vacation. Said he was going to disappear for five days, and that if something should come up about his whereabouts to inform everyone that there was nothing to worry about."

The timing struck Otto. "That was two days ago," he said.

"So he'll be gone another three days," Patterson said. "There's no reason to suspect that he was lying, especially dealing with the grief of losing his wife so tragically. And learning that he has an inoperable cancer."

"Pete Boylan confronted his imposter in London, who told her that his contract was for two more days only."

"Tommy Boyle told me that he arranged an RAF flight to Islamabad for her," Bambridge said. "I ordered him to have it recalled but he couldn't without burning a favor, something neither of us wanted to do. She'll be on the ground in the next few hours."

"That's not the point," Otto said. "Whatever Dave's planned will presumably happen in two days."

"It's actually a moot point, because McGarvey will be under arrest and on his way home before then," Bambridge said.

Otto's temper spiked, but he held himself from lunging across the coffee table between them and breaking the stupid bastard's neck. "What have you done?"

"I authorized it with Sue Kalley's blessing, who thought it was a brilliant way out of the situation," Page said. "The fallout from any more killings over there will be far too costly for us, but outing Mac as a whistle-blower who we wanted returned immediately was something that could be handled politically."

Otto didn't want to believe what he was hearing. "Mac is either on his way to meet with Rajput or he's already there in the Secretariat."

"Yes, we know," Bambridge said.

"Don't tell me that you actually identified Mac?" Otto asked, surprised by his control.

"Of course not. What do you take me for?" Bambridge said. "Austin told Rajput that Travis Parks worked for us, but that he fancied himself to be another Snowden, seeking asylum in exchange for information on this agency's top operations. Ambassador Powers has an appointment with Rajput later today to demand that Parks be turned over to us. On the line will be a significant portion of our continued military aid."

Otto got to his feet.

"Sit down, please," Page said. "We're not done here yet."

"Not by a long shot."

"Where the hell do you think you're going, mister?" Bambridge shouted, jumping up.

"To try to undo the damage you've done before it's too late."

"I'll have Security up here before you get halfway down the hall."

Otto shrugged. "Marty, you little prick, you cannot in your wildest nightmares imagine the rain of shit that is a hair's breadth away from falling on you—on this entire agency."

"Mr. Director!" Bambridge shouted.

"Before you go any further, ask yourself how much Kirk McGarvey has given this country and how much he's lost for it. He's in badland at the president's behest to try to stop something terrible from happening. With no interference from you his chances for survival were next to nothing. He knew it going in, and yet he thought the risk was worth taking. Now if you'll excuse me, I have some work to do catching up."

Otto headed for the door.

"Goddamnit, come back here," Bambridge said.

"Be careful that your political ambitions don't rise up and bite you in the arse one of these days, Marty," Otto said, and he left.

Page's phone call came as Otto got to his office. "Can you repair the damage?"

"I don't know, but first I'll try to save his life."

"This came from the White House."

"From the president herself?" Otto asked.

"Not directly," Page admitted.

"Just understand, Mr. Director, that Bambridge and Susan Kalley are best buds. Talk to the president."

FORTY-SEVEN

In the last hundred meters before the ceremonial front gate to the Secretariat, Haaris felt like Jesus Christ himself—or more like Lawrence of Arabia strutting in his costume. Arms outstretched to either side, he picked up the pace, so that he and the mufti were practically running. The crowd fell mostly silent and those in front respectfully parted for them.

Two armed guards swung open the iron gates at the foot of a shallow rise up which a paved driveway made its way through a stand of trees to the Secretariat's main entrance.

Haaris suddenly stopped and turned to face the crowd that stretched down Constitution Avenue for as far as the eye could see. Now there were absolutely no sounds.

"My dear people," he shouted theatrically, though only the people at the head of the mob could possibly hear him. He felt strong, even invincible.

All of America's nuclear might had not stopped the 9/11 attacks from happening. Nor would her awesome power be able to stop him in time.

"The TTP's mufti has come with me to this place to form Pakistan's new government. A government of peace. A government to serve the people. A government to feed the poor, to heal the sick."

Haaris was aware that the mood of the mufti beside him and the crowd stretched in front had immediately begun to change. Some of the people seemed confused. He looked at the mufti and smiled, then he turned back to the crowd.

"We will be a government of *Islami qanun*," he shouted—sharia law, which meant actual legislation that dealt with everything from crime, to economics, to politics, as well as hygiene, diet, prayer, etiquette, even fasting and sex. All of it based on a strict interpretation of God's infallible laws versus the laws of men.

Sharia was the real reason many Muslims gave for the jihad against the West. Until sharia was universal there could be no peace with the infidels.

Haaris meant to give it to them—or at least the promise of it—for the next two days. In his estimation the righteous attacks of 9/11, in which fewer than three thousand people had died, had not gone far enough. If they had, the backlash would have been even more severe than it had been. More terrible than the killing of bin Laden.

Had the plan been bolder the West would have shoved Islam back to the dark ages.

It's what they wanted and Haaris would give it to him, *insha' Allah*—God willing.

"Read the Quranic verses and follow the examples of our dear Muhammad set down in the Sunnah," Haaris cried. "Be one with Allah, be one with us!"

The mob roared, and Haaris felt not only all-knowing, all-powerful; he also could feel his sanity slipping away bit by bit.

He started up the driveway, the mufti at his side.

"Did you mean all of that?" the Taliban spokesman asked.

"Of course, didn't you believe me?" Haaris asked.

"And I will require your help as well as the help of the military, the same as in Quetta."

The mufti did not answer.

McGarvey heard the roar of the crowd as did Rajput, and the prime minister got up from behind his desk and went to the window. "He's here and he's brought someone with him."

"Who is it?" McGarvey asked.

"I don't know," Rajput said. His phone rang and he answered it. "Yes," he said. "Bring them up."

"If you had to guess who's with him," McGarvey pressed, though he was just about sure who it was.

"Guessing is not needed. The Messiah has brought a representative from the Taliban, almost certainly the TTP, as I suspected he might whenever he turned up here."

"To form a government with you?"

Rajput smiled, though it was clear he was concerned: something else was in his eyes, at the corners of his lips. "I imagine they'll propose forming a triumvirate."

"Will you go along with it? Will the parliament and the military?"

"Do you still insist on your interview, Dr. Parks, even though it has been revealed that you are nothing more than an analyst for the CIA?"

"I'm not an analyst for the CIA," McGarvey said. "I'm a journalist."

"With First Amendment rights."

"Exactly."

"Mr. Austin was lying."

"Yes."

"Why?" Rajput asked.

"I'll ask him if he'll sit for an interview," McGarvey said. "In the meantime, will the ISI be willing now to work with the Taliban? Could be an interesting partnership."

"Indeed," Rajput said. "Do you still wish to interview the Messiah?"

"It's why I came to Pakistan," McGarvey said.

"Then it will be so," Rajput said. "But we have an old saying here that is the same as in the U.S.: Be careful what you wish for; you might just get it."

Haaris and the TTP mufti were escorted up to the top floor of the Secretariat, where the armed guards left them in the broad corridor that led down to the PM's office. Rajput's secretary stood at the open door to the anteroom. A fair number of clerks and other functionaries had gathered at their office doors and in the far end of the corridor, but none of them said anything.

"Peace be upon thee," Haaris said, raising his right hand as he and the mufti moved down the corridor.

Someone responded, "And peace be upon thee, Messiah."

The secretary nodded. "Messiah, Mufti Fahad."

"We're here to meet with the prime minister," Haaris said.

"He's expecting you, sir," the secretary replied, and he stepped aside.

Haaris was the first into the anteroom, the mufti just at his elbow. He stopped short. Rajput, in an ISI uniform shirt, the collar open, sleeves rolled up, stood at the tall doors to his office. Beside him was a man Haaris had never seen, but it was obvious that he was an American. His presence was unexpected, but there was nothing in Rajput's expression to indicate who the man might be or if he was a possible problem.

Rajput met Haaris in the middle of the room and they embraced.

"Who is he?" Haaris whispered close in Rajput's ear.

"You'll see," Rajput said, and they parted. He held out his hand for the mufti, who took it after brief hesitation. "Old enemies meet in peace at last."

"It has been a long time coming," the mufti said.

"Too long for Pakistan's sake. But now we will put everything right."

"Should I know this gentleman?" Haaris asked, indicating McGarvey.

"He is Travis Parks and among other things he claims to be an American journalist here for an exclusive interview with you," Rajput said. "Probably with the three of us."

"Among other things?" Haaris asked. His artificial voice no longer sounded strange in his ears. Nor did his Pashto.

"The CIA's chief of station at the embassy claims that he is a CIA analyst who wants to trade information for asylum here. But his credentials as a writer pan out."

The mufti was visibly affected. "The CIA is here?" he demanded.

"And why not," Haaris replied. "Assuming he's not armed." He switched to English. "Mr. Parks, it was very inventive of you to find me."

"I merely had to follow the crowds, sir," McGarvey said.

"And now that you're here, what do you want?"

"I'm a journalist, but the mufti believes otherwise. He believes that I work for the CIA. I do not."

"Very well, you will have your interview," Haaris said. "But, Mr. Parks, it will be a two-way interview. An exchange, shall we say, of ideas and ideals. Do you agree?"

"Of course."

FORTY-EIGHT

McGarvey was made to wait in the anteroom for nearly a half hour while Haaris and the TTP spokesman met with Rajput. There'd been no hint of recognition in Haaris's eyes when he'd come face-to-face with McGarvey, exactly what Mac wanted. If Haaris had seen through the disguise it would have been impossible to get anywhere near him. But if he was pushed by a journalist, or even someone else from the CIA, he might start making mistakes, especially if there was validity to the two-day timetable suggested by the imposter in London.

It was a double-edged sword for all of them. In the first place, McGarvey knew that Haaris wanted publicity. He needed his identity as the Messiah, and not as a high-ranking CIA operative, to be rock solid around the world—especially in London and Washington. The man could not afford to create a panic. For now he was all about peace and cooperation between the government and the Taliban.

On the other hand, if he suspected that McGarvey was a CIA spy here to gather information, Haaris would be caught between a rock and a hard place; he'd want Mac to report back to Washington that the Messiah was really a voice of stability in the region, and yet the presence of a CIA spy meant someone at Langley might suspect Haaris's real identity.

For McGarvey's purposes, he wanted Haaris to have some serious concerns, not necessarily that the CIA had sent an operative here, but that its purpose was to out him and then either reel him back home or assassinate him.

The prime minister's secretary answered a string of telephone calls with the same reply: "I'm sorry, but the prime minister is in conference at the moment and cannot be disturbed."

But it was in English, for McGarvey's benefit: the government of Pakistan was going on as normal, there was nothing to worry about.

The telephone rang again and the secretary answered it. "Yes, sir," he said. "They are ready for you now, Dr. Parks."

McGarvey went into the office, the secretary closing the door softly behind him.

Three ornate armchairs had been set up in a semicircle across a low table facing a plain office chair. Rajput and the mufti sat on either side of Haaris. This was to be more of an inquisition than an interview.

He took his seat, facing them. "Thank you, gentlemen, for agreeing to this interview on such short notice, but the events of the past few days have been nothing short of stunning. My readers would like to know more."

"I'm sure they would," Haaris said. "Your telephone was taken from you downstairs, a curious device, from what I've been told, protected by a very serious password. I'm assuming that you record your interviews on it. Would you like to use one that the prime minister is willing to provide you?"

"Thank you, sir, but it's not necessary. I have a very good memory."

"As you must in a profession such as yours. How may we be of assistance?"

"May I see your face, sir?"

"There is no need for it at this time," Haaris said.

"Can you tell me something of your background? Experts I have spoken with tell me that yours is a Pashtun accent but with a strong hint of a proper British education."

"It is true I am Pashtun and it is also true that I was taken to England as a young man, where I received a first-class education."

"Do you still hold a British passport?"

"Yes, as well as a Pakistani one."

"May we know under what name?"

Haaris laughed softly, and for just an instant McGarvey thought he recognized it. "'The Messiah' will suffice for now; it is the people's choice."

"One definition of the word is a zealous leader of a cause," McGarvey pressed.

"I think that the people had in mind the deliverer they'd hoped for."

"A deliverer of what?"

"Not *of* what but *from* what," Haaris said. "From the strife that has torn this country apart for most of its history. Before we can expect to be at peace with the world we must first be at peace with ourselves."

"Does that include India?"

Rajput bridled, but Haaris held him off with a gesture. "Especially India."

"And the U.S.?"

"I wasn't aware that we were at war with your country," Haaris said. "I rather thought that we were partners in the war against terrorists." He looked at the mufti. "A war that has gone on entirely too long, at a cost so dear it hurts us all."

"Peace, you say," McGarvey said. "That was begun with the beheading of Pakistan's properly elected president, and the suicide or possible assassination of the prime minister?"

"Both of them were corrupt," Rajput answered. "We have proof that both of them were siphoning aid money, for their own purposes, that we were receiving from the U.S."

"Wouldn't it have better suited your purpose to arrest them and place them on trial?"

"No," Haaris said. "Pakistan was in dramatic trouble; a dramatic solution was needed to get the people's attention."

"By 'dramatic trouble,' are you referring to the nuclear event near Quetta? It's thought that perhaps the Taliban hijacked a nuclear weapon that was being moved and somehow set it off."

"We're investigating that possibility. But there have been other attacks, as you well know. Attacks on the military headquarters, the killing of innocent citizens. Suicide bombers. Tribal warfare along the border with Afghanistan. The list is long."

"Why do you think that the U.S. ordered the strikes against Pakistan's nuclear arsenal? And why has it been kept out of the press? There must have been many casualties on both sides."

None of the three men seemed to be affected by the question. But Haaris took a long time to answer.

"I'm told that you may be a journalist, but that the CIA's chief of station here claims that you are a rogue CIA analyst who's come to trade information for asylum."

"He's wrong," McGarvey said.

Again Haaris took his time in responding. "I expect he might be, but I don't know his reasons, except that you are probably an NOC, perhaps even freelance. But here to do what, exactly? Something beyond your orders, making you a rogue operator but of a different sort than he suggests?"

"Have you heard of a man by the name of David Haaris?"

If any of them reacted, it could have been Rajput, but the changes in his expression and demeanor were so slight as to be scarcely noticeable.

"No, is it significant?" Haaris asked.

"General Rajput certainly knows him. They've worked together for several years, from what I was told."

"Told by whom?" Rajput asked, the look on his face deadpan.

"A CIA insider whose name I can't mention, for his own protection. Haaris worked in a section called the Pakistan Desk and came here often."

"You do work for the CIA," Rajput said.

"I'm not on the CIA's payroll," McGarvey replied calmly.

Haaris again held Rajput off. "I believe that Mr. Parks is telling the truth, so far as it goes. But why," he turned to McGarvey, "are you here at this moment? What does Mr. Haaris have to do with me?"

"Perhaps nothing, but he went to London several days ago and has disappeared."

"And you were sent to find him?"

"No, that would be up to the CIA. I was merely told he'd disappeared and it was presumed that he would naturally come here to find out what was going on. I'd like to interview him, and I'd hoped that General Rajput might lead me to him."

"What do you think I can do to help you find him?" Haaris asked.

"Nothing, sir. But you're news, so I figured that I

could kill two birds with one stone—find a clue to Haaris's whereabouts and interview you."

"I think that you are a liar," Haaris said. "This interview is at an end. It's time that you leave Pakistan while you still can."

McGarvey got to his feet. "Thank you, gentlemen, I believe that I got most of what I came for."

The side door opened and two armed men dressed in the uniforms of the Secretariat Security Service, their pistols drawn, came in.

"You're under arrest, Dr. Parks," Rajput said.

"On what charge?"

"Espionage."

FORTY-NINE

The gruff flight sergeant gently touched Pete's shoulder and she came awake instantly. His name was Bert Cauley and he'd been the attendant for her and the other two passengers who were last-minute additions to the staff at the British embassy. On the flight over they'd mostly stayed to themselves. They'd been told that she was CIA.

"We're forty minutes out, ma'am," Cauley said. "You have a call, but you might want to come forward to take it. You'll have a little more privacy."

Pete went forward to the Citation's tiny galley just aft of the cockpit, where Cauley took the phone from its hook on the bulkhead, pressed one of the buttons and handed it to her.

"It's a secure circuit," Cauley said, and he went aft.

The copilot reached back and closed the cockpit door.

"Yes?" Pete said. She was afraid that it was trouble.

She looked at her watch which she had set to Pakistan time just after they'd lifted off. It was a few minutes before midnight.

"Mac is missing," Otto said.

Something clutched at her heart, and she closed her eyes. "Are you sure?"

"The battery was removed from his phone six hours ago, but he's done it before to avoid detection if he got into a bad spot. But it's worse than that. I didn't want bother you before, but now it looks like you could be walking into a tornado."

"I'm listening."

"It's Ross Austin. He told Rajput that Mac—as Travis Parks—is a CIA analyst sent out to find the Messiah's identity and the man's agenda."

"Goddamnit to hell, Otto. Why? What the bleeding Christ is wrong with the bastard?"

"He's friends with Susan Kalley, the president's national security adviser. Apparently she sidestepped Page and contacted Austin directly. Told him that the president had called off the deal with McGarvey and they wanted him out of there immediately."

"Page could have talked to him."

"It wouldn't have done any good, and you know it," Otto said. "Austin told Rajput that military aid was on the line and that the CIA wanted Mac arrested and turned over to him personally for immediate deportation back to the States."

Pete felt a glimmer of hope. "Maybe that'd be for the best after all."

"There's more," Otto said, and he sounded worried. "Mac went to the Secretariat and bullied his way into Rajput's office as Haaris and a TTP rep were marching up Constitution Avenue. He wanted to interview not only the PM but the Messiah as well."

"If Haaris was told that Mac was a CIA analyst it's

more than possible he'd know that was a lie. The son of a bitch knows just about everyone on Campus. And he'd have to think that Mac was there to spy on him and maybe even assassinate him."

"Louise and I came to the same conclusion. Page knows everything and he has a three o'clock with the president; that's about an hour from how. He has a fair idea that calling off Mac was Kalley's idea and not Miller's."

"Maybe. But I'll be on the ground before then. A couple of British embassy staff are on board with me, and they've agreed to drop me off at our embassy on the way over to theirs."

"Mac wanted me to give Austin the heads up that you were on the way," Otto said.

"Not until I'm practically at the front gate. I don't want him to call his pal Rajput and out me too."

"Walk with care, Pete. He's just doing his job the best way he knows how, and among other things that's protecting U.S. interests over there. He has a big staff, a lot of them in the field at any given time, and he owes them his muscle. By all accounts he's doing a good job."

"He's one of Marty's fair-haired boys, isn't he?"

"Yes, and rightly so, but they are not, I repeat, they are not cut of the same cloth. Not by a long shot."

"We'll see," Pete said, sick at heart. "Call Powers as well. I'll want to talk to him. One way or another I'm going to do my damnedest to save Mac's life."

"Good hunting," Otto said.

After landing they taxied over to the VIP arrivals area of the airport, where a driver and a security officer from the British embassy were waiting with a Range Rover. A Pakistani customs official met Pete and the two Brits and stamped their diplomatic passports, not raising an eyebrow that an American woman was included.

Pete had put on a scarf to cover her hair, but the custom's officer was indifferent; he didn't even bother to check her face against the photo in her passport.

At this time of night the airport was all but closed down and the highway into Islamabad was nearly deserted. She'd watched the replays of the satellite images from last week when this same stretch of road was a battleground: Taliban fighters seemed to be everywhere, and dozens of cars and small trucks were on fire along both sides of the highway, a few blocking the road. There had even been bodies lying in a two-hundred-meter stretch.

Now it was quiet, the city to the west, and the Himalayan foothills beyond, sprinkled with streetlights. This was a nation finally at peace, and she almost felt like a night stalker come to do evil, something to do to break the peace, yet she knew two things: Dave Haaris did not want the peace to last and he was here to change everything, and that Mac was here, and that she loved him and that she would do everything within her power to help him even if it meant giving her own life.

Pete turned to the Brit seated next to her. "So what's your take on this Messiah?" she asked. She wanted some feedback, but mostly she wanted to be distracted for just a little while before she met with Austin or she didn't know what she might do.

He was young, probably not in his thirties, and he seemed a little flustered. "I don't really know, ma'am."

"I won't bite, and anyway, we're allies."

"On the outside looking in, he seems legitimate," the other, much older Brit sitting behind her said. "But nobody in my shop trusts him."

"Why's that?" Pete asked.

"It's all too pat. He shows up out of the blue, lops off the head of Barazani and then supposedly goes on a walkabout with his people. Rubbish, if you ask me. The bastard is up to something, and I don't think it'll be good for any of us in the West."

"Neither do I," Pete said, turning inward again. Getting Mac out of the Pakistanis' custody would take the help of Austin as well as Powers, but it was afterward that worried her most. Mac wasn't going to give up. It was one of his traits she loved most and yet feared the most.

They came into the city's diplomatic enclave and to the American embassy, where their credentials were checked by a pair of marine sentries before they were allowed to drive up to the portico at the main entrance. They were met by another security officer, this one in civilian clothes, who opened the rear door for Pete.

"Thanks for the lift, gentlemen," she said, getting out.

The officer closed the door for her and the Range Rover headed back to Post One.

"Miss Day, if you'll follow me, ma'am, Mr. Austin is expecting you."

Pete stopped just at the entrance to the two-story building and looked back the way she had come. "It's quiet here," she said. Now that she was close she tried to reach out to Mac, but she couldn't feel him, and it disturbed her more than she wanted to admit.

"Yes, ma'am, now. But it was busy this afternoon."

"Did you guys have any trouble here?"

"Not here, but just about everywhere else. And I guess that was the spooky part, no crowds on our doorstep. We're not used to it."

"I hear you," Pete said. "But I don't think it'll last."

FIFTY

Walt Page's Cadillac limousine glided to a stop at the White House East Gate, where the guard, recognizing him, waved it through. Driving into the city from Langley he'd had a lot of time for thought, and nothing he had learned in the past twenty-four hours was of any comfort.

The president had sent Mac to Pakistan but with deniability. If he got into trouble he would be cut loose. The White House simply could not afford to take a hit over the issues in Pakistan. Miller had already gone out on a limb sending her NEST people in to neutralize a fair portion of Pakistan's nuclear arsenal, and so far there'd been absolutely no reaction.

But anything else, even the smallest of incidents, could push Islamabad into some reaction, if for nothing else than to appease its people.

And with the Messiah in the mix, actually bringing at least a temporary peace, it was as if the sword of Damocles hung over all of them. Without a doubt it was why the president's national security adviser had ordered Ross Austin to out McGarvey. Ross understood the president's thinking, but she'd been wrong, and he meant to convince her of just that.

A marine was at the door, and just inside a Secret Service agent was waiting for him. "Good afternoon, Mr. Page. The president will be delayed for just a few minutes, and Miss Kalley asked if she might have a few words with you first."

The woman wanted a chance to explain herself, and Page was more than willing to hear her out. "I know the way," he said.

Kalley's first-floor office was in the corner of the West Wing directly opposite the Oval Office. Josh

Banks, her deputy NSA, whose office was next door to hers, looked up as Page passed. He had a long, hound dog face and he couldn't conceal the fact that he was guilty of something, but he didn't rise nor did he say anything.

The president's NSA looked up and smiled pleasantly when Page came around the corner. "Good afternoon, Mr. Director, it should only be a minute or so," she said. "Anyway, I wanted to have a word with you first."

He closed the door and sat down. "Did the president authorize you to call Ross Austin?"

"Directly to the point, as usual. No, she did not. But if a president had to make decisions on every single issue, our government would grind to a halt. It was my choice, considering the situation."

"Outing an intelligence agent in the field is a capital crime," Page said, holding his temper in check. He'd not had many dealings with Kalley, but in the ones he'd had she seemed a bright, decisive woman, though somewhat egocentric.

"Mr. McGarvey is not on the CIA's payroll."

"You're right, he refuses to take a paycheck. Nevertheless, he works for me, and in this instance under the president's orders, something I mean to bring up."

"There'd be no profit in crossing me, Page. It'd be much easier if we could find a common ground so that we could work together for the good of the country."

"Nor would there be any profit in crossing Kirk McGarvey."

Kalley nearly came across her desk at him. "Don't threaten me, you son of a bitch."

"Don't interfere in an ongoing operation," Page said, keeping his tone completely neutral, which was driving the NSA up the wall.

"The situation out there is critical. The ISI has had absolutely no reaction to our incursion, nor has it allowed any news to leak to their media. Were you aware that they pulled Geo off the air again just two hours ago?" Geo was Pakistan's leading news channel.

"Yes, because they were getting too critical of the Messiah. They want to know who he is and where he came from."

"He's brought peace for the moment. Something no one else has been able to do."

"Don't be so goddamned ivory-tower naive. He has a schedule, and it's set for less than two days from now."

"No reason to think it's not benign."

"The man chopped off President Barazani's head."

Kalley was silent for a long beat as she composed herself. "Is that what you've come here to tell the president?"

"There's more," Page said.

"Tell me."

"And the president," Page said. "She's expecting me."

President Miller was working at her desk, her suit jacket off. She looked up when her secretary brought them in, but she wasn't smiling.

"I thought you would have come sooner," she said.

"There've been a number of developments," Page said.

Miller glanced at Kalley. "You two have spoken," she said. "Under the circumstances I had no other choice but to withdraw Mr. McGarvey from the assignment."

"Having the ISI arrest him was the wrong choice for several reasons, Madam President."

"The only choice," Miller shot back, her anger rising.

"Something's going to happen in less than two days' time. We don't know what it is, but it will possibly be a strike against the U.S. or our interests. Revenge for not only our incursion into Pakistan to assassinate bin Laden but for our strikes against their nuclear arsenal."

"They already tried the first, and it didn't work," Kalley said.

"Because McGarvey stopped them. But there's more. We think we know who the Messiah is, and it's even more critical that we stop him now."

"Who is he?" the president asked.

"David Haaris," Page said, catching them completely by surprise.

"Impossible," Kalley said.

"What's your confidence level, Mr. Director?" the president asked.

"Ninety percent, conservatively," Page said. He told them what had happened to date, including the discovery of Haaris's imposter in London. "McGarvey was at the Secretariat, presumably to interview Rajput, at the same time the Messiah and Mufti Fahad, the new TTP spokesman, showed up. It's more than conceivable that Mac and the Messiah came face-to-face."

"If it was Haaris he would have recognized McGarvey from the start," Kalley said.

"Mac is traveling under false papers and a very good disguise," Page said. "Fortunately, Ross had sense enough to out Mac's work name and not his real ID."

"You're ninety percent sure that Haaris is the Messiah, and you think he has something planned in two days, for which you don't have a clue," the president said. "What's next?"

"McGarvey's operating as a blogger under the name of Travis Parks. Call the prime minister and remind him that we have freedom of speech and of the press, no matter how onerous it might seem to him. And assure him that Dr. Parks is not an employee of the CIA."

Miller swiveled her chair and looked out the bullet-proof windows at the Rose Garden for a long time. "Who else have you discussed this with?"

"Some of my staff, but the number is small," Page said.

"Otto Rencke?" Kalley asked.

"Yes."

"Saul?" the president asked.

Saul Santarelli, the director of National Intelligence, was a bright man, but in Page's estimation little more than a functionary for nothing more than another layer of bureaucracy.

"No," Page said.

"Then don't. The need-to-know list will go no further. I'll telephone Rajput first thing in their morning and ask him to release McGarvey—Dr. Parks."

Page said nothing.

"The Messiah is probably Haaris, but we don't know if he has an agenda, so we can't react until something happens. The next twenty-four hours will tell. But Mr. McGarvey's orders remain the same. Kill the Messiah, whoever he is. Am I clear?"

"Perfectly clear, Madam President," Page said, surprised.

FIFTY-ONE

With the ambassador back in residence the embassy was busy. On the way upstairs Pete's escort reminded her that they, like most of the other embassies whose staffs were returning, were on what amounted to a wartime footing.

"A lot of it has to do with the nuclear incident near Quetta," the young woman said. She looked as if she was just out of college. "We still don't have many answers."

"Is it possible that the Taliban got their hands on one of the weapons and set it off by accident?" Pete asked.

"God help us all, because only one went off and three are still missing."

"No sign of them?"

"Not yet, but everyone's looking."

Ross Austin, dressed in a light pullover sweater, jeans and deck shoes, was in the corridor just outside his office talking to a pair of marines in desert camos and bloused boots. They only carried pistols, but they wore Kevlar vests, pockets bulging with combat equipment.

"I'll just leave you here, ma'am," Pete's escort said, and she hurried down the corridor in the opposite direction.

Austin looked up as Pete approached, then said something to the marines, who headed to the stairs.

"Thanks for at least agreeing to talk to me instead of turning me around at the airport," Pete told him.

He was the perfect chief of station: of medium build, with a pleasantly plain face, an empty smile and a slightly vacant look in his soft brown eyes, completely without guile or aggression. He was a man who would never stand out in a crowded room or on a street corner in just about any city in the world. He could have been easily taken for an American businessman, a British tourist or an employee of a small Swiss bank.

They went into his office. "Wasn't my choice," he told her. "Though with any luck I'll have you on a plane out of here first thing in the morning."

Pete was jet-lagged and her temper rose. "There's a lot you don't know."

"I was briefed by the director himself less than ten minutes ago. I know about Haaris and the imposter you burned in London, and I know what McGarvey's real mission was."

"Haaris has an agenda and whatever he has planned will happen in less than two days."

"I'm sorry but I can't envision Dave as the Messiah. It doesn't fit, and from what I'm told the Company isn't one hundred percent sure. Even Rencke can't nail it."

"Then why the imposter in London?"

"Dave has got something in mind, all right, but I suspect he simply wanted to step off the merry-go-round for a breather. He's been going at it hammer-and-tong forever; time to take a vacation somewhere. An anonymous vacation. And I can't say as I blame him."

"Tommy Boyle said just about the same thing," Pete practically shouted.

The office door was open and Austin went to shut it.

"Are you guys out of your minds? Or has Haaris got something on both of you? Is it blackmail?"

"This conversation will not continue," Austin said angrily. "You're on my turf now, and I don't give a shit who says what, you're out of here on the first flight I can arrange."

"Might not be your station for long. Outing a fellow

agent is a capital offense. It'll be a wonder if you don't end up in a federal penitentiary somewhere, a lot sooner than you think."

"Believe what you will, Boylan, I did it for his own good, as well as for the good of this station and for American interests here."

Pete wanted to smash her fist into his face.

"Hear me out," Austin said. "McGarvey came here to assassinate the Messiah—whether he's Dave Haaris or not—because the president was convinced that the guy is a major threat to Pakistan's stability."

"What stability?"

"Whatever your politics are, we need Pakistan, just as they need us."

"To help us fight the war on terrorists."

"Yes."

"Like the Taliban, whose mouthpiece, I'm told, marched up Constitution Avenue practically hand in hand with the Messiah, right into the office of the prime minister," Pete said. "A man, I might remind you, who probably hired the German assassination squad to take out our SEAL Team Six operators last year. McGarvey stopped them, but you know this. Yet you outed Mac to this son of a bitch."

"I outed Travis Parks, who Rajput promised he would release to my custody this morning."

"Mac almost certainly killed two ISI officers who were sent to take him down after what he did at the reception yesterday. And he caused the death and disappearance of another of them. Do you honestly think that Rajput doesn't know this? Do you honestly think that he's going to order Mac's release?"

Austin just looked at her.

"You stupid, silly bastard," Pete said, because she couldn't think of anything else. She was sick at heart and frantically trying to figure out a way to get Mac out of wherever he was being held or at least get word to him that she was here.

Austin looked over her shoulder. "Mr. Ambassador," he said.

Don Powers, in gray slacks and an open-collar shirt under a dark blue blazer, was at the open door. He didn't look happy. He came the rest of the way in and closed it.

"I have no real need to know the day-to-day operational details of your station except when it has an effect on what I'm trying to do here. Pakistan is in turmoil and I'm here to guide U.S. interests in the long-term. That cannot—must not—include divisiveness at any level in this embassy. Am I clear on this point, Mr. Austin?"

"Perfectly clear, sir."

"And you are?"

"I'm traveling on a diplomatic passport under the name Doris Day. In reality I work for Mr. Page and I've just arrived from London."

"Your being here, I presume, has something to do with the actual identity of this man who the people are calling the Messiah."

"Yes, sir. I was sent to help Travis Parks."

"The other CIA officer that Walt presumably sent over. I can tell you, Miss Day, or whoever you really are, that Dr. Parks has made a royal mess of things and I too want him gone as soon as we can secure his release from the authorities. It's a wonder the ISI didn't send assassins after him."

"They did. But all three of them failed."

"How do you mean, 'failed'?" Powers demanded, but it was clear he knew exactly what Pete was saying.

"He was forced to defend himself. They're dead."

Powers was taken aback. "Murdered? He murdered three ISI officers?"

"It was that or lose his own life, sir," Pete said. "Did Mr. Page explain to you who we believe the Messiah to be?"

"My God," Powers said. "How am I to explain this? The man actually came from Washington with me."

"Explain what to whom?"

"To the legitimate government of Pakistan. To General Rajput."

"Are you suggesting that one of our people face criminal proceedings? You know how it will turn out."

"My hands are tied."

"What about the Messiah?"

"The country is at peace, I don't know if we can ask for more at the moment."

"I want you to demand that Parks be immediately released before it's too late."

"Too late for what?" Austin asked, but it was clear to Pete he'd merely said it for Powers's benefit, because he knew exactly what she meant.

"He's an embarrassment to Pakistan," Pete said. "They'll kill him if they haven't already."

"As I said, my hands are tied," Powers told her. "And I think it would be best for everyone concerned that you leave Pakistan as soon as possible."

"Travis Parks's real name is Kirk McGarvey, Mr. Ambassador. I thought you should know that. Mr. Austin does."

FIFTY-TWO

McGarvey, dressed in only a pair of filthy khaki shorts, sat alone at a small metal table bolted to the concrete floor. His left leg was shackled to a leg of the table. He had nothing on his feet, the soles of which were battered and bleeding, nor anything on his chest, which, like his back, was crisscrossed with welt marks from the repeated canings he'd suffered through the night and early morning hours.

Oddly enough they'd left his face alone, and his eyes were clear, as was his head. Even odder was the fact they hadn't used drugs on him. But they would, sooner or later, and he would break. His only real option at this point was to escape.

A Pakistani man easily as large as McGarvey, dressed in an ISI uniform, walked in and said something indistinct to the guards in the corridor before the steel door was closed.

"Good morning," he said in good English. He took off his baseball cap and laid it on the table before he sat down across from McGarvey. "I'm a lieutenant in the security service, my name is not important for you to know at this time. What is important is that I am considered to be a proficient interrogator. Seems as if you wore out the others. They tell me that you are a man of some stamina—more than they thought possible for even an American spy."

"I'm a journalist," McGarvey said.

The officer had a large square face pitted with what had probably been childhood acne. He smelled strongly of cigarette smoke, and the fingernails on his left hand were dirty with what might have been blood.

"As it turns out one of your own countrymen has

admitted to us that you are a spy for the CIA here to gather information. We were to arrest you and then turn you over to your embassy so that you could be sent home. Unfortunately, Dr. Parks, you were shot trying to escape."

"You might consider setting me free after all, before I kill you."

"The thing is, we need a confession from you so that the repercussions of your death won't be so difficult. We'll turn over your body, of course, and you'll receive a posthumous star in the lobby of your headquarters building, and memories will fade. In the meantime the situation between our countries will not change because of your being here. And do you know why?"

"Do you have a wife and children who'll mourn your passing, Lieutenant? Do families get pensions for soldiers who die in service of their country, or will they be left wanting?"

"We'll get your confession," the lieutenant said. "I'm pretty good at what I do. I have a perfect track record."

"Okay, I confess that I'm a spy," McGarvey said. "You win."

"Oh, but I think that you are more than just a spy. In fact, do you know what I think?"

"I'm all ears."

The lieutenant's jaw tightened but just slightly. "I think that you are an assassin. And I think you came here to kill the Messiah."

McGarvey didn't think that Austin could be so stupid as to tell the ISI something like that. "I was not armed when I was arrested."

"Nor were you armed when you killed two of our officers yesterday, but you took one of their pistols and one of their identification wallets, which apparently you discarded somewhere along the way. We'll find them."

"Then let's get it over with, or do you mean to keep me chained to this desk while you talk me to death?"

The lieutenant got up, his hand on the butt of the pistol holstered at his side, and looked at McGarvey for several long moments. "Interrogating you should be interesting. I sincerely hope you don't tell me everything for a very long time."

He went out and told the guards to bring the prisoner to him in five minutes.

The interrogation chamber was at the end of a short corridor. They were in the basement of ISI headquarters, and when McGarvey had been taken into custody they had made the mistake of not blindfolding him. He knew the way out.

One unarmed guard had removed the shackle from his leg, while the other stood aside, a Kalashnikov at the ready. The armed guard was careful not to get too close as they marched down the otherwise-deserted hall.

The lieutenant had taken off his blouse and laid it on a chair in one corner. He was filling a two-quart metal pitcher with water from a tap in the wall.

He looked up and motioned for McGarvey to be strapped to a wooden table in the middle of the small, dungeon-like room. A car battery and a battery charger were on a metal roll-about. A long set of jumper cables fitted with ten-inch wands ending in large sponges was attached to the battery. No other equipment or furnishings besides the metal chair were in the chamber, which was harshly lit by a single electric bulb recessed behind a mesh in the ceiling.

Blood and what looked to McGarvey like feces stained the top of the table and had dribbled down to the concrete floor.

"This room is my favorite," the lieutenant said. "It reminds me of a coffin."

McGarvey made a show of reluctantly lying down on the filthy table, forcing the armed guard to muscle him down.

"You're going to die here this morning," McGarvey whispered in his ear.

The guard was young, probably in his early twenties, and he was extremely nervous, so that when McGarvey strained at the leather straps around his arms and legs he didn't bear down. He wanted to be anywhere but here.

"Remember what I told you," McGarvey whispered.

The guard straightened and backed off.

"Leave us now," the lieutenant said.

The two guards left the chamber and closed the door.

"What did you say to the boy?"

"That I didn't blame him," McGarvey said, feigning fear. "Maybe you and I can come to some kind of a deal that doesn't involve killing me."

"Let's just see how it all begins, shall we?" the lieutenant said. He got the filthy remnants of an old bath towel that had once been white from a shelf at the base of the table. "You know all about waterboarding, I'm sure. Your Congress is certainly aware of the method. They don't think that it works. But we know better, don't we, Dr. Parks."

He draped the towel over McGarvey's face but then took it off.

"I've not strapped your head down. I would like to see your control. Some of my subjects have died by thrashing around so violently they broke their necks. One poor fellow just two months ago damaged himself in such a way that he suffocated. I looked into his eyes as his face turned purple and he realized that nothing on earth or in Paradise was going to save him. He knew that he was dying, and he understood at the end that I knew it too. And that it gave me pleasure. No more talk?"

"I don't want to die," McGarvey said, again feigning the first glimmerings of fear.

"Of course not," the lieutenant said, and he draped the towel over McGarvey's face again.

A CIA operative working the Calle Ocho Cuban-ex-pat neighborhood in Miami had agreed to water-board McGarvey, who had insisted that he needed to know what it was like.

"It's not good, comp, not at all," Raul Martinez had argued.

"Do it," Mac had insisted.

Pete had been there as a backup in case something went wrong. And her voice had been in his ear through the entire ordeal, which had lasted less than ninety seconds but had seemed like an eternity.

"Just relax with it, Kirk," she had whispered as the water soaked the towel, and went into his mouth and throat, gagging him, drowning him, making it nearly impossible to think about anything except for the incredible pain, the instinct for survival kicking him against his will. He had to fight back. He had to live.

"Go with it, Kirk. Let it happen, I'm here, you'll be okay, I promise you, my darling. Focus on my voice. Nothing else."

The water flowed in and around him. He could hear his accelerating heartbeat even over the sounds of Pete's words close in his ears. She was holding his forehead, her touch gentle, comforting, even though he could feel the muscles of his neck and chest convulsing because of his need for oxygen. One clean breath of air.

Her voice began to fade, as did his need to breathe, and for a moment he and Katy were on their sailboat in the Bahamas at night under a billion stars, pinpricks of light that seemed to descend from above and surround him.

FIFTY-THREE

Pete stood at the corner window looking out across the little piece of the Red Zone she could see. The diplomatic enclave was all but deserted at this hour of the morning. Only a lone unmarked van came up Ispana Road and disappeared around the corner toward the German embassy.

Austin had suggested that she get a few hours' sleep, and he'd assigned her a room in the BOQ section of the building.

"Mentioning McGarvey's name did absolutely no good with Powers, and I think you probably knew it wouldn't," the chief of station had told her earlier. "He's had history with Mac, and none of it very satisfactory. He doesn't like mavericks."

"Not many people do, until they need them," Pete said bitterly.

"Whatever you must think, Miss Boylan, I was merely trying to protect his life."

"You've already said that."

"You didn't believe me."

"No," Pete said. "So now what? Are we just writing Mac off? You're sending me home hoping the situation will all blow over? Well, it won't, you know. I won't let it."

"A military transport will take you to Ramstein, where you'll be able to hitch a ride stateside."

They had been in Austin's office, and she'd taken a step closer. Powers had left and for the moment she and Austin were alone together. "If something happens to him, I swear to God that I'll move heaven and earth to get to you."

"I might take a hit, but I made the decision I thought was best for Mac and for the country."

"I won't file a formal complaint, if that's what worries you. I'll come back here, or wherever you are, and kill you."

Austin seemed to slump. "Get some sleep, Miss Boylan. I'll call Rajput first thing in the morning."

There was nothing left to say.

"It's all I can promise."

Pete laid her head against the relatively cool windowpane and closed her eyes. Almost instantly her throat constricted and she felt as if she were drowning. She straightened up and reared back, her eyes wide.

It was Kirk, she could feel his breath against her cheek. She raised her right hand. She was touching his head. She felt his pain, but she also felt his strength. She knew that he wanted her.

She grabbed her sat phone from her bag on the bed and called Otto at Langley, where it was five in the afternoon. He was still in his office.

"Where would they have taken him?" she demanded as soon as he came on.

"If the ISI has him, which they probably do, he'd be in a holding cell at their headquarters building. Page has been talking with Miller to see what diplomatic pressure can be brought to bear. But they already know that he works for the CIA, so there's a real possibility he'll go on trial and we might have to wait for that to happen before a deal can be made."

"No, listen to me, Otto," she screeched. "They're waterboarding him right now. We can't wait."

"How do you know this?"

"I just know it. Where would he be if they were torturing him?"

"The interrogation area is in the basement of the main building. Heavily guarded, of course. Constant electronic surveillance."

"Can you hack into their computer mainframe?"

"I have. But there's nothing on him, though that's not unusual. They handle their most sensitive cases totally offline. Just paper memos and orders directly man to man."

"The surveillance systems. Can you shut the cameras down, maybe release any electronic door locks?"

"I can do that easily enough."

"Good. I'll let you know when, but it'll be within the hour, hopefully sooner. In the meantime have Page go back to the president; we have to get him out of there right now. We'll use it as a diversion."

"A diversion for what? You're not going to storm the gates."

"Not immediately. But Mac will try to get out of there; you and I both know that's a fact. I want to make it a little easier for him."

"Okay, but what can I tell the director? That you've had an out-of-body experience? ESP or something? You know how far that will go?"

"They're going to kill him. Tell us it was an accident."

Otto was silent.

"Christ," Pete said in despair.

"I'll scramble the mainframe in the Secretariat," Otto said.

"What good will that do?"

"I'll crash their system for sixty seconds and before I bring it back up I'll let them know that it was brought to them courtesy of the U.S.A. Ought to get their attention."

"How will that help Mac?"

"I'll put my signature on it. They've got some pretty bright people over there who'll figure out who did it, and when Haaris hears about it, it won't take him a millisecond to figure out what we want. And as long as he doesn't suspect that the ISI has got Mac and not some CIA contractor, he'll order his release and expulsion from the country just to make this headache go away."

"Do it," Pete said.

"It's going to take the better part of a half hour, so hang in there, Pete. We'll get him out."

Pete used the house phone in the room to call Austin in his quarters. He finally answered after a half-dozen rings.

"What?"

"Meet me in your office in five minutes; we're springing Mac."

"What the hell are you talking about?"

"The ISI is waterboarding him right now, and we're going to stick it to them in such a way they'll not only know what's happening, but who is doing it and why."

She splashed some water on her face, stuck her conceal-and-carry Glock in the waistband of her jeans beneath her shirt and pocketed an extra magazine of ammunition and her sat phone. She grabbed her scarf on the way out.

Because of the nuclear incident outside Quetta and

the transition of the government and the other extraordinary events of the past days—not the least of which were the Messiah's appearance and the Taliban's supposed willingness to cooperate—many of the offices at the embassy were staffed even at this hour.

Austin was on the phone in his office when she showed up.

"She's here now, Mr. Ambassador. But she hasn't explained what she means or how she came by her information."

"I need your help," Pete said when he put the phone down.

"My hands are tied, I'm sorry, but you're leaving in a few hours."

"They have him in the basement of the ISI's main building, where they're torturing him right now."

"How in hell do you know this?"

"Never mind, I just do. We're going to shut down all the electronic surveillance systems in the building as soon as I'm in place with a car and a driver who knows his way around the city and isn't afraid to stick his neck out."

"If it gets that far, which it won't, where the hell do you think you'll go? They'll have the airport closed up tighter than a gnat's ass."

"They'll be too busy trying to take care of another, much bigger issue."

"What are you talking about?"

"We're going to shut down the mainframe in the Secretariat for sixty seconds and let them know who did it, why we did it, and warn them that it could be permanent."

"Rencke," Austin said angrily. He reached for the phone.

"I would think about it for just a minute, Ross," Pete said. "We all know what Otto can do if he's pressed, and we also know what Kirk McGarvey is capable of."

"Doesn't matter."

"Think what they've both done for our country. Are you really willing to throw all of that away?"

FIFTY-FOUR

The single point of light began to blossom into something much larger, almost overwhelming in McGarvey's eyes as he slowly regained consciousness. The filthy towel was gone and he was no longer drowning. He made a great effort to control his breathing.

"Relax," Pete had told him what seemed like a long time ago, and yet he was sure it had been just minutes. He could almost feel her touch on his forehead.

He turned his head to one side as the ISI lieutenant came toward him.

"I admire your control, Dr. Parks. I didn't do nearly as well in training. And it's certainly nothing I'd like to go through again."

"May I have a drink of water," McGarvey croaked.

The lieutenant laughed. "That's the paradox. You have nearly drowned, and yet your throat is terribly dry. I feel your pain, believe me. We could be brothers, Travis. Comrades in arms. Perhaps in different camps, but certainly fellow soldiers."

McGarvey said nothing. His awareness and strength were coming back to him, slowly, and he closed his eyes against the glare of the overhead lightbulb.

"Sometimes the subject even becomes sleepy immediately following a session," the lieutenant said amiably. He pinched McGarvey's cheek.

McGarvey took a long time opening his eyes, as if he were having trouble. "Water."

The lieutenant laughed. "In due time. And I even promise you'll have a reasonably soft bed and something to eat when you wake up. But for now I need your cooperation. The truth, if you please."

The straps, especially the one at his left wrist, were loose. He blinked several times. "I'm a journalist."

"Yes, I've read some of your blogs. And you were quite right about many things. The problem we're having is that no one ever heard of you until a few days ago. It's as if you were invented out of whole cloth, I believe is the correct expression. Something the CIA is certainly capable of doing. So let's start there, shall we? Of course your name isn't Travis Parks. What is it, please?"

"Parks," McGarvey whispered.

"We can do better than that."

McGarvey let his eyes flutter. "Davis," he said softly.

"What's your social security number, Mr. Davis?" the lieutenant asked.

McGarvey shook his head.

The lieutenant slapped his face. "The truth."

McGarvey opened his eyes. "Fuck you."

The lieutenant rolled the battery cart back. He dipped the sponges in the pitcher of water, flipped the power switch and jammed them against McGarvey's bare chest.

A massive pain roared through Mac's body, rebounding from the top of his skull; every muscle, even those controlling the movements of his eyes, went into spasms so tightly he thought for a split instant that his bones would break.

Suddenly it was over and he slumped back, any lingering effects of waterboarding completely gone.

"Your real name, please," the lieutenant said.

"Fuck you!"

The lieutenant pushed the sponges onto McGarvey's chest.

Mac heaved against the restraining straps and roared in pain. He kept screaming even after the lieutenant pulled the sponges away.

"Do I have your attention now?"

McGarvey let his head loll to the left so that he could see the door. The guards had not come despite the noise he'd made. He felt the strap around his right wrist and willed that arm to completely relax.

"Your real name. Let's start there, or I'll be forced to let the current run through your body much longer than one or two seconds."

McGarvey shook his head. "Four-seven-nine," he croaked, barely above a whisper.

The lieutenant flipped the power switch off and laid the wands on the cart. He bent down closer to McGarvey. "Four-seven-nine," he said. "What comes next?"

The man's breath smelled of onions and curry and something else unpleasant.

"What comcs next?"

McGarvey slipped his right hand free. "Six," he whispered.

The lieutenant bent even closer.

McGarvey suddenly reached up and clamped his hand around the lieutenant's throat, compressing the carotid artery on one side.

The lieutenant tried to pull away, but McGarvey was strapped to the table and his grip was too powerful to break. Blood started to gush from where one of Mac's fingertips broke through the man's skin.

He got his other hand free and rolled halfway onto his side, grabbing the lieutenant's neck with both hands, crushing the man's larynx and compressing the other carotid artery. He looked into the man's eyes.

"I told you that I would kill you."

The light slowly faded from the lieutenant's eyes, his faced turned a deep purple and finally his legs collapsed and McGarvey let him slump to the floor.

Torture was a useful tool if it was handled properly. The point was to hurt the prisoner but not damage him permanently, and certainly keep him well enough restrained that he couldn't hurt his interrogator.

McGarvey undid the straps around his legs, got off the table and checked the lieutenant's pulse, but there was none; the man was dead.

He listened at the door but there was nothing to be heard, so he went back to the lieutenant's body, undressed it and got into the man's clothes. The boots were a little tight, but not impossibly so, and the uniform blouse stank of sweat.

Strapping on the holster, he checked the pistol, which was an old American-issued nine-millimeter Beretta, with a full nine-round magazine and one in the chamber.

He listened again at the door for a moment, then eased it open. The corridor was empty, and for all intents and purposes the building could have been deserted or asleep. The red lights on the camera at both ends of the short corridor winked off. The system had just shut down, and the only reason why that he could think of, other than a system power failure, was Otto.

Slipping out he raced to the stairs at the end of the corridor and took them up two at a time, taking great care to make no noise.

At the top a steel door was closed but when he tested the handle it was not locked. He opened it a crack and looked out. A broad corridor led to the right, blocked by a gate about twenty feet away. A lone guard sat at a table, his back to the gate; beyond him was another steel door.

To the left about fifteen feet away was yet another door but no guard. No one was expecting trouble.

Moving on the balls of his feet McGarvey hurried to the left. He glanced over his shoulder, but the guard had not moved. The door was unlocked and Mac opened it and slipped through into an anteroom about ten feet on a side. Stairs led up to the left and another door, this one with a thick glass window, was straight ahead.

Outside was a covered driveway, a closed garage door to the left and a guard positioned behind glass directly across from it. Two uniformed men sat behind a slightly raised platform inside.

This was a sally port designed to admit prisoners into the building, where they would be taken directly below to the interrogation center.

The garage door rumbled open and a truck came in and stopped. Two armed soldiers got out of the back and stood aside as a half-dozen prisoners in ragged clothing, their wrists in manacles, their ankles shackled on short chains, emerged.

The man from the glass booth met the driver and had him sign something on a clipboard. He said something to the armed guards with the prisoners and the driver came across directly to the steel door.

McGarvey sprinted for the stairs and stopped halfway up.

The driver and the two armed guards and the prisoners came into the anteroom and started up the stairs.

FIFTY-FIVE

Pete walked out of the embassy and hurried down the long drive to Post One, where the two marines on duty had been advised she was on her way. They opened the small service gate, but neither of them said a word to her. She just nodded and headed down the street.

A military jeep turned the corner a half block away, but nothing else moved anywhere in the Red Zone so far as she could see.

It was possible that Austin was playing games with her, agreeing just to get her out of his hair, at least temporarily. And if she was to be picked up by the Pakistani police, so be it. Because of her diplomatic passport she would be sent home immediately.

But when she'd mentioned retaliation from Otto and from Kirk he'd got the message loud and clear. She'd seen it in his eyes. The man had a job to do here, but he was no fool, he had respect.

A block and a half farther she came to Khayaban-e-Suhrawardy Road, the bridge across the Jinnah Stream, which flowed south into the lake to her left, when a red Mercedes C-class sedan with a taxi light on its roof came out of nowhere and pulled up at the curb.

The passenger-side front window was open and a familiar figure dressed in a Manchester United sweatshirt and jeans leaned over. "He's already made his break, get in," the driver said in a Texas accent.

"Milt, am I ever glad to see you," Pete said and climbed into the backseat.

Milt Thomas was a deep-cover operative working for the CIA and the Islamabad police. His job for the local cops was to report on any passengers of inter-

est he picked up either at the airport or the three hotels that catered mostly to foreigners. His job for the
CIA over the past three years he'd been in country
was the same. She and McGarvey had met him last
year when they'd been on an op here.

"I talked to Otto three minutes ago. Mac's on the
move."

"Where is he exactly?"

"Right at this moment we don't know. But he was
in an interrogation cell in the basement with Lieutenant Nabeel Khosa, who's the ISI's chief interrogator—
read *torturer*—and just a few minutes ago he
appeared at the doorway in Khosa's uniform. Otto
thinks he got the surveillance system shut down before Mac was spotted. Anyway, there's been no alarm
so far. Otto will warn us if it happens. He also wanted
me to call him when I picked you up."

"I hope you have a plan," Pete said.

Thomas laughed. "Are you kidding? The place is a
fortress." He phoned Otto. "I have her. Anything new
yet?"

"Let me talk to him," Pete said.

Thomas handed the phone back, then made a
U-turn and headed for the bridge.

"How are we going to get him out of there?" she
asked.

"I'm working on it," Otto said. He sounded busy.
"I turned the surveillance system back on as soon as
he cleared the hallway in the basement. Right now
he's in the service stairwell on his way up to the second
floor. He got to the sally port exit, when half a dozen
prisoners were brought in and started up the stairs
right behind him. He had nowhere else to go."

"With the surveillance system on they'll spot him."

"With it off they would lock down the entire compound. And as long as he keeps his face away from

the cameras—which he's done so far—he's just another ISI officer in a very busy building. The ISI is on emergency footing because of the Messiah thing—the media has started calling it a velvet revolution—but the entire compound is crawling with people."

"Someone is bound to spot him as an imposter. He has to get out of there right now."

"I have no way of contacting him, but he knows the layout of the place; he's seen live satellite images and has to figure that the only way out is the rear of the building. To the east, north and south are major roads, already starting to get busy, so his only real option is west."

"On foot," Pete said. "Even in an ISI uniform he'd attract attention and he wouldn't get very far. He'll know that."

"What do you have in mind?"

"Which is the least busy of the three roads?"

"The west service road. It's where he was brought in. It's the gate used mostly for incoming prisoners and outgoing bodies."

"That's how he's getting out. He's going to steal a car or truck and if he isn't waved through he'll crash the gate, and we're going to be there to pick him up."

"Then what?" Otto demanded. He didn't seem the least bit alarmed. They'd all get worried later.

"I don't know, but Milt and I will figure something out," Pete said. "Anything changes, keep us posted. In the meantime, where's Haaris?"

"He's disappeared again."

"Great, great, great." Pete switched off. "Are you armed?" she asked Thomas.

"Of course. What's the story?"

"The west service road gate," she said, and she explained what she and Otto had discussed.

"Are you sure about it?"

"It's the only option. Once he's out, we have to pick him up before they respond in force. But I don't know what after that. We'll have to get under cover ASAP."

"My house," Thomas said without hesitation. "It's down in Rawalpindi, maybe ten klicks from here."

"Won't your place be under surveillance?"

"I'm a fair-haired boy."

"Not after this morning," Pete said.

"I've been thinking lately that it's getting time to pull the pin. You guys will have to get out, and I'll just tag along."

"Right," Pete said. But she had to wonder if Mac would give up so easily. Haaris was still out there.

Thomas made another U-turn on the deserted road and headed back toward the Red Zone. "In another hour, maybe sooner, traffic is going to pick up and it won't be long before we're in a full-blown rush hour. Happens every A.M. and goes on all day."

"We need to wait where we can watch the service road and yet not attract any attention," Pete said.

"The Rose and Jasmine Garden, it's just across the Kashmir Highway. But he's going to have to turn south, toward us."

Pete called Otto again and told him their plan. "Any word yet?"

"He's in the west stairwell on the third floor. A couple of close calls, but everyone is too busy or too stressed out to see him for anything other than an ISI lieutenant."

"It won't hold."

"No. And there's still no way I can get word to him."

"But you can tell us when he gets out and which direction he's taken," Pete said.

"His chances are slim."

Pete laughed, and it sounded like false bravado in her ears. "We're talking about Mac."

Thomas got off the highway and worked his way through the park, finding a narrow road that looped back to the southwest and then north, finally connecting with a tree-lined lane that became the west service road across the Kashmir and Kayaban highways, which ran parallel to each other. He doused the lights and parked.

Pete got out of the car and Milt handed her a pair of Chinese-made binoculars, which she used to scope the walls of the ISI compound and its main building, which rose up into the early morning sky like some squat palace from an ancient time.

She reached out to feel him, but he wasn't there, and she was suddenly very cold and very frightened.

FIFTY-SIX

McGarvey, the Beretta in hand, opened the door to the fourth floor and peered out. This part of the building seemed to be empty; all the lights in the corridor were on and many of the office doors were open, but no one was here. This was the executive floor, and McGarvey had half expected to see Rajput busy at his desk. But the prime minister's office was locked, and listening at the door Mac couldn't hear a thing.

The lights on the security cameras were back on, indicating they were active, so he kept his face averted as he hurried down the corridor and ducked into an office twenty feet down from Rajput's, and closed the door.

A pair of file cabinets stood along one wall, and in

the middle of the fairly small room was a plain desk with a computer and a telephone, but nothing else. The drawers were locked and there were no files or anything else that might have indicated who worked here or what their job might have been.

Two windows looked down at the roof one floor below, and beyond that a driveway that passed an open field and through a thick stand of trees to the rear gate that opened onto a service road, if his memory served. Before he'd headed over on the ambassador's aircraft, he'd taken the time to study the layout of the Secretariat compound as well as the Aiwan. He'd considered it a possibility that he might have to take the fight either here or to the Presidential Palace and he needed to know his way around. Especially if he was in a hurry.

Laying the pistol on the desk he ignored the computer, which would almost certainly be password protected, and picked up the phone. Getting a dial tone he entered the international code for France, and then Otto's personal relay number, which was only ever used if an agent was in trouble and on the run and needed to call home without alerting his pursuers that he was calling the States, and certainly not the CIA.

If there was a central switchboard or a monitoring system of some sort, it wouldn't take long for someone to notice that a call was being placed from an office that was supposed to be empty, and either listen in or send a security officer to investigate.

Otto answered on the first ring. "Yes."

"Me," McGarvey said.

"West service road gate," Otto said. "Head south, you'll be met."

The line went dead.

There was no lock on the door, so McGarvey

wedged a chair against the handle, and holstering the pistol went to the windows, which like those at the CIA were double-paned and likely flooded with white noise. But unlike at the CIA the windows were not sealed; unlatched, they swung open.

The building was constructed like a ziggurat, each lower floor jutting out from the one above. McGarvey climbed out and hung full length for just a moment before he dropped the fifteen feet or so to the roof below. Looking over his shoulder as he ran, he tried to spot someone watching him from a window, or perhaps from the roof above, which bristled with antennas and satellite dishes. And he half expected to come under fire.

But he reached the edge of the roof. The drop here was about the same as from the fourth floor. Many of the offices were lit, the glow reaching through the windows.

Picking a spot between windows, he hung over the edge again and dropped. He landed off balance and fell hard on his side. A stab of pain in his right hip when he got up nearly caused that leg to buckle, but he reached the wall and flattened himself against it.

He waited there for just a couple of seconds before he took a quick look through the window beside him into a large space broken up into cubicles, most of which were manned. As far as he could tell from the brief snapshot, no one was coming to investigate.

Favoring his right leg he dropped to the roof of the first floor, and despite the intense pain rolled to the wall, again between windows. He had a much harder time getting to his feet. Some of the windows were lit on the second floor, but the office he looked into was dark, the only light coming from the open door to the corridor.

Half hobbling, half running, he got to the edge of

the roof and without hesitation dropped the last fifteen feet into a line of bushes just as a jeep came up the driveway and suddenly came to a stop.

McGarvey got to his feet as a slightly built man in uniform, three sergeant stripes on his sleeves, came through the bushes, a Kalashnikov rifle at the ready.

But he was totally surprised. He said something in Punjabi, but then caught the two pips of a lieutenant on Mac's shoulder boards and started to stiffen.

McGarvey lurched forward, grabbed the sergeant in a headlock and before the man could cry out, broke his neck. It took nearly thirty seconds before the sergeant finally lost consciousness.

Taking the rifle Mac pushed his way through the bushes and got into the jeep. No alarm had been sounded yet because of the phone call or because someone had spotted him making his way across the roofs, but the silence wouldn't last much longer. And once it did happen, the entire ISI compound would go into immediate lockdown. At that point getting out would become unlikely.

He propped the rifle on the passenger seat so that he could get to it instantly. Someone came on the radio and barked an order. Almost instantly a one-word reply came back.

The main access road swung around the north and south sides of the main building to the front gate, but a much narrower lane headed west off the south road down a long row of tall, slender cedars. The parade field stretched off to the right, and a row of smaller buildings that could have been barracks for the enlisted men lay to the south. Nothing moved anywhere, and only the brilliantly lit headquarters gave any indication that something out of the ordinary was going on. Pakistan was in what some of the local media were calling a "welcome crisis," to counter the Western media's tagline of a "velvet revolution."

Passing a broad paved driveway that led from the barracks to the parade ground, where troops could march up for review, he had to turn left at the end of the driveway to the back gates, less than fifty feet away.

He pulled up at the double-chain-link fence topped with razor wire. An inner gate opened onto a no-man's section a little longer than a troop transport truck, which was blocked by the outer gate. Vehicles coming in or out would be trapped between the two gates until a positive ID could be made.

A uniformed sergeant came out of the guardhouse, a Kalashnikov rifle slung over his shoulder. Behind him another enlisted man stood at the open door. He had a sidearm but no rifle in hand.

The sergeant said something as he approached, but five feet away he suddenly stopped short and reached for his rifle.

McGarvey pulled the Beretta and shot the man center-mass twice.

The guard in the gatehouse reacted, but McGarvey was out of the jeep and to the doorway as the man was grabbing his sidearm from its holster.

Mac pointed the pistol directly at the guard's head. "Open both gates."

The guard didn't respond, though McGarvey was sure that he understood English by the look in his eyes.

"Now, or I will shoot you," Mac said.

The guard turned to the left to reach the two green levers for the gates, but instead he slammed the palm of his hand into a large red button and immediately a klaxon broke the early morning air.

Mac fired one shot into the side of the man's head,

and as the guard went down, McGarvey shoved his body aside and swung both green levers.

The two gates began to open as Mac jumped into the jeep and drove forward.

Just inside the no-man's-land the second gate, less than half open, began to close.

Mac accelerated, the front right fender of the jeep catching the leading edge of the gate, knocking it just far enough so that he could get through.

Even more lights came on all over the ISI compound as McGarvey hauled the jeep around the tight corner to the left and onto the service road, and fewer than a hundred yards later turned right on what he thought was an empty Khayaban Highway.

A car, lights on its roof, suddenly passed and then turned directly into his path, leaving him no choice but to run off the road.

FIFTY-SEVEN

McGarvey drew the pistol as Pete jumped out of the red Mercedes and ran back to him, a look of intense relief on her face. Searchlights stabbed the air behind them and more sirens started up.

"Are you wounded?" Pete demanded as McGarvey grabbed the Kalashnikov and struggled to get out of the jeep.

"I banged up my leg getting out," he said, almost collapsing.

Pete took his arm, put it over her shoulder and helped him to the cab as Thomas jumped out. Between the two of them they got him in the backseat and Pete climbed in beside him.

Thomas made another U-turn on the still-deserted highway and two blocks away turned onto a side road that led into the Rose and Jasmine Garden. Following even narrower roads he wound his way into the deeper woods to the east. From here they could just make out the highway.

"We can't stay here long," Thomas said. "But as soon as the search widens we'll take a chance on Club Road. I know a couple of shortcuts to get us to my place in Rawalpindi."

"Otto's going to crash the ISI's mainframe," McGarvey said. "Soon as he does it they're going to know for sure that I'm CIA and all hell is going to break loose."

"He's already done it once, and he's going to shut them down even longer just as the morning shift shows up," Pete said. "It'll play hell with their security routines."

"Thanks for picking me up, guys, but what the hell are you doing here, Pete? I told you to stay home."

"Like I would."

Mac was vexed, but without her he wouldn't have gotten more than a few blocks before he'd have had to ditch the jeep and make his way on foot. "Thanks, to both you and Milt."

"Otto's going to set up a SEAL Team Six extraction for us up to Jalalabad, but not until tonight. In the meantime we're going to go to ground at Milt's place."

"They're not going to come to me until they're sure that you managed to escape," Thomas said. "But then they're going to call up all of their assets."

"Time for you to come home," McGarvey said.

"I've been thinking the same thing lately. And despite what the local media is reporting, most people are nervous about suddenly being pals with the Taliban. Everyone is sure they were responsible for the nuclear explosion outside of Quetta, and that maybe more of the bombs are still missing."

A jeep, its siren blaring, passed by on the highway, followed immediately by a pair of open troop-transport trucks filled with helmeted soldiers.

"That took longer than I thought it would," Thomas said. "No one wants to accept responsibility."

"Soon as they find the jeep they'll figure I'm on foot and they'll send helicopters to look for me," McGarvey said.

"And this'll be one of the first places they'll look," Thomas said, slamming the car in gear.

Headlights off, he followed a footpath that snaked through the woods, the lower branches of the trees scraping against the sides of the car. They came out behind a group of buildings, among them a mainte-nance shed. A campground was off to the left. A driveway around front led up to Club Road just above a cloverleaf that connected it with Murree Road. Both were major highways during rush hour, which would begin in less than an hour.

Back to the west two helicopters were rising from the ISI compound as Thomas turned south onto the broad road, passing around the cloverleaf, and then speeding up.

"Did anyone spot you this morning?" McGarvey asked.

"A couple of truck drivers, but no one saw us when we picked you up, I made sure of it," Thomas said.

McGarvey looked out the rear window as one of the helicopters dipped low over the campground and set up what looked like a search pattern. For now they had a little breathing room. But it wouldn't be long before the search expanded.

"How far to your place?" he asked.

"About ten K from here," Thomas said. A blinding

light from above swept over them. "Down," he shouted.

McGarvey grabbed Pete's arm and dragged her with him to the floor, the pain in his hip like a lightning bolt to his system.

Thomas slowed down, stuck his head out the window and waved.

The Aérospatiale Alouette III helicopter swung to the driver's side of the car, and flying sideways about twenty feet up, kept pace. Someone said something in Punjabi over a loud hailer.

"They want to know who I am," Thomas said. "*Gohir*," he shouted in Punjabi. "But police call me the Fox."

The crewman said something else.

"They've ordered me to pull over and stop," Thomas said. "They mean to search us."

"Do it," Mac said. "But be ready to get us out of here."

"Right."

McGarvey switched the Kalashnikov's fire-selecter lever to full automatic. "Stay down," he told Pete as he rose and began firing directly at the cockpit canopy.

The pilot swung hard to the left, exposing the tail section and fuel tanks.

Mac let the rounds walk aft, hitting the crewman perched in the open doorway, who'd managed to get off a few rounds of returning fire, and punching holes in the fuselage, finally hitting the fuel tank and turbine.

The chopper spun farther left, its nose dipping when a fireball rose out of the engine and a split instant later a bang shattered the early morning air and the machine disintegrated as it hit the ground.

Thomas accelerated away.

"Is everybody okay?" McGarvey asked.

"Jesus," Pete said. "I'm fine."

"Milt?" McGarvey asked, checking the magazine. It was empty.

"As long as they didn't get a chance to use their radio, we should be okay. But take off the uniform shirt or at least get rid of the epaulets, and Pete, cover your hair. We're coming up on a residential and business section and there's bound to be people up and about."

Mac pulled off the sweat-stained shirt, noticing some blood on his chest, and removed the epaulets, name tag and unit patches from the sleeves.

Without a word Pete wiped the blood away with her scarf before she covered her hair.

"It's not as bad as it looks," McGarvey said, putting the shirt back on.

The eastern sky was just beginning to lighten as they drove through a rat warren of narrow streets, many of the vendors in the small shops and sidewalk kiosks opening up already. Pedestrian traffic here in the northern section of Rawalpindi was heavy, as was vehicular traffic on the main roads, all of it picking up with a vengeance that wouldn't let up until well after dark.

Down one lane paved with cobblestones they stopped at a tall metal gate. Thomas passed back his keys to Pete. "Open it for me, please," he said softly. "This is home."

Pete jumped out, went around to the gate and undid the heavy padlock. She swung the gate in, and Thomas drove through, parking in the narrow space in front of a three-story hovel. Laundry hung drying outside the open windows on the second and third floors. Several bags of garbage were piled in a corner.

Pete closed and locked the door.

"Be it ever so humble," Thomas said, and he slumped forward.

McGarvey managed to grab his shoulder and pull him back before he hit the horn. Blood had poured down his side and covered the seat.

Pete immediately returned, and between them, they managed to get the barely conscious Thomas out of the cab and to the front door of the house.

"Wafa," Thomas said softly.

The door was unlocked, and half carrying, half dragging Thomas into what had been a spotlessly clean front room, they stopped short. This room and what they could see of the living room through a beaded archway had been ransacked. A woman, her dress hiked up to her waist, her underwear torn away, lay dead. Her throat had been slit, blood pooling like a halo around her head.

FIFTY-EIGHT

Haaris could not remember the last time he had slept, and though he was weary, at this moment he wasn't sleepy. In fact, his mind felt as sharp as it ever had; the feeling was surreal, almost as if he were on a coke high.

Today was the day it would begin. All of his planning over the past five years was coming to fruition. His name and his high position within the CIA, and even more deliciously, his close relationship with the president of the United States, would strike a blow against the West that would be worse than a thousand 9/11's. The very foundations of American prestige around the world would be diminished, as would those of her closest allies, the British—all the bastards at Eton who had used him so hard and who now were in positions of power in Whitehall.

On top of that Pakistan, the country that had turned its back on him when he was a child, and had so foolishly misspent its energy and resources on a stupid religious war with India, would pay dearly.

Standing at the windows in the president's office—the same spot from which he had watched the crowds gather in what seemed like an age ago—watching the start of the dawn, he felt for just that moment like Gandhi. The man had started out as the great pacifier, giving up nearly everything to ensure that India's Muslims and Hindus could learn to live in peace.

He'd been wrong, of course; and as a result Pakistan was born. And now it was the Messiah's turn. He would reunite the two countries in fire. And when it was finished the world order would have taken a paradigm shift.

Not bad, he thought, for a peasant without parents. He threw his head back and began to laugh, all the way from his gut. It wasn't a good feeling, just relief that the end was at hand.

His encrypted cell phone buzzed. It was an out-of-breath Rajput.

"We have trouble coming our way."

"It's too late for that," Haaris said. He felt as if he were in a dreamlike state. Nothing could touch him. His will was supreme.

"Listen to me. Parks managed to kill his interrogator and three others and escape."

"He won't get far. When you find him, kill him."

"You don't understand. He had help. Someone shut down the building's surveillance system long enough for him to get out of the interview cell, before they turned it back on."

"The system isn't hardened, I warned you about it before. Doesn't change anything; he won't get far."

"Our entire system crashed for precisely sixty seconds. My people tell me such a thing is impossible. Yet it happened. Worse than that they believe that a virus has been implanted in the mainframe so that such a thing can happen again. It has made us vulnerable."

"Go back to the factory default settings. Start all over again."

"You still don't understand. It gives them access to operational details. *Your* operation."

"Nothing vital could have been included."

"No, but enough for the right program to unravel it with time."

"With time," Haaris said, but something suddenly struck him, completely dashing his euphoria. "How exactly was the system crashed? Was it simply a power failure? And are you sure about a virus?"

"It wasn't a power failure. Embedded in the virus is a warning that the system will go down again later this morning, and this time it could be permanent."

"Backup systems?"

"All have been infected."

"You have experts."

"To this point they have no idea where to turn," Rajput said. "And that in itself is an extraordinary admission. This isn't the work of some ordinary hacker. Whoever is doing this to us is a genius."

Traffic was building on Constitution Avenue, both vehicular as well as pedestrian. A normal workday was beginning. Functionaries out and about the business of governing 180 million–plus people through a difficult transition. Glad souls, many of them, sad souls, others.

"Rencke," Haaris said, almost as a half whisper.

"Who?"

"Otto Rencke. One of the only men in the world—maybe the only man—who could pull off something like this. He's the CIA's resident computer genius, and he's a close personal friend of Kirk McGarvey's."

"If that's true, how do we stop him?" Rajput demanded.

"You don't, but that's not the most important thing."

It was the look in the journalist's eyes that had been bothersome. There'd been too much confidence in them, or at least a different kind of confidence. Real journalists asked questions; Parks had made challenges. Journalists were gatherers of information, storytellers. Parks had the feral posture of a killer.

"What are you talking about?"

"It's my fault. I missed it. Travis Parks is not the man's real name."

"We know that."

"He's Kirk McGarvey and he came here to kill me."

The line was dead silent for a long time. When Rajput came back he sounded determined. "At least we know who we're really dealing with. We found the jeep he stole and almost certainly the person or persons helping him. One of our helicopters was shot down on Murree Road just south of here."

"What'd they report?"

"Nothing."

"Call out all of your resources, priority one. Kill them on sight."

"We're already on it."

"But, General, listen to me very carefully. Send your best people, and a lot of them, because McGarvey isn't a man who'll be so easy to kill."

"We'll need to hold off."

"Absolutely not," Haaris said, his anger rising. "We have a timetable and we will stick with it. All three packages will be delivered across the border as we planned."

"Too much can go wrong."

"We have come too far to stop now. After Quetta it was too late to quit, because sooner or later it's bound to leak what actually happened up there."

"Yes, and someone like Rencke will put two and two together."

"But not the how or the where or the when," Haaris said.

"I'm not sure," Rajput replied.

"I am," Haaris said. "The next step happens now."

"What next step happens now?" the mufti asked from the doorway.

Haaris pocketed the phone as he turned. The Taliban spokesman, who was sharing the Aiwan with Haaris, stood in his full dress, including his head covering. He'd just come from morning prayers and his eyes were at peace.

Haaris smiled pleasantly. "Prayers this morning were comforting."

The mufti chuckled. "Save me," he said. "What next step?"

"The transfers begin this evening."

"Everything has been arranged?"

"Yes. I want you to get word to your people in Quetta."

"You do me an injustice, Messiah," the mufti said. "All three packages have been waiting at the American and British trucking depots in Peshawar from the beginning."

Haaris couldn't hide his surprise. "I wasn't told."

"No reason. You and Rajput own this part of Pakistan, we own the north. Even you cannot imagine our reach."

"There have been no suspicions?"

"The packages are radiologically sealed and hidden in boxes marked *hazardous*. No one will touch them until they reach their destinations in a few days."

Haaris nodded. Even McGarvey was helpless to stop them.

"And now it's time for me to talk to my people again. Tell them who is really to blame for their woes."

"You mean *our* people," the mufti said.

"My people," Haaris said. He took out a silenced Glock and shot the mufti in the middle of the forehead.

FIFTY-NINE

Thomas sunk to his knees next to his wife's body and arranged her clothing to cover her nakedness. Tears streamed down his face. The bullet wound in his back was merely oozing now. He had lost a lot of blood; his complexion was milky white.

"Is there someplace else for you to go?" McGarvey asked. "They know about you."

"It's not what you think. The ISI didn't do this. It is our neighbors, the men from the teahouse at the corner. They resent my marriage to Wafa. I'm not a Pakistani. They've taught me a lesson."

"Do you want us to go after them?" Pete asked.

"It wouldn't bring her back."

"You won't be safe here," Pete said.

"I won't be safe from myself anywhere," Thomas

said. He pulled out his pistol. He looked up. "Both of you need to get out of here. If you can get to the Marriott, call Austin, he'll arrange for the the airlift across the border."

"We're not leaving you," Pete said. She looked to McGarvey. "Tell him, Mac."

"Don't be stupid. There's not a fucking thing you can do here for either of us. You're on a mission," said Thomas.

"Goddamnit," Pete cursed.

"He's right," McGarvey said. "The two days are nearly up; whatever's supposed to happen will go down today."

"We can't just leave him."

"Yes," McGarvey said.

He took Pete's sat phone, called Otto and explained the situation.

"Sit tight, I'll have Austin send somebody for you," Rencke said. "You'll be safe waiting at the embassy. The chopper can pick you guys up there after midnight."

"Pete and Thomas are going to hole up at the embassy; I have something else to finish," McGarvey said. He had a fair idea what was going to happen sometime this morning, sometime soon, but something else nagged at him. Something he was missing, something they were all missing, had been from the beginning, and it was driving him nuts.

"What are you talking about, *kemo sabe*? Every gun in town is looking for you. And by now Haaris has probably figured out who's screwing with the ISI's mainframe, and once he figures out that it's me, he'll have to know who you are."

"They'll expect me to take refuge in the embassy," McGarvey said. "They won't bother about Pete as long as she's not with me. But they'll keep watch until I show up. Every car, truck, delivery van, anyone showing up on foot, will be searched."

"I'm not going to leave you," Pete said.

"Haaris is going to make another announcement, first on radio and TV, and then he's going to make an appearance on the front balcony of the Aiwan."

"The announcement was made five minutes ago," Otto said. "He's going to speak to the people in person and reveal Pakistan's true enemies."

"*Enemies*, plural?"

"Yeah."

"The crazy bastard's engineered another nine-eleven."

"There's more. One of my darlings picked up a brief mention in the ISI's mainframe about weapons inventories. We took out eighty-seven of their nukes and we know where most of the rest are depoted, but four are missing from Quetta's list. The Taliban detonated one, so that leaves three unaccounted for. If the inventory is accurate."

"London's on the list. He's got an ax to grind because of how they treated him as a kid."

"That'd make him insane as well as brilliant," Otto said. "A bad combination."

"Tell Page what we think might be coming our way and have him inform Sir John." Sir John Notesworthy was head of the British Secret Intelligence Service.

"What about the president?"

"That's her call," McGarvey said. "But I don't think this'll wait for a diplomatic solution."

"You're going ahead with the op," Otto said. "You're going to show up at the Aiwan and try to take him out. With what? You don't have a sniper rifle, so it'll have to be a pistol shot, which means short range."

"It has to be that way."

"Goddamnit, why, Mac? You might get close enough to him to pull it off, but afterwards you'll never get out of there. The mob will tear you apart."

"He's almost certainly compartmentalized the entire thing, which means he's the only one who knows all the details."

"He won't talk to you," Otto said.

"I think he will," McGarvey said. "Now get on it, but, listen, Otto, keep everything low-key. I suspect that he still has a go-to on Campus."

"Your name or the op haven't been mentioned. The list is very tight."

"I know, but if word gets out that we're taking a special interest in incoming flights and ships, especially to DC, New York and London—and if I can't get to him in time—his plans will change. He could postpone everything for a week or a month, even a year. We couldn't keep up the tightened security posture forever."

Otto was silent for a long time, and Pete looked stricken.

"I'm getting word to Austin," Otto finally said. "I don't like this, Mac."

"Do you think I do?" McGarvey asked.

McGarvey borrowed a pair of loose trousers and a knee-length shirt from Thomas, and armed with Pete's Glock and a spare magazine of ammunition he came back downstairs to where she was finishing bandaging Thomas's wound.

"Good luck, pal," Thomas said, his voice strong. He was holding up well. Hate was a powerful motivator.

"Nothing I can do for you unless you go to the embassy with Pete."

"They'd think I was you, and we wouldn't get within a block of the place. Then both of us would be in the shit."

"I'll have somebody come back for you after it's settled," Pete said.

Thomas actually smiled. "Sounds good."

Pete came outside with McGarvey. "I understand what you're doing, though I can't approve. Your chances are slim to none, and you know it."

McGarvey shrugged. "I've faced worse odds."

"I want you to know something first."

"Don't say it."

"Nothing you can do to stop me, Kirk. But the fact of the matter is that I love you."

McGarvey didn't want to hear it, not from Pete, not from any woman. At night when he dreamed it was always of Katy. On the sailboat at anchor; at home in her gazebo on the Intracoastal Waterway on Casey Key; in Washington, Paris, Berlin, Toyko, once even Moscow and another time, Beijing. She'd wanted to see some of the places he'd been.

"So long as no one is shooting at us," she'd said.

But it hadn't lasted, of course. There'd been the *of course* almost from the beginning. All the women he had loved, including his daughter, had been taken from him because of what he did, because of who he was, who he had always been.

"I know that you feel something for me," Pete said.

McGarvey looked away.

"I want to hear you say it. Just once."

"No."

"Even if you don't mean it, Kirk."

He looked at her. "Not yet," he said. "It's the best I can do for now."

She smiled. "It'll do," she said.

SIXTY

Haaris, in his full regalia, including the voice-altering collar, sat behind the president's desk watching a replay on a laptop of his canned announcement, which was being broadcast through just about every media outlet in the world.

The building's staff was at a bare minimum, most of them security officers forbidden to come above the ground floor. No real work of government was being done from here; Rajput handled the day-to-day business of the country, and he was doing a reasonable job, considering the difficult circumstances.

Except for the business with Kirk McGarvey.

"We have come to a new juncture in Pakistan's future, you and I," his image on the monitor was saying. "One that I must apologize for not seeing. The signs were there for me to see even in my blindness."

Haaris smiled. Politics was theater. Even, certainly, American presidents had always known it, especially Reagan, who'd been the consummate White House actor. But his had been an excellent presidency because of it. First, he had known how to hire bright people. Second, he had listened to them. And third, he played well on television.

"I have a way forward for us. Not with guns but with hope. With understanding."

The mufti's body lay where it had fallen, on its back, very little blood from the head shot, its arms splayed, one leg over the other.

"For us there will be no Shiite-Sunni war. We will not become another Iraq, dominated by the U.S. Our future is what we will make of it. And I promise that our future will be a bright one, beginning today."

He got up and went to the double doors to the

balcony. Already people were streaming onto Constitution Avenue. Many were coming from the direction of the parliament building, the National Library and the Supreme Court to the south, as well as the Secretariat to the north. But many came from the west, starting to choke rush hour traffic on Jinnah Avenue,

This time the crowd would be bigger than for his first public appearance. They wanted answers, and he would give them what they wanted.

He phoned Rajput. "Have you found him?"

"We think that he's gone to ground in Rawalpindi at the house of one of our police informers, who works for the CIA but for us as well. We've tolerated the man because he's given us good intel from time to time and we handed him bits of disinformation that we know got back to Austin's people."

"Do not try to take him into custody; this is very important, General. Kill him on sight. Am I clear?"

"Now that we know who he really is, he could be invaluable."

"Am I clear?"

"Despite your clever speech this morning, you are not running this country. You are nothing more than a traitor—three times removed. First against Pakistan, the country of your birth. Second, against Great Britain, the country that educated you. And third, the U.S., the country that gave you employment and listened to your advice. Now where does your loyalty lie?"

"Look out the window," Haaris said.

"I am at this moment. But what if you were to be exposed as an American spy?"

"Are you getting cold feet?"

"I don't know what you're up to, exactly what sort of a deal you've made with the TTP, but I think that it has gone too far. The Taliban have never been our friends. We have used them on the Kashmir border to keep the Indian army occupied, but nothing else."

"Just as the Americans used bin Laden and al Qaeda to keep the Russians distracted in Afghanistan. Need I remind you of that outcome?"

"You need not," Rajput flared. "Perhaps we will take care of Mr. McGarvey, as you suggest, and then perhaps we will come for you before it's too late."

"You would fall with me," Haaris said. "But if you stay the course the outcome will be more than even you could imagine."

"That's what worries me."

"Your name is written all over this operation."

"What operation?" Rajput shouted.

"To strike a blow against Pakistan's real enemies."

"Save me," Rajput said after a beat. It was the same thing the mufti had said just before his death.

Haaris sat sipping tea at the desk for a full half hour, before he went back to the windows. The crowd had swelled enormously, completely filling the broad avenue for as far as he could see. At least eight or ten television vans had set up at the edges of the crowd not far from the Aiwan's security fence. He picked out ABC, CBS, the BBC and Al-Jazeera, along with others.

The international media were here for one of the biggest shows on the planet, which to this point had not involved wholesale bloodshed. It was something unique.

Before dawn he had set up the sound system on the balcony but had not called up the technicians to drag out the Jumbotron screen. It would be enough for his people to see him in person, even if at a distance, and to hear his voice.

He went to the controls and switched on the power, then took the still-bloody machete he'd used to decapitate Barazani from the closet.

As early as six years ago, he'd advised the Pakistani government to strengthen its alliance with the Taliban but to watch them very carefully should the same thing happen as happened with al Qaeda in Afghanistan. The CIA had gone along with him, as had the White House. It was to the Americans' advantage to nurture Pakistan's reliance on their military aid so that the U.S. could fight the war against the Afghani insurgents who took refuge across the border. Pakistan needed the money to fight the Taliban, which had turned on them, as Haaris had predicted they would.

"And here we are," he said to the mufti's corpse. "Come round full circle to the final act, which none of you in your wildest dreams could have predicted."

He heaved the body over onto its stomach, and raising the machete nearly severed the head from the neck, the sharp blade crunching through the spinal column at the base of the skull. He had to strike two more times before he managed to cut through the cartilage and other tissue until the mufti's head came completely free from the body.

Tossing the machete aside, he picked up the head by the hair above the base of the skull. The mufti's black cap fell off, and Haaris awkwardly managed to put it back in place before he walked to the doors, opened them and stepped out onto the balcony.

Immediately a roar rose from the crowd.

"Messiah! Messiah! Messiah!"

Haaris raised the mufti's head high.

A sigh swept across the mob.

"This is the face of our enemy," he shouted. "It is they who exploded the nuclear weapon near Quetta. Their intention was to kill as many of our people as possible. But our soldiers gave their lives to make sure the death toll was small."

An uneasy silence came over the broad avenue.

"This is just the first blow. There must be more. We need to eliminate the terrorists from our midst. We can no longer abide the murders of innocent civilians. Ordinary people like you. The killings must stop now!"

"Messiah!" a lone voice near the front cried.

"We must make a jihad against the killers of our babies."

Several other voices joined the chorus. "Messiah!"

"But the Taliban is just a tool used by our real enemies!"

"Messiah!" The chant rose.

"The Taliban are the messengers sent to us from New Delhi!"

The cries were louder.

"Allies of America! Do not forget! Never forget!"

SIXTY-ONE

McGarvey watched from the partially open gate as the Cadillac Escalade that Austin had sent for Pete turned the corner at the end of the block. The neighborhood was strangely quiet for this time of the morning, but Otto had told him that Haaris was making another major announcement at the Aiwan. The crowds were enormous, people drawn from all around Islamabad and even down here from Rawalpindi.

"I'm not leaving Pakistan without you," she'd told him before she got into the SUV. Austin had sent two stern-looking men to retrieve her.

"Are you coming with us, sir?" one of them asked.

"No. But whatever happens, don't stop for any-one."

"Good luck."

"You too," Mac had said.

He went back into the house to check on Thomas, who lay slumped over his wife's body. He was dead, his hand holding hers.

A lot of sirens began to close in from the north, as Mac went outside to Thomas's Mercedes. Two bullet holes had punctured the driver's-side door, and a lot of blood stained the MB-Tex upholstery.

He found a prayer rug in the trunk to cover the blood, pushed the gate all the way open and drove out, just as the first of two jeeps, followed by two troop-transport trucks, rounded the corner. One of the jeeps was fitted with a rear-mounted sixty-caliber machine gun.

Mac just made it to the end of the block before the gunner opened fire, the shots going wide as he turned down a narrow side street of vendors and tiny shops. Only a few people were out and about and they scattered as he raced past, laying on the horn.

Thomas's house was in a section called Gullistan Colony, dense with homes and small businesses, all serviced by a rat warren of streets. One neighborhood consisted of hovels, while two blocks later the houses were mostly upscale, compared to most others in the city.

He easily outran the jeeps and troop transports, but other sirens were beginning to converge from the north and east. And now they knew the car he was driving.

Suddenly he came to the end of a block, the street opening onto a broad thoroughfare across from which was what looked like parkland, trees and grassy hills but little or no traffic. It was as if the entire city had been drained of people.

A troop truck appeared around a sweeping curve a quarter mile to the north, and the jeeps and trucks that had followed him from Thomas's house were behind him.

He accelerated directly across the highway, crashing across a drainage ditch and sliding sideways down a grassy slope, where at the bottom he just missed several trees, finally clipping one with his right front fender, taking out everything from the headlights back to the door post, and shattering that half of the windshield.

A machine gun opened fire from the highway behind him, several rounds slamming into the trunk of the Mercedes, before he came to a winding drive through the park and turned north.

The busted fender was rubbing against the tire, which within fifty yards shredded, sending him into a sharp skid to the left, off the road, through more trees and finally crashing through some thick brush and deep grass onto a golf course fairway.

Suddenly he knew exactly where he was. The first main highway was the National Park Road, and he'd managed to make his way through Ayub National Park and onto the Rawalpindi Golf Club course. Otto had given him satellite views of the entire twin-cities area of Islamabad and Rawalpindi. He'd not had the time to learn much more than the layout of the main roads and their features, but this place stuck out in his mind because it seemed out of place. An upscale park and golf course in what was mostly a slum city didn't fit.

The course was empty, and slipping and sliding, tearing up the turf, the Mercedes barely under control, he made his way to the maintenance sheds, where he drove directly into one of the garages, slamming into the back wall before he could stop.

A uniformed cop, drawing his pistol, a radio in his free hand, came around the corner in a dead run as McGarvey jumped out of the car.

The cop shouted something in Punjabi that almost certainly meant *stop*.

McGarvey jogged to the left, his leg nearly collapsing under him as the frightened cop fired three shots as fast as he could pull the trigger, all of the rounds slamming into the side of the car.

The sirens remained off to the east and north now, but they were getting closer, and back in the woods someone was firing a machine gun. His pursuers were all on hair triggers. They knew about him, and their orders were simple: shoot to kill.

Drawing the Glock, McGarvey fired two snap shots, both of them hitting the cop center mass, dropping the man.

The shed was filled with lawn mowers and other equipment to maintain the course, but just outside around the corner, a ratty blue Toyota pickup was parked, a key in the ignition. A pair of tools for taking plugs out of greens for hole placements were in the bed, along with a couple of bags of what were probably weed killer, and a large tub of green sand.

More firing came from the woods to the south now.

McGarvey closed the shed's door, then laying the pistol on the seat next to him, started the pickup and headed up an access road that eventually led past the clubhouse and onto another broad thoroughfare, this one the GT Road.

There was some traffic here, most of it commercial, and he stayed with the flow, constantly checking his rearview mirrors.

Another jeep, followed by a troop truck, came

from the north at a high rate of speed, and traffic parted to let them pass.

For now the search was concentrated on the golf course. But in the confusion, with all the shooting at shadows, it would take them some time before they calmed down enough to find the Mercedes and the dead cop in the shed, and perhaps even longer to realize that the Toyota was missing and start looking for it.

The massive crowds were already beginning to disperse by the time McGarvey made it up to Islamabad's Red Section, but they were still heavy enough on Constitution Avenue that he had to take Bank Road across to Ispana, behind the Supreme Court, before he could get anywhere near the Aiwan.

He pulled over across from the National Library and called Otto. The battery on Pete's phone was low and he had trouble getting through.

"It's over, Mac," Otto said. "He made his speech and he left."

"I can't hear you."

"Wait," Otto said, and a moment later the connection cleared. "Your battery is about flat, I gave you a temporary fix. Haaris is gone. He told the people that the Taliban was the tool and India was the real enemy. He held up the mufti's head, just like he did with Barazani's."

"Goddamnit, where is he?" McGarvey demanded, his frustration nearly overwhelming.

"I don't know. He left the balcony, and within ten minutes a convoy of nine cars and four panel vans took off from the Aiwan's rear gate and headed in different directions. My darlings are tracking most of them, but he has the ephemeris of our spy bird, so he knows where to hide. He could be anywhere."

"Still at the Aiwan?"

"I don't think so," Otto said. "But you're going to have to get out of Dodge ASAP. The cops, the ISI, the army, everybody's gunning for you."

"What about Pete?"

"She's safe at the embassy. A SEAL Team Six squad is coming by chopper around midnight to pick her up. The thing is, you're not going to get anywhere near the embassy. They have the place completely surrounded. What's your situation now? Pete said you screwed up your leg or something."

"I'll live," McGarvey said, and he told him what had happened from the time he'd left Thomas's place. "I'll try to make it up to Peshawar."

"You won't get that far. They'll figure out that's where you'll run. You need to ditch the truck and go to ground someplace safe until the ST Six guys can get to you."

McGarvey looked up toward the rear of the parliament building, just beyond which was the Aiwan. He had failed. Haaris had been one step ahead of him—of them all—from the beginning. Now the deadline was here. It was bitter. But Pete was safe.

"Mac?"

"I'm going to the ISI apartment Judith Anderson took me to. It has to be clear by now. They'll never expect me to go back."

"Don't leave the truck anywhere within a mile of the place," Otto said. "And keep the phone with you; especially if you have to move, the guys can home in on it. But switch it off. I gave you a boost but the battery is still low."

McGarvey didn't bother asking how the phone

could be located even when it was off; if Otto said it could be done, it was a fact.

"The important thing is, we're getting you out," Otto said.

Not important at all, McGarvey thought.

PART
FOUR

The Countdown

SIXTY-TWO

Walt Page's limo showed up at the White House East Gate a few minutes after six in the morning and was waved directly through. The DCI was met at the door by one of Miller's aides, who without a word took him directly across to the Situation Room in the West Wing.

The president was sitting at one end of the long conference table, some of the Security Council members gathered around her. They were watching images of Islamabad's Red Section on a large flat-panel screen on the opposite wall.

It was just after three in the afternoon there, and crowds were rioting. Cars and trucks had been set on fire, tall iron fences around the Interior Ministry and adjacent Secretariat had been torn down in some places, and army troops were dispersed in defensive rings.

The crowd had been fired on, many bodies were strewn about the streets, and as Page walked in, a pair of Chinese-made Al-Khalid main battle tanks rolled up Constitution Avenue.

The president looked over. "Is this what McGarvey warned us would happen?" Her tone was brittle.

"I don't know," Page said, taking his place across the table from her. "The Messiah's turnabout came as a complete surprise to all of us."

"Are you up to date on the present situation?"

"As of twenty minutes ago, about the same time the army opened fire."

"I meant with India," the president said. "Their military has gone on full alert. Air force bases at Ayni, Farkhor and Charbatia are on total lockdown, all leaves and passes have been cancelled and all personnel ordered to return to duty."

Admiral Altman, the chairman of the Joint Chiefs, had been on the phone. He hung up. "I've just received confirmation that the *Vikramaditya* is moving from its base at Karwar at a high rate of speed up the Arabian Sea directly toward Karachi." The ship was the Indian navy's newest aircraft carrier. She was capable of launching a full-scale nuclear attack on her own. "A pair of their Kolkata destroyers are accompanying her and we have to assume at least three of her Kilo-class subs are acting as screening vessels."

"It's a goddamned act of war," Susan Kalley said.

"It's a move toward self-defense, according to Gauas Kar," the president said. Mammohn Singh was Indian's prime minister. "And I can't say that if I were in his shoes I wouldn't do the same thing."

"How about Rajput?" Page asked.

"He won't return my calls."

"Don Powers is still over there, and he can't get through either," Secretary of State John Fay said.

"We don't know what it means, but since the Messiah's beheading of the TTP's mufti and declaring India as Pakistan's primary enemy, the Pakistan military has only raised its threat level to DEFCON Three," the admiral said.

"It could mean they're sending India—and us—a message," Page said. He actually wished that Dave Haaris was here to help them sort through the situation.

"What's that?" Miller asked.

"The Messiah does not speak for Pakistan."

"You're talking about a break in their relationship?" Kalley asked.

"My people think it could be a partial explanation for the rioting. Our embassy has been surrounded, but Austin said it looked to him like the military wasn't trying to keep them bottled up. Instead it looked as if they had thrown up a protective barrier," Page replied.

"Two nuclear powers on the brink and your people have zeroed in on the Pakistani army's effort to protect our embassy?" Kalley exclaimed.

Her question didn't deserve an answer. Page said nothing.

"Have you been in touch with Mr. McGarvey since the Messiah's speech?" the president asked.

"Not directly, but he's evidently in a safe place somewhere in the city, until we can get a SEAL Team Six squad to pick him up, along with another of our agents who managed to get to the embassy."

One of the tanks on the flat screen pulled up in front of the Aiwan, its main gun pointed toward the rioters on Jinnah Avenue.

"If they don't calm down soon this could turn out worse than Cairo," Fay said.

"You said they arrested McGarvey, and yet he's someplace safe in Islamabad?" Kalley asked. "It means that somehow he managed to escape."

"That's what I understand."

"I've read his file, Walt. I know what this guy has done in the past. It's why the president hired him to do the job over there."

"Which he warned against."

"Yes, unintended consequences," Kalley said. "How many people has he killed this time?"

"I don't have that number," Page said. "He'll be debriefed when he gets back."

"More than one?" the president's national security adviser pressed.

"I don't know," Page repeated. "The point is, we're not going to leave him there. We sent him to do a job and he took it on to the best of his abilities, no matter how disagreeable he thought it was. Well, it didn't work."

"The man was facing the entire ISI," the admiral said. "The fact that he managed to sidestep the bastards has to count for something."

"Get him out of there, priority one," Miller said.

"Thank you," Page replied.

"But he stays out of politics," Miller said with a slight smile. "It's not his game."

Saul Santarelli's tall, lean frame appeared in the doorway. "Sorry I'm late, Madam President." He was chief of National Intelligence. The agency had been created after 9/11 to do what the CIA had been designed to do—and had been doing—since after World War II. He was dark-skinned, with short-cropped steel-gray hair and the nearly constant look on his face as if he had the weight of America's security on his shoulders, and his shoulders alone. He was a politician, not an intelligence officer.

Page and he did not get along.

"Are you up to date?" Miller asked.

Santarelli took his place and handed a leather-bound briefing book across the table. "My people put it together and I looked through it on the way over." He glanced at Page. "Good stuff from your Watch, but I was surprised to see that McGarvey was in the game over there. I'd not been briefed on his mission."

"No," Page said. "Unless I'm needed here, Madam President, I'll see to retrieving my people."

"I want to talk to him the moment he gets back,"

Miller said. "I want to personally thank him for what he tried to do for me, despite the overwhelming odds."

Page glanced at the flat-screen monitor. The second tank had taken up position a half a block south of the first, its main gun pointed straight down Constitution Avenue. No one except McGarvey had seen anything like this coming their way.

"Be careful of what you wish for, you might just get it," he sometimes warned. Unintended consequences. Blowback.

Page got to his feet. "Thank you, Madam President."

SIXTY-THREE

Assistant Secretary of Defense Robert Fishbine was at the end of an unannounced visit to the U.S. training base at Jalalabad, and the moment he was appraised of the situation with McGarvey and Pete he ordered his Gulfstream held until they showed up. He and his two assistants had been ordered back to DC. That was shortly before midnight.

"What time can we expect the team to get them up here?" he asked the navy lieutenant commander in charge of the SEAL Team Six presence, which had been reduced to almost nothing after the nuclear-neutralizing incursion into Pakistan.

"They're making the pickups now. Should be an hour out, unless they run into trouble, sir."

"We'll wait."

"We were told that your orders said now, sir. Your aircraft and crew are standing by."

"We've developed an unexplained problem with one of the engines," Fishbine said. He'd worked as a military liaison to the CIA during the brief period when McGarvey was the DCI. He didn't know the man well, but what he did know was all positive.

"Yes, sir," the lieutenant commander said, grinning.

The assistant sec def had served in the marines as an enlisted man, until he'd retired and completed his law degree at Northwestern. The president had appointed him to the Department of Defense two years earlier, and it was broadly accepted that he would take over the top spot soon because he was a decisive man who wasn't afraid of making decisions.

"Have they been hurt?"

"Unknown at this point, but there is a medic aboard the chopper."

The battery on McGarvey's cell phone was almost completely dead. For the last couple of hours he'd stood at the fifth-floor window of Judith Anderson's apartment looking down Luqman Hakeem Road toward the Al Habib Market.

Here the neighborhood was quiet, but elsewhere across the city, especially to the northwest toward the Red Section, there had been a lot of gunfire, several explosions and a couple of what sounded like tank rounds.

Television service across all the channels had been shut down. And since around eight traffic had dried up, and even the building had quieted down.

The cell phone switched on and rang once. It was Otto.

"They have Pete, and the chopper is less than five minutes from you. But the ISI apparently got a tip where you were. At least three troop trucks are about the same distance away. It'll be close. They're going to have to fast-rope down and pick you up on the roof. Go!"

McGarvey pocketed the phone, left the apartment and hurried to the stairwell at the end of the corridor.

An older man came out of one of the other apartments and immediately started to shout something.

McGarvey pulled out his pistol and turned around. The man, dressed in baggy pants and shirtsleeves, held a cell phone to one ear and a Kalashnikov in his right hand, the barrel pointed toward the floor.

McGarvey gestured with the Glock for the guy to go back inside.

For a longish moment the Pakistani stopped talking. But then he shouted something into the phone and the barrel of the rifle started to come up.

McGarvey fired one shot, and the man's legs collapsed under him, the assault rifle spraying a quick burst into the wall about knee height before it clattered to the floor.

Immediately a woman inside the apartment began screeching, and what sounded like two young children started to wail.

"Goddamnit," Mac said, half under his breath. He slammed open the stairwell door and raced up to the roof level in time to hear the incoming chopper.

Its lights were out, so it was invisible until it flared directly overhead, about fifteen feet off the roof. Two ropes dropped from the open hatch and two SEALS in full combat gear descended in a rush.

"We're about to get company, sir," one of them said. He tied a loop around McGarvey's waist, and a winch pulled him up.

The other operator went to the edge of the roof. "We've got about five mikes."

"Let's go," the first SEAL shouted.

McGarvey came aboard at the same moment the

chopper dropped down its wheels just inches from the roof.

Both SEALS clambered aboard.

"Go! Go! Go!" one of them shouted, and the stealthy UH-60 Blackhawk leaped into the air, peeling sharply to the north.

Both operators had their weapons at the ready position but the pilot shouted back to hold fire.

Within a minute they were already northwest of the city, heading low and fast directly for the foothills, no sign that the Pakistani air force had put anything up yet to knock them out of the sky.

"Are you all right, sir?" the medic asked, undoing the rope from McGarvey's waist and sitting him down in an aft corner seat just across the cabin from where Pete was strapped in.

"No holes so far," McGarvey told the kid.

"That's a good sign." The medic quickly took his pulse and blood pressure, then shined a small penlight into one eye at a time. "You'll live, sir."

"Glad to hear it."

"But strap in, could be a rough ride."

McGarvey did as he was told. One of the operators looked back, and Mac gave him the thumbs-up. The SEAL nodded.

Pete came out of the shadows, took a headset from a hook on the bulkhead behind her and motioned for McGarvey to do the same.

"They have a Gulfstream standing by for us," she said. "Are you okay?" She was shivering.

"Medic says I'll live, how about you?"

"Austin's not happy."

"Can't blame him."

"Haaris has disappeared. So whatever was supposed to happen never did, unless it's the Taliban riots across the city or the situation with India. Could be war. Powers left earlier this evening, along with some key embassy staffers."

"Any word from Rajput or anyone else in the government or military?"

"Not that I was told, but everyone at the embassy was keeping a lid on things."

It couldn't be over like this; McGarvey could feel something lurking around the corner. Haaris had not gone through all the trouble of setting himself up as the Messiah, and beheading the president and the head of the TTP, simply to foment a possible nuclear exchange with India. It wouldn't do him any good.

Pete stared at him. "I'm glad you're back."

So what would Haaris do? What did Haaris want? Another 9/11 against the U.S.? Maybe England too? The man had terminal cancer with not many months to live, so whatever he had in mind wasn't about his personal safety.

What can you possibly do to a man who had absolutely nothing left to lose?

"Hang on," the copilot shouted back to them. "We have company."

They were well northwest of the city, up in the foothills, and the copilot was on the radio while the pilot dove for the deck, setting down hard in a steep-walled valley lined with big boulders and scrub brush.

Even before the chopper was settled one of the SEAL operators jumped out, ran about ten meters past the nose and shouldered what looked to McGarvey like an American-made Stinger missile. Over the past fifteen or twenty years it had been the most common weapon in Afghanistan other than the Russian AK-47.

There were estimated to be five hundred Stingers

still operational in the field, carried by al-Qaeda, the Taliban and the Mujahideen.

An F-16 jet fighter passed low overhead and the operator fired the missile.

The moment it was airborne the SEAL dropped the launch system and raced back to the helicopter.

The fighter jogged left then right and seconds later the missile struck its tailpipe and the jet exploded.

As soon as the operator was aboard they took off again, flying low and fast.

Pete was smiling. "You sure know how to show a girl a good time," she said to McGarvey.

SIXTY-FOUR

The taxi dropped Dave Haaris off in front of the Connaught's entrance at four-thirty in the afternoon. He'd flown directly to Paris from Istanbul and from there had taken the Chunnel Eurostar to London. He was tired—in part because of the strenuous happenings of the past several days, but also in large measure due to his illness—and he wanted nothing more than to take a hot bath, order up room service and turn in early.

But not yet. There would time enough later to rest. All the time in the world.

He tipped the cabby well and allowed the bellman to carry his single light bag inside, where he handed his passport and Platinum Amex card to the startled clerk.

"Mr. Haaris, we didn't expect you back so soon, sir. Not after the bit of difficulty."

"What difficulty would that be?"

The day manager came out, smiling. "No difficulty at all, Mr. Haaris. Your suite is still available."

"That's fine. I'll be expecting a friend for an early dinner this evening, Say at seven. In the meantime have a bottle of Krug sent to my room. Very cold, if you please."

"Of course, sir."

Upstairs he also tipped the bellman well, and when the man was gone, he stripped and got into the shower, letting the water beat on the back of his neck for a long time. He was bruised on his legs, his right side and on both arms. Dr. Franklin had warned it would happen because of his low blood count, but Haaris had refused treatment to bring it up.

The champagne had already been delivered. He opened it, drank down a glass, then poured another.

In a hotel bathrobe, he checked the street out the window, but if the CIA had picked him up at St. Pancras International, the Eurostar's terminus, they had apparently not followed him here to the hotel. Anyone who thought he was the Messiah was expecting him to be in Islamabad. In the thick of things. Wandering among his people, as he had supposedly done before. Preparing the nation for war with India, while containing the Taliban.

He turned on the television to CNN, which was in the middle of rebroadcasting his latest speech as he held up the severed head of the mufti. The riots and bombings across Pakistan and especially in Rawalpindi and Islamabad, plus the rapidly rising tensions with India, were also the lead stories on the BCC, Al Jazeera and many of the other channels.

Turning the sound down, he poured a third glass of champagne then got an outside line and dialed Tommy Boyle's private number at the embassy.

The chief of station's secretary answered on the first ring. "Who is calling, please?"

Boyle's number was classified, and only a few people in London knew it; almost all of them were government officials who were aware of exactly what he was and would rather talk freely with him than be spied upon.

"David Haaris."

To her credit the secretary hesitated only for a beat. "One moment, Mr. Haaris."

Boyle came on almost instantaneously. "David, I'm surprised to hear from you. You're here in London again?"

"At the Connaught. Wonder if we could have dinner tonight? We have a lot to catch up on."

"We certainly do."

"First off, I need to apologize for the little fiction with Ron Pembroke. I hope you weren't too difficult on him. He's an out-of-work actor."

"I can come over there now."

"I'll meet you in the bar at six," Haaris said. "Dinner at seven. And, Tom, hold off calling Langley. I expect by now that Marty is beside himself."

"Can't promise that. But I'll meet you at six."

"Good enough," Haaris said.

He hung up and went into the bathroom, where he threw up in the toilet, the champagne still cool at the back of his throat. For a long time he sat on the floor, his cheek against the porcelain of the bowl, his head spinning, pain raging through his body from the base of his skull all the way to his backbone and his legs.

"Holding it together is going to become a matter of pain management," Franklin had told him at All Saints. "If you take something for it, you'll not be in agony."

Haaris had smiled faintly. "Nor will my head work properly."

"Only you can decide the balance."

Haaris got up, splashed some cold water on his face and got dressed in highly starched jeans and a white shirt with a button-down collar, plus the British-tailored black blazer. They were the last of his decent Western clothes until he could get back home.

He got his gold watch, cell phone, wallet and other belongings and poured another glass of Krug.

"Alcohol won't do it either," Franklin had warned. "In fact, in a month or so it'll actually make things worse."

Haaris had managed to smile. "There's always pot."

Franklin had returned the smile. "That'll work, for a while."

But for now good wine was the more civilized of his limited options.

Tommy Boyle, tall, thin, lots of angles to his features, walked into the bar at precisely six o'clock. He had been assistant deputy director of operations at Langley when Haaris had first started working for the Company. It was he who'd helped start up the Pakistan Desk. And it was he who'd been best man at Haaris's wedding.

Haaris half rose to greet him and they shook hands.

"How'd Marty take it?"

"Not well," Boyle said. The waiter came and he ordered a martini. "You?"

Haaris held up his champagne glass. He was on his second bottle of Krug, but it was having no effect on him yet.

"Have you been paying attention to the situation in Pakistan?" Boyle asked.

"I've taken a look at CNN and Al Jazeera."

"Where the hell were you? What were you up to?"

"Paris for a day or two, and then Istanbul," Haaris said. "Interesting city."

"Doing what?"

"Getting past Deborah."

Boyle looked away for a moment. "I'm truly sorry about her. Last I heard the police were still looking for her murderer." He shook his head. "Why the imposter?"

"I wanted a few days on my own. If I had stayed here, you know and I know that I would have been recalled to Langley to help straighten out the mess the White House, State Department and Pentagon created. But it was too late. Nothing I could have done, then or now."

Boyle's drink came and he knocked back half of it before the waiter left.

"Another, sir?"

"No," Boyle said, and when the man was gone he shook his head again. "What's your take on the Messiah?"

"I told them that it would be absolutely necessary for someone like him to show up, religious plus secular; but I also warned them that at the very least he would be unpredictable and probably impossible to control."

"Any idea who he is?"

"He was born in Pakistan—the Punjabi accent comes out even though he's done something with his voice. It's not natural. But I suspect that he was probably educated right here in England. You might have your people do a search at least for body types matching his."

"We're already on it. What else?"

"Have Rencke gear up one of his programs for a voice analysis. Might come up with a clue that could help."

"I'm told he started that right after the Messiah's first speech."

"Barazani was a good man but totally ineffective, and from what I saw Rajput isn't doing such a hot job as PM. I assume that he and Miller are talking."

"He's disappeared."

"Who's running the bloody country? The military?"

"For now. But everyone is waiting for the Messiah to show up again and tell them what to do."

Haaris lowered his eyes for a second. This meeting was going almost exactly as he thought it would. All that was left was for Boyle to drop the other shoe. He looked up. "What aren't you telling me, Tom?"

"I've been ordered to have a couple of my guys escort you back to Langley. Technically, you're under arrest."

"On what charge? Desertion of duty because my wife was murdered, and I'm told that I have terminal cancer?"

"Shit. They think that you are the Messiah."

Haaris hid the smile of triumph by throwing his head back and laughing out loud, the effort combined with the champagne making his stomach roil all over again. "It'll be good to get back to work."

SIXTY-FIVE

The Gulfstream heading west was chasing the sun, and the assistant sec def's aircraft landed in Germany at Ramstein for refueling well before dawn. On Pete's insistence McGarvey had managed to catch a few hours' rest, not waking until they took off.

Pete was sound asleep in the seat across the aisle from his, a blanket covering her. Fishbine and one of his assistants were deep in discussion in seats facing each other near the front of the cabin.

McGarvey got up, adjusted Pete's blanket and went forward to the two men.

Fishbine looked up. He seemed pleased. "Good morning, Mr. Director, how are you feeling?"

"Fine. Thanks for the lift."

Fishbine motioned for him to have a seat. The attendant, a young navy chief, came back with a coffee. "This might help," he said. The coffee was laced with brandy.

"Outstanding," McGarvey said. "Maybe you could rustle up a sandwich or something. I haven't had much to eat in the past couple of days."

"Eggs Benedict and hash browns in ten minutes, sir."

"There're some perks to the job," Fishbine said. He motioned for his assistant, a navy lieutenant in ODUs, to leave them.

"I didn't know that you were in Afghanistan," McGarvey said.

"Wasn't made public. I came over to take a closer look after our raids last week and to check if there'd been anything new on the nuclear incident outside Quetta. But I didn't learn a damned thing. Wasted trip. Means just like you I'm heading home to a shit storm."

"You were military liaison to the Company when I was DCI," McGarvey said, suddenly remembering the name. "We've survived shit storms before."

"Indeed," the assistant sec def said. "Miss Boylan briefed me on something you went through. What's your take on the situation?"

"I actually got to meet with the Messiah for just a few minutes. I was undercover as a journalist."

"Good disguise, I would never have recognized you. Did you get anything from him?"

"Nothing worthwhile, except he and the PM knew that I was CIA and considered me enough of a threat to have the ISI arrest and interrogate me."

Fishbine glanced back at Pete, who was still asleep. "She said that you escaped."

"Didn't have much of a choice; they were going to kill me."

"The Messiah beheaded the TTP's mouthpiece and disappeared. And last I heard General Rajput was assassinated and the military took over. But the entire country is falling into civil war and India is doing some serious saber rattling. So what happens next? A nuclear exchange, maybe even all-out war?"

"That'll probably depend on the Messiah."

"What if the son of a bitch wanted this all along? What if he's got a hard-on for all Pakis and just came over to stir the pot? He's sitting somewhere safe now, sipping a mai tai, surrounded by beautiful naked women. His idea of Paradise. Fiddling while Rome burns."

The thought was startling and it caught McGarvey somewhat off guard. "It might be just as simple as that, Mr. Secretary."

"Well, we sure as hell aren't going to put boots on the ground. I just hope that Miller has enough moxie to hold the Indians at bay, and that the Pakistani army can keep the remainder of their nukes out of the hands of the Taliban."

"Four were taken from Quetta."

"What?"

"Four tactical weapons, all of them mated, went missing from Quetta. One of them was detonated, leaves three at large, and almost certainly in the hands of the Taliban or one of their factions."

"Yeah, ain't it a bitch?" Fishbine said softly.

Fishbine went aft to the compact communications center in its own compartment.

Five minutes later McGarvey's breakfast arrived, along with a bottle of water and a refill on his coffee and brandy. When he was finished the assistant sec def still had not returned, and Pete had not awakened.

It was just possible that Fishbine's explanation was correct. Perhaps Haaris had merely shown up in Pakistan to stir the pot; maybe his mission had simply been to lead his country of birth first into a civil war and then into an all-out nuclear war with India.

But why? Where was his personal gain? Simply revenge for being mistreated? But that hadn't been the case in Pakistan, and in any event, he'd been taken to England by an uncle and had led a privileged life there that had continued when he moved to the States and become a U.S. citizen. His position at the CIA was top level, and he was even a regular at the White House.

A man of his education, intelligence and charm could well have eventually become the CIA's director or even the director of National Intelligence. Except for his illness.

What was so important to him that he was willing to spend his last few months doing it?

McGarvey went back to his seat, strapped in and went to sleep again.

Pete woke him. "We're about forty minutes out of Andrews; how are you feeling?"

"Glad to be getting home," McGarvey said, gathering himself. "But still no answers."

"I talked to Otto. He and Louise are coming out to pick us up; they're bringing fresh clothes and a razor for you. Nothing much I can do about my hair, though."

"You look good to me."

Pete grinned. "Thanks."

"Actually, when it comes to your hair—"

"I don't want to hear it," Pete said.

McGarvey went to the head and splashed some water on his face. His eyes were a little bloodshot and it was obvious he'd been under some sort of duress recently. But except for his uncertainty about Haaris's plans he felt in good shape.

Pete had a cup of the chief's coffee for him.

Fishbine came back to them. "I talked to Bill, and he's taking what you said over to the White House." William Spencer was the secretary of defense. "I don't mind admitting that he was just as concerned as I am that the Taliban might have the nukes. We thought it was a possibility, but you seem to think it's a fact."

Otto and Louise came aboard as soon as the pilot taxied over to a hangar, shut down the engines and the chief opened the hatch and lowered the stairs. They brought clothes, even underwear, and something for Pete to use in her hair that didn't require a shower.

Mac let Pete use the head first.

"Haaris showed up in London," Otto said. He was perched on the armrest of the seat across from McGarvey. "Denied he was the Messiah, claimed he was in Paris and Istanbul recovering from his wife's murder, and told Boyle that he was ready to get back to work."

Nothing surprised McGarvey any longer. "Where is he now?"

"About one hour out. Boyle put him under arrest, at Marty's insistence, and sent a couple of embassy types with him. Page and just about everyone else is on Campus, not only because of the situation in Pakistan but because both you and Haaris are back. The president wants to meet with both of you ASAP."

"Keep Dave away from her. No telling what he's capable of doing."

"What about you?" Otto asked.

"I assume we're going to Langley to answer some questions, but afterwards I'll have a few things to tell the president. Stuff she's not likely going to like."

"I want to be on the team interviewing Haaris," Pete said.

"And I want to listen in," Mac said.

SIXTY-SIX

The two minders Boyle had sent with Haaris handed him over to a pair of Langley muscle who'd shown up at Andrews with a Cadillac Escalade. Actually, it felt good to be back, not because this was home—he'd never felt that—but because this was the end game that had been in the planning stages for more than five years.

By now the three packages had arrived at their points of entry. Two had been sent to the joint base at Dover and the third to Farnborough, outside London. They would be isolated with other hazardous materials.

Messy, full of potential troubles just waiting to happen. But the outcome was inevitable. The firing circuits had been connected to cell phones. Any incoming call would immediately start the detonation cycles. All three of the phones had the same number.

He'd given his word not to be difficult, so he'd not been handcuffed by Boyle's people. And the pair from Langley saw no need for restraints either. Haaris was one of theirs.

"Gentleman, thanks for the ride across the pond," he told the two from London. "Must you turn around and get back immediately?"

"I'm afraid so, sir," the one named Masters said. They were both kids, barely in their late twenties.

"Too bad, I would like to have taken you to dinner this evening," Haaris said. They shook hands. "My compliments to Mr. Boyle."

All very civilized, Haaris thought, getting into the backseat of the Caddy. But it was happening the way he'd expected. There'd been accusations that he was the Messiah, but there could be no proof of it yet. On top of that he was cooperating, and he had the sympathy vote on two counts—his wife's murder and his own terminal cancer. And sympathy almost always blinded the observer.

They were passed through the gate, and once they were on the ring road, the security officer riding shotgun turned in his seat. "I was told to ask if you needed to stop first at All Saints, sir."

"Thanks, but no. Nothing Franklin can do for me at this point. I'd like to get my debriefing over with.

The situation is spinning out of control and my people need to be on it."

"Yes, sir."

Marty Bambridge, his tie correctly knotted, his suit coat buttoned, met them at the elevator in the underground VIP parking garage beneath the Original Headquarters Building.

"Glad to have you back, David," the DDO said, shaking hands. He dismissed the two minders, who drove off.

"It's good to be back even though I walked away from a developing mess," Haaris said. He left ambiguous what developing mess he was talking about, the one in Pakistan or the one here on his desk because of Pakistan. He wanted to get Bambridge's reaction. But the DDO missed it.

"Under the circumstances—we're all terribly sorry about Deborah—no one could blame you. Though you did leave us in something of a lurch."

They rode directly up to the seventh floor, which surprised Haaris. "I thought that the director would have waited until after my debriefing to see me."

"He has a few questions first, we both have. Since your trip and your disappearance, you have become operational, under my purview."

"Has my desk been taken out of the DI?" Haaris asked. The DI, or Directorate of Intelligence, was where the analysis of most incoming information was performed. The DO, or Directorate of Operations—most often called the National Clandestine Service these days—did the work in the field. It was tasked with all kinds of spying, including the administration of the NOC program—the spies in the field who worked without official cover. It was their deaths the stars on the granite wall downstairs in the lobby represented.

"At least until what we're facing has been resolved."

The DCI's secretary told them to go directly in.

Walt Page was leaning against his desk, saying something to Carlton Patterson and an attractive woman in jeans, a white blouse, the sleeves rolled up above her shoulders, and a pink baseball cap.

It took just a moment for Haaris to realize who she was because he'd not expected to see her here. He managed to cover the lapse by walking directly to Page and shaking his hand. "Quite a mess, Mr. Director. But not completely unexpected."

"Welcome back," Page said.

"Thank you," Haaris replied. He turned to the others. "Carleton. And Miss Boylan, I'm surprised to see you here this morning."

"Why's that, Dave?" Pete asked.

"Just surprised, nothing more."

"Would you like a cup of coffee or anything before we start?" Page asked. His body attitude was of a man wanting to have a little chat and nothing more. He was saying that this was not to be an inquisition.

It was more than Haaris had expected. "No. I'd like to get this over with so I can resume work. My people have a lot to catch up with."

"They've been holding the fort," Bambridge put in, and Page shot him a look.

"Where've you been all this time?" Page asked. "Boyle says you told him Paris and Istanbul, but we haven't been able to find any traces."

"You wouldn't have. I'm good at my job."

"What were you doing all this time?"

"Grieving, in part, and coming to accept my condition," Haaris said. "But before you ask, I am not the Messiah. I've not been anywhere near Pakistan since I got free from the Taliban. And I only hope that you put a contract on his life. He is directly responsible for the mess we're facing. If we can take him out, we can start to repair the damage he's caused."

"You warned us," Pete said.

"Yes."

"I'm just wondering why."

"It was relatively easy to predict a unifying voice such as his to show up."

"I meant, why were you so adamant about warning the president that she would have to act? She ordered McGarvey to go over in disguise and kill him. You didn't mention the unintended consequences, whether or not Mac was successful."

"Was he? The Messiah has evidently disappeared."

Marty started to say something but Pete held him off. "We lost touch with him."

"He was there in Islamabad?"

"Yes," Pete said. "And I think you were there too."

Haaris sat back, suppressing a smile. He had them. "You still think that I played the role of the Messiah."

"Yes."

"Your proof? Or is it just wishful thinking? Blame this on me, perhaps because of a less than lovely childhood? British public schools do have a reputation. Well deserved, I can assure you, from direct knowledge, though the education they offer is first rate." He looked at the others. "But why, Miss Boylan? Why would I have put everything at risk to pull off such a fantastic scheme?"

"You were dying. One last hurrah, thumb your nose at us and our cousins."

"Something like this would have to have been planned for years. I only just found out about my cancer last week."

Pete didn't respond, and he thought that she looked confused, her lone argument shot down so easily.

"If you want to find out his real identity, where he's disappeared—unless Mr. McGarvey's mission was a success—and the way out of the mess that we ourselves made, then let me get back to work."

No one said a thing.

Haaris got to his feet. "I'll get my people headed in the right direction, and then I'd like to go home for a shower, something to eat and a change of clothes. At some point I'll need to brief the president."

"First we'll need to debrief you, David," Pete said, her voice soft, almost silky, somehow bothersome.

"Then let's get it over with."

Pete got up. "Good."

"Mr. Haaris, a question first, if you please," Patterson said, his voice also soft. "Of course we're all off-base here, about your being the Messiah, but we're just trying to do our jobs."

"I understand."

"When the dust has settled, so to speak, do you contemplate bringing suit against the Company? Taking us to court and all that? Perhaps a memoir you'd refuse to allow us to vet? It's been done before."

"Heavens, no," Haaris said. "I've been an American from the beginning and always will be." He smiled. "Truth, justice and the American way. Is that how it goes?"

No one returned his smile.

SIXTY-SEVEN

Otto went with McGarvey over to Saul Landesberg's studio in Technical Services, at the same moment Pete was walking out of the DCI's office with Haaris. They'd heard everything over an in-house audio feed that Otto had set up. No one else except Pete knew about it, especially not Page, and certainly not Haaris.

"He held his own," Otto said.

"No one accused the man of being stupid," McGarvey said.

"Gentlemen?" Landesberg asked, looking up.

"We were talking about someone else, not you," McGarvey said. "Especially not you." He paused. "The ISI had me for a few hours, during which I was waterboarded."

"What's it like?"

"Sporty. The point is, your makeup job survived."

"Of course it did," Landesberg said. He sat McGarvey down and took the earbud out and handed it to Otto. "Won't work in here. We're shielded against everything except actual human presence. What happens in this room—how it happens—stays in this room."

"Interesting problem," Otto said, grinning.

It had taken Landesberg a little more than two hours to complete McGarvey's disguise but less than twenty minutes to restore his hair color, uncover his natural features and bring back his complexion.

"Nothing else I can do about your hair, but it'll grow back in a few weeks. Nobody recognized you, not even close up?"

"Just Pete Boylan."

"No shit?"

"I'd give you a tip if I knew what you charged," McGarvey said.

"On the house, Mr. Director. And if you ever need me again, I'll be here."

Outside, the section secretary had a phone call for McGarvey from Page.

"The president wants to see you," the DCI said.

"How'd it go with Haaris?"

"About how you expected it would. If he's guilty of anything it's being overly smooth. Miss Boylan just left with him to do the debriefing."

"I want to listen in before I head over to the White House, because I already know what the president is likely to say to me."

"I talked to her personally just now. She said you were to come immediately."

McGarvey hesitated.

"Just get it over with, and try to be polite for a change. There's never been a president who could do without you, but not one of them ever ended up liking you. Maybe this one will be different."

"I doubt it. Have a car brought round for me."

"Do you want a driver?"

"No."

On the way down to Otto's office, McGarvey explained where he was going. Otto gave him a cell phone.

"It should give me decent reception even from the Oval Office."

"Good thing you're on our side. I'm going to make it short and to the point."

"She'll have a witness, probably Susan Kalley."

"Good."

"What are you going to tell them?"

"The truth," McGarvey said.

"I don't think this president will like it very much."

McGarvey was expected at the East Gate and was passed through without a credentials check. He turned the plain Chevy Impala with government plates around so that it was facing down the gentle hill, just past the door into the White House.

The president's adviser on national security affairs had been alerted to his arrival and she met him. "Thank you for being so prompt, Mr. McGarvey." She was dressed in a feminine business suit, medium heels, a scarf around her throat. A serious outfit for a serious moment.

McGarvey, on the other hand, wore khaki slacks, a white polo shirt and black blazer, boat shoes on his feet. His attitude was that he'd stopped over for a chat after just getting back from the front.

"Are you carrying a firearm, Mr. Director?" the marine guard asked.

"No."

He followed Kalley across to the extremely busy West Wing.

"The Messiah has vanished," she said. "Of course I'm sure that you knew this."

"It's a mess over there. Any word yet from India?"

"Their new aircraft carrier is standing about fifty miles off the coast from Karachi, and General Nasiri is screaming bloody murder, threatening to launch the air force to deal with the threat."

"I don't know the name."

"Wasim Nasiri; he was the Pakistani army's chief of staff and served as a defense minister. Sharp man, from what we've been told. Their parliament appointed him as temporary spokesman for the government, and the supreme court confirmed it last night. But I can tell you that he's not made any difference so far. The country is in an almost total civil war. Some of the military units, especially up north and a few in the southwest, have joined the Taliban."

"What about their remaining nuclear weapons?"

"Nasiri assured us that they are safe."

"Do you believe him?" McGarvey asked at the open door to the Oval Office.

"No," Kalley said.

The president, her jacket hanging over the back of her desk chair, was just getting off the phone when they came in. "The Messiah has vanished," she said.

Kalley closed the door.

"Did you manage to assassinate him?"

"I met him face-to-face, and in fact he has not disappeared. He is here in the States, at Langley."

"The CIA has him in custody?"

"Not yet. He's one of ours, and no one else but me is convinced he played the role."

"Haaris," Kalley said.

"Yes."

"I want to see him here," the president said, reaching for the phone.

"That wouldn't be smart, Madam President," McGarvey said.

"What did you say?"

"If I'm right he is a dangerous man who wouldn't hesitate to kill you."

"If he tried to get in with a gun he'd never get past the sentries."

"He wouldn't need a weapon."

The president looked as if she was on the verge of exploding. "You're convinced that David Haaris and the Messiah are one and the same man?"

"Yes, ma'am"

"You idiot," Kalley said. "By your meddling you damned well might have sparked the breakdown."

"That will be enough," Miller said.

Kalley didn't want to quit.

"Leave us now," the president said.

Reluctantly Kalley got to her feet, glaring at McGarvey, and walked out of the Oval Office.

"I asked you here to thank you, not only for what you did in Pakistan, but for what you've done, and what you've given, for your country. Unfortunately, there'll be no medals, nor ceremonies on the lawn." The president got up and came around her desk. McGarvey rose and she extended her hand. "It's all I can do for now."

McGarvey smiled, and shook hands. "It's enough for now," he said.

Miller read something in his eyes. "It's not over yet."

"No, ma'am."

"Then don't let me keep you."

Outside, McGarvey walked down the hall the same way he'd come in. Kalley was nowhere in sight. At the east door he nodded to the marine sentry.

"Have a good day, Mr. Director."

Outside he got in the Chevy, drove directly down to the gate that led to East Executive Drive and was passed through.

He picked up his cell phone. "I'm out," he said.

"Where are you going?" Otto asked.

"After Haaris."

"He's still here on Campus, and you don't want do anything there. He'll fight back, and there could be a lot of collateral damage. Go to my place, out of his way. I'll give Louise the heads-up."

"I'll do better on my own," McGarvey said.

"No, you won't. Anyway, don't be so goddamned stubborn, for once in your life. We've done this bullshit together a long time; let's not change the game in midstream. I'll let you know when he's on the move."

"Depending how it goes with Pete, he might just try to see the president. But whatever happens, it has to be me who takes him down. He'll take anyone out who gets close to him."

SIXTY-EIGHT

Haaris left the small conference room where Pete had debriefed him for the past twenty minutes, his heart skipping a beat in every six or seven despite his outward calm, and took the elevator down to the first floor.

McGarvey had managed somehow to escape from the ISI, and later that night a SEAL Team Six helicopter had picked him up and taken him and Miss Boylan across the border to Jalalabad. The worst of it was that both of them were convinced that he was the Messiah, though apparently they had only the slightest glimmer of his motivations and absolutely none of what was coming next.

She had refused to tell him where McGarvey was at the moment, but it was a real possibility that he could be here on Campus.

"We've determined that the Messiah's voice was electronically modified. We've had a computer program working the problem since the first speech, and we've come up with a number of certainties. The speaker was born in Pakistan, most likely in Lahore. He got his education in England, starting as a young boy, and his diction, grammar and manners are of the old school. He's in his late thirties and has spent some time, perhaps years, in the States. The programs picked up a few traces of an American accent. Northeast."

"Interesting," Haaris had said.

"The profile fits you, Mr. Haaris. Can you explain that?"

"No, I cannot, except to ask if you are formally accusing me of being the Messiah?"

"What do you suppose the Messiah's agenda is? Simply a nuclear war between Pakistan and India?"

"It's what I hope to discover with my team's input. The president will be needing a briefing from my desk sooner rather than later," Haaris had said. "So, if you will excuse me, Miss Boylan, I will get back to work."

Pete said nothing until he was at the door. "You've made a mistake, you know."

He turned and smiled faintly. "Oh?"

"You got Kirk McGarvey involved."

Haaris took the covered walkway past the cafeteria, the sculpture "Kryptos" outside in the courtyard, but instead of taking the second covered walkway past the library, he turned left. At the end of the corridor he scanned his pass and went outside to the parking lot and his Mercedes.

He figured it wouldn't take long for the bitch to realize he had left the building instead of going directly to his office, which didn't leave much room for error.

On the way down to the gate, he called his house from his cell phone and scanned the outside as well as every room in the house. No cars he didn't recognize were parked anywhere in the neighborhood. The crime scene police tape had been removed from the front and back entrances, the sliding glass doors from the pool into the family room, and the garage door. The inside of the house had obviously been searched, but as far as he could tell nothing was missing except for his laptop.

Every closet in the house had been searched with a fine hand; nothing had been pulled out and tossed aside, no holes been punched into the walls to find a safe or a hiding place.

The bathroom where he'd killed Deborah had been cleaned by his service, and using the surveillance detection program on his phone, he could find no traces of any electronic eavesdropping devices other than his own.

A forensics team had checked for evidence relating to Deborah's murder but not for the supposition that he was a spy.

The guard at the main gate didn't bother to look up as he flashed past in the exit lane, the bar code scanner on a corner of the car's windshield automatically registering his identity.

Instead of turning right on the parkway and back toward the city, he turned left, to the north, merging with I-495 a few minutes later and crossing the river into Maryland.

Following the Beltway as it merged with I-270 and heading off to the east, he kept checking his rearview mirrors for anyone keeping pace with him, and the sky for any signs of a helicopter dogging his trail. But if the alarm had been sounded no one was coming after him.

Using one hand he removed the battery cover on the phone and took out the SIM card. Until it was back in place even Otto Rencke wouldn't be able to trace him.

Fifteen minutes later, still certain that he wasn't being followed, he turned south on State Highway 295; a half mile later he pulled up at the gate of a self-storage company and entered his password. No one was around. Arranging for a storage space was done by appointment only, and there was no security except in the evenings. Five years ago when he'd begun to put his preliminary planning in place, he searched for a mostly unattended self-storage place just like this one.

His was a large, two-car garage space, which had been another of his requirements. The lock was an old-fashioned combination, and when he had the door up, he drove inside, parking next to a five-year-old dark blue Toyota Camry, possibly the most common car in America.

So far as he could tell nothing had been disturbed since the last time he'd checked the place the week before he'd left for London. In fact, if someone had tried to break in, the garage and most of the units for fifty feet on either side would have disappeared in a massive explosion of nearly one hundred kilos of Semtex placed in two barrels filled with roofing nails.

He changed clothes from the trunk of the Camry, dressing in khakis with cargo pockets for three fifteen-round magazines of forty-caliber ammunition, plus an advanced Vaime silencer, and a quick-draw holster for the compact Glock 27 Gen4 pistol.

Also pocketing a fold-up knife, several four-ounce bricks of Semtex with chemical fuses, and a thirty-two-caliber revolver in an ankle holster, he backed out of the garage.

Included in his kit were two different sets of identification: one for Rupert Mann, from Brooklyn, and the other, complete with an Irish passport, for Pete O'Donald, from Belfast.

When this was finally over he'd planned on disappearing. Maybe the South Seas somewhere. Maybe even Venezuela. He had enough money in various offshore accounts to buy his way into relative luxury in just about any Third World nation.

But that had been before he'd learned he was dying. Now the money and the escape didn't mean much to him. Only the plan did, and only because doing something was infinitely better than doing nothing except waiting around to die.

He walked back into the garage and armed a switch that would set when the door was closed and fire when the door was opened.

Turning around he came face-to-face with the manager of the property, along with a man in his twenties and a pretty woman of about the same age, both of them dressed in jeans, both of them smiling.

"Mr. Dodge," the manager said. He was a florid old Cuban in jeans and a guayabera, sandals on his feet. "I'm glad you're here. This couple is moving and they have need of one of our largest storage units. Showing an occupied unit is better than showing them an empty one."

It was an irritation, nothing more, except it made no sense to Haaris, and he was suspicious. But the couple were not in the business, it was obvious, and the manager was an idiot. He stepped aside and motioned them in. "Please," he said.

They went inside.

Haaris quickly screwed the silencer on the Glock's muzzle. No one else was around. The couples' car had to be parked in front. He fired three shots, dropping them. And then walked back inside and fired one shot into the backs of each of their heads.

Closing the door, which armed the explosives, he shoved the padlock home and drove away. Sooner or later the young couple would be reported missing and their car discovered here, but there would be nothing to link him to the place.

Unless McGarvey put it together. But time was running out. And no matter what else happened Haaris had the number in his cell phone.

As soon as the call went through the three nuclear devices would explode wherever they happened to be.

He wanted them in New York, Washington, DC, and London.

It was the last stage of his plan.

SIXTY-NINE

In the kitchen at Rencke's safe house McGarvey sat staring out the window at the swing set in the back-yard. He and Louise had sent Audi down to the Farm, where she would be safe until the trouble blew over. And there'd been so many incidents in the past couple of years that she had started to grow up there and was the mascot of the training facility. Everyone doted on her. It wouldn't be long before children's toys like swing sets would be far too tame for her.

Louise came in from outside. "My Toyota is in the driveway. When you leave, take it. The staff car stays in the garage till we get past this. Haaris will know it's someone from the Company, namely, you."

"You shouldn't be involved."

"Don't be silly. You saved my husband's life in Cuba. What would you have me do?"

McGarvey's cell phone rang. It was Pete. He put it on speakerphone.

"I'm on a secure phone in Otto's office. Haaris left the Campus almost forty-five minutes ago, but we didn't catch it until one of his staffers called Marty's office to complain that his debriefing was taking too long."

"He could be practically anywhere by now. Check Dulles, Reagan and Baltimore."

"That's the first thing we tried, but if he's booked

on any international flight there've been no last-minute additions."

"Expand the search to domestic flights. But he'll need documents, money and a clean credit card or two. We either missed his go-to-hell kit at his house, or he's got a stash somewhere else. A storage locker."

"How about an APB on his car?"

"He'll have switched cars by now, and I want to keep the cops at arm's length. Anyone approaches him is probably going to die."

"SWAT teams?"

"We need the man alive, Pete. Three nuclear weapons are missing from Quetta, and I think we have to consider the possibility that they're already here in the country. Only he can tell us where they are and when they'll be detonated. The man has a timetable, and he's going to stick with it no matter what."

"Could be he has a team. Someone local, unless he imported three suicide bombers willing to push a button and sacrifice their lives for Allah. It's not likely he'd be willing to die himself."

"Don't be so sure," McGarvey said. "He only has a few months to live, so he has nothing to lose."

"Something else has come up. There's a federal warrant for your arrest. Came from the White House. The president's national security adviser."

"Kalley."

"That's right. You're to be considered armed and dangerous. Which was stupid, actually, because a lot of people in the Bureau and the Secret Service know who you are, and know damned well that you would not open fire on any cop doing their duty."

Otto broke in, and he sounded excited as he always did when he was on to something.

"Haaris made one call from his cell phone to his house, and pulled up the ADT alarms and monitors.

We made sure that the police tapes were gone and no one was watching the place. Soon as he was finished with that call he pulled the SIM card, so I lost him. At least at first.

"I hacked into his house system and went through the recordings from the time he pulled the SIM card until ten minutes ago. But he never showed up. It's telling me that wherever he's stashed his walking papers, they're not there."

"Why did he go through the bother of doing a surveillance search?" McGarvey asked. "Unless it was to keep you busy."

"Bingo. But it backfired."

"Tell me."

"He had his escape well planned, I'll have to give him that. I figured that he would need not only papers, but he'd need new wheels. Renting a car somewhere was too obvious, so I started a search within a thirty-mile radius of Campus for self-storage facilities that had units large enough for two cars."

"Why two?" Pete asked.

"Because he didn't want to screw around pulling one car out and then parking his Mercedes inside. Might attract too much attention. Just one little detail he figured would help with his margin," Otto said.

"He would have wanted a place that had no onsite security, other than fences and a surveillance system. Mounted cameras."

"Right, but he made a mistake. For whatever reason he missed the cameras and at least three people paid for it with their lives."

"Did someone stumble on to him?" McGarvey asked.

"The manager and two people looking at units. They parked their car up front, and I hacked into the surveillance system and saw it all. He's driving a five-year-old Toyota Camry, dark blue, with Maryland tags."

"Where'd he go?"

"We'll have to put something in the air to find out," Otto said. "But he lured the three people into the garage, shot them all, then locked up and drove off. Five minutes later it exploded, taking out twenty other units. He either set the explosion, or maybe his aim was lousy and one of them survived and tried to open the door, which was wired."

"I can retask Flybaby Prime to find him," Louise said.

The designator actually included a constellation of four Jupiter satellites in moderate Earth orbits, just above the International Space Station, arrayed in such a way that at any given time, twenty-four/seven, one would be above Washington, DC. The program, which had been put in place in the aftermath of 9/11, was classified Top Secret/Flybaby Prime access. It would take practically an act of Congress to retask any one of the birds. But Louise had been one of the designers and first administrators of the system.

"First of all, you can go to jail for the rest of your life, and if Washington is one of Haaris's targets, you'd be leaving the city unprotected," Pete said. She was clearly playing devil's advocate.

"Ten-second snapshots every sixty," Louise said. "I'll send the feed to Otto, and he can insert a loop showing just before and just after the ten seconds that the bird would be off task."

"Make them one second every fifteen, and there'll be no need for a loop," Otto said. "I'm working on a recognition program now. My darlings will pick out every dark blue Camry in the bird's line of sight and read the tag number."

Louise had already taken her laptop from the kitchen desk, opened it on the counter and turned it on.

"We'll need to hustle, sweetheart," Otto said. "We don't have that wide an angle. If he gets more than a hundred miles out, there's a good chance we'll miss him."

"Don't wait for me, I'm on it," Louise said.

Her computer finished booting, and within twenty seconds she had gotten into the NSA's highest security programs' mainframe, had entered all the passwords and was in the Flybaby Prime control program.

"Gotcha," she said. She looked up. "Your call, Kirk. Which way is he heading?"

"Box the compass," McGarvey said. "North first."

"Ready, Bear?" Louise asked. Teddy Bear, or usually just Bear, was her pet name for Otto.

"Go," he said.

Louise expanded the satellite's view and changed its direction to the north for one second, then brought it back to its original parameters.

"Searching," Otto said. "You can't believe the number of dark blue Camrys on the highways. We should send this to Toyota for a commercial." Two seconds later he was back. "No."

Louise reprogrammed the satellite to look east, took the one second-snapshot and brought it back.

"Shit," Otto said.

"What?"

"Dark blue Camry, Maryland tags; it's our man. He's heading east on U.S. Fifty just across the Chesapeake Bay Bridge into Delaware."

McGarvey had it all at once. "Dover Air Force Base."

"Yes," Pete said. "He had to get the weapons out of Pakistan. They were put aboard military transports to Dover."

"From there at least one made it to Washington," Otto said. "A second to New York. And the third?"

"I'm going to ask him just that," McGarvey said. "We still don't know how he's going to get them out. I don't think he'll simply trigger them in place."

"We can get a NEST team in the air within fifteen minutes," Louise said.

"If he finds out he'll push the button," McGarvey said. "Keep looking for his cell phone. I'll need to know the second he replaces the SIM card."

"I'm coming with you," Pete said.

"I need you on Campus to back me up in case this thing goes south," McGarvey said.

"Goddamnit, Kirk."

"If there's going to be any future for us, you'll have to start listening to me. At least every now and then." He could hear her draw a breath. It was dirty pool, but she hadn't left him any other choice.

"Okay," she said.

"Promise?"

"Promise."

SEVENTY

Haaris parked at the Dover Mall just past lunchtime and walked directly into Macy's department store. It was a weekday and the place was almost empty. By now if McGarvey had enlisted Rencke's help, they could know about the incident at the storage center, including the car and its Maryland tags. If Rencke's wife had also become involved it was possible, though unlikely, in his estimation, that she could have re-tasked one of the Flybaby satellites to follow him.

But that led to a number of other unlikely, though

disturbing, possibilities. They knew that three nuclear warheads were missing from Quetta. And if they had traced him here they might have figured out that the weapons had arrived from Pakistan.

A host of *what if*s.

He had passed the entrance to Dover Air Force Base just off Delaware Route 1 a couple of miles back, but there hadn't been any unusual activity. No helicopters circling. No police cars or military cops parked alongside the road leading to the main gate.

In any event, if he was cornered with no way out he wouldn't hesitate to replace the SIM card in his phone and make the call. It would be a waste of five years, but once again people in the U.S., and this time in Great Britain also, would feel the same sense of vulnerability that they'd felt after 9/11. No place would ever seem safe again.

He went to the men's department, where he bought a light-colored poplin jacket, and in another section a Nike baseball cap.

In a stall in the public restroom at the opposite end of the mall, he removed the tags and put the jacket on, zipping it all the way up.

Stuffing the hat inside the jacket he walked down the broad mall corridor to the Sears store, where he found an old-fashioned pay phone, called the number from memory of the City Cab Company and asked to be picked up outside JCPenney and taken to the Dover Downs Casino.

He walked back through the mall to JCPenney, and when the cab pulled up, he put on the cap and walked outside.

The man who had arrived in the Camry had disappeared, as had the man who'd walked through the mall wearing a jacket but no hat.

At Langley, Pete was with Otto in his suite of offices, when the satellite feed Louise had been sending them suddenly shut down. The phone rang, and it was she.

"The system's malfunction alarm came up, so I had to pull out," she said. "Is it Dover?"

"Yes, Mac was right," Otto said. "He parked in front of Macy's at a mall a couple of miles north of the base. We were waiting for him to come out."

"I'm sorry, but I don't think we can use the satellite any time soon. They'll be revamping the malware system, and until I can get the bypass codes we're out of luck."

"Will they trace it back to Louise?" Pete asked.

Otto grinned. "No," he said, at the same time his wife did.

He picked up the GPS signal from McGarvey's phone, then called.

"I'm about thirty miles out," McGarvey said. "Is he in Dover?"

"In the Dover Mall just north of the base. We're waiting for him to come out."

"There's no reason for him to stop at a mall, except to ditch the Camry. He either walked away, or someone picked him up."

"How about a cab?" Pete asked.

"That's possible. It means he knows or suspects that we're watching him, and he considered the likelihood probably from the beginning. He's on his way now to pick up another car."

"You think he'll try to get on the base?" Pete asked.

"Guaranteed," McGarvey said. "Call the commander and get me a pass."

"We still have time to get a NEST team up there," Otto said. "It's worth a try."

"If he so much as gets a hint that those people have shown up he'll pull the trigger."

"Maybe he will anyway," Pete said.

"He's got bigger targets in mind. Somehow he managed to get the three weapons shipped over, and they're sitting in a warehouse or empty hangar somewhere on base waiting for him to pick them up. And from there he'll take them probably to Washington and New York."

"They're sending back lots of military equipment out of Lahore now that most of the operations in Afghanistan have been shut down," Pete said. "Rajput was helping him so it would have been fairly simple to slip three packages through. Shielded crates, maybe, even hidden in boxes of aircraft parts. Anything."

"Medical waste," Otto suggested. "Could be marked *biohazard*. I have a feeling that Dover doesn't have the facilities to dispose of something like that, so it'd have to be shipped to a safe site somewhere."

"Find out as much as you can," McGarvey said. "It's a good bet he's going to get on base with the proper credentials and paperwork to pick up whatever they're packaged in. And at this point I'd guess biohazardous material would be the most likely. The packages would be sealed, and no one would be tempted to open them."

"We're on it," Otto said.

"I'll be at the main gate in less than thirty minutes."

Haaris paid off the cabby and went inside the casino, where he ditched the hat in a trash can. He had a cup of coffee in one of the snack bars, then bought an oversized dark blue sweatshirt printed with a pair of dice with a five and two showing, the casino's name below them.

He left the jacket in the men's room, pulled on the sweatshirt and went back outside, where he caught another cab, giving the driver a residential address on the west side of town just off Forrest Avenue.

Just before he got in the backseat, he looked to the southeast toward the base as a C-5M Super Galaxy troop transport made its approach into the pattern. NEST teams did not ride around in aircraft like that, but he was still worried that something was coming up on his six. McGarvey.

Ten minutes later the cabby pulled up in front of a ranch-style house with a two-car garage in a quiet middle-class neighborhood. It was a weekday, so husbands were at work and wives were either home doing housework or off shopping with friends, whatever housewives did during the week. He'd never wondered about Deborah's schedule while he was away. But then, he'd never really given a damn about her.

The last time he'd been up here for a long weekend he'd taken the ten-year-old Chevy Tahoe out of the garage and washed it in the driveway. One of the neighbors came over to say hi, and they'd chatted about absolutely nothing for ten minutes until the poor bastard had wandered off.

Haaris came across as an okay neighbor who kept his place neat but was standoffish and hardly ever home. No wife, no kids or pets, probably a salesman on the road most of the time. He'd owned the house for three years and most of the time he arrived by cab, just like today. Nothing unusual. *Ted Johnson is home again. Blend with the woodwork. Show them what they want to see.* Just like the Messiah had.

Inside he made a quick inspection of every room, all the doors and windows, to make sure no one had been inside or had tried to get in since the last time he was here. There was dust on everything; no one had been here.

He changed into a long-sleeved white shirt and opened the garage door. The Tahoe started with no trouble, and he pulled out, closed the garage door for the last time and drove directly back to Forrest Avenue, traffic almost nonexistent compared to that in DC. Past the AAA offices, Forrest turned into State Road 8, and six miles out of town he came to what had once been a metal fabrication company behind a tall wire-mesh fence, but was now long since deserted.

He'd bought it through a shell company two years ago and had come out only once in person, at night. The one-story office building was set just off the road, behind it two fabrication buildings and a warehouse and parts inventory facility. The driveways were cracked, weeds growing everywhere.

Unlocking the gate, he drove back to the warehouse, unlocked the big steel doors and drove inside, parking next to a white Lincoln hearse fitted out to transport two full-sized coffins. He pulled the silk cover off the hearse. The tastefully small logo on the driver's and passengers' doors read: THOMAS FUNERAL HOME, WILMINGTON, DE.

SEVENTY-ONE

McGarvey pulled up at the Dover Air Force Base main gate a few minutes before one and presented his ID to one of the air policemen. "General Taff is expecting me."

"Yes, sir," the airman said. He wrote something on

a clipboard. "If you'll park in the visitors' lot your escort will be here momentarily."

About fifty yards back was a small parking lot and visitors' center. McGarvey drove over and parked at the same moment Otto phoned.

"Two Bureau guys were here looking for you. Marty told them that you definitely were not on Campus and probably not in the city. I'll have Page call the White House and cancel the warrant."

"Don't do it. If Haaris thinks that I may be arrested at any moment, he might let down his guard."

"They'll try to search your apartment, if they haven't already tried. Are they going to run into any surprises?"

"Nothing dangerous, but they'll need a damned good locksmith to get in. Any trace of Dave?"

"We're blind for now, but I put three of Stuart's people on ex-comms checking every hotel and motel in town, plus the casino and security at the Dover Mall for anything unusual." Stuart Middler was chief of CIA internal security, and the ex-comms was an extended communications check to places that Haaris might have shown up. "They haven't come up with anything yet."

"Where's the nearest decent-sized civilian airport?"

"Wilmington, about forty miles north."

"Does he have a pilot's license?"

"I'll find out."

"Extend the ex-comms to the airport; see if anyone has reserved an airplane to deliver something. Maybe automobile parts, something fairly heavy. I'm guessing a twin-engine Cessna or better."

A plain blue Chevy Impala with air force markings came through the gate and pulled up as McGarvey got out of Louise's car. A master sergeant whose name-tag read, LARSEN, introduced himself.

"I'll take you to General Taff, Mr. Director. He's expecting you."

The sergeant drove directly over to base headquarters. In the distance, on the far side of the main runway, the Super Galaxy was parked on the tarmac in front of a large building at the end of a row of several equally large hangars.

"What's over there?" McGarvey asked.

"The Carson Center for Mortuary Affairs. Where all the bodies are brought for preparation before their release to families."

"Civilians?"

"Some."

Brigadier General Herman Taff was a slender man with ordinary features who could have passed for the CEO of a medium-sized business just about anywhere. When McGarvey was shown in he got up, shook hands and motioned to a chair across the desk from him. He was slightly annoyed.

"It's been a busy day so far, Mr. Director, so I assume you're going to explain why you came to visit us."

"We don't have a lot of time, General, so I'll be brief. You have trouble coming your way, and it'll probably be here within the next half hour or less. We think that as many as three nuclear devices may have been sent to this base from Pakistan, possibly disguised as medical waste, a biohazard of some sort in sealed containers that would likely not be opened by your personnel."

"Nuclear weapons," Taff said. "From Pakistan."

"Someone will be coming here to pick them up. If it is medical waste, what would you do with it?"

"Depending on the hazard level, it would be sent out by air to Nellis in Nevada."

"What if it were too dangerous to be put aboard an airplane?"

"If it were too risky it would go by truck or unmarked van," Taff said. "We had an incident three months ago involving medical waste from a pair of Ebola victims in Africa. Someone from the CDC came to pick it up."

"If someone shows up with the proper paperwork, do you release whatever it is they've come to pick up without checking with someone? Say, at the CDC?"

"No need if they have the proper orders, and they're on our roster."

"I'd like to see that roster," McGarvey said. Haaris had made his first serious mistake.

"That's not going to be possible. I'm sorry, sir, but I'm going to need more than your word."

"Have your secretary telephone Walt Page, he's the director of the CIA. But do it now."

Taff hesitated for a moment but picked up the phone and instructed his secretary to make the call.

"What about civilian bodies?"

"We get them from time to time."

"Who picks them up?"

"A funeral home sends a hearse."

McGarvey pulled out his cell phone and called Otto. "They might be in coffins," he said. "Haaris will be showing up with a hearse to pick them up."

Taff was alarmed.

"Would the bodies be processed here?" McGarvey asked the general. "Would the coffins be opened?"

"Not if the families requested closed-coffin funerals. We respect their wishes. In any event that sort of processing, identification and perhaps autopsies, would most likely be done before the bodies were shipped to us."

Taff brought up something on his computer.

Otto was back. "Robert Brewster, Thomas Funeral Home, Wilmington, chartered a DeHavilland Beaver in the land version for a flight to Teterboro Airport in New Jersey. It's the only plane like that they had. Cargo is listed as two coffins."

"Only two?"

"Yes. And Haaris is a commercial-rated pilot."

"One's missing," McGarvey said. "Find it."

"Where do I start?"

"England."

Taff's phone buzzed; he answered it and looked at McGarvey. "Get them up here; we'll wait."

"Hang on," McGarvey told Otto.

"There's a federal warrant for your arrest, Mr. McGarvey. We were told to hold you here until someone from the Bureau shows up."

"Call Page," McGarvey told Otto. "It's time to call the Bureau off. If they come anywhere near this place, and Haaris spots them, he'll pull the trigger."

"I'm on it," Otto said.

"Someone from the Thomas Funeral Home with the right documents will be showing up here to pick up the bodies of two civilians," McGarvey told Taff. "Only, the coffins won't have bodies, they'll each have a Pakistani nuclear device. Probably something in the ten-kiloton range. Actually, warheads for tactical missiles. This guy is well motivated, he knows what he's doing and the cell phone he's got with him is almost certainly programmed to detonate both weapons. He doesn't want to do that here. He means to take one of them to New York City and the other down to Washington. He's chartered a private plane from Wilmington and he's filed a flight plan to fly first to New Jersey."

The general suddenly didn't look so sure of himself. He glanced at his computer screen. "A hearse from Wilmington, just the driver, is waiting at the main gate for his escort. We'll delay him there until I can get some help."

"You can't do that," McGarvey said, jumping up.

"We'll take care of it," Taff said.

Two armed air policemen showed up.

"Keep Mr. McGarvey here; the FBI has sent people to pick him up."

SEVENTY-TWO

"An escort is being rounded up for you now, sir," the air policeman at the main gate told Haaris. "If you'll just go back to the parking area and wait there, shouldn't be but a couple of minutes."

"Okay," Haaris said. He made a U-turn and went to the parking lot.

In the distance he could just make out the hangars, the Super Galaxy and the Carson Center, where his two coffins were waiting to be picked up. Something was wrong; he could feel it in his bones.

He glanced over at a Toyota SUV and it was vaguely familiar to him. He'd seen the boxy vehicle somewhere before, but he couldn't place the where or the when. But there had to be hundreds of SUVs just like it between here and DC.

He stared at it for a long time, the uneasy feeling growing.

Taking out his cell phone, he slid the battery cover off, removed the battery and got the SIM card from the jacket pocket of the dark blue suit he'd dressed in at the warehouse.

. . .

McGarvey's cell phone rang. "May I answer it?"

The general nodded.

It was Otto. McGarvey put it on speaker. "The Bureau has agreed to drag its feet for now. But they're not giving us much time before they want you to talk to them."

"What about the Secret Service?"

"They turned it over to the Bureau first thing."

"Haaris is already here, they're holding him at the main gate. In the meantime the general has placed me under arrest."

"Hold on, I'll have Altman call him. . . . Shit, *shit*. Mac, Haaris's phone just went active."

"Can you block his outgoing calls?"

"I can try to shut him down, but he's using one of our phones—one of the phones I modified for field officers—and he'd know the moment I tried something like that. You have to get to him and right now."

"Admiral Altman?" Taff asked. He was impressed.

"Yes. But it's your call now, General. The hearse driver has just activated his cell phone. All he has to do is pull up a number and hit speed dial. We might have just an instant to see the flash when both nuclear devices ignite, but it'll be over with."

"He won't commit suicide."

"They've been doing it in the Middle East for years, and the guys who took over the planes on nine-eleven were willing to die for their cause. Are you?"

The general was deflated. "Can you stop him?"

His secretary buzzed him. "Admiral Altman is calling for you, sir."

"I'd like to try."

"What do you need?"

"A ride over to wherever he's supposed to pick up the two coffins. No sirens. And in two minutes let him through the gate."

Taff hesitated only an instant longer, but then he nodded. "Do it," he told the two air policemen, and then picked up the telephone.

Haaris pulled up the number that would detonate the two bombs here and the one in England. For the longest time, what seemed almost like an eternity to him, he stared at the SUV. From Lahore to here had been a terribly long journey. Along the way there had been some good times, he'd never denied that to himself. Even with Deborah there had been the odd moment, when glancing at her he could see the obvious love for him in her eyes, and it gave him a little thrill of pleasure that somebody actually gave a damn. Unconditionally.

He would have liked to finish his work. Deliver one bomb to his people at the mosque in New Jersey, who would in two days take it to the new World Trade Center. The second to his people in Alexandria, who would at the same moment as the New Jersey driver take it to the fence in front of the White House. The two days would give him the time to reach the funeral home in Farnborough, where he would pick up the coffin and deliver it to Ten Downing Street.

Then he would press the button.

Revenge would finally be his. But sitting here at the wheel of the hearse, the cell phone in his right hand, his thumb over the speed dial button, he tried to visualize exactly what it was that he was taking revenge for.

At that moment a blue sedan with air force markings came through the main gate, and he shut the phone off and put it in his pocket as he powered down the window.

. . .

The two air policemen drove McGarvey directly across to the Carson Center's incoming and processing facility, where bodies were brought in and made ready either for transportation to Arlington National Cemetery or for pickup by families.

The cops parked their pickup truck around the corner of the building, out of sight of anyone coming from the main gate, and hurried back with McGarvey to the loading bay area, where the coffins would be brought out on trolleys

A technical sergeant named Oakley came out. He looked a little green. No one else was around.

"The captain called, said we've got some kind of trouble coming our way?"

"Someone from a funeral home in Wilmington is coming to pick up a couple of coffins," McGarvey said. "Where are they?"

"Just inside. Said this guy was armed; what the hell is going on?"

"The coffins might be wired with Semtex, set to blow up at any moment. So get your ass out of here now."

"No shit," the sergeant said. "That'd spread radioactive crap everywhere."

"What are you talking about?"

"The bodies were from the nuclear explosion in Pakistan. They're hot." He gave McGarvey and the cops one last look and left.

"I want you out of here too," McGarvey told the cops. "Right now."

"Good luck, sir," one of them said, and they headed back to their truck.

In the distance McGarvey spotted a blue air force sedan followed by a white hearse heading his way.

The coffins were waiting on two trolleys just inside the small processing center, which wasn't much larger than a five- or six-car garage. Double doors at the back presumably led to the morgue itself, where coffins were in storage for pickup. The concrete floor was coated with a gray epoxy and the entire space was spotlessly clean and empty. There was no place to hide.

Pulling out his pistol, McGarvey stepped inside just to the left of the open door and flattened against the wall.

The coffins were marked with the three-bladed-propeller symbol: caution radioactive materials. McGarvey had to give Haaris credit for coming up with the way to make certain that no one would try to open the coffins, and at the same time offer a good explanation in case the bombs were leaking and someone detected the radiation.

Haaris backed the hearse to the open bay door and got out. No one was around, which he thought was strange. He could see the two coffins on trolleys just inside the pickup area.

"Will someone be out to help me load?" Haaris asked the escort driver.

"Should be, sir," the driver said through his open window. He swung the car around and headed away.

Haaris didn't know the entire procedure for picking up bodies, but he was reasonably certain that he would have been required to show his papers and sign something.

The hairs at the nape of his neck stood on end.

He took out his cell phone again and brought up the detonation number. He was armed, but getting into a gunfight here would guarantee that he would never get off the base. If this was a trap, he would push the button.

No one else was heading his way, and the escort car had disappeared somewhere behind one of the hangars.

Everything was wrong. Everything screamed at him to make a one-eighty and get the hell out. Survive to fight another day. Push the speed dial button once he made it to Wilmington. Or perhaps when he was in the air, flying away. The mushroom cloud would be interesting to watch.

Maybe back to Pakistan as the Messiah. It would be dangerous but exciting. Revenge came in many different guises.

Perhaps he would go to ground instead. Fight back in a different way, just as Snowden had done. Could be he would become someone else's hero.

He'd never had any belief in fate, though he understood the concept. What happened was of your own making.

Haaris came through the doors, the cell phone in his left hand.

McGarvey stepped forward and batted the phone out of his hand, sending it skittering across the floor facedown. "It's over now, David."

"Fuck you," Haaris shouted. He rolled forward, shoving McGarvey against the concrete wall.

McGarvey's damaged hip went numb, but leaning into Haaris for balance, he slammed a knee into the man's groin.

Falling back, Haaris managed to grab Mac's pistol, but before he could bring it to bear, McGarvey fell forward with him, twisting the pistol away and sending it sliding across the floor.

Their bodies intertwined, they fell down hard, Haaris banging the back of his head on the floor, and

McGarvey further damaging his hip, a very sharp, nearly incapacitating pain shooting up his spine.

Haaris managed to get himself free, roll away and get to his feet. He reached inside his still-buttoned suit coat as McGarvey got up and lurched forward, landing a roundhouse punch to the man's face.

Blood suddenly gushed from Haaris's nose. Dazed, he stumbled backward just out of McGarvey's reach as he pulled the Glock out of its shoulder holster.

"It's not over until I say so," he shouted, a wild smile on his face.

He started to raise his pistol when he was suddenly flung forward, the pistol dropping to the floor the moment before he felt his face bouncing off the concrete, a small hole at the back of his skull oozing blood and brain matter.

Pete stood in the doorway, in the classic shooter's stance, half squatting, the pistol in a two-handed grip, a crazy look in her eyes.

McGarvey turned without a word and went to Haaris's phone. He stared at the display for a long beat, not wanting to comprehend what he was seeing. The number was ringing. Either Haaris had pushed the speed dial before he'd dropped the phone, or when it had hit the floor, facedown, the button had been pushed.

"It's ringing," Pete said just behind him. "But the bombs didn't go off."

McGarvey looked up at the coffins, with their radiological warnings. "He out-thought himself," he said. "In case the bombs leaked. The coffins were lined with lead. The phone signal couldn't get through."

ΕΡΙLOGUE

Three Weeks Later

At the Blessed Savior Anglican Church Cemetery outside London, Charlie Wilde and Manley Stroud used a small front-end loader to guide the aluminum coffin into the grave. It had been shipped here from Pakistan and was marked with the radiological caution symbol and warnings.

The military hadn't wanted a thing to do with it, nor had any family come to claim the body.

"Bloody heavy thing," Wilde said as he picked up a shovel and began filling the grave.

"Lined with lead, I suppose," Stroud agreed, pitching in with the shoveling. "Even if it was my aunt Myrtle I don't think I would have wanted to come here to claim her. Rest in peace, I always said. Rest in peace."

At the kitchen counter in the Rencke's safe house, four-year-old Audi, sitting between her grampyfather Kirk and Miss Petey, was beside herself with happiness. "My boys at the Farm were fun and all," she said. "But this is infinite better."

They all laughed, but Otto and Louise were beaming so hard they could scarcely contain themselves. "Something, isn't she?" Otto said.

"You two are doing good," McGarvey said.

"Okay, Miss Rencke, time for bed," Louise said, taking the girl by the hand. "Say good night."

After hugs and kisses all around Louise took her upstairs and when she got back, she opened a second bottle of Valpolicella as Otto was taking the baby lamb chops out of the marinade, ready to put them on the grill.

"I've been meaning to bring something up," Pete said.

"Things are finally settling down between Pakistan and India," McGarvey said. "So hopefully this has nothing to do with work."

"No, but related. Has to do with a promise made to me."

McGarvey didn't have a clue, but Otto and Louise knew.

"Quote: 'If there's going to be any future for us, you'll'—meaning me—'will have to start listening to me'—meaning you. 'At least every now and then.'"

"I was under duress," McGarvey said, remembering every word.

"I don't know," Otto said. "We've been friends for a long time now, and I've never seen you rat out on a promise."

"This is different," McGarvey said.

"Coward," Louise told him.

"Damned right."

"How about a Rémy?" she asked. "Will that help?"

"A little, I suppose," McGarvey said, and despite the complications he knew damned well would follow, and despite the fear that would ride with him like a tremendous weight on his shoulders, he figured that he hadn't been this happy in a very, very long time.

Don't miss Kirk McGarvey's
next adventure in

Tower Down

DAVID HAGBERG

A freelance killer, code-named
Al-Nassar, "the Eagle," blows
the supports on a pencil tower in
Manhattan and sends it crashing
down. But no one in the White House
or even in the CIA wants to believe
that more Americans are going to die.
Only McGarvey, Pete Boylan, and Otto
Rencke believe that another attack on
a Manhattan skyscraper is imminent.
The trio embarks on a mission to
find the Eagle and stop him before
he strikes again. They're hot on his
trail—but the clock is ticking.

tor-forge.com